MISSION TO
MINERVA

Baen Books by JAMES P. HOGAN

Inherit the Stars
The Genesis Machine
The Gentle Giants of Ganymede
The Two Faces of Tomorrow
Thrice Upon a Time
Giants' Star
Voyage from Yesteryear
Code of the Lifemaker
The Proteus Operation
Endgame Enigma
The Mirror Maze
The Infinity Gambit
Entoverse
The Multiplex Man
Realtime Interrupt
Minds, Machines & Evolution
The Immortality Option
Paths to Otherwhere
Bug Park
Star Child
Rockets, Redheads & Revolution
Cradle of Saturn
The Legend That Was Earth
Martian Knightlife
The Anguished Dawn
Kicking the Sacred Cow (nonfiction)
Mission to Minerva

MISSION TO
MINERVA

JAMES P. HOGAN

MISSION TO MINERVA

A Baen Books Original

Baen Publishing Enterprises
P.O. Box 1403
Riverdale, NY 10471
www.baen.com

ISBN: 0-7434-9902-6

Cover art by Bob Eggleton

First printing, May 2005

Library of Congress Cataloging-in-Publication Data

Hogan, James P.
  Mission to Minerva / James P. Hogan.
      p. cm.
  ISBN 0-7434-9902-6 (hc)
  1. Space warfare--Fiction. I. Title.

  PR6058.O348M57 2005
  823'.914--dc22

                                                        2005001009

Distributed by Simon & Schuster
1230 Avenue of the Americas
New York, NY 10020

Production & design by Windhaven Press (www.windhaven.com)
Printed in the United States of America

10 9 8 7 6 5 4 3 2 1

For Sheryl, Lindsey, and Tara

PROLOGUE

By the fourth decade of the twenty-first century, the nations of Earth had finally resolved or learned to live with the differences that had made so much of their history a story of exploitation and conflict. A major expression of the new spirit of cooperation and optimism toward the future took the form of a joint program of Solar System exploration carried out under the direction of a Space Arm formed as part of the UN. With its redirection of the resources and industries that had once served a bloated defense sector, the program was seen as a triumph of the unifying power of technology and reason, and a prelude to reaching outward toward the stars. As permanent bases appeared on the Moon and Mars, and manned mission ships reached the outer planets, it was confidently assumed that the sciences responsible for such spectacular success were thereby shown to form a solidly based foundation for the continuing expansion of human knowledge. The basic belief structure was secure. While the universe undoubtedly had more revelations and surprises to deliver, the body of fact that had been established was impregnable to any major need in the way of revision.

Such moments of blissful self-assurance invariably come immediately before the biggest tumbles. In just a few short years, a series of stupefying discoveries not only added an entire new dimension to the history of the Solar System, but uncovered a strange, totally unanticipated story of the origins of the human race itself.

Twenty-five million years before the present time, a race of nonviolent, eight-foot-tall giants had flourished across the Solar System and surpassed everything that humankind had achieved. The "Ganymeans"—so-called when the first indication of their existence was discovered in the form of a wrecked spacecraft buried under the ice of Ganymede, largest of the Jovian moons—had originated on a planet christened Minerva, that had once occupied the position between Mars and Jupiter. By the time the Ganymean civilization reached an advanced stage, climatic conditions on Minerva were deteriorating. As would be expected, their voyages of discovery had brought them to Earth, from where they transported large numbers of plant and animal forms from the late Oligocene–early Miocene period back to their own world as part of a large-scale bioengineering research project to combat the problem. Terran life enjoyed a generally greater toxic resistance than that possessed by the Ganymeans, and their hope was to incorporate the appropriate genetic structures into their own makeup in order to render themselves tolerant to altering Minerva's atmosphere in a way that would enhance its natural greenhouse mechanism. These efforts failed, however, and the Ganymeans migrated to what would later come to be called the Giants' Star, located twenty light-years from Earth in the direction of the constellation of Taurus.

In the millions of years that followed, the imported terrestrial animals left on Minerva replaced most of the native Minervan forms, which owing to a peculiarity of early Minervan biology that precluded the emergence of land-dwelling carnivores, were unable to compete effectively. The terrestrial forms included a population of primates as advanced as anything existing on Earth at the time, which in addition had undergone genetic modification in the course of the Ganymean experimental program. Fifty thousand years before the present time, while the various hominid lines developing on Earth were still at stone-using stages of culture, a second advanced, spacegoing race had already appeared on Minerva as the first version of modern Man. They were given the name "Lunarians," after evidence of their existence came to light in the course of twenty-first century lunar exploration. (See *Inherit the Stars.*)

At the time of the emergence of the Lunarians, varying solar conditions were bringing the onset of the most recent ice age on Earth, while the even greater effect on Minerva threatened to render the planet uninhabitable. The Lunarians responded with a concerted effort to develop their space and industrial technologies to a level that would permit mass migration to the more hospitable climate of Earth. But, as with the Ganymeans before them, the ambitious plan came to nothing. When the Lunarians were practically within reach of their goal, the cooperative spirit in which they had worked for generations broke down with the polarization of their civilization into two superpowers, Cerios and Lambia. Resources that could have been concentrated on saving the race were squandered instead on a ruinous military rivalry. The result was a cataclysmic planetwide war, in the course of which Minerva was destroyed.

The Ganymean culture, in the meantime, had entered a long period of stagnation brought about by the unanticipated effects of advancing biological science to the point of prolonging life practically indefinitely. When the consequences became clear, they took a decision to revert to their natural condition and accept mortality as the price of experiencing a life enriched by motivation and change. By the time of the events on Minerva, they had established a thriving interstellar civilization centered on the planet Thurien of the Giants' Star system. The Thuriens were never comfortable with what they regarded their ancestors' abandonment of a genetically mutated sapient species left to take its chances in the survival arena of Minerva, and followed the subsequent emergence of the Lunarians with a mixture of guilt and increasing awe. But when it all ended in catastrophe, the Thuriens relaxed the policy of nonintervention that they had been observing and sent a rescue mission to save the survivors. Gravitational upheavals caused by the emergency methods used to transport the Thurien ships threw what remained of Minerva into an eccentric outer orbit to become Pluto, while the smaller debris dispersed under Jupiter's tidal effects as the Asteroids. Minerva's orphaned moon fell inward toward the Sun and was later captured by Earth, which until then had existed as a solitary body.

Even after all their experiences and the loss of their world, hostility between the Cerians and the Lambians persisted, making them incapable of uniting to rebuild their culture. The Lambians went back with the Thuriens and were installed on a planet called Jevlen, where they grew to become a fully human element of the Thurien civilization. The Cerians, at their own request, were returned to the world of their origins, Earth, only to be almost overwhelmed by the climatic and tidal devastation caused by the arrival of Minerva's moon. Their remnants fell back into barbarism, struggling for millennia on the verge of extinction. Apart from myths handed down from antiquity, the meanings of which were forgotten, all memory of their origins was lost. Only in modern times, when they at last mastered space again and ventured outward to find the traces of what had gone before, were they able to piece parts of the story together. The rest was added when a freak occurrence reestablished contact between the human inhabitants of modern Earth and the ancient Ganymean race that had created them in the form of their Lunarian ancestors. (See *The Gentle Giants of Ganymede*.)

The Jevlenese never ceased regarding themselves as Lambians, and the Terrans as ongoing rivals who would challenge them again if the opportunity arose. As part of a plan to eliminate the perceived threat, they inaugurated a campaign to retard the progress of Earth toward rediscovery of the sciences, while they themselves absorbed Thurien technology and gained autonomy over their own affairs. Fully human in form, they obstructed Earth's development by infiltrating agents throughout history to spread irrational beliefs and found cults of unreason, diverting energies from the path to reacquiring true knowledge.

As the confidence and arrogance of the Jevlenese leaders grew, so did their resentment of the restraint to their ambitions posed by the Thuriens. Exploiting the innate inability of the Ganymean psyche to suspect motives, they gained control of the surveillance operation that the Thuriens had set up to keep a watch over Earth after the catastrophe that had befallen Minerva. The Jevlenese fed falsified accounts to the Thuriens of a militarized Earth poised to burst out from the Solar System, and by playing on the implications, induced the Thuriens to devise countermeasures to isolate and contain the threat. But the Jevlenese intent was to seize control of the countermeasures themselves and contain the Thuriens, settle the score with their Cerian rivals of old, and then take control of the system of Thurien-administered worlds themselves. And the plan would have been fulfilled but for the reappearance of a lost starship from the time of ancient Ganymean Minerva.

The scientific mission ship *Shapieron* was sent to conduct experiments on altering the radiation dynamics of a distant star to assess the feasibility of changing the Sun's output as an alternative solution to Minerva's problem if the attempt based on atmospheric reengineering coupled with biological modification failed. But the star went unstable, forcing the *Shapieron* to make an emergency departure when partway through overhauling its drive system, which operated by creating a local distortion of spacetime. The result was that the ship experienced an artificially compounded time-dilation in which twenty-five million years passed by before it was able to reintegrate with the local solar reference frame, compared to only twenty years of ship's time. Hence, it returned to find the configuration of the Solar System changed, Minerva gone, and a new race of terrestrial humans spacefaring among the planets.

The "Giants" came to Earth, where they were cordially received, and remained for six months. But the most significant outcome of their presence was the opening of the first direct contact between Earth and the Thuriens, bypassing the Jevelenese intermediaries established by longstanding precedent. The story of how the Jevlenese had schemed to retard Earth's development and misrepresent its modern-day situation was finally exposed. In the ensuing confrontation the Jevelenese, who had been secretly making military preparations of their own, proclaimed their independence, staged a demonstration of strength, and demanded submission from the Thuriens. But their hand had been forced; the bid was premature and collapsed when the Terrans and Thuriens working together turned the Jevlenese's own stratagem of deception against them by inventing a fictitious Terran battle force manufactured entirely within the supercomputing entity VISAR, which supported the Thuriens' interstellar civilization. (See *Giants' Star.*)

The Jevelense leaders believed the deception and capitulated, after which the world of Jevlen was placed under Ganymean and Terran administration while a reformed system of government was being worked out. Because of the autonomy and privacy to run their own affairs that the Jevlenese had always insisted on, this was the first opportunity for outsiders to look closely into what had been going on there. What they found was even stranger than anything that had gone before.

Obsession for conquest and fixation on the irrational ideas that

had been imported to Earth was not a general trait common to all
Jevelenese. They stemmed from a small, disaffected but influential
group within the race that had appeared suddenly. Something
about their deeper psychology seemed to set them apart from
the majority of Jevlenese. They were the source of the beliefs in
magic and supernatural powers that defied all experience and
had never arisen among the Ganymeans or Lunarians, yet sprang
from inner convictions that were unshakable. It was as if their
instincts about the nature of the world and the forces operating
in it had been shaped by a different reality.

And it turned out that this was indeed exactly the case. For
the "Ents"—from "Entoverse," or "Universe Within," as the unique
realm where they originated came to be named—were not products
of the familiar world of space, time, matter, and physics at all. In
setting up their own planetary administration, the Jevlenese had
created an independent computing complex, JEVEX, to serve a
comparable purpose to that of the Thuriens' VISAR. In a peculiar
concurrence of circumstances, information quanta took on a role
analogous to that of material particles, interacting and combining
to form structures in the dataspace continuum that corresponded
to molecules and more complex configurations in physical space.
A complete phenomenological "universe" resulted, eventually producing self-organizing entities that were sufficiently complex to
become aware of their own existence and perceive themselves as
inhabitants of a world. But the "forces" that guided the unfolding of events in that world derived not from the physics of the
universe outside, but from the underlying internal rules imposed
by the system programmers.

Following Thurien practice, the primary method for interfacing
with JEVEX was by direct neural coupling to the mental processes
of the user. Some of the Ents discovered that they could interact
with the data streams flowing through their world, and from
them they extracted perceptions of a "higher space" beyond the
one that they existed in, where superior beings lived and impossible things happened. Adepts among the Ents learned to project
their psyches into these "currents" and transfer themselves into
this world "beyond," where they became occupiers of hosts who
had literally been possessed. So the aberrant element among the
Jevlenese were not deviants who had acquired their aggressions,
insecurities, and strange notions of causality in the same world of

experience that had molded the minds of Ganymeans, Lunarians, and Terrans; they were victims of a form of alien invasion more weird than science fiction had ever conceived. (See *Entoverse*.)

Such "possessed" Jevelenese—taken over by Ent personalities—seemed also have been at the root of the schism that subverted the Lunarian enterprise when it had almost succeeded—fifty thousand years before JEVEX even existed! How could this possibly be?

Following from the earlier Ganymean spacecraft propulsion technology, the Thurien interstellar transportation and communications web exploited artificial manipulations of spacetime to bypass the restrictions of ordinary space. The mathematics of the physics involved also admitted solutions that implied the possibility of transfer through time. Since the Thuriens had never been able to put a physical interpretation to this, they regarded it as no more than a theoretical curiosity. But then, in the final stage of the "Pseudowar" in which the Jevlenese believed themselves about to be assailed by VISAR's imaginary Terran invasion fleet, their leadership attempted an escape to a distant planet that they had secretly made into a fortress. When JEVEX initiated creation of a transfer port to transport their ships, VISAR intervened in a countermove to neutralize it. Nobody ever knew quite what happened as the two supercomputers grappled across light-years for control of the same knot of spacetime—except that the fleeing Jevlenese craft were swept into the convulsions. Afterward, all sign of them had vanished. Everywhere.

But the last images to be received from a surveillance probe that had clung in pursuit showed they had rematerialized somewhere. There was a background of stars. And there was a world. The world was Minerva, intact, as it had been. The starfield showed the time to have been the late period of the Lunarians. In fact, it was at just before the time when the Lambians adopted their militant and uncompromising policy toward Cerios. This was surely too much to have been a coincidence.

With Jevlen pacified and on probation while its population adjusted to life undisturbed by the influence of the Ents, the scientists of Thurien and Earth were free to turn their attention to the latest, and perhaps the most baffling mystery of all. (See also the "Giants Chronology" compiled by Dr. Attila Torkos, page 403.)

PART ONE

The Multiverse

CHAPTER ONE

The object appeared out of nowhere on the Earth-ward side of the Sun, roughly halfway between the mean orbits of Earth and Mars. Its bulk ejected the flux of solar-wind particles and cosmic-ray photons that happened to be occupying the volume that it materialized in, and generated a mild gravitational ripple fitting for its mass of several tens of thousand tons equivalent. But otherwise, its arrival was as unremarkable as its appearance.

It was about the size of a domestic washing machine and vaguely cubical in form, although any clear lines were lost in the profusion of antennas and sensor appendages cluttered untidily on all its sides. For a while it hung in space, sampling and processing information from its surroundings and sending its findings back to the realm from whence it had come. Then, as suddenly as it had arrived, it vanished again.

Its corrected position put it inside the Moon's orbit, approximately twenty-two thousand miles above the Earth's surface in the belt used by synchronous communications satellites. One more relocation, and it was in place to intercept the beam from the comnet ground station in Maine, which handled one of the primary trunk routes into the USA. The alien device connected into the system using standard Terran communications protocols and transmitted the phone number of the UN Space Arm's Advanced Sciences Division at the Goddard Center in Maryland, one of the homes of what had been NASA in years gone by.

In a neighborhood bar called Happy Days, a few miles from Goddard, Dr. Victor Hunt leaned back in a corner booth by the window and took in the scene. It was a sunny Saturday morning in June. People were making the best of the fine weekend. Across the aisle, three men who had pulled up earlier in a pickup loaded with timber were downing some preventative thirst medicine on what looked like their way to a home remodeling project. Some younger people at the far end were working up enthusiasm in advance for the Baltimore Orioles versus Atlanta Braves game due to be played later. A couple sat holding hands across one of the tables, blissfully unaware of anything else.

For Hunt, the snatched moment of relaxation was a rare luxury. His position as Deputy Director for Physics of UNSA Advanced Sciences put him at the center of the effort to assimilate Thurien scientific knowledge without disrupting Earth's social and economic structure. Already, some of the most cherished notions once believed to be permanently beyond questioning had been consigned to oblivion. The whole system of values that most had considered as constituting the inescapable underpinnings of commerce and production was having to be rethought in the light of the Thurien existence, proof that deeper, less adversarial ways of motivating creativity and cooperation were possible. Nobody knew what the next ten or twenty years might bring. Paradoxically, for the majority of people this all added up to carrying on more or less as normal. The gigantic forces now in motion that would change all their lives irreversibly were beyond any ability of theirs to control.

A swarthy figure sporting a shaggy mustache and wearing a bright scarlet shirt and shorts turned from the bar and came over, bearing two pint glasses of black, creamy-headed Guinness. Jerry Santello was Hunt's neighbor from the adjacent apartment unit in a landscaped residential development on the edge of town. They had come out for some refreshment after a morning workout at the complex's gym. Jerry deposited the glasses on the table, pushed one across, and sat back down on the seat opposite.

"Cheers," Hunt acknowledged, raising his in salutation as he picked it up.

Jerry took a draft and licked his lips. "I'd never have believed it. I'm actually taking to this stuff."

"About time, too. Beats that fizzy yellow concoction. Too sweet. I'm not sure I like the connotations of Clydesdales, either."

"The bartender asked me if I wanted them mixed with ale. Is that normal in England too?"

"Black and tan," Hunt replied, nodding.

"Oh, really?"

"Half and half. That's what they call it. It was the name of the auxiliary military units the English used in Ireland back it the time of the Troubles ... around 1920, or whenever it was. They had uniforms that were half police and half army."

"Wasn't it two different countries there until not long ago?"

"Right. The North originally stayed with the UK—when the rest became the Republic."

"What was all that shit about? I never could figure it."

Hunt shrugged. "Usual thing, Jerry. Too many Catholics. Too many Protestants. No Christians." He looked away while he took another sip. A girl called Julie, who worked in one of the administration sections at ASD, had come in with two others that he didn't recognize. Jerry carried on.

"Anyway, Vic, as I was saying, this scheme that the guys are buying into. . . . People are working less, retiring sooner, and when the family's grown and gone and they move to a smaller house that's paid for." He made an open-handed gesture. "They've got money. The spendable income isn't with the kids anymore. By the time they leave school half of them are maxed out on credit already."

Jerry was a former employee of the intelligence agencies. The spy business had contracted markedly as the world gradually resolved a legacy of twentieth-century political absurdities by allowing people to live among those they chose to. Having banked a lump severance payment, and finding himself less than enamored by the thought of returning to the corporate style of workplace, he was constantly on the lookout for investment opportunities to provide the wherewithal for preserving the ease and freedoms that a period of enforced paid leave had led him to grow accustomed to. The latest was a plan for a chain of theater-restaurants with lounge bars and dance floors to cater to the more mature clientele. It was an interesting thought, Hunt had to agree. There were probably thousands of such couples, or singles wanting to be half a couple, hidden away in the suburbs with nowhere to go that suited their taste. At just over forty himself, Hunt could go for it.

"I've always wanted to own a nightclub," he said. "I like the image. It must be from seeing *Casablanca* years ago. You know, Bogart in the white tuxedo with the carnation in the lapel. Piano bar and all that stuff. . . . You don't see that kind of style these days. Do you reckon we could bring it back, Jerry?"

Jerry tossed up a hand. "Who knows? Anything's possible. Does that mean you're in?"

"How much are we talking about?"

"The other guys are coming in for ten grand."

"Um . . . I'd need to think a bit more. How soon do you need to know?"

"The option on the deal closes at the end of next week."

"Okay, I'll let you know one way or another by then."

"You can't lose, Vic. Lot's of people have been waiting for something like this, who don't take to the bar scene. Some place to go out and meet your friends, have a meal, see a show. . . . Music that you don't have to be some kind of spastic epileptic or something to dance to . . ."

"Dr. Hunt?" Hunt looked up. Julie had come over to the booth with her two friends. She was tallish and slim, with fair hair, a scattering of freckles around her nose, and just at that moment, a nervously uncertain smile. "I saw you over here and just wanted to stop by and say hi. I hope you don't mind."

"Not at all. Glad you did." Hunt looked at her quizzically for a moment. "Julie, from the main admin section, right?"

"That's right!" Julie seemed impressed.

Hunt glanced at the other two girls, who were hovering behind. "So what are we doing—starting a party?"

"Oh. This is Becky, who's visiting from Virginia . . . and Dana."

Hunt gestured across the booth. "Jerry, my neighbor."

"You live near here?"

"Redfern Canyons—on the west side from here."

"I think I know it. Where they have all the valleys and ridges cut into the hills so it looks like somewhere in California. With a creek and ponds down the middle."

"That's it."

Becky, who was looking mildly awed, found her voice finally. "This is really *the* Dr. Hunt . . . who was there at Ganymede when the aliens came back, and then discovered that whole world inside the computer on Jevlen?" She shook her head. "I always think of people you see on shows and read about in magazines as flying everywhere in limousines and living in places with security gates and fences. But here you are, just a regular guy in the local bar."

"I hope we weren't interrupting something," Dana said.

"We're quaffing away all the benefit from a couple of hours of healthy working out this morning," Hunt replied. "But I've always had this theory that too much health is bad for you."

"So that tastes really good, I bet." Julie indicated their drinks.

"The first one didn't touch the sides going down," Jerry said.

"Actually, Jerry was trying to sell me on a business proposition. Restaurant nightclubs for older fossils like us to get out to and creak around in. What do you think?"

Julie looked perplexed. "I'm not sure what to say. You don't exactly look over the hill or anything like that, Dr. Hunt."

"Oh, don't worry about it," Hunt told her cheerfully. "People have the wrong attitude. What's wrong with getting over a hill? Think what happens on a bicycle. All the hard work's over. You just leave everything to gravity, sit back, enjoy the view, and pick up speed. Life's the same. That's why everyone says time goes so much faster. You know—" The call tone from the seefone in the holder on his belt interrupted. "Excuse me." He took it out, flipped it open, and thumbed the Accept button. The head and shoulders of a young man in a white shirt greeted him on the screen. A caption below gave the sending code and advised that the call was from the UNSA Goddard Center. "Hello. Vic Hunt here."

"Dr. Hunt, this is ASD. We have an incoming off-planet call on hold. The caller is asking for you."

Off-planet? Hunt wasn't especially expecting anything of that nature. UNSA communications from distances farther than about the Moon usually came in as recordings because of the propagation delays. Ironically, an interactive call was more likely to be from the Thuriens' interstellar net, which communicated virtually instantaneously via spinning microscopic black-hole toroids, and linked to the Terran system via Earth-orbiting relay satellites.

"Who is it?" he asked, at the same time conveying an apology with his eyes to the others around him. But the face on the screen hesitated, seeming not to know how to answer. "It doesn't matter," Hunt said. "Just put it through." A moment later, he was staring incredulously in total befuddlement.

The face looking back at him was of a man around forty, with tanned, lean-lined features giving him an alert and active look, and wavy brown hair starting to show touches of gray just discernible on the matchbook-size screen. He seemed amused, even impudently so, waiting several seconds as if savoring the effect to the utmost. Finally, he said, "I suppose this must come as a bit of a shock."

Which perhaps qualified as one of the greatest understatements in all Hunt's years of experience. For the face was his own. He was talking to some bizarre version—existing in some other where, and for all he knew, some other "when"—of *himself*. He could do nothing but sit there, stupefied, unable to muster a coherent response. The three girls exchanged mystified looks. Then Jerry said, "Are you all right, Vic?"

The words jolted Hunt sufficiently to make him look up, though for the moment still only marginally aware of his surroundings. Finally, with an effort, he forced his faculties back to something resembling working order. "Er, I'm sorry," he said, standing up. "If you'll excuse me, I need to take this privately." He crossed to the exit and left.

"What was it, a ghost?" Jerry muttered to the others.

Outside in the parking lot, Hunt climbed into his car and closed the door. The face of his other self was still there, waiting on the screen of the seefone. "Okay, I give up," he told it. "So . . . just what in hell is going on?"

"I'll try to be brief, because there may not be a lot of time," the image answered. "First, the Thuriens are trying the wrong approach. It isn't an extension of the h-space physics the way they've assumed. That only applies within particular wave solutions evolving vertically and manifesting internal space and time separation. Horizontal movement involves a different concept. Think of the dynamics of the data structures that we found in JEVEX's computing matrix. . . . As I said, there may not be a lot of time. This is an early test run. We haven't learned how to sustain coherence for extended periods yet. I've got a compressed file here that will give you what we've managed to figure out so far. The main thing you need to know about is the convergences. But codes can be different, even between nearby regions. Can you send me something to scan for any transmission corrections we might need to make?"

"What . . . ?" Hunt was still numbed by the shock.

"A file out of your system there. Anything. We need to know the codes you're using so the one here can be set to match."

"Oh. . . . Right. . . ." Hunt shook himself into action sufficiently to bring up a directory of his personal library and flagged one of the items for transmission.

"Using the phone," his alter ego observed. "Where have I caught you?"

"Er . . . I'm in the parking lot outside Happy's. I was with Jerry Santello. . . . Here, it's coming through now."

"Okay, got it. Let's see, now . . ." The alter-Hunt looked away. "Which time was that?" he inquired as he worked, evidently consulting some off-screen oracle.

"A Saturday—the time that Julie from admin showed up with a couple of her friends. There's an Orioles-Braves game due to be played later."

"I don't recall that. It was probably different on this time line. The parallelisms can show surprising discontinuities." Then, in a louder voice, apparently to someone nearby, "Have we got it yet?"

"Jerry was selling the restaurant-dance-bar thing again," Hunt said.

"Oh, that. Yes. Tell him to forget it. It's a scam. The pictures in the brochure he's got are faked. It's a shell company set up by a Ukrainian outfit who'll take the money and fold. If you want a better deal, buy Formaflex in Austin. Small pilot experiment. Nobody knows about it yet—limited license to deal in Thurien matter-duplicator technology. It's going to go over big." Alter-Hunt winked, then looked away again. "Okay? Are we ready? Can I send—"

The connection died, as twenty-two thousand miles above the Earth's surface the object that had appeared out of nowhere dissolved into a haze that dispersed and faded, leaving nothing.

Hunt waited fifteen minutes, but nothing more came through.

CHAPTER TWO

Even before the first contact with Ganymeans, when the *Shapieron* from ancient Minerva returned from its strange exile out of normal spacetime, the majority of Earth's physicists had come to favor the explanation of quantum weirdness known as the Many Worlds Interpretation, or MWI. Its claims were so bizarre and counterintuitive that many maintained it *couldn't* have been conceived by unaided human imagination or unwitting self-deception. Therefore, it had to be true. The discovery that a race of advanced, starfaring aliens had reached the same conclusion seemed as strong an endorsement as anyone could wish for and pretty much won over the last of the doubters.

The "quantum paradoxes" that textbooks and popular writers of years gone by had reveled in arose when a system of quantum entities such as photons or electrons existing in some particular state changed to some different state when a number of new states were possible. Examples might be an energetically excited atom that could relax back to its minimum-energy "ground" state via any of several alternative sequences of intermediate energy levels, or a photon hitting a half-silvered mirror, which gave it a fifty-fifty chance of being reflected or transmitted. How did Nature "choose" from the various possibilities the one that actually took place?

On the face of it, the situation seemed no different from that of, say, a gambler's die, which from the rolling state could assume any of six discrete final states, each showing a different number. The mechanics of moving objects was well understood, and only inability to specify precisely the die's shape, mass, and motion prevented the outcome to be predicted reliably every time. In other words there was no mystery. The outcome was determined, but imperfect knowledge made it unpredictable. However, this was only another way of saying that the situations were not the same to begin with. At the quantum level, this was not so. The systems being investigated were identical in every way that could be established. Why, then, should they behave differently?

Quantum objects acted as if they were everything at once while they were not interacting with their environment, but the instant they encountered another entity capable of pinning them down—for instance, a detector in a measuring instrument designed to find out something about them—they abruptly took on one from the available selection of possible states. Hardly surprisingly, such oddness did not sit lightly with beings accustomed to a world in which things knew what they were and continued to be so while nothing was looking at them. The scientific debate about the perplexing accumulation of quantum paradoxes raged through the first two decades of the twentieth century—beginning, ironically, immediately following a series of confident assurances that everything of substance was known and science was effectively a closed book. But there could be no getting away from what the results of countless experiments seemed to indicate. The challenge was to account for them in a way that described what was "really" going on.

Some refused to get embroiled in the issue at all, and instead took the view of science as being simply a pragmatic process for generating numbers to be compared with experimental results, beyond which nothing more could be said. For a long time the predominant view was that nothing really existed in any objective sense at all until an act of observation caused it to assume one of its possible sets of attributes ("states") randomly. Exactly what constituted an "observation" was a further source of contention, opinions covering the range of steps from any interaction with another quantum object, to the final registering of an impression upon a human consciousness. Others avoided the disturbingly mystical implications of this kind of approach by maintaining that the allegedly identical objects weren't really identical but differed in some subtle ways that eluded detection at the present time. The problem with this, however was that it required everything in the universe to be capable, just as subtly, of instantly influencing everything else, a notion which many considered to be every bit as mystical as anything else that was being said, if not more so.

By the end of the twentieth century, the scientific world had come to terms with accepting that whatever answer they settled on was going to be bizarre by normal standards anyway, so they might as well get used to throwing away all preconceptions and focus purely on what the facts seemed to be trying to say. And what the facts said, when the formalism was taken at face value without imposing some arbitrary wave-function "collapse" that the mathematics said nothing about, was that the world showed evidence of being everything at once because it *was* everything at once; the reason it didn't appear that way was that everyday awareness only apprehends a small part of it.

According to the picture that finally emerged, neither an energized atom nor an impinging photon "chooses" one state from an ensemble of possible states—thus provoking endless debates about how, when, and why it gets to make that choice; *every* possibility is actualized—but each in its own separate reality, which then continues to evolve the various consequences of the particular alternative that led to it. The various realities all contain versions of their inhabitants that are consistent with the unfolding of events making up that reality, remaining unaware of all the rest. The dice thrower in one reality rolls a boxcar, double six, breaks the bank, and retires rich; his counterpart in another of the thirty-six possible two-die variants rolls zilch, loses his shirt, and jumps off a bridge. This formed the essence of the Many Worlds Interpretation of quantum mechanics.

Many popular accounts talked about the universe "splitting" into alternative forms, with notions of what constituted a branch point varying from "every quantum interaction" to any event deemed sufficiently significant by humans—the realities continuing thereafter to exist adjacently but separate and discrete, somewhat like the pages of a book. Hence the term "parallel universe." But while perhaps more easy to visualize, this did not accurately capture the strange state of affairs that the formulators of the MWI were proposing. New universes didn't spring into existence out of nothing every time some kind of decision was called for, anymore than New York or Boston suddenly materializes in response to a driver's going right or left at a junction in the highway. They were there already and always had been, just like all the other possible destinations on the road map.

In a similar kind of way, not only all the futures that could possibly arise from a given "now," but all the different "nows" that could have come about, existed as parts of an immense, branching totality, all of it equally real. Within it, every quantum alternative led to a unique consequent reality which in that detail at least differed from all the rest. Rather than resembling a stack of pages, its nature was more that of a continuum of change existing in as many directions as change was possible. The kind of change depended on the direction taken, occurring sometimes gradually, sometimes abruptly. Every conceivable way in which one world could differ from another therefore corresponded to an axis of change within the continuum, endowing it with an as good as infinite number of dimensions. The totality itself was unchanging and timeless. The phenomenon of time measured by physics arose as a construct of the event sequence that arose from tracing a particular path through the tree of branching alternatives. Every such path defined its own discrete reality, or "universe." The perception of time emerged from a consciousness following such a path through the alternatives that it encountered. Exactly how was something that the physicists left to philosophers, theologians, and mystics to explain.

The normal "forward" flow of experience within a universe ran up the tree of branching time lines. Direct knowledge of the other realities existing to the "sides" seemed to be precluded—except for the interference paradoxes that resulted from information leaking across at the tiniest level, from which the necessary existence of the entire stupefying whole had been inferred. Of course, this didn't prevent speculation on whether some kind of communication "horizontally"—between branches—might be possible. Even if it were, nobody had the remotest idea how such a thing would be achieved. It remained just an intriguing hypothesis, good for philosophical Ph.D. dissertations, becoming known in obscure journals, and getting a discussion going at cocktail parties. Nothing in the whole of history suggested any precedent for taking the subject seriously. . . .

And then, the last pictures came back from the probe that had pursued the fleeing Jevlenese spacecraft, showing that they had been hurled across light-years of space and back tens of thousands of years in time to reappear near the planet Minerva in the era of its habitation by the Lunarians, long after the Ganymeans had departed. The proof was there, indisputably, that it had happened. The demonstration that put an abrupt end to any further speculation as to whether such a happening was possible came to be known as the "Minerva event."

After the years he had spent as Hunt's boss in some capacity or other, Gregg Caldwell had thought he was past being capable of surprise anymore. Four years previously, in 2028, when the first evidence of the Lunarians was discovered on the Moon in the form of a fifty-thousand-year-old spacesuited corpse, Caldwell, as chief of UNSA's former Navigation and Communications Division, had set the ebullient Englishman the task of unraveling the mystery of where "Charlie" had come from. Exactly what reconstructing pictures of vanished civilizations had to do with the business of navigating UNSA's spacecraft and maintaining its communications around the Solar System was a good question, but Caldwell had always been a compulsive empire builder. His way of going about things was to stake out a claim on getting something done while others debated the demarcation lines, and possession being nine-tenths of the law, like some of the ideas of quantum physics that he had been hearing lately, he created what became reality. Hunt, along with his biologist partner-in-crime, Christian Danchekker, who now directed the Alien Life Sciences Division, had responded by causing the story of human origins to be rewritten from its beginnings. When Caldwell sent the pair of them to Jupiter to look into some relics of long-vanished aliens that came to light shortly afterward on Ganymede, they came back with a starship full of live ones. Despatched to Jevelen to help pinpoint the source of mass mental derangement among the natives, they turned up an entire functioning universe evolved out of data structures inside a planet-size computer. But this latest was straining Caldwell's credulity, even yet.

He sat at the desk, flanked on one side by a wall of display screens, in his office on the top floor of the Advanced Sciences building, drumming his fingers on the armrests of his chair while Hunt paced in front of the picture window overlooking the

Goddard complex. Caldwell was stockily built, with steely gray hair cropped short and the kind of solidly carved, heavy-jowled face that suggested granite slabs and lunar crags. His expression remained impassive despite the excitement that Hunt was still unable to contain. Just what kind of reaction should be expected from someone who had talked to another version of himself, calling on the phone from another universe, Caldwell wasn't exactly sure. If the story had come from anyone other than Vic Hunt, he would simply have refused to believe it. Hunt had also kicked his lifetime smoking habit not long ago, which probably added to the theatrics.

"Gregg, it means that somewhere in another part of the Multiverse they've figured it out," Hunt said, not for the first time. "Somewhere corresponding to a future ahead of where we are right now." As a rule, he kept his thought processes orderly enough to avoid such repetition. Caldwell granted that these were somewhat unusual circumstances. "It must have been some kind of test to establish a channel across time lines. They were going to send us a file containing what they knew, but the link went down too soon. My God, Gregg! Can you imagine what it would mean if this ever became routine? Suppose you could get a copy of a new Shakespeare play that he never wrote in our history! Or an authentic account of how the pyramids were really built! What do you think that kind of cross-cultural fertilization might be worth?"

"Let's not get too carried away by that for now, and just stick to the basics," Caldwell suggested. "We figure it had to be some kind of communications relay that appeared out there in orbit." The message routing log into Goddard had shown the signal to have come in via a channel that didn't exist. The signal turn-around delay indicated that it couldn't have been much farther away than the synchsat belt, twenty-two thousand miles out. Hunt had reasoned that it had to have been a relay device rather than a manned vessel of some kind on the grounds that the premature termination pointed to an experimental program still in its early days. Hunt, sure as hell, would never have climbed into a conjuror's box like that, to be shot off into another universe at that stage of the game. It seemed a fairly safe bet that no other version of what was, after all, Hunt's same self would have, either. Caldwell couldn't argue with that.

"Interfacing into the Terran comnet in the same way the Thurien relay satellites that we've got now do," Hunt affirmed. That would have made the device massive, though not necessarily huge in size. Information transfer into and out of the realm used by the Thurien interstellar communications system, referred to as h-space, was effected via spinning microscopic black-hole toroids generated artificially. Putting them in orbit avoided the weight problems that would have resulted from locating the equipment on the Earth's surface. The various Terran outposts across the Solar System were being equipped with Thurien relays as well. When the network was completed, it would mean that a link from a UNSA base at Jupiter to Goddard, for example, could be routed via the Thurien system, making communications turnaround delays of hours or more a thing of the past.

"And the gist of what you . . . he, this other Hunt, whatever, had to say was that Eesyan and his guys are going about it the wrong way," Caldwell went on. "It needs a different kind of physics. The Multiverse is more like the JEVEX computing matrix?"

The Minerva event involving the fleeing Jevlenese had demonstrated cross-Multiverse transfer to be possible. Ever since it happened, Thurien scientists had been trying to unravel exactly what had taken place in the hope of being able to reproduce the effect. Porthik Eesyan was one of the Thuriens' principal scientific figures, attached to their culture's highest administrative body at their Government Center in the principal city of Thurios. Hunt moved back from the window and across in front of Caldwell's desk, frowning while he collected his thoughts.

VISAR, the computing entity that managed the technicalities of the Thurien civilization, was a distributed system scattered across all the star systems that they had spread to. The Jevelenese, by contrast, had built their counterpart to VISAR as a centralized system physically located in one planet, where the workload was handled in a gigantic, contiguous, three-dimensional matrix of cells, each combining the functions of computing, storage, and communication. Changes of state propagating through the matrix from one adjoining cell to another in the course of computation behaved in a way comparable to that of elementary particles moving in physical space, which was interesting but amounted to no more than an unremarkable analogy. But things hadn't stopped there. The rules adopted by the Jevlenese system designers to govern the interactions between cells resulted in the emergence of behavior that uncannily mimicked such properties as mass, charge, energy, and momentum. These in turn gave rise to extended structures formed in the manner of molecules by the balance of opposing forces, out of which emerged a universe of worlds orbiting data-radiating "suns," and eventually harboring its own form of peculiar, squabblesome, sentient beings. It sounded as if Hunt was saying that the underlying nature of the Multiverse was something similar.

"It seems as if it could be the key to the whole thing," Hunt said. "Forget all the physics you've heard before, that talks about mass and energy moving through space. That's the physics that happens within a Multiverse reality that you happen to be a part of."

"You mean on some particular time line—like the one we're in here, right now?"

"Exactly. Where serial ordering gives rise to the perception of change, unfolding in ways that differential equations describe. Ordinary physics—and that includes all the Thurien h-space business as well—is expressed in the language of change. But the Multiverse itself is changeless. So crossing it would have to involve something other than physical movement. In the JEVEX matrix nothing actually moves. Cells just flip between states."

Caldwell stared while he digested that. It seemed almost obvious once it was spelled out. "Wouldn't the same underlying cell structure apply everywhere, here included?" he queried. "It's all part of the same MV."

"Yes," Hunt agreed. "In fact, Dirac proposed something very like it: a universe filled with a 'sea' of particles in negative energy states. They become observable when they're kicked up to positive states. Antiparticles are the holes left behind. They can move around too, as if they were particles—like holes in semiconductors."

"Go on," Caldwell said.

Hunt arrived back at the window, stared out for a second, then wheeled around and spread his arms sideways along the sill. "The matrix supports two kinds of physics. One, we just mentioned: the familiar kind that describes change, which applies to the event sequences ordered along time lines. The other involves a different form of cross-propagating cell states."

"What kind of propagation speed might we talking about, do you think?" Caldwell inquired.

Hunt shook his head. "I don't know."

"Have you talked to Sonnerbrandt yet?" Josef Sonnebrandt was a quantum theoretician at the Max Planck Institute in Berlin, who probably knew more about Entoverse physics than anyone else at the Earth end of the Jevlen link.

Hunt nodded. "He thinks we're probably talking about basic elements of the dimensions of Planck length switching in Planck time or something like that, but how any of it would translate into the dimensions that we measure things on is impossible to say right now. The Thuriens might be in a better position to guess. They've been doing the experiments. We and they need to get our acts together."

Caldwell sucked at his teeth while he contemplated the desktop. Silence ensued for perhaps half a minute. Hunt turned and stared out at the dark marble-and-glass bulk of the Biosciences building, looming above trees on the far side of one of the airmobile parking areas.

"Then let's do that," Caldwell said.

Hunt turned back to face him again. Caldwell got the feeling that this was what he had been angling for. "Are we talking about a Thurien trip? That's what it would need, Gregg. Would that be on?"

Caldwell gave him a long, pensive look, then nodded. "Okay."

"Seriously?"

"If I say it's on, it's on." Caldwell studied him for a moment longer. "You know, Vic, you don't seems as surprised as you would have been in days gone by. What's happening? Does it come with getting older?"

"No, it comes from getting to know you. Nothing could surprise me anymore."

"Well, that works both ways." Caldwell turned to one side and touched a key on the desk unit. The face of his secretary, Mitzi, in the outer office, appeared. "Did you talk to Farrell?" he inquired.

"Yes, I did. He says how about ten tomorrow? You're clear then."

"That's fine. And another thing, Mitzi. Could you get on the h-net and see if VISAR can raise Porthik Eesyan at Thurien? Also, I'd like the schedule of the Thurien ships that will be here and when, over, say, the next month."

"Going on vacation?"

"I think we've maybe found another job for Vic."

"I should have guessed. Will do."

Caldwell cleared down and looked back at Hunt. "I think I'm pretty much past surprises, too. The last time I sent you anywhere, you came back with a Universe. This time it's the entire Multiverse. That's it, the ultimate. It has to be. You can't get any bigger than that. Am I right?"

They stared at each other for a second. Then Hunt's face split into a grin. They were in business once again. He obviously liked the feeling. Caldwell allowed his craggy features to soften into the hint of a smile and snorted. "What about Josef in Berlin?" he asked, getting back on track. "Do you figure you could use him along, too?"

"Sure—if he's up to it. Want me to sound him out?"

"Yes, do that. And I guess it goes without saying that Chris Danchekker's going to want to be in on it, too. We can put it to him at the dinner for Owen tonight, after you make the big announcement."

"Sounds good," Hunt agreed.

So far, the story of Hunt's contact with another version of himself had not gone beyond a select few among UNSA's senior management and scientific staff. A dinner was being held that evening in honor of one of the original UNSA founders, who was retiring, at which Hunt was due to say some words of appreciation on behalf of the physical sciences side of the operation. Someone had suggested that this might be a good opportunity to make the news of Hunt's strange experience public. Caldwell's initial reaction had been negative on the grounds that such a bombshell would risk eclipsing Owen on what was supposed to be his night, after all. Hunt had felt that it could just as well work the other way: having one's retirement dinner cited as the occasion when the world had been was told could be the best memorial to a lifetime's work that anyone could wish for. In the end they had decided to put it to Owen and let him decide. Owen's answer was that he could think of no greater honor than to have his name linked with what could qualify as one of the most exciting scientific revelations of all time.

"I take it we're still going ahead," Caldwell said. People did have second thoughts about things like this.

"I was planning to double-check with Owen before I get up to speak," Hunt answered. "I can always switch to a fallback routine of Irish jokes or something if he changes his mind." Caldwell nodded that they were both thinking the same way.

The screen by his elbow came to life again to show an elongated Ganymean head, dark gray in color, with a protruding chin and vertical gothic lines framing large, ovoid eyes. The shoulders were covered by the top of a light orange tunic, with a yellow collar enclosing the neck. The countenance compressed in the way Caldwell had learned to recognize as an alien grin.

"Porthik Eesyan," Mitzi's voice announced. "I told him Vic is with you. He says it sounds like a sure sign of trouble ahead."

CHAPTER THREE

Professor Christian Danchekker was perplexed. One of the cornerstones of what had been regarded as an unquestionable and universal tenet of biological theory looked as if it might be resting on shaky ground. Accepted scientific beliefs had not been arrived at lightly, and he was not of a nature to change them lightly.

He sat hunched in his office in the Biosciences building at Goddard, his lean, balding frame and gangling limbs splayed at an odd composition of angles in one of those chairs that never seemed to be the right size or shape no matter how many models he tried, and frowned at the offending papers strewn around the desk, while he polished the lenses of his anachronistic gold-rimmed spectacles. Then he perched them back on the bridge of his nose and returned his attention to the references that he had listed on one of the displays on the side panel. The reports were on work done in various places around the world to duplicate and extend some experiments performed by a research group in Australia on nutrient-metabolizing pathways in certain strains of bacteria. In general, each type of bacterium depended on a primary food that it possessed the genes to break down and utilize. Probably the most familiar example was the common *E. coli*, found in humans, which required the sugar lactose. It sometimes happened that if the mechanism to digest the primary food was disabled, mutations were possible that could create an alternative metabolic pathway to exploit a different food instead. In the case of *E.coli*, two particular point mutations occurring simultaneously enabled it to feed on a different sugar. The mutation rates were known, and under the conditions of a typical laboratory experiment would be expected to occur together about once in a hundred thousand years. In practice, scores of examples were observed within a few days. But it happened *only* when the alternative target sugar was present in the nutrient solution used for the culture.

What this meant was that the mutations were not random, as biological doctrine had steadfastly maintained for over a century, but triggered by cues in the environment. And that in turn meant that the genetic "programs" for responding to those cues must already have been there, in the bacterial genome to begin with. They hadn't arisen over millions of years of trial-and-error selection from random mutations. The process by which it was achieved had been uncovered in the form of messenger proteins encoding externally acquired information that was written into the genome by special-purpose enzymes—misinterpreted as components of antibodies to viruses that turned out never to have existed, and a cause of a huge medical scandal and a spate of class-action suits in years gone by. One of the central dogmas of evolutionary theory was thus shown to be violated. That the whole business was a far more complex affair than had been confidently supposed was, to put it mildly, the least troubling interpretation that could be put on it.

Danchekker still wasn't sure if a senior directorship in the UNSA hierarchy, with all the attendant bureaucratic chores and deference to academic convention, really suited him. In his quieter moments, when he relaxed in his apartment to the music of Mahler or Berlioz, or sat contemplating the trees by some secluded tributary of the Potomac, his mind still soared with the Jupiter mission ships to the icy wastes of Ganymede and saw again the pale green, orange-streaked skies of Jevlen above the towering alien cityscapes. Across the vast tract of worlds that the Thuriens had spread to, there dwelt more strange and wondrous forms of life than could be so much as glimpsed in the remainder of a lifetime. On Crayses there was a creature that was both animal and plant, rooting itself in the ground when conditions were agreeable, moving on when they changed. Yaborian Two had somehow produced a reversed planetwide chemistry in which oxy-carbon based life flourished in a reducing atmosphere of methane.

He realized that he had drifted away into musings again when Sandy Holmes, his technical assistant, stuck her head in from the lab area outside the office. Divisional director or not, Danchekker wouldn't let administrative matters prevent him from keeping his practical hand in. Taking care of them was what staff were for. He refused to accept calls while he was working.

"Excuse me, Professor?"

"Hm? What? . . . Oh." Danchekker returned reluctantly to planet Earth. He sighed and gestured at the papers lying in front of him. "It appears that much of what we considered to be unquestionable may have to be rethought from basics, Sandy. The development of organisms is much more closely coupled with the environment than existing theory can account for. You need to read this. . . . Anyway, what is it?"

"Mildred is downstairs in reception. You're due to have lunch with her, remember?"

"Ah, yes." Normally, Danchekker blanched at the mention of the name. His cousin from Austria had been camped in the Washington, DC, area for a couple of months while researching her latest book, which was on Thurien culture and sociology. She had latched onto Danchekker as her prime reference and research source. But today he was actually looking forward to seeing her. "Can you organize an aircab to the front door for us, Sandy?"

"It's on its way. I told them, the Olive Tree. Is that okay?"

"That will do splendidly."

"And Ms. Mulling asked me to remind you that you're meeting Vic Hunt and Gregg Caldwell at the Carnarvon at six-thirty tonight." Ms. Mulling was Danchekker's personal secretary, whom he thankfully left to take command of administrative and fiscal matters from her domain on the far side of the top floor, from whence she ruled the building. She had come with his appointment as director in the UNSA reorganizational shuffle and was the main reason for his refusing to take calls when immersed in the things that interested him. Her name was usually sufficient to evoke a reflex grimace too, but on this occasion Danchekker merely nodded matter-of-factly as he slipped off his lab coat and draped it on the stand inside the door. "You seem in great spirits today, Professor," Sandy remarked as she walked with him back across the lab area to where she had been working with a technician preparing microscope slides.

"It looks as if our devious scheme is about to pay off," Danchekker replied breezily. "A week from now, our persistent and pestering authoress will be on her way to distant reaches of the Galaxy, and peace will return to the realm."

"You've heard back from Frenua?"

"Earlier this morning. It's as good as arranged. You know how informal the Thuriens are. I shall convey the joyous tidings forthwith, over lunch, and I have no doubt that cousin Mildred will be suitably thrilled."

"I'm glad it worked out. Enjoy your lunch."

"Oh, indubitably."

Danchekker hummed to himself in the elevator all the way down, oblivious of the clerk carrying a sheaf of papers who got in at the eighth floor and left at the fifth. When the doors opened on the ground level, he sailed out with a broad, toothy smile to greet his cousin, waiting in the lobby area beyond. Mildred was momentarily taken aback but recovered quickly.

"Christian, you're exactly on time! You look quite on top of the world today."

"And why not? I might ask. We should not let the chores of our humdrum lives mar the splendor of such a heaven-sent day. I can see more shades of green from my window on the top floor than would grace a legion of leprechauns." Danchekker held the main door aside graciously to usher Mildred through. She looked at him uncertainly.

"Are you all right?"

"Never better. And you look radiant too—a fitting tribute to spring."

In fact, Danchekker thought she looked mildly ridiculous in one of those floppy, wide-brimmed hats with flowers that even he knew had been out of style for years, a floral dress that was doubtless practical but seemed grannyish, and a pair of equally practical lightweight boots that might have done service on the Appalachian Trail. But beyond that, she *talked*.

The cab was waiting in the forecourt of the building when they emerged. As soon as it lifted off, Mildred was back to the subject of Thurien political society. "I know they don't bother very much about labels and formal organizations and that kind of thing, but when you get down to analyzing the way their system works, it really is a model of the socialist ideal, Christian. And you could hardly ask for better vindication than a culture that travels between stars as a matter of routine and didn't have a word for 'war' until they met us, could you? I know we've made a lot of progress since all the mess at the end of the last century, but you have to agree that too much of the world's thinking is still shaped by insecurity and the compulsion to pointless antagonism. I mean, it's all such an *adolescently* arrested mind-set: the striving for wealth and power—which is just another way of saying fixation on possessions and getting one's own way regardless of the consequences to others. That's hardly what we'd normally perceive as the sign of individual maturity, is it? All this emphasis on competition. We're far more *cooperative* by nature as a species. It makes the Thuriens seems so *adult* by contrast; more ... more *spiritual*. You know what I mean? They're so far past the stage where material gratification means anything. They can think of the longer term. What collapsed in Russia back at the end of the eighties wasn't socialism. What Lenin and Stalin created had about as much to do with socialism as the Inquisition and the witch burnings had to do with Christianity. What collapsed was coercion and the attempt to impose a system by force. But then it always will in the end. People don't *like* seeing being afraid to express an opinion and seeing their neighbors dragged away to prison camps. You'd think that would be obvious enough, wouldn't you? But governments—here, anyway—have always seemed unable grasp it. That's what happens when you can't see further than short-term expediency. Don't you think so?"

"You could be right," Danchekker agreed.

By the time she was squinting at the menu, after rummaging in her purse for a pair of oval spectacles with purple butterfly frames, she had switched to news of the European branch of the family. "Emma—you remember her? You wouldn't recognize her if you saw her today—tall and raven haired like her grandmother was. She took up with a Ukrainian artist of some kind, and they're living like Bohemians in a converted barn in Croatia. Martha that's her mother—is so put out about it. Stefan says he's going to disinherit her if she doesn't come to her senses. He's doing well, by the way. You really could try and stay in touch a bit more, you know, Christian. His firm has just opened a new office in Vienna. They've got a new line on some kind of self-repairing material for spacecraft and things that there was a lot of interest in. But he's worried now that the Thuriens might start importing something superior that would upset everything. I don't think they would, though, do you? I know they don't have an economic system as we know it, or very much in the way of restrictions. But they're just not the kind who would go barging in thoughtlessly and destabilize another culture like that. . . . Seafood Alfredo sounds good. What are you having?"

"Oh, just something light today. I have to attend one of those wretched black tie dinners tonight. In honor of someone who's retiring. Some UNSA people are over from Geneva for it."

"Poor Christian. You never were one for that kind of thing, were you?"

"The primary object appears to be getting seats at the right tables and to be seen, rather than appreciating a good meal. Quite frankly, I'd rather they brought him here."

"The Thuriens would never go for that kind of nonsense, would they?" Mildred said, resurrecting that topic through to the end of the salad course. "From all the things I've read, they just don't have any concept of rivalry or putting the other person down. If you persuade them they're wrong about something, they just admit it. Why can't we be more like that? And it's so idiotic! I mean, how often have you watched someone at a cocktail party who won't back down? . . . because he's afraid of losing face! But he *couldn't* lose more face than by doing what he's doing, could he? . . . when everyone in the room thinks he's being a dolt. But just once in a while you see one who can stop, and look at you, and say, 'You may have a point. I never thought about it that way.' In my eyes, someone like that is suddenly ten feet tall. You think, my God, how wonderful! So why is it so difficult? But all the Thuriens are like that, aren't they? Does it really go back to their ancient ancestors on Minerva, where there were no land carnivores and predators? I've read the things you've written about all that. It explains so much of their social structure today. I really need to learn more."

Danchekker decided that his moment had come. Mildred must have seen him swell in anticipation or caught a glint in his eye through his spectacles, for she paused just as she was about to resume, and looked at him curiously.

"How would you like to learn everything you want to know, firsthand, from the best source you could possibly wish for?" he asked her. Mildred frowned, not knowing what to make of this. Danchekker dabbed at his mouth with his napkin and tossed out his other hand expansively. "From the Thurien psychologists, biologists, and social visionaries themselves! All of them—anyone you care to approach, with all their records and theories, plans and history available and accessible. You said yourself how informal they are."

Mildred shook her head, thrown off track and flummoxed. "Christian, I don't think I quite follow. . . . What, exactly, are you talking about?"

Danchekker beamed in the way of someone finally divulging a secret he could contain no longer. "I have managed to arrange precisely such an opportunity for you: to go there personally, to Thurien, and meet some of their most prominent scientific figures and social leaders. They will be more than happy to help with everything you need to know. A writer's chance of a lifetime!"

Mildred stared at him incredulously. "Me? Go to Thurien? . . . Are you serious? I . . . I don't think I quite know what to say."

Danchekker brushed an imaginary crumb from his lapel with a thumb. "The least I could do as a modest contribution, considering the acquaintances I have been fortunate enough to make there," he told her. "Frenua Showm, an inner member of their highest policy-making organization, will take care of you personally and arrange the right introductions."

"My God, this is . . ." Mildred put a hand up to her mouth and shook her head again. "Quite a shock, you understand."

"I am sure you will rise to it admirably."

Mildred emitted a long, shaky breath and gulped from her water glass. "When is this supposed to happen?"

"A Thurien vessel called the *Ishtar* is in orbit above Earth currently, in connection with a technical and cultural exchange mission visiting eastern Asia. It will be returning seven days from now. I took the liberty of reserving you a place on it."

"*Seven days!* My word. . . ." Mildred put a hand to her chest weakly.

Danchekker waved a hand carelessly. "I know the Thuriens are obliging, and one only has to ask. But it means that places on their ships tend to be filled quickly. And the *Ishtar* is only a small craft, apparently. I didn't want to risk your being disappointed."

"Christian, was this your idea?" A suspicious note had crept into Mildred's voice.

Danchekker spread his palms with the expression of bewildered innocence of a boy insisting he had no idea how the frog had gotten into his sister's bed. "I talk to Frenua all the time, and happened to mention your project and its research needs. The offer was entirely theirs." A mild feeling of discomfort flickered for a moment as he said this, but lightning didn't strike.

Finally, Mildred absorbed what he was saying. She sat back in her chair and looked at him disbelievingly. "Well . . . what do I say? I knew I'd come to the right person."

"Does that mean you're agreeable?"

"It'll be a bit of a rush getting organized at this kind of notice. . . . But of course. As you said, a writer's chance of a lifetime."

"Splendid. It calls for a bottle of wine, don't you think?" Danchekker turned his head from side to side, searching for a waiter.

"I thought you didn't drink," Mildred said.

Danchekker pursed his lips for a moment, then shrugged. "There are moments in life when a rare exception might be permitted," he replied.

He was still cackling to himself an hour later, when he paid the cabbie off at Goddard, having dropped Mildred at her hotel on the way back to begin making her arrangements.

CHAPTER FOUR

A friend of Hunt's named Rita, who was widowed, attractive, sophisticated, and, remarkably, unattached, ran a Turkish-cuisine restaurant that he visited from time to time in Silver Spring. A couple of months previously, she had prevailed upon him to escort her to a wedding she had been invited to of an old friend from college days. It had all gone very pleasantly, and he in turn enlisted her as his dinner companion for Owen's retirement dinner at the Carnarvon. She appeared promptly when he collected her shortly after six o'clock, tall and shapely, her honey-blond hair worn high, and wearing a white stole over a sparkling orange gown, high-necked and sleeveless, Oriental style. "Susie Wong tonight, are we?" Hunt quipped as she took his arm to walk to the airmobile that he had arrived in—rented.

"It goes with the tuxedo image of this James Bondish–looking Englishman. Are you packing a gun, too?"

"I knew I'd forgotten something." Hunt saw her in to the passenger seat, closed the door, and walked around to the driver's side.

"Is it going to be stuffy and horribly technical with all those scientists and UNSA people?" Rita asked as he climbed in.

Hunt okayed the destination for the flight computer and started the turbine, taking an unnaturally long time to reply. The announcement he was due to make was going to be public knowledge soon enough anyway, he started to tell himself. But on the other hand, there was such a thing as professional decorum. He would be left in an awkward situation if he started going into it now, and Owen had second thoughts. "Oh, I think you'll find it interesting enough," was all he said finally.

They were among the early arrivals at the reception, but the room filled quickly. Caldwell arrived with his wife, Maeve, and had also brought Mitzi, his secretary, and her husband. Danchekker showed up on his own, looking about as at home in black-tie attire as an ostrich in ballet tights. Hunt and Rita did the requisite social round, swapping shop and small talk, meeting the two visitors from Geneva, and paying their respects to Owen. Rita carried it all through with poise, fitting in easily and naturally in a way that warmed everyone they talked to. Hunt found himself wondering, not for the first time, if he should be thinking seriously about settling into a more conventional role and finding himself a permanent companion in life. By all the criteria that were supposed to matter, he wouldn't do any better than this person clinging to his arm and captivating his colleagues right now—even Danchekker. And yet . . . He couldn't put a finger on just what it was that didn't feel right. Deciding there was an empty slot in life and looking around for someone to fill it didn't seem to be the way. The right person would make their own slot. Or was it that for someone of his restless, loner disposition, compulsively changing his life whenever it threatened to close in by becoming too secure and predictable, there couldn't be a "right" person?

They were seated at the table presided over by Caldwell, which also included Danchekker, Owen, and the two Europeans. The conversation came around to what Owen planned to do with his time now. Owen said he was going to write an autobiography, giving his account of the extraordinary events that UNSA had been involved in during his time of office. Caldwell agreed that an insider's story was needed. Did Owen know that Danchekker had a cousin who wrote books? No, Owen didn't. Caldwell looked across at Danchekker. "In fact, isn't she visiting here right now, Chris?"

"Doing research for a book on the Thuriens," Mitzi put in.

"It must be very fortunate for her to have such an authority on the subject as her cousin," Maeve commented.

Danchekker looked flattered but sighed regretfully. "It appears, however, that our professional association is to be short lived," he informed the table. "Cousin Mildred is a woman of considerable resourcefulness. She has contrived to avail herself of a far more comprehensive repository of materials than anything I could hope to provide: Thurien itself, no less."

"You mean via a virtual travel hookup?" Owen said. Much of the Thuriens' business among worlds was effected by bringing information from the destination to the "travelers," rather than the other way around. Sensor data derived from the source was imparted into their neural systems in a way that made the experience indistinguishable from actually being at the remote location. Neurocouplers connecting into the Thurien system had been installed at several locations on Earth, including Goddard.

Danchekker shook his head as he took a spoonful of soup. "No, she's actually going."

"Really? To Thurien?" Rita exclaimed. "What an experience!"

"One of their vessels is leaving here to return, somewhere around a week from now, I understand," Danchekker confirmed. "She has a reservation on it."

"It's unbelievable," Leonard, one of the Europeans, said, taking in the table in general. "There isn't anything like having to pay a fare. You just ask them. If there's room, they'll take you."

"So we won't be seeing very much of Mildred after all, Professor," Maeve concluded.

"Tragically so, I fear." Danchekker returned a solemn nod. Hunt saw Caldwell look at him keenly for a second or two, as if about to take the subject further; but then he caught Hunt's eye and turned to say something to Sarah, the other European, instead

Hunt looked across at Owen, cocking his head in a way that singled him out from the general talk. "Are you still happy for me to talk about it, Owen?" he asked. "It's still not too late to change if you've had second thoughts. We can make the news an official release tomorrow. It's your call."

"Well, yes I have thought some more about it," Owen replied. For a moment Hunt thought that he had changed his mind. But Owen went on, "What I'd like to do is make the broad announcement myself, in my acknowledgment speech. Then I can hand over to you to fill in the details. What do you think?"

"Even better," Hunt said. "This is your show. Go over with a bang, eh?"

"What's this?" Rita asked. She kept her voice low, picking up their tenor. "Are we in for some news tonight?"

"You'll see," Hunt answered. "I said you'd find it interesting." Rita raised her eyebrows and smiled resignedly in a way that said she could wait.

But Caldwell, who rarely missed anything, waved a hand for him to carry on. "It's okay, Vic," he said. "We're only talking about a few minutes from now. And it'll be public before tonight's out, anyway." Hunt looked inquiringly toward Owen. Owen shrugged, indicating that it was fine by him. Hunt looked back at Rita.

"I got an unusual phone call the other day," he told her.

"Oh?"

"Do you know much about quantum physics and alternate Multiverse realities?"

Rita regarded him reproachfully. "I thought you said it wouldn't get technical."

"Trust me. This will be worth it."

"Something about all possible universes. . . . We only live in a tiny part of what's going on. Everything that could happen is happening somewhere."

"That puts it pretty well. And they contain other possible versions of ourselves. According to traditional theory, apart from interference at the microscopic level, information doesn't flow between them. They can't communicate. We thought. . . . And then, when Broghuilio and his last hangers-on took off from Jevlen, their ships were somehow kicked back to a version of early Minerva." Rita would know about that, of course. At the time, it had been dissected in the news for weeks. Imares Broghuilio had been the leader of the attempted Jevlenese coup.

"So what are you . . ." Rita broke off as what he was implying sank in. Her eyes widened. The other talk around the table died as one by one the rest of the company tuned in. Rita was now speaking for all of them. "You're not saying this call was from some other . . . reality, universe . . . whatever?"

Hunt nodded, deadly serious now. "Precisely that."

Rita tried to absorb it, smiled incredulously, shook her head. "On the phone? A regular call on the phone? Surely that's crazy. . . ." But at the same time her expression said she wasn't sure why.

"What better way to communicate?" Hunt replied, looking around now to address the whole company. "We think it came via a relay device that was projected into Earth orbit somehow—like the satellites that connect into the Thurien h-net."

Those present who hadn't known about it already returned disbelieving looks, almost as if expecting this to be a joke. Leonard waited for a moment to avoid sounding provocatively skeptical, then said, "How can you be sure it was from another reality, Doctor? Can you positively rule out the possibility that it was a hoax?"

Which was what Hunt had been expecting. "Oh, absolutely," he assured them. "The caller couldn't have fooled me. I know him too well." He glanced around to emphasize the point. "You see, it was me. The person I talked with was another version of myself."

And over the rest of the meal, the whole astonishing story came out. The conclusion that the call had originated from some alternative future brought up the question of time-travel contradictions, which Sarah confessed to having been unclear about ever since the business with the Jevlenese. Going back to the past changed it, she maintained, and that didn't make sense.

"Not with the old notion of a single reality and one time line," Hunt agreed. "But going back to an earlier point on a *different* time line avoids the contradictions. It could be arbitrarily close to the one that you came from, but nevertheless not the *same* one."

Owen came in. "You couldn't change your own, exact past—where no one from the future had ever shown up to bring about any changes. That's true."

"But you're changing the other one just as much," Sarah objected. Owen looked at Hunt.

"The Multiverse totality itself is timeless," Hunt said. "Nothing in it ever really changes anyway. "

"So what's this change that we all see? Where does it come from?" Leonard asked.

"Now you're getting into philosophers' and theologians' territory," Hunt answered. "I just deal in what the physics says."

"Some kind of construct of consciousness," Caldwell offered. "Consciousness navigates its way through the totality somehow." He shrugged. "Maybe that's what consciousness is."

This aspect intrigued Danchekker. His first reaction was usually to reject anything radical, but Hunt had been through this with him several times by now. It seemed that Chris had been doing some more thinking. "The ramifications are profound," he told Caldwell. "Perhaps one of the most significant developments in the history of science yet. The bringing together of physical and biological science at the quantum level. Generalizing 'consciousness' to mean any form of self-instigated behavior modification gives us a whole new way of looking at living systems."

"You sound as if you want to get more involved in it, Chris," Caldwell commented. His steely gray eyes had an odd twinkle.

"Well, absolutely," Danchekker agreed. "Who in my position wouldn't? I mean—" The clacking of the MC's gavel from the podium above the head table interrupted.

The clattering of dessert cutlery had died away by now, and the waiters were serving coffee, port wines, and liqueurs. The MC looked around while the last murmurs of conversation faded. "Thank you all, ladies and gentlemen. Now that everyone is wined, contented, and fed, it's my pleasure to bring us to the prime business of the evening. . . ."

A buildup followed, outlining Owen's career and achievements. Several speakers followed, relating their personal anecdotes, and Hunt went up last to deliver the keynote address. It went over well. The MC called Owen up from the floor to respond, and at the end the room rose to give him an ovation. But then Owen remained at the podium. Puzzled looks traveled this way and that around the room. Even the MC seemed thrown off balance.

"And now I have something further to tell you all," Owen said. "Something that will set tonight aside as a truly memorable occasion in all our lives. Several days ago, an event took place just a few miles from where we are sitting now, which I believe could signal one of the most startling developments in the entire history of our species, with incalculable implications for the future. It's fitting that I should be saying this as my last official duty on behalf of UNSA. For the era of discovery that I represented is over. A new one is about to begin. . . ."

By the time Hunt got up again to complete the story, the thunder for the evening had truly been exercised where it belonged. All fears of stealing Owen's show were forgotten. The room was all but stunned into silence and immobility, except for one or two figures making inconspicuously for the exits, who Hunt guessed to be media people hurrying to send off their stories.

Some questions followed, generally echoing those already heard at Caldwell's table, but not a great many—no doubt because most of the listeners would need time to fully grasp what they had heard. Hunt thought it just as well. This was a celebration dinner, not a technical conference.

But it seemed to have achieved its aim. Owen expressed satisfaction that the occasion had been immortalized. People were staying at their tables and talking in intense, animated groups instead of breaking up and starting to leave in the way that would have been typical. "That would be a tough one to follow," Rita said as Hunt came back over and sat down after exchanging contact details with a number of people wanting to know more who had stopped him on the way.

Caldwell waited until he had Danchekker's attention and looked at him fixedly for a moment as he sipped from his glass. "And now that it's all official, I have some more news—for you, Chris," he said.

"Me?" Danchekker frowned quizzically. "What kind of news?"

"I've been talking to Calazar about Vic's matrix propagation ideas." Calazar headed the planetary administration on Thurien. "He agrees that their scientists and our scientists need to get together on this. And before the speeches, you'd just started telling us about how bioscience and physics are all implicated together. So we've arranged for you and Vic to transfer to Thurien with a small team and work with them."

"Vic and me? To Thurien? ... When?"

"A week from now—on the ship that you mentioned. It's called the *Ishtar*. Some Thuriens who have been visiting places in Asia are going home in it."

Maeve looked delighted. "Why, that's wonderful, Professor!" she exclaimed. "The same ship that your cousin will be going on. So you won't have to lose contact with her after all."

"That's what I was thinking, too," Caldwell said. "I've no doubt she can take care of herself, but an alien culture at another star needs a lot of adjusting to. I've had a taste of it myself. Even if she did make her own arrangements independently, we are still Earth's official space agency, and I feel we have a responsibility. So I'd like you to keep an eye on her, on UNSA's behalf, Chris, if you would." Danchekker appeared to have frozen. He sat, holding a grape that he had taken from a dish on the table suspended halfway to his mouth. Caldwell's brow furrowed. "Okay, Chris?"

"I'd be happy to, of course," Danchekker managed finally in a flat voice.

The sides of Danchekker's mouth moved upward mechanically to bare his teeth, but the rest of him remained immobile. Only then did Hunt see the look of stark horror in the eyes behind the gold-rimmed spectacles. Then the pieces of what must have happened fell suddenly into place. Hunt grabbed his napkin from the table and clasped it to his mouth with a spluttering sound which he disguised as a cough. Rita, to one side, saw the expression that he was struggling to conceal.

"What is it?" she hissed in his ear. "What's so funny?"

"I'll tell you later," Hunt muttered, brushing away a tear.

CHAPTER FIVE

One of the things about working for Gregg Caldwell that suited Hunt was that Caldwell was able to function within a large bureaucracy without acquiring the mind-set of one. Through his career as a nucleonics scientist in England before joining UNSA, Hunt had found that small groups of capable and dedicated individuals were more effective than the armies assembled for large, managerially inaugurated research projects, where too much energy tended to be dissipated fruitlessly on communicating more and more about less and less. Caldwell expressed it succinctly by saying, "If a ship takes five days to cross the Atlantic, it doesn't mean that five ships will do it in one day." Danchekker was necessarily led to the same philosophy, since the number of people he was typically able to tolerate limited the effective horizons of his personal work space in any case.

The team hastily organized in the course of the following week comprised just four more people in addition to the two senior scientists, Hunt being nominally designated the head, since the subject was Multiverse physics, and physics was—literally—his department. Accompanying him would be Duncan Watt, his longstanding assistant from the Navcomms days, who had also moved to Goddard, while Danchekker in like fashion would be taking Sandy Holmes, one of the few individuals to have mastered his filing system, and who could decipher his notes. Duncan and

Sandy had also accompanied Hunt and Danchekker to Jevlen on the investigation of mass psychoses that had led to the discovery of the Entoverse. Josef Sonnebrandt had been recruited without too much persuasion. And he in turn had urged for the inclusion of a Chinese theoretician that he had been working with, a Madam Xyen Chien, who had set up a laboratory in Xinjiang that was already duplicating some aspects of earlier Ganymean physics involving artificial spacetime deformation. Direct as always, Caldwell had contacted her personally, and she had as good as agreed before the end of his call. The rest had been pretty straightforward. Although China still retained some vestige of the authoritarianism of times gone by, nobody there was going to argue with an invitation to send one of their leading scientists to Thurien. In fact, Madam Xyen was on the list that the party of Thuriens currently in eastern Asian had arranged to visit, and she would be returning with them directly to the orbiting *Ishtar* to meet the rest of the Terran group there. UNSA administration needed a name for the project. Since the aim was to investigate TRAns Muliverse communication, Hunt settled on "Tramline."

Sonnebrandt joined the rest of the group at Goddard a day before the *Ishtar*'s scheduled departure for an overview and briefing. They flew out early the next morning to be shuttled up to orbit from the UNSA launch terminal in Virginia. As fate would have it, the flight up turned out to be the same one that the travel agency had booked for Mildred, who was also traveling from the DC area. "What a wonderful surprise, Christian!" she declared when she came aboard, festooned with bags and purses, and found them there. "You were holding back on me. You had this planned all along!"

"What can I tell you?" Danchekker answered. Which was as good a way as any of saying something while saying nothing.

Thurien interstellar transportation worked on the same basis as their communications, which involved spinning artificially generated charged black holes up to speeds that drew them out into toroids. The singularity deformed to become aperture through the center, which could be approached axially without catastrophic tidal effects and gave access to the hyperrealm known as h-space that connected the universe (or, more strictly now, "our" universe, out of the countless universes making up the Multiverse) by paths that bypassed the limitations of ordinary spacetime. The difference, however, was that while communications could be effected via microscopic-size ports located conveniently close to Earth in satellites or, at the cost of some heavy structural engineering, down on the surface, transportation required ports large enough to admit whatever was being transported. Projecting such ports where and when they were needed was one of the things that VISAR handled as part of its function as general manager of the infrastructure that the Thurien civilization rested on. The energy to create the toroids was also directed through h-space, produced by the consumption of matter from the cores of burnt-out stars at colossal generating systems constructed in older parts of the local galaxy. Projecting transportation-size ports into planetary systems would have produced gravitational disturbances sufficient to create havoc with clocks and calendars. Standard practice was therefore to project them far enough away outside for such effects to be negligible. Hence, vessels were needed to get to them. Thurien interstellar craft used regular gravitic drives—essentially the principle that the *Shapieron* had been built around—to travel to an entry port, and from the exit port to the final destination. This meant that a typical point-to point journey between star systems would take in the order of a few days.

The Thurien craft that took Hunt and the earlier group to Jevlen had been immense—more in the nature of a mini artificial world that Thuriens used for long stays in remote parts of the Galaxy, and in which some chose to reside permanently. The *Ishtar*, by contrast, was more in keeping with what most Terrans would have thought of as the dimensions of a "ship." It grew larger on the forward display screen inside the cabin as the shuttle from Virginia closed: bright yellow-gold in color, sleek and stream-lined, flaring out into two crossed, curvy delta forms at the tail, designed like most Thurien craft for descent through planetary atmospheres without the rigmarole of intermediate transfers in orbit. At Earth, however, the several planned surface bases with facilities to service them were still under construction. In the meantime, there was no need for such clumsy provisions as fitting Thurien and Terran vessels with compatible docking hardware. The *Ishtar* simply projected a force shell from its docking-port side to enclose a zone between itself and the shuttle, and filled it with air. The passengers were conveyed across the intervening space, open to the void and the stars, by similar means, on an invisible conveyor—somewhat unnerving for first-timers, but fast and easy. With the larger Thurien craft things were even simpler: they contained internal docking bays that opened to admit the entire surface shuttle, capable of accommodating a dozen or more at a time.

A small reception committee of Thuriens was waiting to greet the arrivals inside the entry port. The first formality was to issue each of the Terrans with a flesh-colored disk about the size of a dime that attached behind the ear and coupled into the neural system to provide an audio-visual link to VISAR, which could then act as interpreter. The devices were known as "avcos"—for audio-visual coupler—and could be used down on Earth where equipment existed that could communicate with the orbiting Thurien h-space relays. This was true at Goddard, and Hunt still had one of the devices in his desk drawer from his last trip. But for little better reason than habit, he preferred to stick to a regular old-fashioned seefone when he was at home. A few people there wore their Thurien avco disks ostentatiously as a status symbol, making great shows of removing, reattaching, and pretending to clean them.

"Welcome back, Vic," the familiar voice of VISAR said, seemingly in his ear but actually activated inside his head. "I see you're getting restless again." The disk also projected images into the visual field when required. This wasn't the full Thurien total-neural experience, but it afforded universal voice communication to anywhere, with supplementary visuals that could be generated from the optical neuronics of senders using their eyes effectively as TV cameras. Once it caught on, it would be the end of the line for the Terran phone business, Hunt supposed.

"Hello, VISAR. Yes, we're back in your territory again." Hunt faced the waiting Thuriens. "So who have we here?"

The deputation was headed by the *Ishtar*'s first officer, Bressin Nylek, who had come to pay compliments on behalf of the ship's commander. It seemed that Calazar had sent a note personally to make sure that Hunt's party was well taken care of. Madam Xyen Chien was aboard and would join them after they had settled in. As was normal Thurien practice by now with vessels sent to Earth, a section of the ship had been adapted for Terran tastes and proportions—the average Ganymean was around eight feet tall. After taking them there, the Thuriens would stop by the lounge area later.

"Who is this that I'm hearing from?" Mildred inquired, looking around after experimenting with her disk. "Are you the driver?"

"In a manner of speaking, I suppose you could say," VISAR answered, coming in on everyone's circuit since she had made the question general.

"Can you tell me about Lynx? Is she all right? She came up in her case with the baggage."

"Who's Lynx?" Hunt asked subvocally.

"Her cat," VISAR returned. Then, in a more public-sounding voice, "Never better. A steward will bring her to your cabin."

"Ah, splendid. I couldn't leave her in Washington. I know nobody there would have fed her correctly. She's very highly strung and diet-sensitive, you know."

"God help us all," Hunt heard Danchekker mutter, turning his head away.

As in their cities back home, the Thuriens also employed their gravitic technology to shape the environments inside their space-craft. Since "up" and "down" could be defined locally and vary progressively from place to place, interiors didn't conform to the layers-of-boxes theme reflected in practically all Terran designs regardless of the attempts to disguise it. Everything merged in a confusion of corridors, shafts, and intersecting spaces, surfaces that served as floors in one place curving to become walls somewhere else with no sense of rotation as one passed from one to the other. Through it all, Thuriens were being conveyed unconcernedly this way and that on by currents of force similar to that which had brought the new arrivals across from the shuttle, traversing the ship in all directions like invisible elevators. But when they came to the Terran section of the ship, everything suddenly became rectilinear, verticality reasserted itself, and recognizable walls and floors emerged around corridors leading past lines of doors. Because that was what Terrans were used to, and how they liked things to be.

Hunt's bags had already arrived in his cabin when the party's Thurien escorts delivered him to the door. VISAR could have guided them, of course, but the personal touch was nice—presumably a part of the crew's response to Calazar's prompting. The interior was comfortable and showed the usual Thurien knack for think-ing of everything, Hunt saw as he deposited the office case that he had carried with him and hung his overjacket in the closet. A coffeepot and ingredients stood on a side table, and a robe and slippers were laid out in the bathroom. He came back out to the main room of the cabin and checked the selection of drinks and snacks in the cold storage by the coffeemaker and cabinet above. "Aha, gotcha, VISAR," he murmured. "You're slipping. No Guinness."

"On tap at the bar in the lounge area," the computer replied. Hunt sighed and went back out from the cabin to find the lounge area, where he had arranged to meet Josef Sonnebrandt.

Sonnebrandt was already there, sitting in an armchair at a corner table with an Oriental woman that Hunt recognized from pictures accompanying various writings of hers that he had read as Xyen Chien. Danchekker and Mildred were a short distance away with two Thuriens who seemed to be the focus of Mildred's attentions. A number of other Terrans that Hunt hadn't met were also dispersed around the room, many of them again Asian. Apparently, a group was going back with the *Ishtar* to reciprocate the Thurien visit. The bar was appropriately stocked with Eastern beers, wines, other beverages, and foods too, Hunt noticed.

The German stood as Hunt joined them—a gesture one didn't see very often these days. He was medium in height and build, with a somewhat overgrown mane of dark, curly hair, dressed casually in a khaki bush shirt with chest pockets and epaulettes, and over it a Western style brown leather vest. "Dr. Hunt. We meet face to face at last," he greeted. "So this is a Thurien starship. You have been in them before, of course. At least, we will remain sane in this part of it, yes? Out there is like being carried through an Escher drawing."

Madam Xyen was perhaps around fifty, as far as Hunt could judge, allowing for the tendency he'd noticed for Orientals to look younger than Westerners thought they should. Her hair was tied high, secured by a jeweled silver clip, and she wore a plain lilac dress with a dark blue shoulder cape. She had a composed air about her, taking in Hunt with a long, penetrating look from dark, depthless eyes that seemed to read everything that external appearances could convey; but her face softened into an easy enough smile when he introduced himself. Hunt's first impression was of a person totally in control, who saw the world for precisely what it was, without pretensions or delusions, and revealed back to it in turn just as much of herself and her thoughts as she chose to.

A four-foot-high serving robot floating a few inches above the floor on some kind of Thurien g-cushion arrived at the table to ask Hunt what it could get for him. He settled for a pot of green Chinese tea and an Indonesian dish that sounded like a spicy meat-and-vegetable pita bread sandwich. "Do you have a name we should use?" he asked the table attendant.

"No, sir. Such has never been the custom." Uncannily, whatever was guiding it reproduced a perfect Jeeves intonation.

"Then from now on, you are . . ." Hunt eyed its silvery metallic curves, carrying tray, and manipulator appendages thoughtfully for a moment, "Vercingetorix. . . . No, wait, *Sir* Vercingetorix. Aptly to be known as Sir Ver. What do you think?"

"As you wish, sir."

Chien chuckled delightedly. "Brilliant," Sonnebrandt, acknowledged, raising his glass toward Hunt. It looked as if it contained a lager beer.

"Is this one of your sidelines, VISAR?" Hunt inquired as the robot glided Jeevishly away.

"I suppose you could say, a distant cousin," VISAR replied in his head. "Mainly locally autonomous, but when it gets hit with something like that, it checks back with me."

After some initial socializing, the conversation got down to the business at hand. The first thing that Sonnebrandt and Chien wanted to hear was Hunt's account of the encounter with his alter ego in his own words. It was one of the few occasions when Hunt regretted not availing himself of the option to keep a recorded log of his phone exchanges in the way many people did. Maybe it had something to do with his English upbringing, but it always seemed to him to smack of lawsuit phobia, security paranoia, and other practices of the neurotic society now fading into history. It was persistently rumored that the communications companies still kept copies of everything that flowed through their channels anyway, but requests from the top levels of UNSA, stressing the importance of the matter, had produced only apologetic denials and assurance that the claim was an urban legend from way back that just wouldn't die. He went through what had been said during the exchange and all the analyses that had been repeated since, and gave his reasons for believing that the device had been an unmanned relay injected into orbit. His tea and snack arrived while he was talking.

"The analogy with the Dirac sea is interesting," Chien said when Hunt had finished. He had reiterated in his communications with Sonnebrandt the point he had made with Caldwell, and Sonnebrandt had passed it on to Chien. "Propagation in the manner of the Jevlenese processing matrix very well could explain pair production and annihilation." The same thought had occurred to Hunt and Sonnebrandt.

"What do we know about the actual propagation mechanics?" Chien asked. "Can we say anything yet about the kind of physics involved? What is it that actually switches 'states'?"

"I've got a hunch that it results from a longitudinal mode of what we observe as electromagnetic radiation," Sonnebrandt said. "I've been playing around with the possible implications. I think this might be it." Hunt and Chien were aware that the standard forms of Maxwell's equations only yielded a transverse vibration. They described electric and magnetic fields varying in a direction perpendicular to the direction of the wave's motion, like waves traveling along a jiggled rope, or a cork bobbing up and down as a water wave passes by. There was nothing comparable to waves of alternating compression and rarefaction in the direction of propagation, as occurs with sound, for example.

"Would that mean we're talking about a comparable velocity, too?" Hunt asked.

Sonnebrandt shook his head. "Not necessarily. The velocity constant c comes out of the differential equations that apply to the kind of changing universe that we perceive. Longitudinal propagation would involve a different set of magnitudes entirely. The same underlying matrix, but completely different physics—in the way that water can carry both sound waves and surface waves. But they're totally different phenomena." Hunt nodded. It was about what he'd told Caldwell.

"What about these 'convergences' that this other version of you mentioned?" Chien asked. "They sounded important. Have you been able to make anything more of what he meant?"

"Not really," Hunt confessed. "At first I wondered if it was a reference to this line of thinking that we're talking about here—matrix propagation—converging with the h-space approach that the Thuriens have been experimenting with, but that seems too vague. We pretty well know that much already. As you just said, it sounds like something more important."

"I thought it might have referred to some kind of mathematical convergence, but I've found nothing that it could apply to," Sonnebrandt said.

"VISAR went through the equations that Josef sent, too," Hunt told both of them. "It couldn't come up with anything either." Sonnebrandt shrugged in a way that said he could add nothing to that.

"Then let's hope more turns up when we get together with the Thuriens," Chien concluded.

Hunt finished his snack and wiped his mouth with a napkin. "Tell me more about this project you've got going with them out in the desert in Xinjiang," he said to Chien. He knew that the object was to set up an experimental tap into the Thurien h-space power grid with a view to later extending its availability on Earth. Misgivings had been voiced in some quarters about the economic implications.

"Perhaps the simplest thing would be for you to come and visit us and see it for yourself when we get back," Chien suggested.

"I'd like to," Hunt said. In fact, he had been thinking of trying to arrange just that. "What are the prospects of it coming into general use in the foreseeable future?" he asked. "Seriously. I've heard a lot of worried talk about it."

Chien smiled faintly in a distant kind of way that seemed very wise and worldly. "Worried talk in America?"

"Well, yes, sure. . . ."

"It will happen, Dr. Hunt. You can't turn the clock back. We will soon be immersed in an economy of universal abundance. It will be the end of the line for capitalism, which functions on the basis of manipulated scarcity. But it was inevitable eventually, even without the Thuriens. The world will just have to learn and get used to new ways of thinking a little sooner than they otherwise would have."

Hunt finished the last of his tea while he thought about that. It wasn't the first time he'd heard such sentiments expressed, but he wasn't sure if this would be the time to go into it with someone he hardly knew yet. He decided to keep things on the light side for now. "You should talk to Chris Danchekker's cousin," he said, indicating the table where Mildred was sitting. "From what he's told me, it sounds as if you'd have a lot in common there."

Chien straightened up in her seat. "Yes, I must do that. I haven't met them yet." She dropped her voice to a whisper. "I've been racing through one of her books since I learned she was coming with us. The one about how brainwashed and conditioned to political ideology professionals in corporations are. Very interesting and insightful. Have you read it?"

Hunt shook his head. "I'm afraid not. Come on over. I'll introduce you."

"Would you excuse me?" Chien said to Sonnebrandt.

"I'll be right back," Hunt told him.

"Of course. We'll talk more later." Sonnebrandt rose again as Chien got up to go with Hunt. Hunt wondered if this was going to be a permanent thing. As they moved away, Sonnebrandt beckoned Vercingetorix over and ordered another beer.

"And one for me," Hunt called back.

Hunt introduced Chien and told Mildred she was a fan. Mildred seemed delighted and flattered. Danchekker and the two Thuriens responded with appropriate pleasantries.

"Duncan and Sandy went off to explore the ship just before you came in," Danchekker told Hunt. Duncan and Sandy had been dating cozily since their return from the expedition to Jevlen. "It seemed like an excellent idea. We were just about to do likewise. Would you care to join us?"

"Just imagine, an alien starship!" Mildred enthused.

"Of course. How could I refuse?" Chien agreed. Hunt declined, saying that he had only left Sonnebrandt for a moment; in any case, he had seen enough of alien starships. After exchanging a few parting words and seeing them on their way, he went back to the other table.

"So you never married, I think you told me once?" Sonnebrandt said, leaning back and taking in the room.

"Never did."

"Never found the right woman, eh?"

"Oh, yes, pretty close, once or twice. Only trouble was, they were still looking for the right man. How about you?"

"Oh, I was once, some years ago now, but it didn't work out. They can be such demanding creatures. I thought marrying them would be enough. I didn't know you were supposed to live with them as well."

They talked about life in UNSA's scientific divisions compared to German academia. Sonnebrandt had worked for a while with the large European nucleonics facility near Geneva. In fact, he had met a number of Ganymeans from the *Shapieron* then, when they were accommodated in Switzerland during their stay on Earth. Although Hunt had been around at the time, their paths evidently hadn't crossed.

Sonnebrandt's work there had been on Multiverse interference experiments and the teleportation of quantum-entangled systems. At first, it had seemed to many people that this had to be the key to explaining how the Jevlenese ships had been hurled back to ancient Minerva, and more recently, following the media furor over the revelation at Owen's UNSA retirement dinner, the projection of the relay into this universe from whichever other one it had come from. But Hunt and Sonnebrandt agreed that quantum teleportation of the kind that was familiar in Terran laboratories and which the Thuriens used routinely in various ways wasn't the answer. The problem, in essence, was the impossibility in principle of being able to synchronize in advance any receiving apparatus at the other end, which was what enabled such effects to be achieved. Transporting to another universe would require something "self-contained" that could be "projected"—like sending a message in a bottle as opposed to transmitting to a tuned radio that was already there. But how did you get a bottle to go where you wanted it to, and then know enough to be able to announce itself when it was there? Clearly, a lot of onboard capability was indicated. But their counterparts in at least one place had managed to work it out.

"We'll start making progress all of a sudden when VISAR gets properly involved," Hunt said.

"You think so?"

"That would be my guess if I had to."

"What do you mean, 'properly'?" Sonnebrandt asked.

"New insights and intuition still seem to be a biological specialty," Hunt answered. "We don't know how we do it, so it's kind of difficult to specify the essence of it to a machine, however much it might be wrapped up in associative nets and learning algorithms. Induction doesn't come easily even to a Thurien system.

But once you've given it the idea, it will run with it and tell you in minutes what does and doesn't follow from your assumptions. VISAR did an astounding job of authenticity faking the Pseudowar that panicked Broghuilio's Jevlenese. But it was us who suggested it in the first place."

"Who? You mean you and Chris Danchekker?"

"Oh, there was a bunch more involved, too, at the time. But all Terrans, yes. The Thuriens admitted that something like that would never have occurred to them. Devious thinking and deception isn't their thing."

Sonnebrandt touched a finger to the avco disk behind his ear. "Just out of curiosity, is VISAR tapping into this conversation?"

Hunt shook his head. "It doesn't eavesdrop. Thuriens are finicky about things like that."

"How do you know when it's online and when it isn't?"

"You learn to cue it. It's a knack that you pick up."

Sonnebrandt rubbed his fingertip lightly over the device, tracing its outline. "This isn't the Thurien total-sensory thing that people talk about, right?" he checked. "It's just an audio-visual subset. That's what avco means."

"You've never tried the full Thurien system?" Hunt was surprised. For some reason he imagined all major scientific establishments like the Max Planck Institute as having a Thurien neurocoupler or two hidden away somewhere. But Sonnebrandt shook his head. Hunt flipped the mental switch to raise VISAR. "I assume you've got couplers installed at various locations around the place?" he checked.

"Sure. It's a Thurien ship. Comes with all the fixings."

"Josef's never used one. Think we could give him an introductory ride?"

"No problem," VISAR replied. "Finish your beers, and I'll guide you to the nearest ones that are available right now."

CHAPTER SIX

Thurien engineering tended not to be intrusive or ostentatious. VISAR directed Hunt and Sonnebrandt along one of the corridors from the Terran lounge area of the ship to a space divided into a number of partitioned cubicles. They entered one of them to find what looked like a fairly standard padded recliner, with panels of multicolored crystal mosaics positioned behind and alongside the headrest in a manner vaguely suggestive of sound baffles in an acoustic room. An array of video and other sensors covered the area from high on the walls and other directions to capture the subject from all angles for an accurate virtual surrogate to be produced. Otherwise, apart from a convenience shelf to one side, coat hanger, and a mirror, the cubicle was bare. A pattern of intriguing artistic designs relieved the monotony of the walls. "That's it. Take a seat," Hunt said, gesturing.

Sonnebrandt looked around, evidently mildly surprised. "What, no flickering lights and forests of wires? You don't stick your head in a helmet, or anything like that?"

"It all went out with steam radio. This is easier than having a haircut."

"Steam radio?"

"Oh, an English expression. Here. Hop aboard the VISAR express."

Sonnebrandt turned and sat down, looking mildly self-conscious.

"This couples into the total nervous system, yes?" he said. "What exactly do I do?"

"It activates when you relax back into it. VISAR will guide you through. Your sensory inputs are suppressed and replaced by what the system channels straight into your brain. Likewise, it monitors your motor and other responses and manufacturers a total environment, complete with a surrogate self, that you think you're actually in. So instead of sending your body to China to experience what's going on there, it brings the information to you. Much faster and flexible. Hop from Thurien to Jevlen and another dozen of their star systems in an hour and be home for lunch."

"It wouldn't know what's going on in China," Sonnebrandt pointed out.

"I picked a bad example," Hunt conceded. "Thurien worlds are fully wired. They can send the data to reproduce what's happening anywhere. So you get injected into an authentic backdrop—the way it actually is there."

"It seems like a lot of effort to put in."

"Thurien psychology is different. They have this hangup about having to get everything exactly right. If something like this ever becomes standard on Earth, you're right—we'd never go to all that trouble. We'd probably make do with lots of extrapolations and simulation. VISAR does that to a degree, too, such as when you want to get the feel of being somewhere that's uninhabited or inhospitable. But where they can, Thuriens have this thing about getting it like it is. . . . Anyway, lie back and enjoy, as they say. I'll hook in next door. See you in psy-space."

Leaving Sonnebrandt to privacy, Hunt went into the adjoining cubicle, sat himself down, and lay back. This had long ago become a familiar routine. A warm feeling of total ease came over him. He sensed the system tuning in to his neural processes. And in moments it was in passive reception mode, waiting for his directions. With Sonnebrandt, things would take a little longer the first time. The system needed to run a series of sensory calibration tests to fix a user's visual and auditory ranges, thermal and tactile sensitivity, and so forth in order to create inputs that seemed normal. Once done, however, the profile was stored and could be invoked immediately on future occasions. It was a good idea to have it updated periodically—a bit like getting one's eyes checked from time to time when approaching the age where things start to get fuzzy.

Hunt swung his legs down and sat up. Or at least, everything in his vision, realistic feelings of pressure against the recliner and friction of his clothes, and simulated internal feedback from his muscles and joints, told him that he did. It was only because of his past experience with this that he knew he was really still immobile in the recliner and would remain so until he decoupled from the system. In earlier days he had found it necessary to convey his wishes, for example as to where he wanted to "go," or whom he wanted to contact, as explicit instructions to VISAR. Now, his interaction with the system had grown subtle enough for it to respond to his unvoiced volition.

When he got up, the recliner behind him appeared empty. What he was seeing was coming into his head from the coupler now, not from his eyes. He walked back around to the adjoining cubicle and leaned casually against the side of the doorway. Sonnebrandt was to all appearances comatose, still undergoing the profiling process. It took a few minutes but was subjectively telescoped to seem a lot less. "Locate him here, too," he said inwardly, evoking VISAR. "Let's see how long he takes to twig it."

"Still can't resist playing a joke, eh?" VISAR observed.

"Consider it an experiment. Purely scientific curiosity."

Sonnebrandt stirred and focused back within the confines of the cubicle. For a moment he seemed unsure of where he was, like somebody coming out of a deep sleep. He saw Hunt, turned his head first one way, then the other to take in the surroundings, then sat up and turned to look at the recliner. He was clearly confused. Finally, he looked back at Hunt. "Do we have a technical hitch?"

Hunt shrugged. "I guess it can happen to anyone," he said noncommittally. "Want to take a tour around? We can try back here later."

"Sure." One of Sonnebrandt's shoes had a scuff mark near the toe, Hunt had noticed earlier. It we there, faithfully reproduced on his virtual shoe. *Amazing*, Hunt thought to himself.

"I hope it's not a very common thing," Sonnebrandt joked as they exited the cubicle. "I mean, stuck in this starship crossing the Solar System in hours. It's not very reassuring to realize that things can go wrong."

"Oh, I think you can trust the Thuriens, Josef," Hunt replied mysteriously. Then, vocalizing aloud so as to include Sonnebrandt, "VISAR, care to be the tour guide?"

"How about Control and Command Deck, Communications Center, on-board power pickup from the h-space grid, and propulsion control?" VISAR suggested. Since Hunt had initiated a public conversation, Sonnebrandt heard the response, too.

"Does that sound good?" Hunt asked Sonnebrandt.

"They won't mind? Tourists coming in and gawking in places like that?"

"I can see you're not used to being around Thuriens yet."

"Well, I'd say that is about to be corrected in the not very distant future." Sonnebrandt turned his head to glance at Hunt as they walked. "Is there anything I should know about Thuriens?—in dealing with them, I mean. Anything they get upset about? Things that offend them?"

"You won't offend them, Josef. They don't have the competitive grounding that makes humans get defensive from feeling inferior or inadequate. It just isn't in their nature. For the same reason, it's no use trying to win your point by being aggressive or making an argument out of it. They won't respond. What we think is firmness and take pride in, they'd be more likely to see as being pointlessly obstinate and mildly ridiculous. If you realize you're wrong, just say so like they do. If you're right, don't crow about it. See my point? There isn't any gaming for one-upmanship points going on. Their minds don't work that way."

"Hm. . . . You make them sound very patient. Is that something that comes from being such an old civilization?"

"They make you feel like children at times," Hunt agreed. As an afterthought, he added, "Maybe you should talk to Chien."

They came to a cross-corridor and turned in the direction of the Thurien part of the ship. Danchekker, Chien, Mildred, and the two Thuriens were around the corner, studying a live mural display of scenes from various Thurien planets. For a moment, Hunt could only stand and stare at them, perplexed. This didn't make sense.

Hunt and Sonnebrandt were surrogates—virtual creations that existed in their own minds, projected into a VISAR-supplied environment, which in this case happened to be the interior of the ship as captured by the senors that Thuriens embedded in everything they built. And it was true that VISAR could include as part of that environment the images of people who happened to actually be there—or edit them out; it depended on what the user that the experience was being delivered to wanted. But in such a composite situation, the "background" figures—like Danchekker and the others, who were physically there, where the imagery was coming from—couldn't interact with surrogates—like Hunt and Sonnebrandt—who were not. But Danchekker *was* interacting—by gaping speechlessly, showing all the signs of being as surprised at their meeting as Hunt was. The only explanation that came to Hunt in his befuddlement was that Sonnebrandt had been right, and Hunt was the one who had been fooled. For some reason, unprecedented in Hunt's experience, Thurien technology had failed to function. . . . Or was VISAR the one, maybe, who was playing a joke? Hunt had come across some of its weird ideas of humor before.

"Dr. Hunt. You've caught up with us," Chien said. "We didn't get very far, I'm afraid. Your colleague, Professor Danchekker, was going to show us the Thurien virtual travel system. But it seems to be down at the moment. I hope it's not a general indicator of Thurien engineering."

"That's extraordinary!" Sonnebrandt exclaimed. "We did the same. And I said exactly what you just said." Chien laughed. The two Thuriens, who were still with the other group, remained detached in a curious kind of way.

But Danchekker wasn't laughing. He looked at Hunt with an expression of somebody confronting the impossible and not knowing how to frame a question to express it. It seemed he was having the same problem, which would mean that he thought the same that Hunt did—or had until a moment ago. But that could only be because he had tried to pull the same trick on his companions, too.

"Okay, VISAR, a good one," Hunt fired at it.

"What do you mean, Vic?"

"The joke's over. Come on, level up. What's going on?"

Mildred, however, was acting differently from the others. She stood, staring uncertainly at Hunt for several seconds, and then moved a step nearer, bringing her face close. For a moment he thought she was about to kiss him on the cheek. She stepped back, her eyes twinkling mischievously. "Christian told me you used to be a smoker until not very long ago. Is that right?"

"Well . . . yes." He shook his head. "What does that have to do with—"

"Ah! Gotcha, VISAR," Mildred said softly. "You're getting lazy."

"What did I do?"

Mildred smiled at Hunt as she replied. "You used your old stored profile to create Dr. Hunt. It included a hint of the aroma that smokers typically have. It's there now. But it shouldn't be. It wasn't earlier, or when we came up in the shuttle." She explained to the others who were listening, but who still hadn't figured it out, "The system is working just fine. We are inside it right now, as I speak—all of us! I'm amazed. Congratulations, Christian. You really had us fooled." Danchekker was looking too astonished to reply. Behind him, the two Thuriens were grinning.

"Okay, you win," VISAR conceded. "So shall we continue with the tour?"

"But of course," Chien said. At the same time, she sent Mildred an approving nod.

It occurred to Hunt that this would be one way of making sure that the crew in the Command Deck and elsewhere wouldn't have to be bothered by gaggles of tourists coming through. Sonnebrandt moved close as they started moving again. "She's sharp," he murmured. "It may be as well that she's coming along."

Hunt had to agree. He was still getting over the surprise himself. It was the first time ever that he had known VISAR to be caught out on something.

CHAPTER SEVEN

From records pieced together in the course of investigating Charlie and the other Lunarian remains uncovered on the Moon, it had been established that the Lunarians knew of the lost race of giant-size bipeds that had inhabited Minerva long before their own time. Lunarian mythology told that this race still existed at a star known as the Giants' Star, which could be identified on the charts. At the time of these discoveries, the scientists of Earth had no way of knowing if the legend was true. But they kept the star's name, and it had persisted since.

Giants' Star, or Gistar, was located approximately twenty light-years from the Solar System in the constellation of Taurus. It was Sun-like in size and composition but somewhat younger, and supported a system of five outer gas giants and five inner terrestrial-type planets, all of them attended by various gaggles of moons, that came uncannily close to duplicating the pattern back home. This was hardly surprising, since ancient Ganymean leaders had searched long and diligently to find a new home for their race that would present as few hazards in the way of unknowns and surprises as possible.

Thurien was the fifth planet out from its star, as Minerva had been, a little smaller than Earth, and cooler, which suited the Ganymean range of adaptation. However, the composition and dynamics of the atmosphere provided a more equalized pattern of heat distribution than Earth's, resulting in polar regions that were smaller than a simple comparison of distances would have indicated, and equatorial summers that were seldom hotter than the equivalent of marginal subtropical to Mediterranean. The surface was roughly seventy percent water, with four major continental land masses distributed, unlike those of Earth, fairly equally across both hemispheres, but with a greater variation in height between the deepest ocean chasms and highest mountain peaks.

The Thuriens had been pursuing their unsuccessful attempt to unravel the mystery of trans-Multiverse movement in terms of their existing h-space physics at a place called Quelsang, close to the city of Thurios, the planet's administrative and governing center. Thurios was where Hunt and his group would be staying, as would most of the other Terrans aboard. It stood near the coast in a setting of lakes connected by gorges and waterfalls on one of the two southern continents, called Galandria. There was none of the complication of docking at a transfer satellite and having to board a surface shuttle as happened when Terran interplanetary craft arrived at Earth. The *Ishtar* went straight from its approach into a descent that brought it down into the great space port situated by the water just over a hundred miles east of the city. Even Hunt, who had probably had as much dealing with Thuriens as any Terran, was awed by the vast complex of launch and loading installations, with starships the size of ocean liners lined up like suborbitals and freighters on a busy day at O'Hare or JFK.

Thurien architecture delighted in immense, soaring compositions of verticality, adorned with towers and spires, some of the larger cities extending upward for miles. A flying hotel lobby that looked like a flattened blimp from the outside but was burnished gold in color carried the arrivals to the city. Their first sight of it came before they were halfway there. It appeared on the horizon as a slowly growing cluster of whiteness and light, at first belying the distance by the suggestion being of some kind of monolithic structure. But as they drew closer and its true proportions revealed themselves, what had seemed to be facets of a single structure gradually unfolded and resolved into entire precincts of colossal frontages and vistas, terraced skyscrapers, canyons, and cliffs of architecture woven amid festoons of bridges and arcades around towering central massifs in a tapestry that sent the mind reeling.

There was as much greenery as glass and sculpted stone filling the progressions of tiers and levels, with lakes connecting via a system of canals, and waterfalls constrained between the faces of buildings, while above, layers of cloud wreathed the topmost pinnacles. It wasn't so much a city, Hunt found himself thinking, as an artificial mountain range.

By the time the ray-shaped blimp brought them to what appeared to be the city's transportation center—or maybe just one of them—Hunt had lost track among the compositions of cityscape that they had passed between and over. They sailed into a vast, hangar-like space high in a stepped block of city vaguely reminiscent of an outsize ziggurat, disappearing below into a tangle of curving traffic ramps and lesser structures. From here, conveyances of every description seemed to come and go, from a web of tubes radiating from the lower levels like an integral circulation system built into the city, to streams of objects following the ubiquitous g-conveyor lines across the spaces above and between, which were as much a part of Thurien city-building as the edifices themselves. It was not always easy to tell what constituted a "vehicle," for pieces of the architecture seemed capable of moving and reattaching elsewhere. On leaving the blimp, the Thurien hosts took Hunt and his group down a couple of levels to a dining area for lunch. When they had finished, they emerged to find that the room had become part of their hotel. A little under thirty-five hours had elapsed by their watches since the *Ishtar* lifted out from orbit above Earth.

Earlier Terran guests had christened it the Waldorf. Originally provided for the convenience of Jevlenese making short visits to the city, it was designed to human proportions rather than Ganymean. Although it included accommodation, catering, recreational and other facilities, "hotel" didn't really describe it since it wasn't set up as a commercial venture. But it was near enough. The rooms had all the comfort and extras that Hunt had come to expect, including a full Thurien neurocoupler in each. There was also a section of cubicles for public use at the rear of the main entrance level, behind the lobby area. The gymnasium below included a gravitically sustained freefall pool where the water was spherical inside a trampoline-like elastic surrounding wall, and swimming combined with power diving became a whole new experience.

The main socializing focus seemed to be a sunken area of

booths and seating alcoves set around a more open floor to one side of the lobby, screened behind planters and partitions and doubling as a bar and coffee shop. The sign in Jevlenese by the entrance gave it as the Broghuilio Lounge in recognition of their esteemed leader, but later Terrans, probably on account of its situation a few steps down from the lobby, had dubbed it the Pit Stop, which the Thuriens obligingly added in English. No arrangement had been made for the Terrans to see the Thurien Mutliverse work until the next morning. The rest of the day was for relaxing and acclimatizing. So after unpacking, freshening up, and settling in, it was to the Pit Stop that Hunt and the rest of the team gravitated, as well as others who had been on the *Ishtar*. The Thuriens who had been detailed to take care of them were either there already or drifted in later as time went by. It was a strange contrast that Hunt had observed before. Nothing ever seemed hurried or strained in Thurien day-to-day personal life. Yet when they put their minds to something like a construction or scientific project, the speed and efficiency with which they went about things could be astounding.

Preoccupation with rebuilding their culture back on their home world had reduced the numbers of Jevlenese coming to Thurien compared to those seen in times gone by. On the other hand, Terrans in some capacity or other were becoming a regular ingredient of life, so the demand for accommodation at the Waldorf was as brisk as ever. The *Ishtar*'s complement had included a school group from Oregon on their way to summer camp on a world that had real dinosaurs; an Estonian choir that had been commissioned to give a series of performances across Thurien; and some technical support people from Formaflex Inc. of Austin, Texas, who were conducting an experiment on the economic effects of introducing Thurien matter-duplicating technology to Earth—the same outfit that Hunt's alter ego had tipped as an investment, which Hunt had passed on to his neighbor, Jerry. There were also some Jevlenese, but they tended to keep themselves apart, conditioned by tradition and upbringing to see Terrans as their implacable Cerian rivals.

Hunt found himself sitting with Sonnebrandt, Chien, and a Thurien called Othan, who was attached to the project at Quelsang in some kind of technical capacity. Sandy and Duncan had gone sightseeing around the city, Danchekker was away, checking something to do with the arrangements for tomorrow, and Mildred was making sure that the Waldorf staff were briefed on Lynx's foibles, aversions, and preferences.

As was the case with many Thurien materials, the table they were sitting at could be made opaque, transparent, and take on various textures. Currently it was glass-topped and functioning as a holo-tank, which Othan had been using to give them a visual tour of Thurios. The image contained in it now, however, was of the Quelsang Institute, where they would be going tomorrow. It was like a miniature version of Thurios, interconnected high-rise structures standing amid parkland and trees, but more curvy and exotically styled. Othan said it was named after a long-deceased Thurien notable. "Institute" was the term that Terran linguists had applied when nothing better really matched the original Thurien word.

"So what kind of a place is it?" Sonnebrandt asked.

"I'm not sure I know enough about Terran organizations to be able to compare it with anything," Othan replied.

"I met an Australian who was there, studying Thurien propulsion," Chien said. "He described it as a mix between advanced-physics research and teaching laboratories, and a philosophical academy."

"Who runs it?" Sonnebrandt asked. Othan looked perplexed.

"The administration sounds a lot less centralized than what we're used to," Chien said. "There doesn't seem to be much in the way of any coordinating policy."

"Different groups use the facilities to pursue their own programs, depending on what interests them," Othan said.

"So how are they coordinated? What unifies them in their approach?" Sonnebrandt persisted. . . . Suppose they have different theoretical foundations. Or even contradictory ones. Would Quelsang be supporting all of it?"

Othan didn't seem to understand the problem. "Well, yes," he agreed. "How else would we find out which was true?"

"The Australian told me it was like a scientific artists' colony," Chien said.

Hunt couldn't make out whether she approved or not. The kind of tradition she was from would not have accustomed her to see the beneficial side, but from his previous dealings with Thuriens he knew something about how they worked. There was no Thurien Establishment to pronounce the approved consensus on a given subject, or any institutionalized reward system that would encourage conformity to it. Ideas either worked or they didn't; predictions succeeded or failed; evidence said what it said, regardless of anyone's preferences or preconceptions. Without political pressures or fears of losing face—which didn't especially affect Thuriens in any case—individuals left alone to make their own assessments in their own time would eventually come around to playing a part in an act that was going somewhere, rather than be left out in the cold with one that wasn't.

Sonnebrandt seemed to get the picture. "I can't see something like that being made to work back home anytime soon," he remarked, looking at Hunt.

Hunt shook his head. "About as likely as the tribal witch doctor hanging up his mask and starting over as a bottle washer in the village clinic," he replied. "The Thuriens don't have police forces. What does that tell you about something just a little bit fundamentally different in our natures?"

"Ah, excuse me. It is Dr. Victor Hunt, the English?"

Hunt turned to find a pretty girl of about fourteen or fifteen standing by his chair, dressed in a sailor-suit school uniform. She looked Japanese and was holding a red, cloth-bound book and a pen. Hunt grinned. "None other. Who are you?"

"My name is Ko."

"Hi, Ko. What can I do for you?"

"Sorry for intrusion. But I collect many famous autographs. I would be honored if I could add also the great scientist."

"A pleasure. The honor is mine." He took the book, and while the others looked on, smiling, wrote,

> To Ko, who came a long way from home. I hope you
> didn't follow me here just for this.
>
> > *Victor Hunt*
> > *Thurios, Planet Thurien*
> > *In the system of the Giants' Star*
> > *October, 2033*

Ko looked uncertainly at Othan. "Could have Thurien, too?" she inquired a shade timidly.

VISAR came in on the circuit—it had to be involved for her to talk to the Thurien. "You can speak Japanese, Ko. I'll take care of it."

It took Ko a moment to realize what was happening. Then she handed Othan the book. "I already have Bressin Nylek's," she said as Othan penned something in heavy Thurien Gothic-like script. "He's an officer on the *Ishtar*. That was the ship we came here in. I have the captain's, too."

"Very enterprising," Sonnebrandt commented.

Not wanting to leave anyone out, Ko passed her book to him and Chien in an unspoken invitation when Othan had finished. "I was hoping to find Professor Danchekker," Ko said, looking around while they complied. "The scientist who went to Ganymede, too."

"He's away right now, but—" Hunt started to say, and then caught sight of Danchekker coming down the steps from the lobby area and looking around. "No, wait. You're in luck. Here he is now." Hunt caught Danchekker's attention with a wave, and Danchekker came over. "Your fame knows no bounds, Chris. This is Ko, who collects autographs. She wants your moniker."

"What? . . . Oh. Yes, of course. . . . My word, you have been busy, young lady." Danchekker sustained a smile while he added his inscription. Ko trotted away happily.

"How goes life in the rest of the universe?" Hunt asked as Danchekker pulled up a chair to join them.

"Cousin Mildred has been drilling the unfortunates who work here on the art of living with her blasted cat. Luckily, they are mostly Jevlenese. Many Thuriens are uncomfortable around carnivores. For a while there was pandemonium. She thought they'd lost it."

"The missing Lynx?" Hunt threw in.

Danchekker groaned under his breath and tried to ignore it. "Everything is arranged for Quelsang tomorrow."

"Did you find out if Porthik will be here?" Hunt asked. Porthik Eesyan was the scientific adviser from Thurios that they knew from the Jevlen expedition. He had been playing a leading part in the Multiverse work.

"Yes, he will. He has some news that he wants to give you personally, Vic. The ideas you forwarded were right on. The Thuriens have been looking into them intently. It seems they were a lot closer to success than they thought. In fact, it appears that they have actually been sending things into other universes and not realizing it!"

CHAPTER EIGHT

UNSA had, of course, communicated to the Thuriens the message from Hunt's universe-traveling other self, and the Thuriens had immediately begun exploring theoretical models and preliminary experimental setups to see what could be made of a matrix propagation approach to the problem. It turned out that a reinterpretation of some of the work they had been doing ever since the Minerva event showed they had been closer to making a breakthrough than they imagined.

Their experiments before Hunt's input had led them to propose a hypothetical particle that Duncan Watt referred to whimsically in a UNSA report as a "thurion," and the name had stuck. The thurion was invoked to account for an energy deficit observed in certain quark interactions, but direct evidence of its existence had never been observed, even in situations where predictions of finding it came close to certainty. So either thurions didn't exist, in which case the theory that said they should was flawed, or something was wrong with the methods being used to look for them. But after careful reanalysis and double checking, both the theoreticians and the experimenters insisted that their side of the house was clean. Thurions had to exist; yet the facts said they didn't.

At that point VISAR pointed out that this resolved logically if "the facts" were taken as referring to this universe, while the thurions existed in a different one. In other words, the Thuriens had stumbled on what they were trying to achieve without realizing it. The reason why they hadn't realized it was that nothing indicating such a process came out of the conventional h-space physics that they had been trying to apply. But when they reran the data using an approach based on longitudinal matrix waves of the kind Hunt had proposed, the effect followed immediately. In fact, fluctuations at the quantum level would be expected to produce something like it all the time naturally—spontaneous transfers of energy across the Multiverse "grain" that would reveal themselves as sudden appearances and disappearances of virtual particles at the smallest time scales. It perhaps accounted for the quantum-level "foam" permeating the vacuum, which physicists had known about and measured for a long time, but never been able to really explain.

Hence, the arrivals from Earth found the Thuriens in a state of considerable excitement. This was not only on account of the thurion mystery being solved, but additionally because things had already progressed significantly further. The key to the whole business, it turned out, was Thurien gravitic technology. The reason why Maxwell's equations didn't yield a longitudinal wave component was that they related only to the aspect of the underlying matrix that was described electromagnetically. Charged objects in motion experienced an electrical drag that increased with velocity. This meant that the faster they moved, the more they resisted further acceleration, which was another way of saying they exhibited an increase in mass. Energy supplied in excess of what they could absorb by changing their motion was disposed of as radiation. Eventually, all of the energy being applied would be radiated, beyond which point no further acceleration was possible and the effective mass would be infinite. This, of course, described all the experimental work carried out on Earth through the previous century and interpreted in terms of relativity theory, which had pronounced the limit on velocity to be universal. But in fact it only applied to electrical phenomena—which was neither here nor there as far as Terran scientists were concerned, since they had no means of accelerating electrically neutral matter to high speeds anyway. But the Thuriens did.

Applying their gravitic methods to the matrix dynamics proposed by Hunt produced a more general form of field equations that contained a longitudinal component with solutions perpendicular to all of the four dimensions contained in the electromagnetic tensor, which could only mean trans-Multiverse propagation. Now that they were on the right track, the Thuriens at Quelsang were already transporting away to elsewhere in the Mulitiverse—the term they used was "multiporting"—electrons and protons, the building blocks of tangible matter. The next step would be to try simple molecules.

A peculiar implication of the whole state of affairs was that if they were sending particle-energy quanta into nearby other universes, then at least some versions of their other selves who lived in those universes would be doing the same thing too. This suggested that, in principle anyway, it might be possible to detect electrons, protons, molecules, or whatever materializing here as a result of corresponding experiments going on next door. The Thuriens had been looking for such events, but the results so far had been negative. From VISAR's latest computations, it seemed that such a result was to be expected. Porthik Eesyan explained why to Hunt while they were observing some of the test runs to multiport molecules. It was several days since the Tramline group's arrival. The introductory tours and demonstrations of the Multiporter, as the project had come to be designated, were over. The combined team were getting down to business. Hunt and Eesyan were both physically there, not neurally coupled in remotely to a composite creation. Experimenters couldn't do much real experimenting in one of VISAR's virtual-world settings.

"Is your head in a mood for big numbers today, Vic?" Eesyan stood over a foot taller than Hunt, dark gray, almost black in hue, his torso covered by a loose-fitting coat that reached to the knees, brightly colored in an elaborate woven design. Ganymeans did not posses hair, but the skin at the tops of their heads roughened into a ribbed, scaly texture, a bit like candlewick, that could range through as many color combinations and hues as bird plumage. Eesyan's was blue and green, taking on streaks of orange toward the rear.

"I'm ready to risk it. Try me," Hunt said.

"Multiverse branches really are as thin as some of us have speculated. In theory, they could differ by as little as a single quantum transition. There could be as many of them as the number of discrete quantum transitions in the entire lifetime of the universe. Pick anything you like for the number of zeros. It won't make any difference that matters."

Hunt pursed his lips in a silent whistle while he thought about it.

Considering the enormity of what it implied, the Multiporter was really quite a modest piece of hardware as Thurien constructions went. The projection chamber itself, which was where the actual multiporting happened, took the unremarkable form of a square metal housing about the size of a microwave oven, upon which an array of shiny tubes converged at various angles from pieces of equipment mounted in a supporting framework extending around the sides, overhead, and into a bay beneath. A forest of sensors and instrumentation filling the remainder of the framework, a worktop and monitoring station, several desks, and banks of conduits, tubes, and other connections disappearing behind the walls and down through the floor completed the scene. The chamber at the center was where matter was being induced to disappear into other realities. It was adequate for the type of experiments being conducted currently. Should success later lead to more ambitious attempts involving larger objects, it was anticipated that a scaled-up Multiporter would be operated out in space, away from Thurien. Eesyan already had some designers looking into it. Short-term budget cutting was meaningless in a system that had no concept nor need of cost accounting.

A volume of space inside the chamber was also where the attempts were being made to detect matter multiported from other realities. By the bizarre logic of the situation, if other nearby selves were multiporting matter out of their universe using their version of the same equipment, then it seemed to follow that this would be the place to look for it in this universe. Hence, the Multiporter's time was divided between operating in sending and detecting modes. This raised the question that if their other selves were working to the same schedule, nobody would detect anything because they would all be sending when no one was looking, and looking when no one was sending. The answer adopted was to use a local quantum randomizer to switch between modes. Assuming their counterparts would think the same thing, the idea was that random generators driven by a different sequence of quantum processes—which was what, by definition, made a different reality different—would yield a different pattern of switching times, giving periods of overlap between modes of sending from one universe and attempting detection in another. The negative outcome had caused this line of supposition to be reexamined without any obvious flaw turning up, but Eesyan was now saying there were other reasons why it was to be expected.

A "segment" was the term that had been given to a "vertical" slice of the Multiverse—a self-contained universe that beings like Thuriens and humans inhabited, and within which change in the form of an ordering of events was perceived to happen. In terms of the not really accurate but more easily visualized analogy of pages in a book, it appeared that the pages were astoundingly thin. "It seems to be the way some people guessed," Eesyan confirmed. "A particle traveling through a segment would exist in it for a vanishingly short time, making it indistinguishable from background quantum noise. Impossible to detect in practice."

Hunt had hoped for some kind of bulk averaging effect whereby individual quantum events would seldom give rise to any discernible difference at higher, more macroscopic levels. That would, in effect, have made the pages thicker. But he wasn't about to argue with VISAR over a matter of computation. "Do macroscopic probabilities get bigger?" he asked Eesyan. In other words, would larger objects take longer to traverse a segment, making their detection easier?

"Not significantly," Eesyan answered. "Multiporting propagation is fast." He made a tossing-away motion with his six-fingered hand. "But we're working toward sending larger configurations of matter. We will upgrade the detectors to look for the same kind of thing, too, anyway. You never know. We might glimpse something passing through."

Hunt rested his elbows on the guard rail in front of them and snorted in a way that said this still took some effort to believe. By the strange reasoning that guided the planning, there would be little point in looking for objects from next door that they were not themselves yet in a position to send. He stared up at the resonator mountings, where the tubes emerged from overhead. That was where the energy was imparted and the matrix waves—"M-waves," by the terminology being formulated—generated to initiate the multiporting process. Thurien technicians assisted by maintenance robots were working on parts of the equipment.

Josef was up there, too, with Chien, hovering in a Thurien gravitic bubble, to see what they could learn.

"So what happens finally to the extended structures that you've been sending?" Hunt asked Eesyan. "The molecular configurations."

"We've no way of knowing for sure. From what we can tell, they just keep going and disperse as an expanding wave function."

Hunt nodded distantly. How, then, had the relay device that had appeared in Earth orbit been able to maintain itself there long enough to initiate and support a dialogue? Did it mean that only objects that were complex enough to contain some means of "stopping" themselves somehow could be multiported into another reality in the meaningful sense of being able to stay there?

"There's a lot to be done yet," Eesyan said, as if reading his thoughts.

At that moment, VISAR came though via avco in Hunt's head to say he had a call from Mildred. Since it was disconcerting—and certainly not the best of manners—for someone to suddenly start talking to thin air when they were with company, VISAR would have announced the event to Eesyan, too. Such courtesies were not possible on Earth, where most people didn't have avcos behind their ears, which was another reason why Hunt generally refrained from using his when back home. Those who did were not the kind who worried unduly about manners anyway. He accepted, and Mildred appeared as a framed head and shoulders superposed in his visual field.

"Victor, hello. And how is the . . . what do you call it . . . multiporting . . . lab?" She had decided it would all be beyond her, and instead gone off with Danchekker somewhere in Thurios to meet some of the Thuriens that she wanted to get to know in connection with her book.

"It makes our national labs back home look like alchemy shops," Hunt replied. "And they got it up and running in less time than we'd have had committees arguing about it. How's it with the sociologists?"

"Oh, unbelievably useful! They're all so helpful! It's as if they have all the time in the world and nothing is so important that it can't be interrupted. Or is it just their way of being polite? I haven't really decided which yet. At first I thought it was a result of their ideas of what we'd call economics—or absence of them. You know what I mean—when anyone can have unlimited anything, you'd think that spending your life trying to get more would cease to mean anything, wouldn't you? But then, it isn't that way with us at all, is it? The more people get, it seems the meaner and nastier they become. I always found it was the poorest people who had nothing who were the most generous. So it must be something innately different in the Thurien nature."

The frame widened to include an image of Danchekker. "Get to the point," he muttered, at the same time sending Hunt a toothy grimace of a smile. "Vic, good day to you."

"So, what's up?" Hunt asked, taking the cue gratefully.

"Oh, I was just calling to remind you that it's close to ten," Mildred said.

"And?"

"You're due to meet us at ten."

"Where?"

"Well, not really actually 'meet.' . . . You know, in one of those couplers, or whatever you call them."

"What for?"

Mildred looked puzzled. "We arranged to go on a tour of VISAR space. You and Christian said you'd show me some Thurien planets, and we were going to say hello to the Ganymean friends of yours in the ship that's on Jevlen."

Hunt's brow furrowed. "There must be some confusion. I've no idea what you're talking about."

Danchekker interjected, "We called you this morning, Vic. The h-space tour, with a visit to the *Shapieron*."

Hunt searched back through his memory but could recall nothing. He shook his head helplessly. "Well, sure, I'll come along, no problem. It would be great to see Garuth and his people again. And I'm sure you mean it. But I honestly never said anything about this."

"Well, we're about ready to depart," Danchekker said. "But we'll wait until you get yourself organized." He sounded a trifle irritable, as if he didn't believe Hunt's denial and saw it as a somewhat lame excuse for having forgotten.

"I'll be right there," Hunt said, and cleared down. He looked back at Eesyan. "Would you excuse me? Chris and Mildred are asking if I could join them at short notice about something."

"As you wish," Eesyan replied.

"Where are the nearest couplers?"

"There's one right here." Eesyan indicated a partitioned space next to the monitoring panels. "It's free now."

Hunt took his leave and entered. He felt a little irked by Danchekker's attitude of uncompromising certainty, when it was obvious there was some kind of mixup. Could he really be getting that doddery? he asked himself. But the flicker of doubt passed. No, the downhill bike ride felt smooth and reassuring, without wobbles, he decided as he eased himself back into the recliner. He hadn't forgotten anything.

CHAPTER NINE

Vranix was an old Thurien city located on one of the north-ern continents, famous for its art centers and museums, and as a cultural repository. It was also noted for some of the most spectacular Thurien architecture, which in the years of the city's growth had flourished as perhaps the most extreme of Thurien art forms at the time. Hunt and Danchekker had "been there" before, in their first virtual visit to Thurien. It seemed a suitable place to include in the itinerary that she and Danchekker still insisted Hunt had helped draw up to give Mildred a preliminary overview of Thurien society—but by unspoken mutual assent they had stopped talking about it. In the evening they would rejoin the rest of the group physically for dinner.

They were standing in a large, saucer-shaped space, inside which circles of tiered seating rose to an enclosing rim. Hunt and Danchekker watched as Mildred gazed up at the three slim spires of what looked like pink ivory, converging above their heads before blending into an inverted cascade of terraces and levels broadening and unfolding upward for an inestimable distance. . . . And then she frowned in puzzlement. For beyond, where the sky should have been, the scene mushroomed out into a fusion of forms and structures of staggering dimensions extend-ing as far as the eye could see in one direction, while forming the shore of a distant ocean in the other. They were looking over the entire city of Vranix. But it was all hanging over their heads, upside down. They waited, seeing how long it would take Mildred to figure it out.

"My God!" she said after a lengthy pause. "All that topsy-turvy wonderland we came through inside. It turned us completely over somehow, and we didn't realize it . . . at least, I didn't. But you said you'd been here before. This has to be underneath. We've walked out like flies on a ceiling."

"Right on," Hunt complimented. The three spires "rising" around them surmounted an enormous tower dominating the city, and supported a circular platform that contained the place they were in—actually a small amphitheater used for various events and social gatherings. But the amphitheater was on the *underside* of the platform, not on top.

"Is it . . . I mean, is it real?" Mildred asked, looking down and from side to side as if checking her other senses. "Or something that VISAR is putting into our heads?"

"Oh, it exists precisely as you perceive it," Danchekker assured her. "A whim exercised by the Thurien architects of long ago, probably to show off their dexterity with the new science of integral gravitic structural engineering, which was developed at around that time. The Thuriens use it extensively, as you will already have gathered."

"So is that why I feel normal? . . . No, wait a minute. VISAR can inject the right stimuli to make you feel normal, anyway, can't it? What I'm trying to say is, if we were really here physically . . . there, whatever . . . would we still feel normal, with everything just looking wrong? Not upside down. The local gravity is normal but inverted?"

"Precisely so," Danchekker confirmed.

A Thurien who had been pacing slowly out by the rim when they appeared from one of the ramps from the interior, and who was now only a short distance away, changed direction toward them. The Terrans turned to face him as he drew closer. His face was lined and seemed old, his furrowed crown a subdued mix of streaky browns and grays that gave the impression of being faded.

"Forgive me if this is an intrusion," he said. "I am not familiar with the ways of Terrans. But it's the first opportunity I've had to speak with people from your world."

"Not at all," Hunt said cheerfully. "It would be a long way to come and not want to talk to anyone." He introduced himself and the others and added, "All in Thurios." When meeting in a virtual recreation of a setting, it was customary to state where one was located physically. It was evident that the Thurien was actually somewhere else also; had he been physically at the tower in Vranix, and therefore not neurally coupled into the system, he wouldn't be interacting with them. "Mildred is writing a book on your society. We're giving her a quick introductory tour of Thurien."

"My name is Kolno Wyarel. On Nessara, a planet of Callantares, a star you've probably never heard of." His manner became more relaxed. "But I was Thurien-born originally . . . a long time ago, now."

"With a system like this, you're never really away," Mildred observed. "Has it changed much?"

"Oh, Vranix never changes much."

"Is Vranix the part of Thurien that you're from?" Danchekker inquired, making a heroic effort at being genial.

"I studied music and philosophy here." Wyarel looked around. A faint smile touched his features. "It is where my wife, Asayi, and I met when we were young. Our favorite memories are of these places. So every once in a while we come back here to relive them a little."

"Will she . . ." Hunt wasn't sure if Wyarel meant that they came here together, or that Wyarel came to be reminded. He broke of the question that he had begun to frame, realizing that it might be indelicate.

The Thurien understood and gave a short laugh. "Yes, she's fine. She was supposed to be here by now, but no doubt she got distracted by something. VISAR says she isn't online yet. Don't worry about it. It happens all the time. She's somewhere in the same house as me."

"A universal proclivity of the female, it would appear," Danchekker observed.

"Oh, don't pontificate so, Christian," Mildred chided. "What do you do now on . . . where was it? . . . Nessara," she asked Wyarel.

"It's what I suppose you would call a tropical planet, teeming with forests and life. Warm and humid by our standards, but you get used to it. We retired there to be among the life, and to contemplate. There is an inner awareness that learns to open out to these things."

"There used to be teachings like that on Earth, but we seem to have turned away from them." Mildred glanced at the two scientists with her. "Such things seem to be considered as gone out of style." Danchekker humphed and rocked from one foot to the other, refusing to be goaded.

"That's only natural. But it will be temporary," Wyarel said. "A culture must attend to its material needs before it can rise beyond them, just as we must eat before we can create the works that are to be found in Vranix. Thuriens have discovered and mastered the physical universe. Now we are discovering ourselves."

"Christian, this is *exactly* what I wanted!" Mildred said. Then, to Wyarel, "Could I feel free to get in touch again sometime, and talk more about this?"

"Of course. But there are times when we retreat from external affairs, you understand."

"It wouldn't be an imposition?"

"We would be honored. . . . Excuse me for a moment." Wyarel stared distantly for a few seconds, then returned to the present. "That was VISAR with a message. Asayi had something to attend to concerning one of the *klorgs*—that's a domestic animal. We have several that come and go around the house. Now she's in the middle of a call from our daughter. Please, don't let me detain you any further. She would love to meet you, I'm sure, but it can always be another time. I am content enough here, alone with my thoughts."

"Females and cats," Danchekker murmured to himself, but not quite below his breath.

"Christian!" Mildred admonished.

They added the planet Nessara to their tour list and visited it next out of curiosity. The part that VISAR brought them to looked like the green rain-forest hills of the upper Amazon with a snow-capped wall of the Himalayas behind, but with greater richness of color and on an even grander scale. The waterfalls tracing their way down from the heights looked like chains of sparkling necklaces draped over the hills. VISAR supplied sensory inputs that faithfully reproduced the heat and the sultriness of the air, the scents and the sounds, even a realistic touch of clothing

sliding clammily over moist skin. Hunt was amused to note that
Danchekker unconsciously removed his virtual spectacles to wipe
the lenses with his virtual handkerchief—there was no reason why
VISAR should cause them to fog up.

"How careful do I have to be about what I'm thinking when
we meet someone like Wyarel?" Mildred asked. "I mean, I can
actually *feel* myself breathing more deeply up here, which I'm sure
I'm really not doing. From what you've said, it must be VISAR
doing things inside my head. How much else of what's inside
there can it pull out?"

"You don't have to worry," Hunt told her. "In principle, yes, it
could. But it doesn't. The Thuriens have strict codes about things
like privacy. Unless a user specifically instructs otherwise, VISAR
is limited to supplying primary sensory data and monitoring
motor and a few other terminal outputs only. It communicates
only what you'd see, hear, feel, and so on if you were there. It
doesn't read minds."

"Well, that's good to know, anyway."

They floated immaterially like cosmic gods above a world that
Danchekker had discovered before and insisted on visiting again.
It described a complex orbit about a double star to produce
conditions so extreme that its surface alternated between being
ocean and desert. Nevertheless, it supported a range of astonishing life forms that were able to adapt, including a part-time fish
that dissolved its bone structure and morphed into a lizardlike
sand dweller when the dry part of the cycle approached. They
visited a newly born world that was still an incandescent caul-
dron of lava flows and outgassing—instantly lethal in reality, but
with just enough of the flavor imparted by VISAR to give them
an idea of it. They stared in awe at an immense Thurien space
construction thousands of miles in extent that formed part of
one of the mass-conversion systems consuming burnt-out stars,
from where energy was beamed through h-space to create the
interstellar transport ports. They saw a world of vapors and
canyons, where the population lived on artificial islands floating
in the sky; a fairyland city carved out under an ice crust; and
an extraordinary football-shaped world that spun about its short
axis with its ends protruding beyond the atmosphere, where it
was possible—after an enormous climb that required life-support
gear—to jump off and be in orbit.

Finally, they found themselves inside what to Hunt and Danchekker were the familiar surroundings of the Command Deck of the ancient Ganymean starship, *Shapieron*. This was the vessel that had left the Solar System at the time of pre-Lunarian Minerva, before the Ganymeans migrated to Thurien, and returned only a few years ago, when Hunt and Danchekker were at Ganymede. The half-mile-high tower of once-gleaming metallic curves, pitted and discolored now as a result of its enforced exile, currently stood on the outskirts of a city called Shiban, on Jevlen. The exiles from the distant past had found adjusting to Thurien practically as difficult an experience as it was for Terrans. But they had found themselves a niche supervising the rebuilding of Jevlenese society after its deterioration and final collapse under the previous regime. Since the Ganymeans were interacting via Thurien neurocouplers, too, the "meeting" could as easily have taken place anywhere. But for reasons of nostalgia and old time's sake, everyone concerned had preferred to make it their old ship.

Garuth, who had been the commander of the *Shapieron* mission, greeted his two old friends and their guest warmly. With him were Shilohin, the female chief scientist, Rodgar Jassilane, the ship's engineering chief, and Monchar, Garuth's second-in-command. The Ganymeans from old-time Minerva were taller than Thuriens on average, not as dark in hue, and their crown coloring was less vivid. Also in attendance was ZORAC, the ship's controlling AI, an early precursor to VISAR, now coupled into the Shiban net to stand in for the decommissioned JEVEX.

The first topic that the Ganymeans wanted to hear about, of course, was the latest on the Multiverse project. Thuriens had no concept of secrecy, and bulletins detailing progress were produced regularly, but Garuth and the others wanted to hear Hunt and Danchekker's personal account. Hunt was able to fill them in on the fine structure of Multiverse segments and consequent ethereal passage of objects propagating through them, which he had learned himself only hours previously from Eesyan. The question again arose of how anything could be halted and stabilized so as to remain in one reality that a coherent picture could be derived from.

"Would it be feasible to create some kind of complementary M-wave that interferes destructively everywhere except at the target distance?" Shilohin wondered aloud. "Would that preserve the transmitted object as a standing resonance? It would probably still extend through many segments . . . but so what? Maybe you could fine tune your connection to any one of them." Nobody could argue with the thought, certainly; but just at the moment, it was purely abstract.

"It's an interesting idea. I'll bounce it off Eesyan," was all Hunt could offer in reply.

"You're still firing blind, though," Jassilane pointed out. "You called it a 'target.' But there's no form of feedback to identify one." He looked around. "You see what I mean? Suppose you wanted to send . . . oh . . ." he waved a hand, "the orbiting relay that this other universe sent to you. It seems to have appeared where and when it was supposed to. How did the senders know how to get it to where they wanted it?"

"I don't suppose we know enough about the Multiverse structure to preprogram the device to recognize features it's looking for?" Monchar ventured. "Like terrain-following flyers."

Hunt shook his head. "It depends too much on the way change occurs from one segment to the next—gradually or abruptly. And that varies with the MV dimension you move in. You could have practically stasis going one way, and total discontinuity if you choose another—a single quantum event being magnified, maybe, and triggering a transition to an entirely different reality. We have no idea how to model effects like that."

"To get where you want, you need a map. But you have to be there to draw one," ZORAC commented.

"Does this mean you're about to deliver one of your profound insights, ZORAC?" Hunt asked it.

"No. Just my take on the situation."

"Thanks."

There was not a lot more to be said on that for now. The talk shifted to the work of Garuth and his administration on Jevlen. The program was progressing well, with the Jevlenese getting over their total dependency on JEVEX and learning to mange their own affairs competently. Hunt had noticed from some of the outside views showing on the Command Deck's display screens that the city was looking cleaner and in better shape than the run-down, decaying condition it had been in when he last saw it. He wondered what Garuth and his people would do when their task here was complete. It seemed a question best not brought up at a time like this. But the *Shapieron* was not decommissioned or stood down from being launch capable in any way. It had played key roles in the ruse that had brought down Broghuilios's Jevlenese regime in the Pseudowar, and afterward, in defeating the mass mind-invasion of Jevlenese that the mental transplants from the Entoverse had intended. Hunt got the feeling that they would be hankering for an excuse to fly their ship again.

And then, after the usual promises to stay in touch more regularly that busy people are always making but seldom keep, they exchanged farewells for the time being. Moments later, Hunt was back in the recliner in the neurocoupler next to the Multiporter at the Quelsang Institute. "Thanks for the ride, VISAR," he said by way of signing off.

"We try to please."

Hunt stretched to take in a yawn, held the pose for a few seconds, and flexed his limbs a few times before getting up and ambling out into the lab area. "Who's still around?" he asked, reverted to avco mode now.

"Only Thurien techs," VISAR replied. "Eesyan left earlier. Josef Sonnebrandt and Madam Xyen Chien have gone on ahead and will see you at dinner with the rest of the Terran group."

"Ah, yes. How long do I have?"

"Little over an hour."

"Does that give me time to get back to the Waldorf to freshen up and change first?"

"No problem. There are some available flyers on the terrace outside the cafeteria area two levels below where you are. Take the door at the back and turn right, follow the wall with the windows in it to the concourse, and step onto the downgoing g-line."

CHAPTER TEN

The venue for dinner was a semi-garden setting of flowers and shrubs, glazed on two sides to look out among the city's heights, which incorporated high-level urban rivers and waterfalls shaped by invisible contours of force. Only the seven Terrans were present, the Thuriens having withdrawn for the evening to leave them some time to themselves. Since this was Thurien, the fare was vegetarian—but delicious. Meat-eating was unknown among Ganymeans, since land carnivores had never evolved on early Minerva. Apparently there were Jevlenese-run places in Thurios that catered to the tastes of visitors of their own kind, but the group from Earth hadn't considered it an especially important matter. The most talkative was Mildred, still enthralled by her recent experiences.

"Do you have any idea how many light-years Christian and Victor and I traveled today?" she said to the others at the table. "VISAR told me it took in a sizeable part of our region of the Galaxy. Yet I feel as fresh as a spring morning in the Alps. And nobody even had to pack a bag! it really is amazing. Can you imagine what it would be like if this kind of thing was extended one day to include the whole Multiverse—you know, all these other realities that I keep hearing about? We'd be able to travel around in history—even all the ones that never happened. . . . Well, they do happen, if I understand it all correctly, but not where we are. Is that it? . . . Oh, you know what I mean."

"Connecting all the VISARs together," Duncan said in a slow voice. He stared at her, obviously fascinated by the thought. It evidently hadn't occurred to him before. As the junior element of the team, he and Sandy had been delegated the chore of organizing the work space that the Terran group would be using. Things there were going smoothly, which didn't leave much to report, and they were happy to leave the talking to others. Sonnebrandt and Chien were strangely quiet, and Hunt thought he detected some strain between them. Danchekker was absorbed in investigating the Thurien organic preparations. Hunt stared at Mildred, his mind boggling at what she had just said. It hadn't occurred to him either.

She went on, "But the part about it that I don't buy, I'm afraid, is this business about every one of these little jiggly . . . what do you call them? The changes that can go one way or another."

"Quantum events?" Hunt supplied.

"Yes. I just can't accept that they lead to every reality that could possibly exist. Every combination that all the atoms that make up the universe could conceivably create. That's how you're saying it is, isn't it?"

"It's what the mathematics says," Hunt replied, treating it cautiously. He didn't want to get in a situation of having to contradict.

"Well, I'm not a mathematician," Mildred declared. "So I don't have to believe it,"

Danchekker eyed her curiously for a moment, seemingly thought better of getting involved, and returned his attention to dissecting a bulbous curiosity garnished with a yellow sauce, vaguely suggestive of a purple artichoke. Hunt smiled. "Numbers that are totally beyond anything you can grasp are just something you learn to live with after a while in this business," he told Mildred.

She shook her head. "It's not the numbers. It's the believability. You're telling me that every universe that could possibly physically happen does happen somewhere. But I don't believe it. I don't believe that a universe exists in which, say, my books are printed with all the pages blank, and they're stocked on shelves, and customers buy them. You see what I mean?" She looked around the table, inviting anyone to comment. Nobody did. "Your mathematics might say there's nothing to stop quantum . . . jiggles from making atoms come together to make a universe like that, but I don't believe it will happen. It just doesn't make any sense. The people in it would never behave that way."

Hunt stared at her while he thought to compose a reply . . . but then found that he couldn't compose one. She'd obviously missed a point somewhere . . . but he was unable to pinpoint exactly what. He needed time to think about this, he realized.

"But I've listened to too much of all this today," Mildred went on. "It was fascinating to meet some of the Ganymeans from the *Shapieron*, but I didn't understand a lot of what you were saying with them either. The most interesting for me were that couple, right at the beginning, in that upside-down superbowl in Vranix. Philosophers and artists," she said, addressing the ones around her who hadn't been there. "They've retired to live on an incredible world of rain forests and mountains that we also saw. They want to discover their inner nature. It seems that Thuriens see that as the main purpose in life. I've always thought it."

Hunt smiled again, amused at Mildred's flights of imagination. "It wasn't a couple," he reminded her. "Just Wyarel. He was waiting for his wife to show up."

Mildred gave him a reproachful look. "What are you taking about, Victor? They were both there. Asayi was charming. Surely you couldn't forget that gold and lilac gown that she was wearing. It was gorgeous!"

Hunt hesitated, not sure how to handle this. The evening seemed determined to get him into an argument over something. "I'm sorry, but you must have made this up somehow. Wyarel was alone at Vranix. . . . He was still waiting for Asayi when we left."

"Victor, I don't understand . . ."

"Cousin Mildred is correct, Vic," Danchekker said quietly. "We talked with both of them. You complimented Asayi on the gown yourself." He was giving Hunt a worried look, but at the same time shook his head almost imperceptibly, indicating that it was not something to make an issue of now. Hunt sat back in his chair and finished the rest of his meal in relative silence. He was as sure of himself as he had been that morning when Mildred and Danchekker called him at the Multiporter, insisting that he had agreed to accompany them.

"VISAR, you handle all the neural traffic involved in these situations," Hunt said. He had brooded for some time after getting back to his room at the Waldorf, then told VISAR of the problem. It was still troubling him. "Do you keep records of what takes place? That would be the way to resolve something like this."

"No, I don't," VISAR replied. "The purpose is purely to provide a communications medium between users."

Hunt had been fairly sure that was the case. It was more a way of broaching the subject. "But could you, if a user asked? Suppose I wanted you to keep a log of everything you channel into my datastream?"

"That would necessarily involve other users, too," VISAR pointed out.

"Does that mean you couldn't?"

"I'm not permitted to. It would require a change of standards and operating directives from the Thurien authorities who decide those things. And a change like that would not be approved easily—if it were ever approved at all." In a mild dig at Terran history that it apparently couldn't resist, VISAR added, "Thuriens don't have a background of obsession with surveillance and keeping tabs on each other."

"Even if the other parties were to agree?"

"It would get impossibly complicated," VISAR said. "Every user wanting to come into the circuit would have to be informed. And for Thuriens something like that would take a lot of explaining. They look at life very differently."

Hunt sighed. "Okay, it was just a thought. Forget it for now." He lay back along the couch where he had been pondering and stared up at the ceiling. It was ornately molded, fashioned from a material that generated light internally, either uniformly diffuse or concentrated in whatever places were desired. Something very strange was going on. He felt confused and disturbed. As disturbed as Josef and Chien had seemed earlier at dinner, from the moment they sat down.

He checked the time. It was just after midnight. "VISAR. Can you connect me to Josef?"

An avco frame opened up in Hunt's visual field a moment later, showing Sonnebrandt's head and shoulders. "Hi, Vic. What's up?"

"Are you doing anything right now? There's something I'd like to talk about."

"Sure, no problem. Do you want to meet in the Pit Stop? Or

you could come here for a drink. I was just getting ready to turn in."

"No, it's okay. I'll come there. See you in a couple of minutes."

Hunt arrived to find Sonnebrandt in house robe and slippers, with a squat, long-necked bottle and two glasses waiting on the table in the lounge section of the suite. "So what is it, an insomnia problem now?" he greeted as Hunt sat down. "I've probably had too much going around inside my head, too."

"Cheers." Hunt examined his glass after Sonnebrandt had poured. "What is it?"

"Some kind of wine the Jevlenese drink, that's stocked here. A bit like hock."

"Not bad."

Sonnebrandt indicated the direction of the door with a motion of his head. "I was talking to a couple of the Estonians earlier in the Pit Stop. I never realized before that Ganymeans can't sing."

"Their vocal apparatus is totally different," Hunt said. "It restricts them to that guttural speech that we have trouble reproducing." The voices that VISAR manufactured when it translated were synthesized to sound normal both ways. "And you're right. It doesn't give them a range that would permit song."

"Our choral music awes them. The Estonians are a huge sensation. Did you know?"

"I haven't really been following that side of things much."

"I thought it was strange . . . not the physiological thing; but that Thuriens should be so surprised. I mean, they've had the Jevlenese around for long enough. They're human."

Hunt shrugged. "Then I can only guess that maybe the Jevlenese aren't so musical. Come to think of it, I didn't see much sign of it when I was there."

"Maybe." Sonnebrandt settled himself back and regarded Hunt over the rim of his glass. "But anyway . . . So what is it that's so urgent that it can't wait until a more civilized hour of the morning?"

"It's not so much that it's urgent, Josef. But possibly personal. I thought that a little privacy might be in order."

"Oh. Now you have got me intrigued. Please go on."

Hunt had been trying to think of the best way to approach

this, but he still found the situation awkward. "Look, first, don't think I'm trying to pry, or that I have any interest in what might be your own personal business. My questions may sound a bit odd, but there's a good reason for asking them."

Sonnebrandt eyed him uncertainly. "Yes . . . ?"

"At dinner earlier tonight, you and Chien . . ." Hunt gestured briefly. "I couldn't help noticing that there seemed to be, oh . . . for want of a better word, something a little strained. A bit of edginess; not a lot of talking. Know what I mean?" He waited. Sonnebrandt stared into his glass without responding. Hunt read it as he'd feared—a tacit way of telling him as politely as possible to mind his own business. "Okay, look, I said at the beginning that if I've gone and trodden into something personal that's going on—"

Sonnebrandt cut him off with a short laugh. "You mean with me and Chien? Oh, come on, Vic. I've only known her face-to-face as long as you have, and it isn't as if we've exactly had nothing else to be concerning ourselves with." He took a quick drink. "Mind you, I wouldn't say no, to be honest. She has this magnificently 'spiritual' quality about her, don't you think? A lesson to the women of the world on how grace and attractiveness should improve with the years. At least, that was how I thought until today."

"You went very quiet when I mentioned it. I thought maybe you were offended."

"Hah." Sonnebrandt wrinkled his nose and thought for a few seconds. "A little silly, rather than offended, if you really want to know," he said finally.

"To do with why you had second thoughts about Chien?"

"Well, yes, if you want the truth."

Hunt knew then that his hunch had been right. "Let me guess," he said. "Something so stupid that it should hardly have been worth mentioning. Yet you found yourselves contradicting each other vehemently, like kids. Something that you knew you were right about, and which should have been easily resolved. But she insisted on making an issue of it and wouldn't back down."

Sonnebrandt's eyes widened in surprise. "That's it, exactly! How did you know?"

"I'll tell you in a second. So what happened."

"Earlier in the day, when we were at the Multiporter, we found ourselves arguing about things all the time—as you said, stupid little things. She'd tell me I was repeating something that I knew I hadn't said; or insist that she'd said things that she never had. Another time, she started to explain what had been happening for the last ten minutes, as if I'd been away, when I was there all the time. Anyone can make mistakes, of course. But when someone that you'd think would know that doesn't seem able to admit it . . . well, after a while, it gets to you."

"I know. Annoying, isn't it."

Sonnebrandt seemed about to go on, then checked himself as he saw the pointed look on Hunt's face. "Are you telling me it's been happening with you too?" He stopped and thought back. "Oh, of course! That business with Chris and Mildred over dinner about the Thurien couple."

Hunt nodded slowly. "I've known Chris Danchekker for years. He can be a bit cantankerous at times, but this isn't at all like himself. There's something very odd going on around here, Josef. It's affecting all of us, not just Chris. And just at this moment, I have no idea what it is."

CHAPTER ELEVEN

But it was not affecting all of them. The next morning, Hunt talked discreetly with Duncan Watt and learned that he and Sandy had experienced no problems of the kind that Hunt described. On the contrary, Duncan assured him, their day organizing the work space that they would be using and checking through the various items shipped from Earth had been a pleasant one, with the routine nature of the work being offset by the exhilaration and novelty of being on a new world.

Hunt decided that it was time to talk with Danchekker. A call established that the professor was in a tower of the Quelsang complex adjacent to the block housing the Multiporter, which was where the space assigned for the Terrans was located. They had agreed that they would prefer to work alongside the Thurien scientists that Eesayan had brought together for the project, rather than be segregated on their own. That was fine by the Thuriens, of course. VISAR navigated him across to the other building and up through exotically styled spaces of curving architecture and ornate interiors that gave Hunt more the feeling of an Arabian palace or a Spanish cathedral than anything he was accustomed to thinking of as a scientific working environment. The robelike garb that seemed common among the occupants added to the effect. It could have been Plato's Academy adapted to hard engineering. The Thuriens made no hard and fast division between what Earth had come to views as arts and sciences. Everything they did, from carving a mural beside a path through an elevated park in Thurios to powering a spacecraft was an art, while every process that involved evaluating a matter of objective truth was "science."

Hunt found Duncan and Sandy familiarizing themselves with some of the Thurien equipment, guided by one of the Thurien students who had volunteered to help out. Sonnebrandt was elsewhere—very likely gone to make his peace with Chien, Hunt suspected. Danchekker was out on the balcony fronting the room, Duncan informed him. Hunt went on through and out the glass-panel doors. It was more a terrace garden than what Hunt would have thought of as a balcony. Danchekker was standing at the outer rail on the far side of some foliage and an artificial stream, admiring the surroundings. Hunt crossed the stream by a small footbridge and joined him. The edifices of marblelike surfaces and glass making up the rest of the institute bodied as much thought and expression as a sculpture, rising from landscaped rock and greenery amid gigantic Thurien trees.

"I thought the view from the top floor of Biosciences at Goddard was stimulating," Danchekker commented. "But after this, I fear it will never seem the same again. If I possess an artistic streak somewhere, I'm sure this is the kind of inspiration that would be required to express it. Did you ever read Oswald Spengler? He believed that human cultures are born, grow, flourish, and die to express a unique inner nature, just like any other living organism. The Thuriens are no different. Everything they do is a statement of what they are and how they view the world. It's probably impossible to change, anymore than you can make a sunflower seed grow into a rose. A ready answer, it would appear, to the futile attempts of one culture to impose itself upon another that make such a sorry story of so much of our history, don't you think?" Danchekker was in one of his expansive moods, which might make things easier, Hunt thought to himself. He was happy to remain out on the balcony, out of earshot from those inside.

"Where's Mildred today?" Hunt inquired.

"Off on travels of her own already. She's meeting with Frenua. A challenging encounter, possibly. But I have no doubt she will handle it well." Frenua Showm was the high-ranking Thurien female who would be Mildred's prime guide in organizing her researches. She had been among the few Thuriens to have suspected Jevlenese motives before the exposure of Broghuilio and his plans, and tended to generalize her reservations into a wary suspicion of humankind in general.

"Chris, about that minor disagreement at dinner last night . . ."

Danchekker turned from the rail, beaming magnanimously, and made a throwing-away gesture. "Oh, think nothing of it. We all have these lapses from time to time. This kind of travel is disorienting and stressful, even if it is measured in a mere day or two. And such abrupt switching to a totally different social and physical environment can only exacerbate it further."

"Yes, but I don't think it's anything like that. There's—"

Danchekker went on, "But I've been thinking about some of the other things that were talked about last night, that I wanted to bring up. The implications could be quite extraordinary. It goes back to something that Mildred said, again." Danchekker had already dismissed the former matter as a triviality, best forgotten, Hunt realized. He groaned inwardly to himself. It was almost impossible to effect course-change once Danchekker launched off into an idea that had seized him. The professor brought his thumbs up to his lapels in an unconscious mannerism signaling that he was in lecture mode. "You may recall that she refused to countenance the suggestion that literally every reality that's physically capable of existing does exist somewhere in the Multiverse. To be frank, Vic, I have long entertained reservations on that score myself, despite what you physics people tell us the formal mathematics might say. But I was never able to identify where, specifically, the model breaks down. I think Mildred may have put her finger on it."

This was the person who grumbled about how his cousin talked unstoppably, Hunt told himself.

Danchekker went on, "She said there isn't a universe anywhere in which her books are produced and sold with blank pages. And of course she has to be correct. What could be more preposterous? But what does your mathematics have to say about it, eh? How does a purely mechanical process distinguish a reality that's humanly plausible from one that unaided common sense says couldn't exist—ever, no matter how remote a probability is assigned to it? It can't. Therefore, your quantum formalism can't be an adequate description of reality, regardless of how successful it might be at predicting the outcomes, over a limited range, of certain kinds of experiments."

Hunt felt again the same confusion he had when Mildred brought this up. There had to be an answer, but he couldn't bring to mind what. It wasn't something he had been giving much thought to since.

"The implications could be profound indeed," Danchekker continued. "Consider this. Physics asks us to accept that the Multiverse in itself is timeless, yes? The sequence of change that we perceive is created by consciousness navigating a path through its succession of alternative branchings. Precisely how it does so is a mystery—and to dispel any rising hope that you might be entertaining at this juncture, not one that I am about to cast further light on now, I fear." Danchekker showed his teeth briefly at his concession to humor. "But the fact that it is able to do so at all perhaps furnishes us with the essential defining criterion for what consciousness is. In fact, I should go beyond that and say 'life.' For by what I'm proposing, it follows that all life is conscious to some degree. Let's not confuse it with self-awareness, which is a qualitatively different subset of the phenomenon I'm talking about."

"So what are you proposing?" Hunt asked, resigning himself. He was obviously going to have to hear it through in any case.

"This. An inanimate object is subject solely to the laws of chance. The future that it comes to experience—or the particular reality that a given version of it exists in, if one wishes to be pedantic about it—is determined by forces and probabilities external to itself. And that is the world that physics accurately describes. But a conscious entity—and by what I said a moment ago, I mean *all* living organisms—by altering its *behavior*, has the ability to change those probabilities. It can *steer itself* toward a future different from the one that it would otherwise have experienced—presumably one which by some means it evaluates as more desirable. The degree to which it is able to do this is, perhaps, a good indicator of how conscious it is. It's a criterion that could conceivably apply equally well within a sapient species, such as ourselves, as across all of life in general."

"Are you talking about plants as well? Bacteria? Fungi?"

Danchekker waved a hand dismissively. "Yes. They all react

to environmental cues to improve their odds for living a better life."

Hunt was losing the thread. "So where does Mildred come in?"

"By pointing out, unarguably in my estimation, that conscious beings like ourselves will act to eliminate whole swathes of futures which, although the mathematics of the purely physical might allow them, will never come remotely close to happening for reasons that are *only meaningful in terms that consciousness deals in.* At some point along the way from the existence of every possible configuration of matter that quantum physics allows, to the actual realities that make up the Multiverse, some kind of 'plausibility bound' sets in that limits the forms they take. Consciousness intervenes to inhibit the quantum transitions that would lead to the excluded realities. How it does so, I have no idea. But it goes a long way toward explaining the somewhat limited success that has attended our efforts to apply physical theory to biological and social phenomena. Much of what the Thuriens talk about suddenly makes a lot more sense." He looked at Hunt expectantly.

But Hunt was still feeling irritated by the condescending air with which Danchekker had dismissed the subject Hunt had tried to bring up, which had been Hunt's prime reason for coming here. Now Danchekker was telling physicists where they had erred in their own domain and offering unasked-for advice on how to fix it. "Well, thanks, Chris, but physicists really are capable of handling the physics," he heard himself say, more shortly than he had intended. "The main job right now is getting the Multiporter to stay connected to somewhere. I don't see how this kind of metaphysical speculation is going to help much."

Danchekker's mouth clamped shut. He drew a long breath, clearly displeased at this reception. "You've constantly reminded me in the past that I should be more open-minded to some of your own wider-ranging conceptions," he said stiffly. "When I venture precisely that, you tell me to stay in my own field. Well, what do you want, for God's sake?" He produced a handkerchief and proceeded to wipe his spectacles. "At least I've always had the good grace to admit as much when, upon further consideration, I concluded that you may have been correct. I do trust that on this occasion I will be accorded the same courtesy." He replaced his spectacles and looked around. More voices were coming from inside. "And now would appear to be a good time to see how our young colleagues are getting along. I do believe that Josef and Chien have joined them." With that, Danchekker turned away, crossed over the footbridge, and disappeared inside through the doorway.

Hunt propped his elbows on the rail of the balcony, sighed, and stared out at the scene. Some Thuriens who looked like students waved up at him from a terraced enclosure some distance below. Hunt acknowledged with the brief raising of a hand. Yes, he knew he'd been out of line. What was getting into him? A fine way to begin a research project, he told himself glumly.

CHAPTER TWELVE

Christian was always telling Mildred tactfully—as closely as he was capable of getting to the meaning of the word, anyway—that she talked too much. If it was true—and she had to concede him something of a point at times, she supposed—then she must try to watch herself and control the trait when she was with Thuriens, she reminded herself. She was here to learn, after all. The trouble was that she always had so many thoughts boiling around inside her head, and she was afraid that if she didn't give vent to them while they were there, they'd sink back below the surface and never come up again. Very probably, it could be exasperating for others sometimes. But surely it was preferable to being like all those people she met everywhere who never seemed to have a worthwhile thought of any kind at all.

Poor Christian! She knew she'd been a pest back in Washington, and he had always been dedicated to his work, even without all the responsibilities of his new job at Goddard. But this project involving a whole, totally different alien culture was so *exciting*! He was simply too valuable an authority on it all to have just let pass. And he had been a dear to try and extricate himself in such a gracious way, instead of just telling her bluntly that he didn't have the time, in the boorish way that most of the pompous professors she had met over the years would have done. So she had resolved to do her best not to be a deadweight and to cultivate some interest in this Multiverse business that he and the others were getting so involved in with the Thuriens. Actually, it *was* turning out to be far more interesting than she had ever imagined, even if some of the things they talked about didn't make sense; and she would strive to be independent in pursuing her own work, staying out of their hair as much as possible.

The office the Thuriens had given her to work in couldn't have been better contrived to make her feel at home. It had shelves of reassuringly solid books; a desk and furnishings of polished mahogany and walnut that suited her tastes, along with drapes and a carpet that blended in; a clutter of homey bric-a-brac that included a china-laden mantlepiece, flower vases, and a cuckoo clock; and diamond-paned windows looking out over a valley of the Bavarian Alps. This was hardly surprising, for VISAR had contrived it all to achieve just that. None of it was real, of course, but it all came with a simulated filing cabinet and notepads that she understood, and a work terminal on the desk that used the formats and procedures that she was familiar with back home. The nice thing about it all was that everything she produced while she was on Thurien would find its way back via VISAR and the phone system somehow, and be waiting for her in her own files when she returned. She could even change the pictures on the walls anytime she got tired of them.

Mildred had made the point that if VISAR could create just about any sensory illusion that might be desired, it should be just as capable of putting together a reference system made up of things that *she* understood, as one incorporating all those annoying menus, options, icons, and incomprehensible boxes that computer people understood. The result was a set of bookshelves unlike any that she had even dreamed of. They were bookshelves because Mildred had insisted that a writer's office had to have books in. But the books arrayed along them changed to suit her particular needs of the moment. If she wanted to check some historical facts, a selection of volumes covering the period she was interested in presented themselves; if something geographical, a variety of atlases, physical, political, biological, and geological, along with travel guides and a picture library; and similarly for biographies, quotations, literature, arts, and every other form of reference that she had experimented with. And she could find her way to anything from indexes that made sense on pages she could turn in the way she had grown up with—except that the indexes rewrote themselves to point to whatever she happened to be researching. It was fantastic!

The other thing she had agitated for was a usable way of keeping track of all those notes, clippings, lists, letters, and so forth that you used to be able to rummage through in a folder, but which none of these desktops on screens ever seemed able to find unless you already knew where to look. In response, VISAR had come up with its single-drawer virtual filing cabinet, which Frenua Showm was just finishing explaining. The drawer looked normal enough, with a wood finish to go with the general decor of the room. It stood on a table at a comfortable height for access, no stooping or stretching to other drawers being necessary because that one could contain anything that was wanted.

"It works the same way as the bookshelves," Showm said. "The label on the front gives the topics the contents are organized under, and the folders inside follow." At the moment, the label was blank. Showm opened the drawer to reveal a set of familiar-looking hangers and tabs, but with all the inserts blank. "Let's try an example. What's a subject that you might be interested in?" she asked.

Mildred ran a virtual fingertip along the line of plastic tabs, feeling them flex slightly and causing a ripple of snapping sounds. It was uncanny. A faint scent of mountain meadows came with the breeze through the open window. She still had to work to remind herself that she was really in a recliner somewhere in the Government Center at Thurios. "One thing I wanted to cover was the Thurien political organization and how it functions," she replied. "How your leaders are appointed, and what guides their decision making. What would all that come under? 'Politics,' I suppose." She was still mildly astounded that somebody of the position that she had been told Frenua Showm held would be taking her through something like this personally and not delegating it to a junior clerk. Thuriens' ideas of priority seemed to be very different from the norms of Earth. Back there, every other value or consideration in modern life seemed subordinated to the great god of "efficiency." The Thuriens didn't seem even to have a concept of the word—at least, not in any economic sense.

Showm gestured. The word POLITICS had appeared on the label above the drawer handle. "The inside will organize itself according to the structure you create as you use it. Suppose you wanted to collect material on, say, how various services across Thurien are managed . . ." In response to her vocal cue, a subhead *Planetary Administration* added itself to the label below POLITICS. Inside the drawer, a group of folders acquired contents, along with suitable tabs to mark them. Showm lifted one of the folders out, riffled briefly through the papers inside, and handed it to Mildred. "And you can take it back to your desk and use it in the way you are used to, with no screens or confusing dialogs to worry about," she said.

"Splendid!" Mildred exclaimed. The folder was marked "Regional Congresses," and contained a selection of articles, maps, charts, and tables that VISAR had compiled together as a starting point on the subject.

"Everything is very local here," Showm commented. "Nothing as bureaucratic as the kind of thing you're used to. Much of Earth's ways of going about things results from the need to resolve conflicts. That's not a problem that we see a great deal of. Conflict arises from competitiveness, which isn't a big part of Ganymean nature."

"Yes, I'd gathered that. On account of your different origins."

"So it would appear."

Mildred dropped the folder back into its place in the drawer. She was still finding her first experience of being able to study one of the aliens alone, at close quarters, too fascinating to make as much of the opportunity for plying Showm with questions as would have been her normal inclination. And besides, her resolution to herself to heed Christian and not talk too much still held sway. There would be other times.

Showm not only towered over Mildred in height, but was built more broadly and massively in proportion, with long, firm limbs, revealed by a short-sleeved tunic to be magnificently contoured and muscled in an athletic kind of way that made Mildred confess inwardly to a feeling of seeming pudgy in comparison. Her skin was a blue-gray, darkening to purplish blooms at the elbows, backs of her hands, and back and sides of her neck, blending onto the black, crinkly head covering that functioned as hair. The effect was somewhat reminiscent of an old-style Roman or Norman helmet adorning the elongated Ganymean skull with its protruding, counterbalancing jaw. It was a strange irony, Mildred thought, that a race so totally devoid of aggressiveness should possess the physique and appearance that evoked images of the warrior caste.

"Is there no competition for office?" Mildred asked. "The leaders who decide your policies. How are they appointed?"

"Terrans have asked me that before," Showm said. She frowned, evidently still having difficulty with it. "There doesn't seem to be a way of answering that is readily comprehended. What you would call leaders here are not so much 'appointed' as 'recognized.' The qualities have to be there already. Devising some process that declares someone to be suitable when in fact they're not would be pointless. Such a person would never be accepted."

"Well, let's take Calazar as a case in point," Mildred suggested. Calazar had spoken for the Thuriens in the dealings with the Jevlenese and seemed to have functioned in the capacity of a planetary ruler or figurehead. The Thurien word for his title seemed to bear out what Showm had said, the nearest translation being "father-found." Terran translators had played safe by opting for the neutral "Identified One" to describe his position. According to Christian, Calazar was due to come over to the Quelsang Institute some time in the next day or two to see the the Multiporter for himself and add his own personal welcome to the team from Earth. "How did he come to occupy the position that he has?" Mildred asked. "What kind of process put him there?"

"He was selected and trained from an early age. The process . . . ?" Showm seemed at a loss. "How could I describe it? It embodies much tradition and experience that has come together over a long time. I suppose that the form of Terran government that comes closest would be a form of monarchy . . . but not hereditary or elective. The nearest word would probably be 'consensual.'"

This still wasn't getting to the core issues that Mildred wanted to probe. "What if others were able to organize enough supporters with the ability to place one of their own there regardless?" she said.

"You mean forcibly?"

"Yes."

Showm made a gesture of incomprehension. "Why would anyone want that? Should it please me to have the power to compel you to live your own life otherwise than as you would choose?"

"But when all have to live by the same decision, there have to be differences at times," Mildred persisted. "How do you resolve them?"

"You're thinking in terms of Terran militarism and commerce," Showm replied. "They are both systems for allying against threats and rivalries that arise from the competitiveness that Ganymeans don't have. Our enemies are ignorance, delusion, suffering, and the natural hardships that the universe throws against all of us. Why would we pit ourselves against each other? This is where the gap between our cultures becomes unbridgeable. You have to be Ganymean to understand. It isn't something that can be explained, and you then know. It's something that you grow up with; that you *feel*."

Mildred pushed the file drawer closed and gazed at the skyline of mountain peaks beyond the window. "Actually, I do think I know exactly what you mean." She sighed. "The people of Earth have been blundering around for thousands of years, perfecting systems for following the absolute worst kinds of individuals. They let themselves be made to hate each other and be turned into tools for serving the narrow interests of others, when they could be building a better future for all. From what Christian tells me, I think you know enough of our history to be aware of the consequences."

"Christian?"

"My cousin: Professor Danchekker."

"Ah, yes." Showm stared for several seconds with her deep, ovoid eyes. "I don't think I've heard a Terran be that frank before. Is it truly what you believe?"

The remark was so refreshing that Mildred was unable to contain a short laugh. Christian had described to her how Frenua Showm had been the least credulous among the Thuriens in the face of Jevlenese duplicity, and the most suspicious of all human declarations and motives thereafter. "Some of us Terrans are able to see reality as it is, and not as we're told it is, you know," she replied. "It's not a question of believing anything; it's seeing with your own eyes and common sense what *is*. . . . Or until quite recent times, what was, anyway. It could be starting to change." She meant since the Jevlenese scheming that had gone on for centuries was exposed. "Victor thinks so. You've met him, of course."

"Hunt, the Englishman? Yes."

"But as for our parade of illustrious princes, conquerors, and shapers of society?" Mildred made a sad face. "The worst of the thieves and the scoundrels. None of their fortunes was ever amassed honestly. They all came from living off the backs of the real producers of anything, however else it might have been camouflaged. There's something defective about people who find satisfaction in that or admire it in others; they're not complete as human beings. But they're the ones who have always had the positions of power. Very rational materialists, no doubt, and highly capable when it comes to pursuing this goal of 'efficiency' that they seek in everything. But lacking in the emotional capacity and feeling for human values that a healthy and sane culture needs to be founded on."

Showm was warming to this echoing of her own feelings that she evidently hadn't expected to hear. "The organized violence that you call war is not only abhorrent but incomprehensible to us," she replied. "No person capable of experiencing empathy and compassion could be capable of ordering such things. And subordinating a life to obsessively accumulating possessions in place of cultivating the works that make life truly rewarding is mystifying indeed. Thuriens behaving in such a way would be regarded with concern and sympathy." She paused to eye Mildred searchingly for a moment. "But I'm not sure that our differences are attributable purely to our respective origins in the way you assume. Ours is also a far older culture."

"You think it might be a matter of the Thuriens being more mature as a race?" Mildred asked.

"Possibly. In part, anyway."

"They certainly show more of the characteristics that I'd describe as 'adult,'" Mildred agreed. "It makes so much of what we've seen on Earth appear as the antics of spiteful adolescents in comparison." She had made the same point to Christian on several occasions. Showm seemed surprised to hear this assessment coming from a Terran—impressed, even. Mildred paused, then went on, "Although it is true that Thurien progress came to a halt for a long time, isn't it?" She was referring to the period of stagnation that occurred following Thuriens' attainment of immortality after their migration to the Giants' Star, which they later abandoned.

"Even without that, we were a spacegoing race long before humans existed," Showm pointed out.

"Well, all right, yes, I suppose so . . ."

"And in those earlier times we went through a phase of what you would probably call hyperrational materialism, too. Before the migration from Minerva, our ancestors considered moving to Earth. They sent survey missions there and set up bases. But nothing in their experience had prepared them for the ferocious competition of life that they found there. They knew that they could never coexist with such a pattern. And so, they . . ." Showm's voice faltered. She was unable to finish the sentence.

"I know," Mildred said quietly, and nodded. "You don't have to explain. Christian told me about it." The early Ganymeans had embarked on a program to exterminate the higher forms of Terran life with the aim of clearing the territory for their own kind and forms of life compatible with it to move in. Parts of Earth subjected to the pilot experiments had remained deserts to the present day. But the experience had proved too traumatic and filled with unexpected consequences for the Ganymeans involved. So the notion of moving to Earth was forgotten, and the program to move the entire race to a new star system took shape in its place.

"It isn't something that Thuriens normally talk to Terrans about," Showm said. She appeared to be a little taken aback. "Because of uncertainty as to the possible reactions. I was prepared to tell you because you seem more understanding than many might be."

"It came from Victor," Mildred replied. "He learned the story from the Ganymeans of the *Shapieron*—before there was any contact with Thurien."

"Ah, yes. . . . In that case, I see." Showm nodded. "And you don't hold it against us? I find that . . . curious."

Mildred smiled, at the same time snorting scornfully. "I don't think anyone from a species with a record like ours would be in any position to condemn the lapses of another," she replied. "Especially when you were able to learn so much from it—about yourselves and about the true consequences of one's actions. That's more than can be said for the geniuses who led Terrans by the millions from one slaughter to another through millennia, and learned nothing."

"You are wise," Showm commented. "You understand truth. So why don't Terrans allow people like you to lead?"

Mildred laughed delightedly. "We've been through that! I'd never be appointed. They don't want to hear what's true. They want to hear whatever justifies their prejudices."

"Like children who think they can change reality by wishing it so. On Thurien you would be listened to."

"Well then, there's your difference, Frenua."

A movement outside the window caught Mildred's eye. A bird had come out of a tree to swoop down over the stream tracing a rocky course along the valley floor. She watched it climb again until it was soaring against the sky. Behind it in the distance, incongruously, the long, slender shape of a bright yellow zeppelin with red markings was hanging above the mountains. "VISAR, what's *that* doing there?" Mildred demanded in astonishment.

"Oh, just an experiment I dreamed up to add in some variety. Would you rather I stuck strictly to authenticity?"

Victor had mentioned that one of the tasks VISAR had set itself was trying to plumb the subtleties of Terran humor, and it had taken to injecting peculiar effects into its creations in an effort to arrive at some understanding of what worked and what didn't. He had told VISAR to be sure to let him know if it ever figured the answers out, because as a human he'd like to know, too—which apparently hadn't done much to help the machine draft its game plan. But it was persevering. "No, it's okay," Mildred responded. "Now I'm curious to see what comes next." She thought for a second. "Although, thinking about it, you could put Lynx here. My office really isn't complete without her, you know." The cat promptly appeared, curled up asleep on the window sill.

"I've been developing a theory that a culture's picture of science reflects the level of maturity that it has reached," Showm said. "In the same kind of way as the worldview of an individual. Fairies and enchantment are the stuff of childhood."

"It's true of Thuriens, too?"

"Oh, yes. Materialism and pragmatism of the kind you talk about come with adolescence. We went through it long ago, and Earth is perhaps just beginning to emerge. It goes with the fixation on the shorter term and inability to see beyond self that are the prelude to maturity. But eventually the realization comes that the important things are not all the mysteries that the materialist sciences can explain, but the things that they can't."

"The Thuriens concern themselves with such things?" Now it was Mildred's turn to be surprised.

"The purpose of life and of mind," Showm said. "Where the quest for greater understanding becomes directed when physical knowledge alone proves inadequate."

"You don't think they are just accidental byproducts of physics, then, the way our scientists would have us believe?" That was another area in which Mildred had provoked her cousin's ire over the years, by steadfastly refusing to accept his pronouncements—although lately there had been signs that he might be having second thoughts about some things.

Showm made an expression coupled with an utterance that Mildred was unable to interpret. "No more than that VISAR is just an accidental byproduct of the configuration of optronics that supports it. Only a culture in its materialist phase could have conceived such an impossibility and believed it."

"Adolescence," Mildred said. "Having banished the fairies of childhood, it makes itself the lord of all that exists. Mindless matter is all that it can allow."

"Yes, exactly."

"So what exists beyond Thuriens and humans?"

"We don't know. The desire is to find out is our greatest motivation."

"Was that why the Thuriens gave up immortality?"

"Not exactly. But we realized later that it was a necessary thing to do in order to ask and understand the question."

There was a drawn-out silence. Mildred had the feeling of sharing a commonality of understanding with this alien that ran deeper than most she could remember. She was still reflecting on the strangeness of the situation, when Showm said, "Well, as I said earlier, I do have another pressing matter to take care of now. I'll leave you to experiment with your office at your leisure. But we must pursue our talk further, Mildred. It's not the kind of thing I'm used to discussing with Terrans. I live in the mountain region to the south of Thurios. You'll have to be my guest there next time—I mean in actuality, in person. But for now, I have to take my leave."

"Thank you. I'd like that," Mildred said. "Au revoir, then." And she was alone in her Bavarian office, staring out at the valley and the mountains, with the yellow-and-red zeppelin growing larger above. Lynx opened an eye, stretched, and yawned. Mildred was too filled with new thoughts to be in a mood for playing with the cat right now. VISAR seemed to pick up on it, and Lynx settled down again.

"I just think I ought to point out what an unusual honor it is to be invited in person to a Thurien's home," VISAR said. "And especially with someone like Frenua. You're the first Terran she has ever said that to. I just thought it was something you should be aware of. You've evidently made quite an impression."

CHAPTER THIRTEEN

Bryom Calazar had a silver-gray crown flecked with white, extending down at the sides to bracket a pair of large, vertically elliptical, violet eyes. His protruding lower face with its blend of hues from mahogany to ebony always put Hunt in mind of ancient Egyptian depictions of Nubians. He arrived in the tower block next to the Multiporter building accompanied by Eesyan and a small retinue, clad in a short open coat over a tunic of embroidered green. It had never ceased to amaze Hunt that the effective head of at least an entire planetary administration—he wasn't sure how Calazar fitted in with the running of other Thurien-inhabited parts of the Galaxy—would travel as casually as a sightseeing tourist and show up with less fuss and ceremony than a regional manager back home visiting the local office. It seemed that Thuriens were as unimpressed by pomp and symbols of grandeur as they were by overassertiveness or attempts at intimidation. Reputation was what counted.

All of the Terran team were present to greet him, with the exception of Sandy, who had gone down with a Thurien bug or rebelled against something in the diet, and was holed up back at the Waldorf. There was also a heavy attendance of Thuriens, both from the project itself and other parts of the Institute, eager to pay their respects or simply to be part of the occasion. Hunt, Danchekker, and Duncan were old acquaintances of Calazar's from the time of the Jevlenese troubles and then afterward, when the first Thurien delegation came to Earth. Despite the demands for a word here, an introduction there, Calazar made a point of finding time to get to know Sonnebrandt and Chien better, to their unconcealed surprise and delight.

"This is unbelievable," Sonnebrandt said to Hunt when Calazar had moved on. "I've just talked to an interstellar overlord. He was interested in my fish and wanted to know if Berlin was like Geneva."

"Stick around. I said you'd be joining the right team. . . . What fish?"

"I keep tropical fish."

"I didn't know that."

"You see. And he found out already!"

After the social preliminaries, Eesyan's scientists updated Calazar and his companions on the latest developments. Then it was time for the visitors to proceed to the adjacent part of the complex to see the Multiporter itself. Eesyan had arranged for some demonstrations of the machine in action. As the throng around the labs began thinning out, Hunt noticed that Danchekker was missing from the group assembling with Calazar to follow Eesyan across. "What's up?" Sonnebrandt asked, seeing the way Hunt was looking perplexedly around.

"We seem to have lost Chris." A mental nudge activated his avco. "Hey, Chris? It's Vic. Where are you? The party's moving on."

"What? . . . Oh." Danchekker came through on audio only, presumably not wanting to be distracted by visuals just now. "I'm in the office." He and Hunt had opted to share office space adjoining the area that the Thuriens used; Thuriens seemed to prefer working communally to being isolated in individual cubbyholes. "I'll catch you up."

"Lost something?" Hunt inquired.

"Yes, as a matter of fact. Sandy made some notes that Eesyan will be needing later. I thought I'd brought them in, but I can't seem to lay my hand on them. Maybe I forgot to pick them up at the Waldorf. It's extremely annoying."

"I'll come back there and help you look."

"Really, there's no need."

"No problem. I've seen the show enough times before, anyway. I'll be there in two minutes." Hunt cleared down and looked back at Sonnebrandt. "He's in the office, looking for something. You carry on, Josef. I'll go back and give him a hand." He winked. "You know how it is with Chris. I'd hate it if he got lost trying to find his way over."

He found Danchekker rummaging around among piles of papers and boxes from Earth that had not yet been emptied. The working space was bright and spacious, with an attention to detail in the fittings that was not functional in any utilitarian sense and carried the surreal feel of an almost Victorian fondness for ornamentation that blended with the quasi-oriental decor of traceries and pointed arches. But it was a hard scientific working environment nonetheless. The walls were graphically active—in effect, complete floor-to-ceiling screens—that could be directed to display images, text, communications windows, lighting panels, or when nothing more demanding presented itself, background designs of whatever mood suited the moment. Just now, one of the larger mural areas was showing a scene from a world that had taken Danchekker's fancy in one of his "travels." It showed a stand of strange trees looking like ice-cream cones made out of broccoli, except that they stood two hundred feet high, their tops fashioned into nests for leathery, long-snouted flying creatures vaguely reminiscent of pterodactyls.

Things had been shifted around in the muddle of moving in, and a few sheets of notes could have been put anywhere. "One of the more exasperating characteristics of the female of the species," Danchekker grumbled. "Here we are on a planet who knows how many millennia in advance of our own, with universal access to a system capable of transferring any information instantly between star systems, and she resorts to handwriting notes. Is there any hope for our race, do you think?" Hunt noticed with amusement that Danchekker was searching inside a briefcase full of papers that he himself had brought from the Waldorf, but said nothing.

"Have you tried calling her?" he inquired instead.

"VISAR says she's blocking calls. Probably sleeping it off."

"Oh . . . right. Okay."

They went over the office one more time and satisfied themselves that the notes were not there. "I'll have to go back to the Waldorf and get them," Danchekker said. "It shouldn't take too long. If I leave right away I'll be back before Eesyan's bit."

"Want me to come along, too?"

"No, Vic. This time I insist. It was my own stupidity. You go on over and explain what's happened. They're probably missing both of us by now."

"Okay, then. Catch you later." Hunt turned to leave.

"Oh. There is one thing you could do for me, though," Danchekker said.

Hunt checked himself. "What?"

Danchekker opened the briefcase again and took out a book with a red, cloth-bound cover. "Sandy asked me to give this to Duncan."

"Ko's autograph book?" Hunt said, recognizing it.

"Yes. Duncan said he'd try and get Calazar to put his in it."

"Oh, dear, it wouldn't do to forget that, would it? Okay, Chris, I'll pass it on."

"I would appreciate it."

Hunt flipped curiously through the pages as he went back out and along the corridor. The collection included an assortment of names from the entertainment world, some notable public figures, various artists and writers, and a number of news celebrities. A youngster with some initiative and energy, Hunt thought approvingly. He found the entry belonging to Bressin Nylek, First Officer of the *Ishtar*, and also the *Ishtar*'s commander. Hunt wondered what Calazar's autograph might be worth back home in years to come.

He exited the tower about a hundred feet above ground on a g-conveyor that deposited him on the terrace outside the cafeteria two levels below the Multiporter, and went up to the lab area with the square chamber standing in its frame at the focus of the array of projector tubes. The machine was running. Hunt seemed to have arrived just at the completion of one of the demonstrations. Eesyan was taking questions from Calazar and his company, who were standing with some of the project scientists. Others, were scattered loosely in the general vicinity, including Sonnebrandt and Duncan, with Chien standing a short distance away, the total numbering perhaps twenty individuals. One of Calazar's company was speaking.

"Let's think ahead and assume that you do find a way of stabilizing a transported object. That means it will stop in some particular universe. It will have rematerialized there—unlike that whatever-it-was just now that was just traveling through."

"Yes," Eesyan agreed.

"Fine. But suppose the process is subject to some kind of positional error, such that it doesn't reappear in precisely the same corresponding place there? It might not be inside their detection chamber at all. Or it could be a universe so different from ours that it doesn't even have a chamber."

"That's possible."

The questioner sent around a quick appealing look that said this could be serious. "Then it could rematerialize inside solid matter. So what happens when you start sending larger objects than these little specks that you've been showing us? You'd have an explosion!"

"We plan to move the project off-planet and operate it remotely in space when we reach that phase," Eesyan said. "A scaled-up projector is being designed as we learn from this one."

"I hope that our neighbors in their other realities are equally considerate," one of the Thurien scientists remarked, which brought laughter.

"Does it have a name?" someone asked.

"We just call it MP2 at the moment," Eesyan said.

As Hunt began edging toward the three Terrans, he passed by Othan, who had met them at the Waldorf on their arrival there, and another of the technicians. They were muttering irascibly in a way that was strange for Thuriens.

"I wish you wouldn't keep repeating yourself, Othan. I'm really not deaf or slow, you know." VISAR automatically supplied any background that would normally be overheard. It seemed to be another part of the Thurien obsession for authenticity. Hunt had grown so used to it by now that it no longer registered as a translation.

"I am *not* repeating myself."

"Why do you deny it? I heard you perfectly well the first time. It's not as if . . ."

Hunt moved on and drew up beside Duncan. "How's it going?" he asked.

"They've transmitted a few molecular configurations. Now we're going to go to try some crystal structures."

"What was that about something passing through?"

"A bit of excitement. There might have been a transient of something coming in a few minutes ago. VISAR's analyzing the detector data now." Hunt raised his eyebrows. If confirmed, it would mean the fleeting trace of something passing through from parallel experiments being conducted in a nearby universe. There had been some previous instances but they were very rare.

"Did you and Chris find what you were looking for?" Sonnebrandt asked.

Hunt shook his head. "No luck. It was some notes of Sandy's that he was supposed to give Eesyan. He thinks he must have left them at the Waldorf. He's gone back there to get them."

At that moment, VISAR came in on the general-address channel. "Attention, please. A positive detection is confirmed. We have evidence of an object passing through from a different reality."

A ripple of murmurings and some applause went around. "Your visit here has been marked as auspicious," one of the scientists said, smiling, to Calazar. "Let's hope it's a good omen."

"I wonder if we've been considerate enough to send them one back," Calazar mused.

"Highly improbable, if my understanding is correct," one of Calazar's party said. Another of the scientists was interpreting further details from VISAR. Eesyan took the opportunity to detach himself and come over to where Hunt and the others were. At the same time, he was turning his head from side to side and looking puzzled.

"Where did Professor Danchekker go, Vic?" he asked. "He's supposed to have something that I'll be needing later."

"You mean some notes from Sandy?"

"Yes—on possible biological implications. It sounded interesting."

"It looks as if he left them at the Waldorf. He's gone back for them," Hunt said.

"Oh. Very well. . . . I hope he won't be too long."

"I shouldn't think so. He's probably halfway there already."

Eesyan snorted. "Then he must be propagating through h-space. He was here just a moment ago."

Hunt frowned. "Chris? No."

"Sure he was, Vic. I saw him come in with you."

"You couldn't have. He left the tower at the same time I did, heading back into town."

Eesyan looked to Sonnebrandt and Duncan in appeal.

"Gentlemen, tell me I'm not imagining things. Didn't Vic arrive here with Professor Danchekker a few minutes ago?" They looked at each other, then back, and shook their heads.

"Vic was on his own," Duncan said.

Chien, who was watching and had partly overheard, came closer. "Professor Danchekker was here," she said. "I saw him."

"There!" Eesyan proclaimed.

This was getting silly again. Sane, intelligent adults unable to agree on what was happening literally in front of their faces. "There's a simple way to settle this," he said. "There is obviously one person who ought to know where he is. VISAR, connect me through to Chris Danchekker."

"Yes, Vic?" Danchekker's voice responded in Hunt's head a few seconds later.

"This may sound like a strange question, Chris, but where are you exactly?"

"There's no need to be sarcastic. I'm on my way. I'm sorry I wasn't there when Calazar arrived, if that's what's bothering you. I was nearly there and then realized I'd forgotten some notes from Sandy that Eesyan needs, so I turned around and went back for them. Is that permissible, might I ask?"

Hunt faltered. The others with him, who were also tuned in, looked equally baffled. Danchekker wasn't making any sense. "Chris . . . what do you mean, you turned around and went back? You mean you were here and went back, yes?"

"I meant precisely what I said. Shall I spell it out? I took a flyer from the Waldorf, as I am now about to do again. I was almost to the Institute when I realized I'd forgotten Sandy's notes. And so I turned it around and went back to Thurios. No, I haven't been there at the Institute yet this morning. What is this, another of your aberrations?"

"But, Chris, I talked to you myself here, across in the tower."

"You're being absurd."

Chien came in. "Professor, Eesyan and I both saw you in the machine area too—which is where we are now. You came in with Doctor Hunt. But he insists he was alone."

"Then all I can say is that you're all living in different realities. I know where I am, for God's sake. And I'm just in the process of boarding a flyer again, in the roof-level lobby of the Waldorf." A view of the surroundings extracted from Danchekker's neural system and superposed as a window upon Hunt's visual field confirmed it.

It was all going from "strange" to plain crazy. They could go on arguing like this all day and get nowhere. Hunt struggled for some continuation. Then he remembered the autograph book that Danchekker had handed to him when they were in the tower. He ran his hand down over his jacket and felt its solid outline in his pocket.

"Chris," he said. "Bear with us. There's another thing. Ko's book. Sandy wanted you to give it to Duncan."

"The autograph book?"

"Yes."

Danchekker sounded surprised. "How did you know about that? You were already gone when Sandy gave it to me this morning. She told me that Duncan should have collected it from her last night."

"Never mind for now how I know," Hunt said. "But do you still have it?"

"Of course. It's in my briefcase, where I put it."

"Could you check that, Chris? . . . Please. It's important."

Muttered sounds came over the audio of Danchekker grumbling beneath his breath. The window appeared again, showing his hands opening the briefcase and searching among the contents. They found the red-bound autograph book and drew it out into view. "There," Danchekker's voice pronounced. "Is that satisfactory? And now may I ask what the purpose is of this melodramatic cross-examining and interrogation?"

For a moment, Hunt's mind seized up. Stunned, he drew the book from his pocket and stared at it to reassure himself. Yes, it was the same. He was even more stunned when Duncan, moving as if in some kind of trance, produced another one.

"I *did* collect it from Sandy last night!" Duncan said numbly.

Danchekker arrived around fifteen minutes later. Three copies of the book lay side by side. The ones from Hunt and Danchekker were identical. The one that Duncan had supplied contained in addition as its most recent entry the signature of Serge Kaleniek, the lead tenor of the Estonian choir visiting Thurien. Duncan had obtained it at breakfast in the Waldorf that morning. He had thought that Ko would be pleased.

So had Duncan collected the autograph book from Sandy the previous evening, or had she given it to Danchekker that morning? Hunt called her to find out what her version was. Her account tallied with Danchekker's: She had given the book to Danchekker that morning, but he had forgotten to pick up her notes for Eesyan. He had returned for them without reaching the Institute, and then departed again.

Everyone was still too shocked and befuddled to begin debating coherently what it all meant. But Hunt was hearing again the chance words that Danchekker had used earlier: "Then all I can say is that you're all living in different realities. . . ." His thoughts went back to the bizarre conversation in the Happy Days parking lot on that memorable Saturday morning. "The main thing you need to know about is the *convergences*," his briefly appearing other self had said, and then never had the chance to elaborate.

The glimmer of a suspicion of what might be happening began forming in Hunt's mind. But he didn't say anything. He wasn't sure himself if he believed it yet.

CHAPTER FOURTEEN

In his office atop the Advanced Sciences building at UNSA, God-dard, Gregg Caldwell chewed on the butt of a cigar while he scanned over the latest interim report from Hunt on one of his deskside display screens. It had been sent from Thurien on the day after Calazar's visit to the project. Hunt believed he had the germ of an explanation, but he was giving it time to consolidate more in his head before sounding out the reactions of the rest of the team. He didn't say what the explanation was.

"That's Vic: Keep us guessing," Caldwell muttered to himself as the anticipation that had been rising while he read down the page evaporated with the realization that it was the last. In the meantime, he didn't have the beginnings of a clue what to make of it. Senior scientists falling out over petty obstinacies that would shame adolescents; even Thuriens bickering among themselves; and now allegations of things that were flatly impossible. Caldwell seriously wondered if there might be something about the transition through h-space that could disorient Terran nervous systems to the extent of inducing hallucinations; or maybe some side effect of Thurien neuro-coupling technolgy. Terrans had only started using it recently, after all. He went as far as calling several names he knew in medical and psychological fields to see if they had heard of any such phenomena, but none of them had. Caldwell leaned back in his chair and drummed his fingers absently while

125

he frowned at the desk. He was still searching for an angle that seemed remotely plausible when the intercom tone sounded from Mitzi in the outer office. "Yes?" Caldwell acknowledged, straightening up.

"Nothing on the web, internal resource list, or the library net," she advised. "I also checked the Thurien link. Nothing there either."

"Okay." It was what Caldwell had been expecting by now. One of the thoughts that had crossed his mind was that something might be infecting VISAR in the way the Ents had infected JEVEX.

"And a Lieutenant Polk of the FBI called while you were talking to Doctor Norris."

"FBI? What have I done now?"

"He didn't say. Want me to get him back?"

"It's the only way we'll find out."

"And Weng's presentation that you said you wanted to hear is due to start in ten minutes."

"I'll be out as soon as I'm done."

"Fine. I'll let them know."

Mitzi cleared down. Caldwell retrieved the memo that had been circulated a few days previously from his Pending tray and glanced over it to refresh his memory. The presentation was titled, "What We Can Learn from *The Prince*." Its premise was that the books, seminars, studies, and policy guides attempting to devise effective management strategies for the miniature feudal states known as business corporations and administrative bureaucracies were largely a waste of time. Machiavelli had figured it all out five hundred years ago. An interesting concept.

The tone sounded again. "Lieutenant Polk," Mitzi's voice announced. The call appeared on one of Caldwell's free screens.

The face was of what appeared to be a heavy-set man in a white shirt and dark tie, smooth-shaven and fleshy, with beady eyes, hair combed back from a broad brow and receding at the temples, giving a moonish impression. Caldwell could almost imagine the flat feet, size 13.

"Mr. G. Caldwell?"

"This is he."

"Lieutenant Polk, Investigations Branch, Finance and Fraud Division." The voice was as neutral as his expression, which hadn't altered by as much as a flicker when the connection was completed.

"How can I help you, Lieutenant?"

"I understand that you are director of the Advanced Sciences Division there at Goddard?"

"That's correct."

"So that would make you the immediate superior of a person that we would like to contact—a Doctor Victor Hunt?"

"That's right. He's deputy director of Physics."

"He appears to be unavailable at present, and so is his assistant, Duncan Watt. I was routed to a Professor Danchekker's secretary, Ms. Mulling, but her attitude was not cooperative. She referred me to you."

Caldwell smiled inwardly at the vision of a relentless, plodding force meeting the unthawable, immovable object. "Hunt and Watt are both away on an assignment right now, I'm afraid," he replied.

"When will they be back?"

"It's impossible to say, Lieutenant. The duration is indefinite."

"Can you tell me where this assignment is?"

"About twenty light-years from here. They're in another star system."

"I see. . . ."

Caldwell could almost sense the methodical stepping through of recalled procedure manuals for a continuation. "Can you give me some idea of what this is about?" he asked, both to fill the silence and get them out of a possibly endless loop. There was a slight pause while Polk executed a context switch.

"Does the name Gerald Santello mean anything to you, Mr. Caldwell?"

In fact, it did. Caldwell had been over Hunt's exchange with the alter-ego Hunt countless times. But Caldwell had no intention of going into any of that. He frowned, knitted his brows, and shook his head at the screen. "Not that I recollect. Who is he?"

"Hunt's next-door neighbor in Redfern Canyons."

"If you say so. Okay."

"Mr. Santello recently approached a broker in Washington, expressing intense interest in acquiring stock in a certain commercial enterprise of a highly sensitive and confidential nature that has not made any public offering yet. We've established that Santello acted on the strength of privileged inside information, disclosure of which could constitute a felony. It appears that this information came from Doctor Hunt."

Caldwell made a show of digesting the information. "I'm amazed," he said. Which was true enough—amazed not at the fact, but that it should have such repercussions. "I've known Hunt for years. He's an exceptional scientist. I don't think I've met anyone with less interest in matters like that. You're sure there isn't some mistake?"

"We can only go by the facts we have," Polk replied.

"Well . . ." Caldwell showed an open hand and made a face. "That's about as much as I can tell you, Lieutenant."

"If anything further comes to mind, would you let us know? You have my contact details."

"Yes, of course."

"Thank you for your time."

"You're welcome."

Caldwell remained staring disbelievingly at the screen for a while after it blanked out. This had to be the strangest case of leaked investment information ever. Finally, he grunted to himself, folded the memo about Weng's presentation, slipped it into his jacket pocket, and left his office.

"Are they coming to get you?" Mitzi asked as he emerged into the outer office.

"Oh, it seems I'll be okay for a while longer. He was trying to get ahold of Vic."

"Vic? Why? What's he been doing?"

"Not our Vic. The other universe's Vic. Apparently, that stuff he passed on about investing in Formaflex is still classified information. The feds think there's some financial scam going on."

"You're kidding."

"I don't think the unflagging Lieutenant Polks of this world are the kind who kid about anything."

Mitzi shook her head despairingly. "As if this whole business wasn't getting crazy enough already. I want to know what Vic thinks has been happening on Thurien. Can we call them when you get back, and ask him?"

"He's not ready yet."

Mitzi sighed with obvious impatience.

Caldwell stopped. There was a glass vase on a ledge above Mitzi's desk, containing a cluster of rose buds just starting to open. Caldwell gestured at it. "Things happen in their own time," he said. "The job descriptions call us managers, but you can't manage creative people. What we really are is gardeners. We put them in a place where the soil is right, make sure they get enough water and sun, and then wait for them to do their own thing. Vic and Chris may not have Thurien depth know-how, but put 'em together and they can think sideways. That's what they've got going for them in this. But only if you give them their own space, far away from where people like me might be tempted to meddle." He nodded toward the vase again. "It would be like pulling the petals of those open to try and help things along."

Mitzi's eyes narrowed as a pattern became clearer. "That was why you sent them to Jupiter when the Charlie business needed a new angle, wasn't it? . . . Then Jevlen. And now Thurien. It's all the same style."

"You know what the two worst inventions were?" Caldwell asked.

"What?"

"The telephone and the airplane. Because they made it too easy for Head Office or the General Staff to go messing around in details that the people on the spot should know how to handle. So they ended up with mediocrities out there. But the Romans managed to do pretty well for six hundred years without any of that. You gave the general his objectives and the wherewithal to carry them out, and after his baggage train or his boats disappeared over the horizon that was the last you knew until a messenger came back. So you had to make sure the guys you picked were good. We have to be careful that we don't make the same mistakes just because we've got Thurien h-space communicators, eh?" Caldwell glanced at the clock display on Mitzi's terminal. "Anyhow, here the lesson endeth. I gotta go."

"Hey, Gregg," Mitzi called after him as he reached the door. He stopped and looked back as he opened it.

"What?"

"How come you're just attending this thing about Machiavelli? Why aren't you giving it?

CHAPTER FIFTEEN

Eesyan ordered the cessation of further experiments until there were at least the beginnings of some understanding of what was going on. On the day following Calazar's visit, Chien sought out Hunt in the office that he and Danchekker shared in the tower. Hunt was alone, contemplating a wall display showing the results of some calculations that he had been running with VISAR. Danchekker was embroiled in a discussion with the Thuriens in their larger office. Sandy, who had recovered to the point of feeling little more than a mild queasiness, was with him.

"I've been having some thoughts about yesterday," Chien said.

"All of us have been having thoughts about nothing else," Hunt replied. He swivelled in one of the human-scaled chairs that the Thuriens had provided and leaned back. Chien was looking neat and trim in a scarlet, high-necked, oriental style trouser suit, eyes and lips tinted, her hair tied high. "So what's your take?" He gestured invitingly to one of the other chairs but Chien perched herself on the edge of a desk and rested her hands in her lap, fingers interlaced.

"Actually, I thought of it yesterday, but I wanted to let it sit for at least one night." She made a brief motion indicating vaguely the direction of the building housing the Multiporter. "The discrepancies all occurred with people who were in the vicinity of the machine. When you disagreed with Professor Danchekker and his

131

cousin over the Thurien couple at Vranix, you were in the coupler located next to the monitor station; the professor and Mildred were elsewhere. Your account was the one that differed."

"Go on."

"That silly falling out that I had with Josef Sonnebrandt. Going back over it, the things we argued about were all to do with events that took place around the machine while it was running; never about anything that happened when it was quiescent, or while we were away from it. Sandy and Duncan had no such experiences, and they were in this building the whole time. And then yesterday, all the anomalies happened over there around the machine, during the demonstrations. The Thuriens have been comparing their own recollections of odd things that have been happening, and checking the records. It shows the same pattern. I've made a list."

Hunt crossed a foot over his other knee, rested his chin on a hand, and regarded her curiously. "So what do you make of it?"

"Will you promise to put it down to Oriental eccentricity and no more if this sounds just a little bit crazy?" Chien asked him.

"Well, I'll say I will, even if it's not true," Hunt offered.

"How gallant. I'm impressed."

"Breeding and all that. You know the English."

"No, that's the carefully cultivated English image."

"I refuse to get into politics. So what about the Multiporter?"

Chien opened her hands briefly. "The machine is affecting its surroundings somehow. It induces inconsistencies in the events taking place around it." She hesitated. "How can I put this? . . . When everyone was disagreeing with each other yesterday, Professor Danchekker said we were all living in different realities. I think he was right . . . well, in a sense. Obviously we were all in the same reality then. But the *pasts* we were talking about were different." She eyed Hunt questioningly for a moment. He made a gesture inviting her to continue. "The normal Multiverse structure that we're used to thinking about consists of paths branching apart toward different futures. But perhaps it's possible for things to be otherwise. Suppose instead that . . ." Chien stopped and frowned to herself. She seemed unsure of how to proceed. "We've been wondering what these 'convergences' were."

Hunt said it for her. "Timeline lensing." It was as he had suspected: Chien had arrived at the same conclusion he'd been nursing since yesterday. The description seemed as good a term for it as any.

Chien's eyebrows lifted in surprise. "You're saying that you think so, too?"

"Instead of diverging, they can come together," Hunt said. "That's what my other self was trying to tell me. In his universe, they discovered that it was the single most important thing to understand before they could make any real progress. And it's easy to see why. Instead of a single point in the present leading to multiple alternate futures, you have got the opposite: a present that's a composite of people, memories, even physical objects, that arrived there from different pasts. How could you get anywhere with the kind of insanity that would generate? The gist of it occurred to me yesterday too. But I wanted to mull over it before mentioning it to anyone—like you did."

"Have you made any kind of a start toward explaining it?" Chien asked.

Hunt waved at the wall behind him, half filled with tensor differentials and M-wave propagation equations. "There are some guesses that I've been asking VISAR to look into out of curiosity. It's going to need Eesyan and his people to really make a dent in it. I just wanted to feel I was halfway toward knowing what I was talking about before putting it to them. But it is starting to make a weird kind of sense—if that's the correct word. After all, convergence is just a special case of bending time lines away from their normal direction. And that's what cross-Multiverse propagation *is*. It's what the Multiporter was designed to do."

"But you just said a moment ago, we'll never get anywhere with the kind of confusion it can produce. How could any complex piece of equipment ever work?" Chien made a helpless gesture. "Is there some way of stopping it, do you think?"

Hunt thought for a second, then grinned. "Well, there has to be, doesn't there?" he replied. "They got the relay working in that other universe. But you and I aren't about to solve that here and now. Come on. I think it's time we took this to the others."

It turned out that just about everyone else had been thinking something similar. But as with Hunt and Chien, the conclusion had seemed so extraordinary that they had all been sounding each other out privately to seek some kind of moral support before risking any general statement of the fact. When Hunt prevailed upon Eesyan to call all of the team together in the tower and presented the argument that he and Chien had talked about, there was little surprise or dissent—even from Danchekker. The general reception was one of relief that someone had brought it into the open at last, since they had all either arrived at some similar suspicion themselves or had one bounced off them by others.

Several groups of Thuriens, independently and unknown to each other, were working with VISAR to try and lay down the basis of a mathematical treatment in the same way as Hunt. Duncan and Sonnebrandt had conceived the idea of an equivalent "M-field mass," causing a curvature Multiverse space in an analogous way to that in which physical mass curves Einsteinian spacetime. Danchekker and Sandy had been wondering if the effect was a result of the Multiporter altering quantum probabilities in the kind of way that Danchekker maintained living organisms were able to do. All of them were using VISAR to test and help develop their theories, but VISAR had said nothing to alert any to the work of the others. Its operating directives precluded informing on the activities of individuals without being asked to.

But now that the debate was general, VISAR was able to construct a graphical depiction of the consensus, showing the event sequences that must have merged. Astoundingly, it followed inescapably that the reality all of them were now sharing and living in had to included individuals who were from at least four different past universes.

In universe "A" that Duncan remembered, he had collected Ko's autograph book from Sandy the night before. If the electrical and chemical patterns in his head were not sufficient evidence of its reality, there could be no denying the book itself, which came with him. But there was also another universe, "B," in which he had neglected to collect the book and so Sandy had given it to Danchekker instead the following morning, along with her notes for Eesyan. Danchekker had apparently met Hunt sometime after arriving at the Institute and gone with him to the Multiporter building. It wasn't possible to check with that particular Danchekker because he didn't seem to be around anymore, but both Eesyan and Chien in Universe "B" had seen them arrive together. The Danchekker who existed in the present reality had diverged into Universe "C" by forgetting to pick up the notes, and then remembered them when on his way to Quelsang and turned back. Since Sandy attested to this, she had to be from Universe

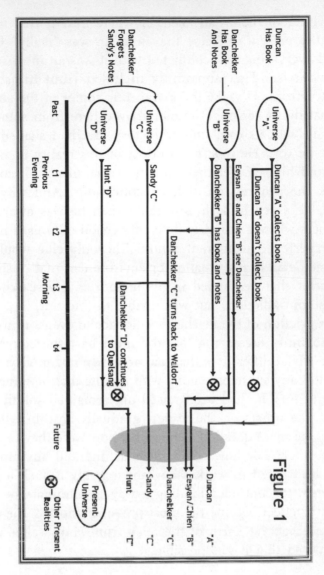

Figure 1

"C" also. Finally, a Universe "D" variant of the Danchekker who forgot the notes hadn't remembered them until after he arrived at Quelsang, and had left to go back to the Waldorf. This was the sequence that Hunt remembered, and so it followed that Hunt was from Universe "D" also. The lines that terminated represented continuations into other realities.

As if all this wasn't discombobulating enough, there was a further aspect of it that Hunt found even more eerie. If the operation of the machine was inducing a local convergence of time lines, it made sense that Danchekker "C" and Sandy "C" should agree, since neither of them had been anywhere near it that morning. Hence, the present universe they were in was "really" Universe "C," and everything that conflicted with it was an intrusion from someplace else. That apparently included Hunt himself, who originated from "D." Like the extraneous copies of the autograph book that didn't "belong," he had arrived here from some different reality with its own unique history that had shaped him to be what he was. He wasn't a product of *this* reality in which he now found himself. Yet there was no sense of any discontinuity to mark the progression of his recollections. And why should here be, he asked himself, any more than he was aware of the divergences where a minutely different version of himself branched off to experience a different future? The only clue would be to find some detail of his situation or environment that clashed with the imprint that he carried in his memories. He searched hard for such contradictions but was unable to find any.

The restriction of the machine's influence to events in its immediate proximity meant that for the most part the convergences involved trivial differences that had arisen comparatively recently. The past of any substance, along with the life that he remembered and the history he had been raised on, remained solidly immutable. As the others on the project gradually absorbed the same message, the main question came to be, how were they to advance things further? For how could the machine and anything in its vicinity be trusted to work safely and reliably if such a state of affairs were to continue? Finding a way to eliminate or at least contain the effect became the most pressing priority. The original appearance back at Earth of the relay from Hunt's alter ego had demonstrated that it was possible.

CHAPTER SIXTEEN

Frenua Showm's home and its setting could conceivably have provided the inspiration for a Wagnerian crescendo of full orchestra and chorus ringing out terror and magnificence in a minor key. It was not a single structure sitting on one level in the way that most Terrans would have thought of as a "house," but consisted of a number of interconnected units distributed across a prominence of rocky crags looking out over a breathtaking Thurien scene of plummeting gorges and near-vertical precipices rising toward distant bastions of jagged peaks. "Villa" might have been a better term to describe it. Although no two parts were at the same height, moving from one to another was speedy and effortless, thanks to the inbuilt system of g-lines that came as part of most Thurien structures. The spaces between provided harmonizing chords of rocky watergardens filled with Thurien flora and greenery, and included a pool held by natural rock forms, warmed to producing a hint of vapors at its surface and fed by a cascading waterfall.

Mildred didn't yet know if it was a general Thurien trait, but it seemed that Showm kept the different aspects of her life separate and apart, as if each functioned in its own exclusive compartment of her awareness, where it could enjoy the full focus of her attention for whatever time she was disposed to allot to it. When she was engaged in tasks connected with her ambassadorial role in

Calazar's administration, she worked tirelessly and single mind-
edly, permitting no distraction. When she turned to the interests
that she pursued to express her creative instincts, which ranged
from writing a revision of Earth's history in the light of the
now-revealed Jevlenese deceptions to creating neurally composed
thought music that acted on the emotions directly as lucidly as
sound upon the senses, Calazar and politics would be as far away
from her thoughts as the star systems that most of such affairs
pertained to. And when her mind sought the times of quiet and
contemplation that all Thuriens looked upon as essential to a
meaningful existence, if not the very point of it, she withdrew
totally into herself and it was as if none of the rest existed. Her
abode separated itself out to reflect those same functions. It was
in a way, Mildred found herself thinking, a symbolic rendering
in program-grown organics, metal-ceramic composites, and opto-
active crystal, of Frenua's life.

The part they were in now, Mildred took to be the abode of the
contemplative and relaxing Frenua. It was the high point of the
layout, an eagle's eyrie of two spacious rooms to the rear of a deck
projecting out over the abyss below the promontory into which
the house had been blended. The shell enclosing the deck could be
varied from place to place in transparency and in hue to take on any
combination of the functions of windows and wall. At the moment
it was predominantly clear, giving an uninterrupted view out over
two vast gorges diverging away on either side below, each carrying a
portion of the flow from an immense system of waterfalls tumbling
down a facing wall of mountain that must have been several miles
away, amid a permanent cloud of mist tinted faintly orange by the
angle of the sun. The only things missing, Mildred thought, were
flying dragons circling among the peaks, and Tolkeinesque castles
clinging impossibly to the skyline.

They sat in a lowered area of the floor on the very edge of
the structure, in a crescent-shaped bay of outsize Ganymean
seating that faced out over the chasm. It reminded Mildred of a
helicopter she'd been in once, and when they first sat down had
produced the same reaction of mild vertigo. She had said nothing,
but reassured herself with the thought that if Thurien engineering
could bring them all safely from Earth in a matter of days and
beam energy invisibly from one part of the Galaxy to another,
their constructions ought to remain where they put them. The

meal had been a thin but tasty soup, not unlike lentil, followed by a mixed vegetable preparation on a pastalike base, vaguely reminiscent of quiche, and a dessert of chilled fruit pudding with a honey sauce. They finished with a selection of cheeses and breads, accompanied by a sweet and tangy, pale green Thurien concoction which from the slight headiness that Mildred found herself experiencing after a second glass, contained a functional surrogate for alcohol molecules.

"I don't know why those scientists are making so much fuss about it," Mildred said. "I mean, this business about universes getting mixed up and people not agreeing on what the past was. Isn't it obvious that it happens all the time anyway? Don't you ever find yourself listening to somebody who denies they said something that you heard them say quite clearly? Or found something staring you in the face in a place you've looked a dozen times, and it wasn't there?"

Showm smiled as she sliced one of the morsels on her plate— Mildred could read Ganymean expressions by now. She was at ease and relaxed, not at all the curt, businesslike Frenua that Mildred knew from the Government Center in Thurios and in their daytime dealings. In place of the tunics that accompanied the professional image, she was wearing a loose, richly embroidered robe of dark, satiny blue. Mildred wondered if she had a different style of dress for each part of the house and the personality that inhabited it. "You mean it happens to you, too?"

"Doesn't it to everyone?" Mildred said.

"I'm not sure. Even if I thought it did, I wouldn't say so. It might make you think that we argue and disagree as much as Terrans." A mild gibe that Freuna could now comfortably feel wouldn't give offense, Mildred was pleased to note.

"I still don't really grasp how this Thurien ability to come to agreements that seem to suit everybody works," Mildred admitted. "Maybe you're right. Maybe you have to be a Ganymean to understand it . . . or feel it, rather, you said, didn't you? You described the system as a consensual monarchy. On Earth it couldn't happen. You'd never get the consensus. It's absolutely as you said. I've been thinking about it. Everything's settled in the end by some form of warfare, camouflaged or otherwise. We're told it's unavoidable. The dominant ideology says that competition drives everything. But Thuriens are living disproof of that."

"An ideology that would suit those who see no significance in life beyond achieving that kind of success," Showm commented. "Its effect would be a society shaped to support and preserve a plutocratic minority, rather than to advance general prosperity and well-being. Wouldn't you think so?"

Mildred struggled to select one of the directions that her mind immediately wanted to go off in at once. "It's supposed to be what produces motivation. . . . Well, that's true of course. But it can't be the whole story, can it? There has to be something that goes deeper . . . farther. . . ."

"It comes from inside," Showm said, answering the unasked question. "You see, it works the other way around too. I am unable to comprehend what the satisfaction can be from devoting a life to outdoing others in contests that don't matter. What kind of people does it influence or impress? Adolescents of all ages, you told me once. I agree. But adolescents given power can do immeasurable damage."

"So what motivates Thuriens?" Mildred asked. This was getting closer to one of the things she wanted to explore more deeply. "You spend much of your time in Thurios or traveling, taking on fearsome responsibilities. Others build starships and energy conversion systems, or decorate buildings with landscapes from other worlds. Why? What's the reward? What do they get in return for the effort? . . . It's not as if their livelihood depends on it. They'll always have food to eat and a place to live, because others here continue to produce such things. But why *should* they?"

"Because there's nothing to prevent them."

"I don't understand."

Showm had spoken as if the answer were obvious. She checked herself and thought for a second. "Think about what you said just now. You asked why a person would do such things if their livelihood didn't depend on it. What does that mean? That their means of staying alive has to be controlled and restricted before they will take part in this mania for competition that Earth thinks is the ultimate meaning of existence? In other words, they have to be induced by need, and if that fails, compelled by violence. What kind of reward should require that? Can an organism that has to be forced be living in a way that is true to its nature? Of course not. It gets sick and it rebels. No wonder Earth has so many hospitals and prisons. . . . Thuriens know that their nature is to build, to create, to help others achieve the things that will bring fulfillment to their lives also, not to profit at their expense. And everyone has something that it's in their nature to contribute. Discovering it is their reward. A true reward. Thuriens would have to be subjected to force *not* to seek it."

Showm paused, looking at Mildred searchingly for several seconds. But Mildred had too many threads of thoughts to untangle to respond immediately. She stared out at the falls where the gorge ended, tumbling in their slow, endless majesty. Such notions were not entirely unknown on Earth, she thought. The old monastic orders with their abbots had accepted the primacy of their own Calazars and worked to contribute each their share to the prosperity of the community that fed and clothed them. Could it be that the most appropriate model for the Thurien social order was a monastery scaled up to interstellar dimensions? She smiled distantly at the thought.

"What do you find amusing?" Showm asked.

"That perhaps not all Terrans are so alien in their philosophy. You should meet Xyen Chien, who's with Christian and his group."

"The Chinese scientist?"

"Yes. She's like you in many ways. She says the world must change as it moves out of its adolescence and comes of age. I think you and she would get along. You'd understand each other."

A serving platter with a domed cover glided silently down from the level above and behind them to hover by the end of the table. The cover opened to reveal a jug containing a hot reddish beverage, two drinking goblets, some ancillary dishes and bowls, and a dish of what looked like confectionary. Mildred helped Showm set the items out on the table and load the things that they had finished with. The platter closed itself and departed. Showm remained strangely silent throughout.

"Now it's my turn," Mildred said. "What are you thinking?"

"This is called *ule*. The small cup is to try a sample and blend ingredients to suit your taste. The colored flakes range from tart to sweet, and the syrups add body and smoothness. When you know what you like, you can mix it again in the goblet."

Mildred made a few choices and tried the result. It was sweet and spicy with a delicious reverberation of aftertastes that died away like echos in a cathedral. "You haven't answered my question," she said as she began mixing a larger version.

Showm made her own selection without needing to use the sampling cup. "I was thinking about what you said . . . Earth moving out of its adolescence and entering maturity. There was a world of humans who would have passed through that phase long ago. Yes, their roots lay in the predatory jungles of Earth, and our ancestors abandoned them to perish as genetically impaired biological misfits. But they didn't perish. With no choice but to play by the rules of the environment that they found themselves in, they braved and survived every challenge that it could throw at them. They emerged finally to dominate that world in a way which was, despite all the things you've heard me say, stirringly magnificent." Showm was talking, of course, about the Lunarians, evolved from terrestrial primates that the ancient Ganymeans had transported to Minerva. She went on, "But they overcame the limitations that my ancestors inflicted on them, and developed a cooperative technological culture in a fraction of the time that it had taken Ganymeans to progress to the same level. It was astounding. You see what I'm saying, Mildred? This Terran compulsion to fight adversity, the refusal to accept defeat, if tamed and directed at the real obstacles that stand in the way of life and the growth of consciousness and spirit, instead of against each other . . . it could prove a more potent force than anything we have encountered in all our explorations of the Galaxy."

"I've heard Christian talk along exactly those lines," Mildred said. She hoped this wasn't going to turn into a Thurien guilt-trip over the destruction of Minerva. Had she been the one who had gotten them onto it? She was unable to recall. It was time to change the subject before they got morbid, she decided. Showm sipped her *ule*, testing it, then added a drop more of one of the syrups and stirred it in. "Is your whole life taken up with public affairs, Frenua?" Mildred asked her. "How about personal things? Do you have any family?"

"Children, you mean?"

"Yes."

"Oh, indeed. I have a son who's away on a distant world these days, working among the natives. They're quite primitive there. And two daughters. One excels me by far in musical talent. The younger one is in Thurios, raising a family of her own."

"So, their father? . . . Are you together still?" Mildred had heard no reference to another occupant of the place.

"That was a phase of living that we completed and fulfilled. But there comes a time when we are called to do other things. He is finding his inner self now. But we remain companions in life. How about you?"

Mildred waved a hand to and fro. "Oh . . . a few flirtatious things in younger years. But I really don't think it's for me, you know. I enjoy solitude with my own thoughts, and the freedom to do things in my own peculiar ways. I don't think I've met a man yet that I didn't end up driving to distraction. Did you know that the only reason I ended up on Thurien was because Christian was trying to get rid of me?"

"No. How could that be?"

Mildred related the story and was relieved to see that it got Frenua chuckling—at least, shaking and making funny cackling sounds that she took to be a Ganymean chuckle—and away from her threatened downward slide over Minerva. Suddenly the thread of a thought came into Mildred's mind that if Eesyan, Christian, and Victor got their machine working, then maybe they could go back there somehow and change what had happened. But she didn't want to get Frenua onto that topic again. "Are you going to let me hear some of this music that you compose?" she asked instead.

CHAPTER SEVENTEEN

Overwhelmingly, it was the short-term capriciousness of human actions that produced the kind of disparities among local time lines that would be experienced as the clashing of incompatible events. But given that the effect was confined to a localized domain, even a complex physical device could be expected to function consistently. While the innumerable quantum transitions involved in its existence and operation would continue to define realities of their own that were, it was true, theoretically discrete, within the immediate locality of the surroundings and the recent past, the likelihood of their adding up to anything discernibly different at the macroscopic level was remote.

Eesyan therefore concluded that the indicated course of action would be to put everything at Quelsang on hold and relocate the work off-planet where it could be directed remotely. Indeed, the scaled-up MP2 Multiporter already under design was intended to do just that, but for a different reason: to safeguard researchers from the catastrophic consequences if a sizable object from a parallel experiment happened to materialize within solid matter. But when Eesyan mentioned the prospect matter-of-factly in the course of a discussion in the Terrans' office in a way that presumed such a decision to be as good as agreed, he was taken aback to discover that they saw no real need for halting the Quelsang program at all.

"Why?" was Hunt's simple rejoinder. Hunt's assistant was there too; also the German and the female scientist from China.

It had seemed obvious. Eesyan made a helpless gesture. "Well . . . you've all seen the kind of chaos it can create around itself. How would it be possible to conduct any work that makes sense with that going on? We've got two extra versions of an autograph book from other realities. Suppose they had been copies of you or me, or anyone else out there?" He motioned toward Hunt. "The Professor Danchekker that you talked to here in this room is now in another universe. What if another one hadn't replaced him in this one?"

"So now we're beginning to understand it better," Hunt said.

Sonnebrandt came in, "We can reduce the operating power to keep the core of the convergence zone within the chamber. That would eliminate the risk of any major discrepancies like the ones you're talking about. Maybe some slight fringe effects, yes."

"Disagreements about minor things, possibly," Chien said. "But none of us will be blaming each other now." She paused, seeing that Eesyan was readjusting his view only with some effort, and then went on, "Professor Danchekker's cousin even thinks it happens all the time anyway as a result of quantum fluctuations, but it took something on this scale to get our attention. And I think she may have a point."

They waited. "What better way could there be to learn more about it?" Duncan asked.

Eesyan had been caught unprepared. He had taken it for granted that differences would generate disagreement and disagreement implied strife, which Thuriens strove to avoid. But Terrans thrived on it. To them it was a challenge. They saw the situation not as a source of disunity to be feared and avoided, but as an enticing and amusing curiosity to be studied. Eesyan deferred making a commitment and went away to consult with Calazar.

"I've found there are times when an old race like ours could use some reminding of the spirit that drove it when it was younger," was Calazar's response. "Our ancestors were able to deal with the universe as they found it, without defensiveness projected out of their own inner fears. When the occasion demanded, they were able to rise to conceiving schemes on scales of audacity that in comparison make the most celebrated of the Terrans' heroics seem pale. I think we should keep that tradition in mind now."

The upshot was that there would be two facilities investigating trans-Multiverse propagation. The original pilot system at the Quelsang Institute would continue running micro-scale experiments to explore the physics, and in particular to delve further into the strange phenomenon that Hunt had dubbed "timeline lensing." In parallel, construction would go ahead of the larger and more powerful MP2 project remotely in space to handle objects that a nearby other universe might not appreciate having materialize under the floor of one of its laboratories. The two complemented each other. Choosing to live with the peculiarities of converging time lines was probably the quickest route toward learning more about the effect, while the larger-scale project offered the most effective means of devising some method of countering it. With Calazar already involved and now personally intrigued by the latest developments, completion of MP2 was accorded highest priority. Although the Terrans were not in a position to contribute much to the actual construction, Hunt was curious to see some Thurien space engineering in progress. He had a feeling that it would be very different from the UNSA projects that he had found himself involved in from time to time.

The original reason for locating the higher-power system remotely in space had been to safeguard against the hazard of objects materializing from corresponding experiments being performed in other parallel realities. The risk of such an occurrence was eliminated by taking advantage of a fact long-familiar to Terran physicists: that no two quantum systems could exist in precisely identical states—where a system's "state" was defined by an appropriate set of "quantum numbers." On an ordinary map, no two points can have identical coordinates. If they did, they would be the same point. In a similar way, for two quantum systems to exist as unique entities in the universe, they have to differ in at least one of the numbers ("quantum coordinates") specifying them.

MP2 was located a few hundred thousand miles from Thurien. Although that was admittedly still in their own back yard on the typical Thurien scale of going about things, statistical calculations indicated it to be sufficient for the purpose. The position had been randomly chosen from the stupendous number of possibilities that existed throughout the volume contained within an even larger radius. The intervals between permissible coordinates being such that the available possibilities would be safely far apart. Yes, it was possible that other parallel systems might use a different method. But the near-infinity of possible sending universes was balanced by the near-infinity of possible universes that an object sent could arrive in, and some arcane statistical calculations performed by VISAR gave the probability of collision at the end of it all as about the same as that of two positions randomly chosen within the entire prescribed volume of space happening to coincide.

There was no real need for Hunt to travel there physically, since VISAR could produce an indistinguishable simulation, but it seemed that Terrans either just didn't share the Thuriens' attitude regarding the equality of surrogates or else they hadn't developed it yet. After experiencing some virtual previews of the work going on at MP2, and since it wasn't taking place in some distant part of the Galaxy, Hunt decided he wanted to go out there. He couldn't exactly pinpoint why; it seemed that coming all this way from Earth only to remain confined on the same planet was missing out somehow. Duncan, Josef, and Chien felt the same way. When they mentioned it to Eesyan, such being the Thurien disposition, he put arrangements in hand to accommodate their wish. A craft appeared the next day at the space base along the coast from Thurios to transport them to the site of MP2.

If the Terrans' desire was to experience the reality of "being there," the Thurien response came as close as was alienly possible to granting them just that. The vantage point they were provided with suffered from none of the distancing effect that would have been induced by viewing the operation through windows or on a screen inside some kind of enclosed structure. Hunt had told Eesyan they wanted to be "out there," and that was exactly what they got.

When the ship arrived at the project, they were conveyed through a connecting g-field "tunnel" to a room-size platform equipped with seats and containing an assortment of housings, compartments, and pieces of strange equipment, all surrounded by a low parapet rail but otherwise open visually to the surrounding vastness of space. From VISAR's description the vehicle—for want of a better term—created a local gravity comparable in strength to that of a planet but with an abrupt cutoff distance, limiting its range. It thus imbued the occupants with normal bodyweight, while a force and filtering shell retained a breathable atmosphere and shielded out radiation and particle hazards. Thus, warm, comfortable, yet wearing only everyday clothing, they looked around, speechless, at the wonders of stars of every hue in the stellar spectrum, ghostly nebulas, and radiant filaments of color all around on every side, above and below, seemingly near enough to touch or infinitely distant. The perspective shifted spontaneously like the optical interpretation of a wire cube. There was no standard that they were familiar with to set a scale of size or distance. Despite his years of experiences from the Moon out to Jupiter, and the previous Ganymean and Thurien ventures that he had been involved with, Hunt had never before known such an overwhelming feeling of experiencing the immediacy of space. It was intoxicating, a sensation of total immersion—like someone who had seen the ocean all their life from the inside of a submarine, swimming for the first time. The children and younger Ganymeans who had been borne during the *Shapieron*'s strange exile and known no other existence than life within the ship had tried to describe similar impressions after emerging onto a planetary surface when they arrived, finally, on Earth.

"You . . . certainly never let up on the surprises, VISAR." Duncan was the first to speak.

"We try to please." The phrase was by now familiar.

"You didn't make this exotic celestial tour bus just for us?" Sonnebrandt queried.

Eesyan, who was not actually present but coupled in via avco from Thurios, replied. "Actually, it's a pretty mundane, regular maintenance platform that we use for external work on vessels and structures. The shell can be molded to the surrounding contours, leaving the crew free and unencumbered. We thought it would be just right for the job. What do you think?"

"Impressive," Sonnebrandt said.

"Good. Well, I'm signing off now," Eesyan said. "Enjoy your visit. We'll see you back here at Thurien in due course."

While they were taking in the spectacle and speaking, the platform had been moving closer to the MP2 construction they had come to see, which had now grown to dominate the view on one side. Chien was studying it silently. About the size of a city block in Hunt's estimation, it had the form of a roughly spherical core with external lines flowing to blend into shapes of perhaps a score of symmetrically arranged protuberances—no doubt the ends of a converging system of projectors comparable to the ones on the smaller-scale prototype at Quelsang. Two larger, pear-shaped lobes extended from opposite sides of the sphere, again consisting of curviforms blending into the general body, instead of the cylinders and boxy modules that made up a typical piece of Terran space engineering. Even with a purely scientific experimental endeavor, it seemed that the Thuriens were incapable of refraining from imparting some art and aesthetics into their creations. The region of the sphere forming its "equator" between the lobes was still incomplete, as were the extremes of the lobes themselves and some of the projectors.

The vicinity around the construction was dotted with all manner of devices, objects, and machines, hanging in space to perform unidentifiable functions or moving on various errands. The majority were concentrated around a white, featureless hump, fifty or more feet across, sitting on a section of the structure's unfinished equatorial band. Chien glanced at Hunt. "It's an assembly processing zone in action, isn't it?" she said. This was something that Hunt had said he was particularly curious to see.

"We picked a good time for you," VISAR interjected. "This phase is just completing now."

The Thuriens didn't build things by bolting parts together the way Terrans did, in ways that had changed little since the times of Victorian factories. They grew them from the inside, by methods that were closer to the way Nature created organisms. The white hump was actually composed of fluid, constrained by a g-field shell similar to the one surrounding the maintenance platform. The fluid contained a supply of materials in various dissolved forms, and also a population of trillions of nano-assemblers programmed to extract the elements needed and incorporate them into the growing structure in precisely the way that was required at every point. In this respect, the process resembled that of organic cell differentiation, in which the cells of a developing embryo are able to activate just the correct parts of their common DNA program to turn into bone, blood, muscle, or whatever else a particular cell in the overall plan is destined to become. As they watched, the fluid inside the hump became cloudy and patchy, and seemed to go into some kind of agitation. It looked like a washing machine going into its rinse cycle.

This was new to Sonnebrandt, and in response to his questions, Duncan outlined the idea. Sonnebrandt nodded as he listened, but then frowned. "Every assembler would have to know exactly where it is to do the correct job," he said. "You said it was like biological cells. But cells can sense their relative positions in a growing organism and know which functions to switch on and which to suppress."

"They use things like chemical concentrations and electrical gradients," Chien put in.

"Yes, that's what I mean. But nothing in what Duncan just described seemed to play the role of a physical cell matrix that positional information can relate to. So how do they do it?"

Duncan looked to Hunt, who had studied the Thurien accounts more. "It's neat," Hunt said to Sonnebrandt. "The design is encoded into coordinate operators that define a high-density standing g-wave pattern throughout the construction volume. In effect, it translates it into a unique signal at every point. The assemblers decode the appropriate signal for whatever place they're at, and that tells them what to do."

"That's amazing." Sonnebrandt shook his head wonderingly. "What must be involved in computing a function like that?"

"Don't even think about trying. You'd need something like VISAR to do it."

Out on the construction, the containing shell was suddenly turned off as the process terminated. The fluid dispersed to vanish away into space in a few seconds, revealing a gleaming new layer of walls, decks, and structural members ready to be fitted out.

"Voilà," VISAR commented, sounding matter-of-fact.

Chien was looking at Hunt with an amused, slightly wry expression. "You love this kind of thing, don't you?" she remarked. "It fascinates you. As you said, 'neat.'"

Hunt didn't know quite how to reply. "Original, at least. You've got to hand it to them," he said finally.

"Were you like that as a student? Is it what Americans call nerdy?"

"Not Vic," Duncan chimed in. "He gets on with people too well. One of those popular types. Nerdy people have a problem in that area. That's why they turn to nerdy things."

"I'm not so sure," Hunt said. "I'd say it's more the other way around. Being popular is nice enough, sure . . . if it happens. But it's not worth spending all your time working on. There are too many things that are more *interesting* to spend it on. Anyway, all this business about having to be popular with everyone all the time is an American student obsession." He shrugged and looked back toward Chien. "Wouldn't you say so? What are kids like in your part of the world?"

But he saw then that Chien wasn't listening. She had turned her head and was staring at the construction in front of them again, the look in her eyes a million miles away. "Standing waves," she murmured after Hunt had waited several seconds.

"Eh?" he returned.

"Standing waves." She turned her head back and focused on him. "Defining a structure distributed through a volume of space. *That's* the way to halt a test object! It propagates as a longitudinal M-wave function. If we project an interference function to create a standing wave in resonance with the normal transverse solution, it will lock it into the target universe. It would force the object to materialize there."

Chien didn't have to elaborate. The others understood immediately what she meant. It sounded plausible. Forgetting all about MP2 construction methods for the moment, they put the proposition to VISAR there and then. From a theoretical standpoint, the machine could find no flaws. But only experiment could give the final word. "Can you connect me to Eesyan again?" Hunt asked.

"He is in conference right now," VISAR cautioned. Which was about as close as Thuriens were likely to come to refusing. Hunt knew it would be a violation of normal protocols to press the matter. But this was too exciting to sit on.

"I'll risk it," he said. "Offer apologies, but tell him I insist."

Eesyan appeared in a window in Hunt's visual field after a short delay. "Yes, Vic?" he acknowledged. While Eesyan's manner remained polite, VISAR injected an unmistakable undertone into its voice reconstruction that said this had better be good. Hunt summarized what had been said as briefly as he could and asked Eesyan's opinion. Eesyan was silent for what began to seem a long time. For a moment, Hunt feared that he really had offended Thurien sensibilities in a way he hadn't been prepared for. And then he read from the Thurien's face that he couldn't have been more wrong. This *was* good. Eesyan was going over the implications intently in his mind, far removed from whatever other business he had been attending to. Then VISAR came through for Hunt again.

"And I've just got an incoming call from the link to Earth comnet."

Earth? Probably Gregg Caldwell. It would have to be something urgent. "Sure, put it through," Hunt said absently while he waited for Eesyan's reaction.

But the face that appeared in VISAR's window was unfamiliar: fleshy and rounded, wearing an expression of implacable relentlessness. "Dr. Hunt?" it inquired.

"Er . . . yes."

"Dr. Victor Hunt, of the Advanced Sciences Division, UNSA at Goddard?"

"Yes. Who's this?"

"Lieutenant Polk, FBI, Investigations Branch, Finance and Fraud Division. I understand that you are acquainted with a Gerald Santello, Dr. Hunt."

What in hell was this? It couldn't have come at a worse time. "Not now, VISAR," Hunt muttered. "Cut the link. Tell him there's a technical hitch or something."

"I don't have technical hitches."

"Well, get rid of him somehow. It's only some stupid piece of bureaucracy. We're on the verge of a major breakthrough in physics here."

Polk vanished, and there was a short pause. "Okay, you're off the hook," VISAR said. "I faked a message into the comnet saying that the Terran end is having problems. Can I ask you not to make a habit of this? I have a reputation to consider."

"I'll bear it in mind," Hunt promised. At the same time, he saw that Eesyan was waiting for his attention.

"It makes a lot of sense," the Thurien said. "So much so, that I can't think why it wasn't obvious before. Yes, Vic, I think that Madam Xyen and the rest of you are onto something. This has to be the way."

CHAPTER EIGHTEEN

Frenua Showm sat alone in the part of the house that she called the eyrie, staring out at the cliffs and ridges and the distant peaks. The falls at the far end of the gorge, dyed orange in the light of the setting sun, were being eaten up slowly by advancing shadows. The crescent of Doyaris, one of Thurien's two moons, hung brightly above, waiting to take charge of the night. It was one of those times when Showm withdrew from the world of duties and day-to-day affairs, and turned her focus inward to this being that her mind and her body served, exploring its thoughts and feelings. The ability was rare among Terrans, and the few who knew their true nature and inner souls were not understood by the others. Their impetuousness and the compulsive violence with which they attacked everything, or else were themselves attacked by others, drove them to lives where attention was permanently externalized. Perhaps it was another quality that developed in its own time as a race matured.

She had thought much about Terrans and their nature as a result of her studies of Earth's history. Life had its seasons like the year, and when one came naturally to its close it was time not to dwell on false attachments to the past but to move on into harmony with the next. Showm's life was in its autumn now, the season for returning nourishment to the soil, when the wisdom and experience accrued along the way made it possible to give

155

back what the earlier stages had necessitated borrowing. Spring had been the season for creating, and summer, that for nurturing and sending forth life. For the Thurien, the spiritual delight of experiencing life and growth, of creating and building, was the most precious reward that the universe had to offer. It was the reason for existing, and making it possible was the reason why the universe existed. The universe was a desert waiting to be brought to life. Although the aberration was not entirely unknown in the long history of their species, the notion of willfully killing a sapient being was about the most abhorrent that most Thuriens were capable of conceiving.

They believed that in a way similar to that in which the observed universe was an infinitesimal grain of the totality making up the Multiverse, so the Multiverse itself was merely an aspect of something incomparably vaster. In this domain dwelled the true soul that the heart of a thinking, feeling being connected to. It continued to exist while the personas it created came and passed, each of a nature and formed in such circumstances as the soul needed to heal and to grow. Although the personas might be discarded, the things their experiences had revealed and taught were retained and absorbed, much as with the characters that were temporarily manufactured for some kinds of game. Although the death of a persona, when it came, was thus seen as merely the closing of another season, to cut short the soul's connection would be to starve its essential growth.

Even more, the transient lives of the personas served as nurseries for developing such qualities conducive to the soul's higher life as understanding, creativity, gentleness, and compassion. But the act, or even the contemplation, of killing and destruction invoked all the emotions and insensibilities that were the precise opposite. The perpetrator was debased and deformed, violating the self's inner nature in a way far exceeding any outrage done to the victim. To the Thurien, it represented the ultimate denial, a rejection of all meaning to the universe, and any reason for it to exist. Small wonder then, Showm reflected, that in the world reduced to mindless matter that they had created, and themselves to purposeless accidents of it, that the majority of Terrans knew of no higher aspiration than the accumulation of money or a craving to control the minds and lives of others.

She had known close love and the tenderness of motherhood,

the ties of friendship, the privilege of being able to help others find happiness in their lives, the joys of creating and accomplishing, the feelings of admiration and gratitude toward those whose work made hers possible. The high moments of significance, when the splendor of existing and the meaning that the universe stood for were revealed, she saw in the bright eyes and enraptured faces when sages inspired the minds of the young; in colonizing ships lifting out of orbit to head for a new world; in the communion of elderly sharing dreams and reminiscences as they neared the end of their journey; in worlds clothed in forests, mountains, and oceans. These were the things that the universe existed for, in accord with its nature, that brought it to life. Life and the universe produced a music that was heard by the soul. Everything that grew was an expression of it.

She still had disturbed nights and moments of cold, gnawing horror at some of the things she had learned in her researches of Earth: children forcibly regimented into cults of mass murder; industries dedicated to death, the annihilation of cities, eradication of whole cultures. She had read accounts of armies seized by blood lust, hunting defenseless innocents down like vermin and hacking them to pieces; of families burning and screaming under collapsing buildings; of people starving, people drowning, people driven from their homes into the snow to die. And all of it was planned, deliberate, celebrated by some side or other as heroic and glorious. Showm had watched the recordings of aircraft pouring bombs down upon the dazed and terrified survivors of towns already turned into smoldering rubble; ships and vehicles packed with human beings incinerated, cut to shreds, blown apart; people fleeing and falling like blades of *arui* grass in a hailstorm. She had stared numbly at pictures of the corpses, grotesque and stomach-wrenching: charred, mangled, dismembered, disemboweled; twisted in ditches, ensnared in wire, crushed in mud, rotting in heaps. She had watched the sorry processions bringing back the limbless, the blind, the maimed, the insane wreckage of what had been husbands and sons, brothers and lovers, youth with its dreams. At one point she had appealed to VISAR for guidance on how such things could be. VISAR was unable to offer any. And so she had wept. How could beings who were capable of thought and feeling do such things? How could they believe the lies?

Even more incomprehensible, how could those who ruled and

commanded promote such lies? Not just to advance petty ambitions or carry out their schemes of conquest, but in every sphere where humans struggled, plotted, allied, and betrayed to set each against all, everyone a threat or a rival, to gain some advantage one over another. The whole philosophy underlying their dealings with each other was not only predicated on but exalted and glorified self-seeking and exploitation, oppression, rapacity, cruelty, and the enslavement of the weak to serve the strong, all rationalized in the ruthless calculus of money that recognized efficacy of contributing to profit-making as the sole measure of an individual's meaning or worth.

Mildred had described the leaders as the worst of thieves and scoundrels, and didn't listen to them. But Mildred was the exception, resigned to the private life of a minority with no voice. Among Thuriens, the quality most looked to for leadership was benign maturity and the selfless compassion that it engendered. Government office or the power to make responsible decisions were looked upon as privileged opportunities to serve the people. To abuse such a position for personal gain or to coerce the unwilling beyond basic restraints essential for a community to live together would be the most heinous of offenses. To say such transgressions had never occurred would have been untrue . . . but it came close to being unthinkable.

Only Terrans could have produced the myths that mindless, undirected matter could organize itself into living organisms able to communicate emotion and thought, or that the universe had begun in unimaginable violence out of nothing. They projected their inner natures into what they saw, and then convinced themselves that what they were seeing was external reality. The Thuriens knew that the programs that directed life did not originate on planets, although planetary systems were the assembly stations where the programs found expression in the bewildering number of ways that conditions across a galaxy made possible. The seeds were brought by the cosmic wind. Where they came from, how they were produced, by what agency, and for what purpose were the prime mysteries that had become the quest of Thurien science to answer, and one of the imperatives driving their expansion. There was evidence of strange conditions behind the obscuring clouds and increasing star concentration at the very center the Galaxy—and the core regions of other galaxies too. But the Thuriens had not penetrated far enough yet to learn more. Their period of apathy and stagnation, when they achieved immortality and as a consequence little else that was of any importance for aeons, had cost them much. To be inspired by dreams and embark on quests to make them come true required the constant reinvigoration of youth. That realization was what caused the Thuriens to revert to the old way and accept nature and its seasons.

Was the violence of humans an inescapable flaw in their makeup? Or was it a perversion of something irrepressible that might be harnessed to direct at constructive ends the same furious energy with which it was able to destroy? Perhaps it was because of their unique origins in ancient Ganymean genetic manipulations, but the Thuriens had met nothing anywhere that compared with them. From what had seemed hopeless beginnings in the face of impossible odds to just before the tragedy that eventually befell Minerva, the speed at which the ancestral Lunarian civilization had emerged and advanced was astounding, mocking the Ganymean experience—which itself surpassed every other race they had encountered since. Eesyan had reported that despite their younger science and limited technical grounding, Hunt and his group were already having a significant impact on the project. What might the impact be of both cultures fully mature, working in combination?

Showm's thoughts went back again to her conversation here in this same place with Mildred. Exactly that situation might long ago have come to be, if the Lunarians hadn't been deflected from their path by the intrusion of Jevelenese fugitives. The Lunarians before then had worked cooperatively toward the goal of migrating to Earth. Could it be that the later pathological instability of the Terrans was not something innate to their humanness at all, but a product of traumas they had undergone? The catastrophic war that had dashed the hopes they had been building for generations, culminating in the destruction of their world; the experiences of the last, tiny band marooned on the lunar desert; the renewed hope of beginning again when they were transported to Earth, only to be devastated once more in the convulsions unleashed by the capture of the orphaned Moon. What else could they have become but creatures brutalized to self-preservation as the first instinct for survival? What other philosophy of life and the cosmos would they be capable of producing?

Such reflections assailed Showm insistently. Maybe she had been too harsh in her judgment of humans. And that was important, because the answer the Thuriens finally accepted as to why Terrans were the way they were would determine their eventual decision on how Earth would be dealt with. The debate had been continuing privately among the Thuriens ever since the Jevlenese plans and machinations were exposed.

Showm felt an excitement stirring deep inside her as the thought that had been forming for days finally crystallized. Maybe it was no longer necessary for such a crucial matter to depend on debates and speculation. Eesyan's scientists were talking about sending out packages of instruments to explore and sample the Multiverse from the facility they were building at MP2. Another universe had already transported the communications device that contacted Hunt back on Earth. Broghuilio's Jevlenese ships had actually gone back to Lunarian Minerva.

The technology to do it was all there. Why grow weary debating to exhaustion how much like Terrans the pretrauma Lunarians might or might not have been—with all the attendant risk of coming up with the wrong answer anyway—when the matter could be settled objectively by observation? They could send reconnaissance probes there and find out! Now that it appeared they had the ability, it would be an injustice to the human race not to make the effort. And Showm couldn't abide the thought of that. The humans had suffered enough injustice from Ganymeans already.

As a child, Showm had listened to stories of the world their race had come from long ago, and the barbarians who inherited it and destroyed it. It was the standard, simplified fare that Thurien parents told their children. Only now was she beginning to realize how much those images had shaped the attitudes she had been carrying all her life. Her way of interpreting the realization was that the soul whom her experiences served, in its realm that existed beyond the Multiverse, had learned something worthwhile and significant already.

CHAPTER NINETEEN

To the Terran mind, the extent to which Thuriens went in "wiring" their cities and other environments with sensors to provide authentic inputs for their reality simulations seemed bafflingly elaborate. Even regions that were sparsely populated, or in cases not inhabited at all, were subject to broad surveillance by satellite and other means to enable plausible reconstructions of local scenes and conditions by interpolation. It seemed that the dictate of balancing cost against benefit that was the first consideration of every designer, project planner, and program manager on Earth played no part in whatever process the Thuriens applied in deciding what was to be done, and how. Either that, or the concepts of "cost" and "benefit" meant very different things from what they did on Earth.

Even the voids of space around planets and other habitats, and the regular traffic lanes within planetary systems, were monitored to a degree that would have struck Terrans as pointless. It meant, however, that a network of imaging pickups and other detectors likely to spot any unusual events was already distributed through the volume affected by the MP2 experiment. VISAR estimated that the chances of at least one intruder from a different reality appearing somewhere in that region of space were about even. The surveillance system was primed to be on the lookout accordingly.

It happened when MP2 was being readied for the first attempts at transporting sizeable and more complex test objects. Hunt was

161

in the tower at Quelsang, going over proposals that had been put forward for the kinds of objects that should be sent, when VISAR came through to announce that the sensor scanning processor covering a region about a hundred thousand miles out on the far side of Thurien had reported anomalies consistent with the sudden appearance of something that shouldn't be there. A replay of the image captured by analyzers directed at the location showed what appeared to be some kind of instrument package: an open framework containing antennas, and other bits of engineering, the whole about the size of a regular upright chair. It sustained itself for just over eleven seconds, and then broke up. But not in the sense of coming to pieces; it more, just faded away—growing indistinct and then dissolving into nothing. It was exactly what the scientists had been hoping for. Without even bothering to convene together, they excitedly suspended whatever else they were doing in the various places they happened to be, to go over the information the detectors had recorded and see what could be made of it.

It was clearly Thurien in origin, although there had never been any doubt about that. Some of the devices were of recognizable function, others more obscure. A number of optical and other imagers were identified, busily scanning the surroundings. One of the appendages suggested a Thurien gravitic transponder used for relaying into h-space.

"The cluster at the left-hand end looks like an antenna array for the local planetary spectrum," another Thurien commented, this time in the Institute.

"The design is unfamiliar, but the dimensions check," VISAR agreed.

"Are my eyes playing tricks, or is that an UNSA emblem painted on the side—at about coordinates 1.2 and 3.7?" Sonnebrandt queried, across in the other building at Quelsang.

"I wouldn't be at all surprised. It's the kind of thing I can imagine Vic doing," Danchekker said. Hunt shot him a pained look across the two desks separating them.

"Let me see if I can enhance it," VISAR said. "It could be just a trick of the light."

VISAR also reported that transmissions had been received across a number of standard Thurien communications signal bands. But they were garbled and defied all efforts to extract anything meaningful. Nevertheless, it was encouraging. A proof as bizarre as anything that could be asked for that project's immediate aims, at least, were realistic.

Most significant was that if the device was equipped to collect data from the place it arrived at, it followed that it had to possess also a means of sending its findings back to where it had come from. Otherwise, what would be the point of collecting anything? It implied that even at the stage the scientists were now at, they should be close to achieving the communication across the Multiverse that the original brief visit of Hunt's alter ego had demonstrated as being possible. The fact that the device had remained only for seconds indicated that although the versions of themselves who sent it seemed to have solved the problem of getting a transported object to stop, they were not yet able to stabilize it. Chien had already proposed a halting method that the Thurien experts agreed sounded promising, and so with luck they couldn't be very far behind.

The manner of dispersion when the device vanished was consistent with the idea of its being locked as a standing wave pattern that had lost coherence. VISAR was already analyzing the decay profile, from which it was hoped a lot more would be learned. From what could be ascertained at the present, it seemed to the scientists that they were on the right track. This boosted their confidence to push ahead even more vigorously with implementing a similar instrument package of their own, which they just happened to be working on. But given the strange nature of these parallel realms of existence, it probably wasn't such a strange coincidence really.

The first visit by an artefact from another universe, and the ensuing conversation between Hunt and an elsewhere-existing version of himself, had been announced publicly at Owen's retirement dinner a week before Hunt and the others' departure. With no precedent to compare with it in the whole of history, it could only be a godsend to the media and entertainment industries, the publishing world, and the entire spectrum of scientific debate from supermarket tabloids and chat shows to the proceedings of the most eminent institutions. News from Earth was that the whole subject of Multiverse physics and the implications of effectively unlimited "twin" realities had become the latest sensation to capture the popular imagination. The discovery of "Charlie" was old now; the subsequent speculations regarding the supposedly extinct race of Ganymeans, died when they showed up very much real and alive; and the more recently revealed computer-evolved world of the Ents was already starting to wear thin.

A British sitcom entitled *Sorry, That's the Universe Next Door* was roaring up through the ratings, and a number of games had been rushed out in which players at different terminals hopped in and out of each other's realities. Old song titles that had inspired top-selling spoofs included "Welcome to my World," "Don't Blame Me," and "Out of Nowhere," while a remake of *The Wizard of Oz* was in the works with a time-line warp replacing the tornado and providing the lead-up to the classic-line warp: "This isn't *our* Kansas, Toto."

Inevitably, the public was saturated with misconceptions which, once formed and launched into circulation, took on a life of their own through uncritical repetition. One of the most common was a revival of the old notion of the universe "splitting" at critical junctures, "critical" usually being taken to mean as judged from the standpoint of human affairs. That the fundamental processes of physics should be responsive to events in the day-to-day lives of cabbage-growers or kings was evidently no obstacle to the popularizers, some of whom didn't hesitate to embellish the notion with articles bearing such titles as "How Your Flip of a Coin Can Change the Universe," and even a book-length decision-making guide on how to get the better deals in life at the expense of other selves competing for them in other universes. And, of course, Multiverse phenomena in some form or other became the latest explanation for telepathy, telekinesis, psychic visions, visitations, ghosts, and the basis for a new interpretation of UFOs, various "triangle" mysteries of interchangeable geography, and the list of usual suspects from the JFK assassination all the way back to the builders of the pyramids.

Hunt remained serenely detached from it all with a mixture of amusement and despair . . . until VISAR put through a call from Caldwell's secretary, Mitzi, at Goddard, saying that someone from a company from California had been in touch, who wanted to offer Hunt a part in a movie.

"You're kidding," was Hunt's hardly original reaction when she delivered the message.

"Yeah, as if I don't have anything better to do than make practical joke calls to busy scientists at other star systems. He's serious—as serious as anyone out in the Granola farm gets, anyway. His name's Arty Strang. From Premier Production Studios."

"PPS? . . . Are you sure this isn't a joke?"

"It's not even April one, Vic."

"Hm. Okay. What kind of movie is he talking about?"

"How would I know? The only way you'll find out is to call him and ask."

"I guess so. . . ." Hunt realized that he was stalling for time while he tried to organize his thoughts more coherently. "Oh yes, and while were at it, do you know anything about a Lieutenant Polk of the FBI?"

"Yes. He was trying to get hold of you too. How did you find out about him?"

"He tried calling me here. How did he get the access codes?"

"Well, they are the FBI."

"So it wasn't you, then?"

"No. We just told him you were out of town. Gregg figured you had better things to do too."

"Any idea what it was about?"

"Do you remember giving an investment tip for Formaflex in Texas to that neighbor of yours out at Redfern Canyons?"

"Jerry Santello? Yes, right. What about it?"

"You got it from the other version of you who showed up here, right?"

"That's right. Jerry had been bugging me about investments for a while. I thought it might keep him happy. So?"

"Well, it seems your other self was privy to information that's still not for general consumption yet in this universe we live in. Like, illegal? That's what Polk was on about. He wants to know where you got it from."

Hunt stared at the window in his visual field that Mitzi was speaking from. "That's it? We're on the verge of opening up new universes on a scale that would make colonizing all the galaxies look like camping in your own back yard, and he wants to talk about shopkeeper economics and bookkeeping?"

"I told you Gregg figured you'd have better things to do."

"Gregg never fails us. Look, if you hear more from this guy, which I've a feeling you will, hold him off until I've thought of how to handle it, would you?"

"Will do. How's everything else there? Has cousin Mildred driven Chris nuts yet?"

"Pretty good. We had another object materialize. I've sent through a report. Actually, you'd be surprised. Mildred is turning out to be a great hit with the Thuriens. She's possibly the best ambassador we could have picked to send. Chris doesn't quite believe it either. But he isn't complaining."

"Wow! Sounds fascinating. I can't wait for you to tell me all about it. But right now I have to go. I'll watch out for your name on the Oscar list."

"Don't hold your breath. Talk to you again soon, Mitzi. Say hi to Gregg. Take care."

Hunt leaned back in his chair and stared for a minute or two at the wall screen, which was showing some results of VISAR's decoherence analyses superposed on a background of an alien undersea scene somewhere. Danchekker, who had been at his desk earlier, had gone out of the office while Hunt was talking, leaving him on his own for the moment. On impulse, he activated VISAR again.

"Do you have a number for Arty Strang at Premier Productions?"

"Of course."

"What's the time there?"

"Almost three in the afternoon, Tuesday."

"See if you can raise him for me, would you?"

Perhaps what they had in mind was some kind of science documentary, Hunt reflected. Hosting something like that would be appealingly different from the regular workaday routine, he had to admit. Even if he did say so himself, he thought he could do a much better job than many of the overrated celebrity names whose efforts he had witnessed. And given some say in the content and presentation—which his position in UNSA would surely give him some leverage to negotiate—it could go a long way toward correcting some of the deluge of nonsense that the world had been drowning in.

A window appeared, framing the upper view of a heavy-set man in his mid-to-late thirties, perhaps, with a pink complexion and collar-length blond hair, wearing a bright yellow jacket with a red shirt collar turned over the lapel, and sunglasses. Hunt shifted his field of view to bring the wall around as background. "Dr. Hunt!" The face creased into a rubbery smile.

"No less."

"Fantastic!"

"My office at Goddard says you were trying to contact me."

"That's right." Strang's image peered out questioningly for a moment. "Just to make sure I've got this straight. Right now, as we speak, you're talking to me from some other star out there, that right?"

"The Thuriens' home star, twenty light-years away," Hunt confirmed.

"Unbelievable! You know, they used to tell us that could never happen. I never believed it. They said that about too many things, and now they happen every day and nobody even notices. But it was all there in the old movies from way back. Did you ever see one called *Starward Imperative*? Kevin Bayland at his best, before he went into all the weirdo stuff. That was where Martha Earle first got noticed."

"I can't say I did. . . ." Hunt waited for a moment, then hazarded, "I, ah, was told you had some kind of proposition in mind."

"This is you, I suppose? Not one of these doubles of yours that comes zipping in and out of other universes or whatever?"

"What? . . ." Hunt brought a hand up to his brow. How did one handle this kind of thing? "I'm not sure I—"

The pudgy features contorted into a grin again. "Just a joke. But it's more than a joke really. That's what we want to make the movie about."

"What is?"

"*You!* Your story. I mean, come on, don't you know you're a big name these days? Regular on the shows; pieces in all the mags. And all to do with the kind of stuff that everybody's interested in and kids are wild about: The mummy on the Moon; real starships and aliens; people inside a computer. And now this latest! . . . It's a natural that's screaming out to be made. It beats me why nobody's done it yet. It'll be the blockbuster of years."

"Well, that's an interesting thought, I suppose. . . ."

"Trust me. I know the business. It's got all the potential. But to really make it fly, we're gonna give that something-extra zip, know what I mean? We want you in it, playing yourself."

Hunt shook his head as if to clear it. Strang raised a hand in the manner of forestalling an interruption.

"We've got the angles figured. Some of those Jev lines about our guys having all that military out there at Ganymede when the Ganymeans show up are dynamite. And it's already put together. All we have to do is weave it in." He was talking about the faked surveillance accounts that the Jevlenese had fed to the Thuriens. This was already getting insane. "We've got a couple of writers working on some action scenes that make them into great paranoids to begin with—but only until they come around to realizing that we're only defending ourselves and underneath it Earth guys are really okay. Then the act comes together. It needs more sex too. We want to give you a real dazzler as a partner, to work in some good hot scenes. Somebody like Kelly Heyne, maybe. Does that sound good? She plays Danchekker. We make it a female role. The balance is perfect, and the opportunities for—"

Hunt shook his head. "No. I'm flattered and all that, but I don't think it's my kind of line."

Strang showed both palms in a conciliatory gesture. "Okay, well I kinda figured that might be the case. But we'd still be interested in having you on board as an advisory consultant. I mean, we want to make sure we get everything right, right?"

Hunt almost choked. "Really. . . . Thanks again, but I do have more than enough to do here as it is."

"What kind of money do they pay you?" Strang inquired.

"Enough to get by."

"Whatever it is, we'll double it."

"You don't seem to understand, I don't need it. I wouldn't have the time to make use of it," Hunt said.

Strang had to stop and think about that one. His script evidently didn't allow for such a possibility. "What do you mean? How can anyone not need it?" he asked finally. "It's what it's all about, isn't it?"

"Is it? What what's all about?"

Strang seemed momentarily at a loss, as if he were being asked to explain the obvious. He made a face and threw up his hands briefly. "Everything. . . . The works. The ball of wax. I mean, it's the thing that get's you what you want, right?"

"No, Arty, you've got it backward. The only use it has is for buying junk I don't need. Not having to waste time making it gets me what I want."

"I don't getcha. What kind of sense is that supposed to make?"

Hunt made as if to reply, then changed his mind and shook his head wearily. "Forget it," he replied. "It could be just being out here for a while. Maybe I'm starting to think like an alien."

CHAPTER TWENTY

Mildred joined Hunt and Danchekker at breakfast in the Waldorf. The others of the group hadn't put in an appearance yet. She was quite pleased with the way she had been keeping to her resolution of finding her own way around and not being a burden to Christian by distracting him from his work. At the same time, there was no reason to ostracize herself from the others socially.

"I hear you've got your machine out there working—MP2, or whatever you call it. . . . Thank you so much. Oh, it looks delicious! What kind of bread is that?" Her last words were directed at the young Thurien girl who had brought her dishes to the table. Although serving robots and platters that floated in the air like the one at Frenua Showm's house were universal, there was no shortage of volunteers wanting to perform services for the Terrans. Apparently, waiting personally on one's guests was an old Thurien custom that denoted high honors, and that was gratifying. But more to the point in the present circumstances, it was a way of meeting the aliens from Earth that so much had been heard about. Notions of any implied role or status were lost on Thuriens.

"It's called *deldran*, made from a sweet grain with fruit pieces, lightly toasted. The jams are for spreading on it. Very nice to start the day."

"And that smells like real coffee."

"It is. The catering manager here ordered a list of things on the last ship that came from Earth."

"Much appreciated. Do pass it on," Danchekker said.

"We try to please."

"You've been talking to VISAR," Hunt quipped, and then even as he said it, remembered it was VISAR's translation that he was listening to. "What should we call you?" he asked to move away from the subject.

"Ithel. I live here in the city part of the time, and also on a world called Borsekon. The surface is all ice and snow, ocean and mountains. We make long journeys there alone—disconnected from VISAR for days at a time. You're really, totally 'there.' The solitude is very spiritual."

"What about school?" Danchekker asked. It seemed a fair question by what Mildred guessed to be Ithel's age. "Do you take care of that here, on Thurien, or is it divided between the two?" Ithel didn't seem to follow the question. "Where youngsters go to learn," Danchekker said. "To prepare them for life."

Ithel smiled uncertainly. "Life is its own preparation," she answered, but still without seeming really to have understood. However it was instilled, politeness seemed to come naturally to young Thuriens, Mildred had observed. Unlike the situation that had become depressingly the norm in some places on Earth, they didn't confuse courtesy with subservience or equate assertiveness with being obnoxious and rude. Thurien education system was another item on Mildred's long list to investigate. In fact, it was first on her agenda today.

"I'd like to talk with you if I may, Ithel," she said. "When you have some free time. There are a lot of questions I think you could help with in connection with the work that brings me here. How would you like to be in a book read all over Earth?"

"Really? Of course!"

"What do I do to get in touch? Just ask VISAR?"

"Yes."

"I'll do that, then. Thank you very much."

"My privilege."

Ithel went away. Danchekker poked curiously at preparation that looked like a cheese omelette with some kind of chopped, red vegetable mixed in, garnished with herbs and covered with a clear gravy. Hunt answered Mildred's earlier question.

"MP2's working, but so far with nothing very exciting to report. Yes, we're sending objects off into other universes that are bigger and more complex than the specks of molecules and crystal flakes that the machine over at Quelsang handles."

"My word," Mildred remarked. "That just goes to show how quickly your ideas of what's exciting deteriorate. A couple of months ago you'd have been leaping around the room and whooping if you'd been able to say that."

Hunt acknowledged with an upturned hand and went on, "But we've no idea where they end up—or even if they end up anywhere. They might just keep on going until the wave function disperses."

Whatever that meant. "I thought Chien had come up with a way of stopping them," Mildred said, at least managing to construe that much.

"We think so," Hunt agreed. "But so far there's no way to be sure. The Thuriens have done tests that involve moving things from here to there around Thurien, and even via h-space to other star systems. And in those cases, sure, it seems to work. But that's all still within *this* universe. It doesn't prove that it works when you're going transversely across the MV."

"Going horizontally, between universes," Mildred said.

"You are coming along," Danchekker told her.

Hunt continued, "The only way we'll be able to find out is by sending something that's able to communicate back. But we still haven't overcome the problem of time lines coming together around the projector and getting mixed up. It means that any message you get back out of it is a composite of different inputs all scrambled up. Totally incoherent. You can't get any sense out of it. It's clear now what that other version of myself was trying to tell us back at the beginning. Convergence is the big thing we have to solve."

Mildred thought about it while she stirred her coffee. "But *they* must have solved it—in the other universe that he was from. Because you were communicating."

"Exactly. That's the galling part. And I'm certain he was going to tell us how, but we lost the connection. If we'd had a battery of Thurien sensors and detectors in the area they way they have here, we'd probably have stood a good chance of figuring out how they did it."

"It sounds a bit like tuning a radio," Mildred said. "You know, you've got signals everywhere from all these stations at once, and somehow you have to pick out just the one you want. I've never really understood how that works. Well, yes, I know you 'tune a circuit.' But what does that mean?"

"Close," Hunt granted. "But in this case you're more jumping from one channel to another all the time instead of having them all there at once. If you could find some way of locking on to just one, that might work. But what is there about it, exactly, do you lock on to? As far as we can make out, It would involve identifying some kind of quantum signature that's unique to that particular universe. VISAR has been churning through permutations for a while now, but with no luck so far. The computations are horrendous, even by Thurien standards."

But it was a touchy matter with him, and on reflection she decided it would be more tactfully broached when they were alone. So they spent the rest of the meal talking about Thurien social customs and the latest stories about weird time line convergence effects instead. Then, Hunt and Danchekker left to collect the things they needed for the day. Mildred waited to have a few more words with Ithel, and then proceeded from the dining area to the space at the rear of the building where the cubicles containing the full-neural virtual travel couplers were located. She could have used the one in her room, but these were closer. The feeling of slipping out of reality as her mind opened into a vast internal void was by now familiar. She had asked VISAR to see if it could arrange for her to visit a Thurien "school."

Mildred found herself out of doors beside what could have been a river or an inlet of sea, surrounded by a small, rambling town. The houses were ornate and colorful, mixing all manner of styles, modest in scale, simple and functional compared to some of the things she had seen. She got the feeling this was an old town that hadn't changed much in a long time. Steep, tree-covered hills gouged by valleys rose behind the houses. The sky was sunny with a few clouds, the air warm, stirring enough to carry a hint of forest scents. Mildred was standing inside an area of yard by the water's edge, screened by a fence from a row of buildings. In the upper parts of one of them, some Thuriens were sitting out on a deck in front of a window opening through to the interior. The yard contained a few sheds by the water, another building behind, complicated-looking things with hoists and tackle, and a small dock. About a dozen Thurien children and two adults that Mildred could see were busy around the dock. They were building a boat.

"Oh. . . ." Mildred looked around again, as if to check her bearings. She knew by now that if she was careless and stepped on a rope or something she would trip and feel the tumble—without actually bruising herself or breaking anything, of course. Her voice carried a note of doubt sufficient to cue VISAR.

"You rang?"

"Yes, er . . . this is all very nice, VISAR, but maybe I wasn't clear enough. What I wanted to see was a school—you know, where children learn the basic things they have to know for living in a community."

"Yes, I know. This is how they learn them. Or it might be laying out a garden and tending it to make things grow; renovating a theater and creating a play for it; building a machine with hands and tools the ancient way; exploring the arts of athletics or dance; learning to handle animals. . . . It depends on what they're interested in or think they can do. This is where they find out."

"Isn't there any standardizing process that they all have to go through to conform?" She realized as she heard herself using the words that some part of her was already anticipating the response.

"Not really," VISAR answered. "We're not seeking conformity. The intention is to discover and cultivate differences. Everyone is unique. Thuriens believe it's for a reason. It makes every individual priceless. They have a saying that if any two people were the same, one of them would be unnecessary."

Mildred saw that one of the Thuriens had left his charges and was making his way across through the jumble of boat parts, materials, and work tables. Naturally, he was "here" and not connected through another neurocoupler somewhere else—which would have made it difficult to build a boat. Mildred knew the system sufficiently well by now to guess that VISAR had superposed her visually via his avco disk that Thuriens were seldom without. Protocol would have required that VISAR announce Mildred's "presence."

"Armu Egrigol," VISAR said by way of introduction.

Egrigol was one of the smallest adult Thuriens that Midred had come across, measuring somewhere around six feet. He also had one of the lightest crowns, sandy yellow, with skin varying from purple to dark red, in contrast with the normal tones of blue-black and gray. He greeted her with a broad smile, obviously expecting her. VISAR updated him on Mildred's impressions and questions since arriving. Egrigol nodded and seemed amused, apparently prepared for it. Mildred suspected that VISAR had given him some kind of briefing beforehand. He spent a short while explaining what they were doing and pointing out details. When the boat was finished, they were going to sail it along the coast and then out on the ocean to an island that sounded alarmingly far away. Mildred was struck by how young some of the Thurien children seemed for such a venture. But there seemed no shortage of enthusiasm.

As yet, they were either too engrossed to notice that he had moved away and was talking to thin air, or it was too common-place an occurrence to warrant attention. Either way, they were not showing any signs of registering her existence themselves, although they were wearing the ubiquitous avco disks. Mildred queried this, and VISAR confirmed that her image was not being fed through to them yet.

"I think they'll forgive us if I let you snoop a little bit," Egrigol chuckled. "I wanted to let you see them working naturally for a while. They'll start showing off if they know they have an audience. Are Terran children the same?"

"Probably worse," Mildred said. "But I was just starting to ask when you came over, what about the basic skills that they have to have, surely, before they can learn anything like this? Things like being able to read and write, carry out elementary calculations. . . . Those are what I think of as 'school.' But VISAR says you don't have anything like that. Is that really true?"

"Do you need schools on Earth to teach children to walk and to talk, to open their eyes and know what objects they see?" Egrigol asked.

"But those are natural instincts," Mildred objected.

"Yes. And so is the desire for inner satisfaction that comes from creating and from doing worthwhile work. We all want to measure as best we can in our own eyes and in the esteem of others. The skills you're talking about are what you have to know to become what you can be. When they understand that, they learn them."

"But *where* do they learn them?"

Egrigol shrugged. "At home, from their friends.... Many who are so disposed teach themselves. Each finds the way that is right, when they are ready. It has to come from the inside."

He turned his head to look back as he spoke. Mildred followed his gaze, and she began to see it all in a different light. A short distance away, a girl called two of the others across and pointed at something that one of the boys was doing at a bench. "Look at how Kolar can cut these joints!" It was a genuine compliment. There was no jealously or put-down. They were learning, Mildred realized, that the most important lesson life had to offer was that they all needed each other.

"Kolar was a late starter," Egrigol commented. "He had trouble working out some of the dimensions at first. We helped him with some basics." He shrugged again. "And he picked up the rest from somewhere.... But anyway, it's about time we introduced you, don't you think?"

Egrigol called for attention and announced that he had a surprise, and also a mild apology to make. "One of the Terrans, who has come here to find out more about Thuriens and is going to write a book about us when she gets back, is here virtually and would like to say hello. Her name is Mildred." A moment later all eyes turned toward her as VISAR put her onstage.

At first they were awed and little reserved. But as their inhibitions melted they became first curious, then talkative, and finally eager to show her the things they could do. This was not an artificial world existing apart from the realities of adulthood, living by its own invented standards and measures that were meaningless outside. The adults were the acknowledged experts in skills they all needed to acquire, and respect was the natural outcome. Mildred found she was among young people who were loved, secure, with growing confidence in themselves and exuberance to experience this adventure ahead of them that was called life.

But it was no stranger, she realized. For she had seen it before. She had seen it kindergartens in every country she had been to on Earth. She had seen it in the eyes of the children in villages of the Amazon headwaters; of desert margin tribes in Namibia; of peasant families in Croatia. "Come and see, Johnny can stand on his head!" "Chano gave it to me. She made it herself!" "Bannuti caught three fish today!" "Juliusz, show me how to ride a horse too." What made it genuine was that their confidence came from knowledge of things they could *do*, as opposed to just knowing how to talk—from which stemmed every form of phoniness and delusion.

It was then that Mildred became conscious of something she had always known, but for some reason had never been able to articulate to herself before. This was their true nature: generosity; sympathy and empathy; helping others to succeed; finding security to face the world in companionship. It always had been. In themselves, they knew nothing of hatred or fear, mistrust and treachery. Such things had to be taught to them, by adults. Overcoming the selfishness and destructiveness of infancy to prepare for a fulfilling life was the proper business of youth. But on Earth, selfishness and destructiveness were idealized as virtues. Earth had things backward. It suppressed the spontaneous expression of life seeking to mature, and taught regression back to infancy instead. Then it twisted reality to fit by manufacturing cultural myths enshrined in what it believed was science. Like all organisms forced to live against their nature, nations, empires, or whole cultures that sought life by killing, wealth by destroying, security by preying upon each other, would rebel, sicken, and eventually die. The whole of Earth's history was a testimony to it.

"Where did you go to this morning?" Frenua Showm asked. They had arranged to "meet" on Borsekon, the ice world that Ithel had talked about at breakfast in the Waldorf. Mildred wanted to see it. She and Showm were standing on a cliff top below vast slopes of white broken by lonely crags, sweeping up to a rocky ridgeline standing sharp against a pale blue sky. Below, a maze of water channels weaving among islands and fantastic floating sculptures of ice extended away into mists. VISAR had injected just enough cold into the air to make the simulation feel authentic. Because anything else would have felt wrong, they were wearing padded coats with hoods.

"I went back to a time I had forgotten," Mildred said. "Most of the people on Earth have forgotten it." She waited for a response, but Showm let her elaborate. "I was interested in Thurien education, and I asked VISAR to arrange for me to see a school. . . ." Mildred wasn't sure how she wanted to put it. She was still wrestling with a flurry of competing thoughts.

"Actually, I did hear about it," Showm said. "They were making a boat. Armu Egrigol was delighted. I hope they find a place in your book."

Mildred was silent for a long time. Absolute stillness hung on every side. "But that wasn't what I saw," she said finally.

"What did you see?"

"I saw . . . I'll tell you what I saw. I saw young people who were not sitting in rows and being lectured to know their place, when they could speak, and what they were allowed to believe. They weren't being taught to hate or to despise, or whom they were superior to and whom they must obey. They weren't learning to recognize and submit to authority, in preparation for accepting the authority that would exploit them for the rest of their lives, and command them into believing it was natural. I saw minds that were free to grow into everything they could become. . . . Maybe for the first time."

This time it was Showm's turn to fall silent before answering. Eventually, she sighed. Her breath made white vapor in the air. "We've talked this way before. Those are not the values that rule Earth. Terrans like you are so few—who can feel and think the way you do."

Mildred shook her head. "No. They are the majority. But they are silent and invisible: the poor, the hungry, the defenseless, the oppressed. Perhaps these are things you can have no concept of, Frenua. How can people think of the stars when they labor morning to night day after day, and all they have to show at the end will barely put a meal on the table for their children? How do people who can't even imagine escaping from crushing debt or the fear of destitution discover their inner selves? How can they build boats when every morning they might be dragged out of their homes and thrown into prisons?"

"But why can't they see the things you see?" Showm asked.

"Because they are deceived by those that they trust. They believe the lies that turn them against each other." Mildred turned her head. There was hope in her eyes. "But that could be changing now. Much of the evil that dominated Earth has been rooted out with the exposure of the Jevlenese influence throughout history. And now that we've made contact with Thurien, Earth might open its eyes finally. Thurien can teach the people of Earth how to reject the lies."

Mildred had expected that Showm would welcome hearing such words. They were little more than a distillation of things that Showm herself had voiced on various occasions, after all.

But for some reason Showm turned away abruptly and seemed strangely disturbed.

CHAPTER TWENTY-ONE

Duncan Watt christened it the "Conveyor Belt." The Thuriens launched a succession of probe devices off into the Multiverse from the MP2 station, each being projected as a component of a standing wave function, which in theory should cause it to materialize in another reality somewhere. Each of the probes possessed some variant of a communications transmitter set up to send back a recognition code as confirmation that it was at least continuing to exist "somewhere" as a coherent, identifiable object. This signal was sent from wherever the probe found itself in the aggregate of realities making up the Multiverse—the realm the scientists termed "M-space"—relayed back to Thurien as a signal through ordinary h-space by the remote-operated equipment at MP2. However, because of the time line lensing effect that this equipment produced in its vicinity, the parts of the incoming transmission being processed from instant to instant were from different versions of the probe, launched by different versions of MP2 existing in other realities. Since they were all designed to transmit their own unique identifying codes, nothing intelligible could be made of the resultant jumble from all of them.

The main object of the exercise was to provide VISAR with data to attempt construction of what Hunt had described to Mildred as a "quantum signature" unique to a given reality. If such a function could be defined, the hope was that MP2 might be able to "lock on" to one of the converging time lines, selecting only the universe associated with a given signature. This would be demonstrated when a coherent, decodable signal was received, instead of the scrambling of signals from different universes that was coming in at present.

The probes being sent out via the Conveyor were just that—simple signaling beacons. Unlike the instrument package that had been glimpsed briefly after coming the other way, they didn't at this stage carry detectors and sensors to find out something about where they had arrived at. One thing at a time. All the scientists were interested in at that point was being able to establish that a probe had arrived somewhere. The rest could come later.

Hunt's awareness of all this had tended toward a somewhat abstract immersion in trying to follow Thurien mathematics. Its more palpable meaning was brought home one afternoon, when VISAR came online suddenly while Hunt was using the neuro-coupler in his room at the Waldorf, taking a break to get in some virtual sightseeing around Thurien.

"Josef asked me to interrupt. Something's just happened that he thinks you should be in on."

"What?"

"Another intruder has been detected. It's a long way out from Gistar, not anywhere near Thurien. There are just a few long-range readings at present. I'm shifting more detectors through h-space to get a closer look at it."

"Okay, take me there, too."

The tower city that Hunt had been staring up at from the sprawl of suburbs and parkland surrounding its base vanished, and he found himself sitting in a glass-enclosed observation room looking out into space. The room didn't really exist; VISAR knew that even the illusion of being out in the void unenclosed and unprotected made biological beings feel insecure and had decided that something more substantial than a maintenance platform would be in order.

The object that had materialized was represented for now by a featureless white oval standing out against the black backdrop, appearing the size of an egg held at arm's length. Sensors were still evidently gathering the details. Hunt got up and moved to one of the stools at the virtual bar that VISAR had considerately provided along one wall, where he poured himself a virtual drink.

He didn't have to pour it, of course. He could have asked VISAR to simply produce it. But omitting it would have made the familiar ritual seem incomplete. The smooth, mellow sensation of Irish whiskey warming his palate was induced perfectly. And with no negative after-effects to be concerned about. It still never ceased to amaze him. For a moment he fought with the temptation to add a virtual cigarette, then dismissed it. The thought of VISAR's probable sarcastic comment, had he yielded, was enough to affirm his resolution.

"It's showing more stability than the previous device," VISAR reported. "Stress gradients and energy distribution in the surrounding h-space manifold are consistent with a standing wave pattern." The patch enlarged and began resolving itself into discernible structure as the vantage point closed. "Envelope dimensions in the order of ten feet by six feet, and eight feet deep. You're fifty feet away from it now. A flat base with pagodas pointing outward on both sides. This is very different from the one we saw before. It's not so loaded with instruments. More for communications. We're picking up strong h-resonances. It's trying to access the Thurien interstellar grid and get our attention. I think it's succeeding." A comical scene flashed in a temporary visual window of Eesyan's scientists elsewhere on Thurien frantically falling over each other to get to terminals or neural couplers.

Hunt got up from the bar and carried his glass over to the observation window. Moments later, Eesyan appeared, standing a few feet away. Hunt realized that this grandstand that VISAR had invented would where it would "bring" everyone else to who was neurocoupled into the system (it was the information, of course, that went to them) and who wanted to be in on the event too. As usual, VISAR had been ahead of him in its anticipations.

"I assume you got VISAR's update," Hunt said, turning his head to acknowledge Eesyan's presence. "It's beaming out in h-band. Stable this time. It sounds as if we might be doing something right. Chien's standing wave idea seems to be the right way to go."

Eesyan didn't reply. Hunt was still preoccupied with studying the object outside, and it took him a moment or two to register that the Thurien was just standing and staring at him strangely. He turned to face the other fully. Eesyan seemed too overpowered by something to speak. Hunt realized there was something odd. He had talked with Eesyan only a short while before; Eesyan had been dressed differently then. And his crown texture, which Thuriens periodically trimmed back in the same way that Terrans had haircuts, was more full. He looked around wonderingly, and then spoke at last, in a voice that was little more than a whisper. "This is really there?" Hunt was still trying to make sense of it when another Eesyan materialized in the floor area behind them. At least, this one looked "right."

Then VISAR came in, a little belatedly. "Sorry. I'm having a lot to deal with here. It seemed the best place to put him. The relay out there is communicating in virtual-travel protocol. They must be coupled in neurally at the other end."

Another Thurien appeared, sitting in one of the seats. Danchekker popped into existence, positioned incongruously behind the bar—one of VISAR's whimsical touches. It evidently didn't have time to make the announcements that would normally have been customary. The two Eesyans stared at each other. The second to arrive took the initiative. "Well, welcome to our world, as I believe a Terran song says. And congratulations. You're obviously ahead of us. What date is it where you are?"

Hunt had to take time out to remind himself, step by step, of what was going on. None of this was really happening. It was all inside his head. He was lying in a recliner in his room at the Waldorf in the city of Thurios. A device sitting out somewhere in the Gistar system, relaying to Thurien via h-space, was connecting the Thurien virtual-reality net into that of a different universe. VISAR was bringing together transmissions originating both from that universe, and within this one, that Hunt and the second Esyan existed in.

"Ah, Vic." Hunt looked back. Danchekker was coming out from behind the bar, where coffee and fruit juices had been added to the selection. "It seems we progress."

Hunt wasn't sure how to answer, since he didn't know which universe this Danchekker belonged to. "Hi, Chris. Which team are you with? Home or away?"

"What?" Danchekker apparently didn't appreciate the situation yet. He came closer, then realized that the two Thuriens with Hunt were both Eesyan, and stopped dead. "Good God!"

Hunt was about to suggest to VISAR that it ought to make them different colors or something, when another Danchekker filled the space behind the bar that the first had just left. The first whirled about as if about to be attacked, and the two gaped at each other. More Thuriens were appearing around the room, as had Josef Sonnebrandt, Sandy Holmes, and two copies of Duncan Watt. The chatter among them grew as those with some grasp of what was going on tried to clue in the others. The throng was growing faster than Hunt could keep track of, while at the same time the room enlarged subtly to accommodate it. His alter egos in other universes surely wouldn't be far away from something like this, he told himself, and scanned around. Sure enough, another Hunt was coming across from the area where the seats were, smirking shamelessly. "I see you found the bar first," he said. "What is it, Irish? How close does VISAR get in this universe?"

"Oh, I think you'd find it up to standard." Even after Hunt's brief experience at the Happy Days back on Earth, this was uncanny.

"No doubt. But today I think I'll settle for a beer." A glass appeared obligingly in the away-team's Hunt's hand. "Cheers." He tasted it, nodded approvingly, and seemed about to say something; but then instead, he frowned and stared in obvious puzzlement from one to the other of the two Eesyans, who were talking intently.

"What's wrong?" the Hunt who belonged here asked. "Can't remember which one's yours?"

The other Hunt ignored the flippancy. "I don't get this." He looked again and shook his head. "Neither of them is."

"This is preposterous!" Danchekker's voice came from behind, rising above the rest. The two Hunts turned. Now there were four Danchekkers, all glowering indignantly at the others as if they had no right to be there. Then one of them vanished. Another seemed to change position instantly by several feet.

Hunt turned back in bewilderment to his other self. "What in hell's . . ." But he was talking to thin air. "Where'd he go?" he demanded, cuing VISAR with a mental prompt.

"He disappeared out of the datastream from MP2. I only inject what comes through."

One of the Eesyans had also disappeared; Hunt was too non-plused to know which. A Hunt appeared fleetingly by the bar and was gone again, leaving three Duncan Watts staring in bemusement—then four, then three again, and then back to two.

A new Hunt on the far side of the room was being assailed by a Danchekker who looked like a reincarnation of the first one. The same thing was happening with the Thuriens. The whole room was a madhouse of figures appearing and vanishing, shifting randomly from one place to another, some gesticulating and arguing incoherently.

VISAR came through. "I appreciate that this may not be the best time, Vic, but I've got Lieutenant Polk on the line again and—"

"I've never told a computer to perform impossible biological acts with itself before, VISAR, but . . ."

"Yes, sir! I'll take care of it."

Hunt turned and stared out again at the relay hanging in space, where the datastream that VISAR had referred to was coming from.

Incoherence. . . .

Behind him, the confusion of voices cutting in and out blended into a meaningless hubbub. And then it was gone.

He was back in the recliner in the Waldorf, amid sudden quiet and stillness. For a few seconds he lay savoring the feeling. It was like waking up from an insane dream. But the thought that had started to form was still there.

The images of other persons that VISAR injected into the perceptions of a user coupled into the system were animated by activity monitored in the speech and motor centers in the brain of the individual that the image pertained to. Thus, a user saw and heard what the other users elsewhere thought they were doing and saying. The difference in this case was that a part of the perceptual experience that VISAR was creating for each of the users coupled in to the situation—Hunt, for example—was coming not from the regular Thurien virtual net in this universe, but through the relay device from another universe. Or "universes."

The relay device had to possess some kind of communications channel back to its universe of origin—achieving what the scientists in this universe were still struggling with. And that channel would terminate at some kind of multiporting projector: the other universe's MP2 or equivalent. But that Multiporter was mixing up the pasts represented by different time lines. So the scientists in the universe the relay was from hadn't solved the convergence problem yet.

So why had Hunt been suddenly cut off like this? As far as he could see, the job of generating the composite images would be no different from what VISAR normally did. it shouldn't make any difference where the inputs were coming from. Once the relay materialized, the link to it would function the same as to any other part of the Thurien h-net. Having clarified that much, he called up VISAR to check.

"I thought you didn't have technical hitches."

"*I* don't. But something was obviously wrong with the experiment that you bioforms were conducting at the other end. They pulled the plug."

"You mean that device didn't destabilize and break up?"

"No, they seemed to have that problem licked. It wasn't a dispersion pattern. The whole thing just wasn't there suddenly, as if it had been switched off. Since things were getting a bit out of hand and everyone was confused, it seemed better to terminate the show. There's nothing left to see out there now, anyway."

"You're probably right. But I hadn't even finished my drink."

"Couple back in. I can fix that."

Hunt sat up, swung his legs down, yawned, and stretched. "No, I think that after an episode like that I could use a shot of the real thing. Is anyone else heading that way downstairs?"

"Duncan, Josef, Sandy . . . it seems most of them have the same idea. Be warned, though. It's got Chris Danchekker going."

"Oh, I think I'm used to dealing with that."

Yes, convergence was the most important issue. Nothing else was going to matter much until they had that cracked. Hunt's other self had tried to pass on the right advice, all that way back at the beginning. In view of that, it seemed odd that whoever had sent the device responsible for the recent pandemonium should have fitted it for communications capability while the convergence problem still remained evidently unsolved. Hunt could only suppose that the inhabitants of different universes would find reasons for going about things differently. Or, of course, there was always the possibility that the particular team he was a part of would find out why in good time.

Others were already in the bar area, including a few Thuriens, with a vigorous debate already in progress. Hunt could hear Danchekker remonstrating above the rest as he approached. He wondered if there were other realities out there in the Multiverse

in which the inhabitants had not been so prudent as to operate their MP2 remotely, confining timeline effects to streams of
neurocoupler information, not the actual bodies. If there were,
then the kind of chaos he'd just witnessed could be real, not just
a virtual experience. How would anyone deal with four Danchekkers in their universe, three of them marooned and unable to get
back? It didn't bear thinking about.

CHAPTER TWENTY-TWO

Frenua Showm met with Calazar in "Feyarvon," his official retreat away from Thurios—his counterpart of Showm's "eyrie," where he withdrew from the world of Thurien and its affairs. Its rooms and galleries rose around a central dome from terraces of gardens and groves bounded on the outside by an enclosing arcade—the whole forming a floating island drifting among Thurien's cloud tops. Showm was present physically, clad in the full purple robe and headpiece that signified her formal role. Calazar, likewise, was wearing his gold tunic and green cloak. By long custom this meant that their dealings were between the two offices that they represented, not the persons. Thuriens were able to separate such functions when necessity called for it. Private interests and preferences had no place in administering for the general good.

They walked slowly along beside the parapet wall above the perimeter arcade, flower banks and miniature fruit trees below them on one side, bottomless canyons disappearing down among cloud on the other. "I must say, such second thoughts are about the last thing I would have expected from you of all people," Calazar said. "You have always been one of the most intransigent when it comes to distrusting humans. I'll credit you with being the least surprised of all of us when we finally discovered the deceptions of the Jevlenese. And you were always of the opinion that the Terrans were more than willing pupils of the agents the Jevlenese infiltrated to set them against each other. Doesn't everything you've studied for this history you're working on uphold it? At one point you were all for writing them off as beyond hope, and going ahead with the containment option immediately. It's strange to hear you sounding as if you might be going soft now."

Yes, it was true. Calazar's last remark referred to a measure the Thuriens had been preparing to defend against the insatiable Terran lust for conquest that the exaggerated Jevlenese accounts had painted. It was not the Thurien way, nor in the Thurien nature, to meet a threat of violence with counter-violence. In accord with the colossal schemes they had devised when the occasion demanded, such as building webs of engineering around burnt-out stars, or power distribution grids that spanned sizeable portions of the Galaxy, their response had been to begin the construction of immense g-warp engines that would be positioned in a configuration to create an impassable shell of deformed spacetime enclosing and isolating the entire Solar System. And the Thuriens would have done it. As some previous episodes in Ganymean history had demonstrated, the same faculty that enabled them to divorce professional life from personal factors made them perfectly capable of setting sentiment aside when higher considerations depended on it.

"I admit it," Showm replied. "I don't know how much of Terran history you've studied yourself, Calazar. There are magnificent and stirring chapters, but most of what's recorded, century after century for millennia, is . . ." she shook her head, looking for a word, "horrifying. Even allowing for the Jevlenese distortions, I came to the conclusion that there was simply something inherently wrong in the human condition—Terrans, Jevlenese, all of them. Something innate and incurable, going back to the genetics involved in that biological experiment on Minerva long ago. If that were the case, then we owed it to ourselves and the other races that depend on us to be protected from it. It couldn't be allowed to break out into the Galaxy. But they are sentient living beings nevertheless, and we couldn't destroy them. It was ironic: Although the Jevlenese had been deceiving us to advance an agenda of their own, the solution that it induced us to devise was correct. Except that it didn't go far enough. I would have contained Athena as well." Athena was the star of Jevlen and its companion planets.

"Yes, I remember. So what has caused you to think again? The progress they seem to have been making in more recent times?" It had been Terrans, after all, notably those associated with the irrepressible Dr. Hunt, who had figured so much in the events concerning the Ganymeans. They had gone to extraordinary lengths to save the *Shapieron* from a Jevlenese plot to destroy it, made contact with Thurien, and it had been they who first awakened the Thuriens to what was going on.

It would have been easy for Showm to go along with the rationalization that Calazar was unintentionally offering. But to do so would have meant deceiving him. To speak or imply anything but the truth when functioning in a formal official capacity was unthinkable. Earth had seen periods of hope and apparent progress before, only to slide back again, sometimes to a worse state than had existed before. Their European culture of the late eighteenth and nineteenth centuries had actually concocted a code of what they called "civilized" warfare to the point where by the end of that period some optimistic commentators had seriously believed the end of war and oppression as instruments of human affairs to be within sight. . . . But the century that followed witnessed the two most savage and destructive wars ever, the perfection of industries of mass killing and mass destruction modeled on their methods of mass production, and some of the most murderous and repressive regimes the planet had ever seen. Even America, formerly hailed as the champion of individual freedom and the rule of law, had sunk for a while to plundering small and defenseless, resource-rich countries. It was now fashionable there to blame the Jevlenese and say that epoch was over. Showm would have liked to think so, but the cautious side of her nature overrode the temptation to wishful thinking. No, she couldn't pretend that she was convinced.

What way was there to explain that what had caused her outlook to change, and forced her to look again at habits of thought she had never before questioned, was listening to a lonely Terran woman of little consequence and no influence, tolerated by her cousin and regarded amiably but depreciatingly by her co-worlders as mildly eccentric? Showm replied finally, "We belong to a culture in which work that serves the well-being of all is morally fulfilling in itself. It gives us our sense of worth. To seek personal gain through the loss or detriment of others would be incomprehensible. In a world that lives by such an ethic, truth becomes the rule, and justice follows naturally. So naturally that we take it for granted. Thuriens have no concept of the brutality and suffering that can result from injustice. I hadn't, until I started delving into the story of Earth and saw what happens when injustice becomes not just the norm, but a mark of distinction for those possessing the power to inflict it—to be envied and emulated. . . . I don't want us to risk being guilty of inflicting an injustice, Calazar."

They came to the end of the parapet and entered a small cupola marking an angle in the perimeter wall. Inside was a seat, an intriguing design of tiled mosaics on the walls, and a g-well going down to the arched cloister below. They emerged onto the continuing ambulatory on the far side. Calazar paused to admire the garden below, where one of the staff was cleaning the edge of a fish pond at the base of stepped lawns leading up to the house. Showm allowed him time to ponder on what she had said. He seemed to have no questions or demurrals so far. When they began moving again, she resumed.

"I believed that humans suffered from an inherent, ineradicable flaw. Now I find I can no longer be so certain. They have undergone cataclysms and traumas that our ancestors never knew. I suspect now that something else which once existed and should have flowered might have been destroyed. Something noble and magnificent, with the potential to transcend everything we have become, just as their ability to endure what they have defies our imagination. But it's still there. I see glimpses of it in their tenacity, their determination, the way they will always come back and rebuild again after the worst calamities the universe can throw at them, and refuse to give in against odds that every Thurien would know are impossible. And if so, then perhaps the damage can be undone. We abandoned them when we left them as primitive hominids on Minerva. We abandoned them to the savagery of Earth after Minerva was destroyed. They were denied their right to grow into what they could have become, just as Minerva was. Let us not abandon them again, Calazar. This time, let us show the patience and guidance that we failed to before. We owe it to them. Not the punishment of isolation from the rest of the universe."

"Profound words, indeed, Frenua," Calazar commented, clasping his hands behind his back and glancing out over the clouds.

"I've been doing some profound thinking."

Calazar looked down for a few moments longer, measuring his steps. "But we're not talking about isolating them now. That goes back to the time when we were laboring under the deceptions perpetrated by the Jevlenese."

"The stressors are still there at the construction centers—thousands of them. They're an abomination. It's to our shame that we ever could have conceived such a deed, let alone commenced implementing it. We went against our own nature and let ourselves be corrupted by the Jevlenese."

"They're no more than a precaution now. . . ."

Showm shook her head firmly. "No, Calazar. They represent far more. Their existence says that we have yielded to the same arrogance of power that we condemn in the Jevlenese and in the Terrans: the right to impose our will; to equate superiority of force with superiority of virtue. For us to remain true to ourselves, they must be destroyed."

Calazar frowned and made an appealing gesture, in the manner of one reluctant to explain something that should have been obvious. "But you said yourself, you cannot be certain. The human problem could be impossible to rectify, something that goes all the way back to their origins. What would you have me do, Frenua? You, yourself had the strongest misgivings about our decision to adopt an open policy of making our knowledge available to the Terrans. You said it would only enable them to make more ghastly and powerful weapons. Are you saying now that we should leave them with that capability, but take away our one means of protecting ourselves, should our worst fears prove true? Would you want such weapons unleashed upon the Galaxy?"

"No, of course not. But what remains is a relationship that at the bottom is based on suspicion and distrust. What poisons it is uncertainty. If we knew for a fact that the cause was hopeless, we could avoid the disillusionment that would be inevitable sooner or later by going ahead with the containment option now, and at least be consoled in knowing there was no choice.

"But if we knew we were dealing with a sickness that was acquired, we could commit ourselves positively to a future grounded in optimism—which might well prove to be the most important ingredient for succeeding—without need for an escape option that we have to keep secret, the very existence of which demeans us.

Terrans call it 'burning your boats.' It's a good phrase. It signi-
fies determination and the commitment to press on, without the
choice of being able to run back again."

"It could also be construed as signifying certifiable recklessness,"
Calazar pointed out. "It would be a bit late to decide you'd made
the wrong guess when you've got planets being overrun, looted,
despoiled, blown up, and who knows what else all the way from
here to Sol and out to Callantares, wouldn't it? Your boats are
gone, and a volcano just erupted in front of you. What do you
do then?" Calazar threw out his hands. "We can't be certain. So
we try to be prudent. We're giving the humans the benefit of the
doubt, and yes, I agree we owe it to them. But we have insurance
if we are wrong. We owe ourselves at least that much."

"All of which is inarguable on the basis of the premise that you
advanced to support it," Showm conceded. "But the premise is
invalid. There *is* a way in which we can be certain." She stopped,
compelling Calazar to do likewise and face her directly.

Calazar's features creased into non-comprehension. "How. What
way? What are you talking about?"

"The Multiverse project," Showm said. "What it points to, if it
succeeds, is being able to contact other realms that exist—or have
existed! And I think it will succeed. We already know that it's
possible to reach the time of ancient Minerva." Showm looked at
Calazar unwaveringly. She had never been as serious in her life.
"What were the Lunarians like before Broghuilio and the Jevlenese arrived? Supposedly, they were industrious and cooperative,
but nobody knows for sure. Were they, in fact, and was that the
beginning of a chain of events that changed them? Or is it just
a fable, and were they already showing traits that the Jevlenese
merely exploited? Your argument presumes that we have to try
and guess as best we can. But maybe we will soon possess the
means to know for certain."

CHAPTER TWENTY-THREE

Gregg Caldwell was in trouble on the home front again. His wife, Maeve, said she had told him two weeks before that Sharon Theakston's wedding would be on May 15, before he'd arranged his getaway golfing weekend in Pennsylvania. He was certain he had heard nothing about it. Maeve insisted that he had assured her he wouldn't forget (again). He had no recollection of any such fact. The battle lines at breakfast had been unyielding. She'd said that he must have been in one of these other realities that everyone was talking about. And suddenly Caldwell grasped what Hunt had been getting at in these reports about "lensing" and time lines coming together instead of branching apart.

He was still turning it over in his mind when he came out of the elevator at the top of the Advanced Sciences building after having lunch with some visiting Brazilians, and ambled back to his office. Mitzi was watering the plants in the miniature Thurien rock garden that Sandy Holmes had sent back on behalf of Danchekker. Apparently, Danchekker didn't trust Ms. Mulling to tend it with the requisite love and care until they returned. "Well, at least they haven't turned into monsters that run around the building eating people," Caldwell commented, inspecting the colorful array of fronds, flowers, and cactuslike lobes.

"They seem to thrive here. Francis says it's because Earth has more carbon dioxide. Plant food."

"Thirty years ago they were panicking about it."

"Well, life wouldn't be normal if they weren't panicking us about something. . . . Oh, and you have a visitor." Mitzi indicated the direction of the inner office with a nod. Caldwell took a pace, then stopped.

"It isn't that FBI guy, is it?"

"No, nothing like that. It's Chris's cousin Mildred, on a quick trip back. I took her to lunch. She's got some fascinating stories. I can't wait to see the book."

Caldwell went on through. Mildred was sitting at the meeting table that formed a T with his desk, clad in a long, rust-colored dress and reading some papers in a folder. Her hat, a bag crammed with more folders and what looked like items of shopping, and an equally laden purse were parked on chairs on either side. "Well!" Caldwell exclaimed as he came in. "The surprise of the day. Sorry you had to wait. But I gather Mitzi has been taking good care of you."

"She's wonderful. I hope it's all right . . . my just dropping by like this, unannounced. I've been dashing all over the place and really had no idea what time I'd be this way. I know that someone like you must be always incredibly busy."

"Don't even think about it. You're family around here." Caldwell moved behind his desk and sat down. As luck would have it, she had chosen a good day. "I didn't even know you were in this part of the Galaxy. You, ah, sure get around. Mitzi says it's just a quick visit."

"For a few days. There was a ship leaving to bring some Thuriens for some kind of cultural mission or something, that they want to set up here, and I hitched a ride. They really are *so* obliging. It's not that much different than hopping on a plane from Europe."

"Yes, I know. In South America. The mission. I just had lunch with some people who are connected with it." Caldwell inclined his gaze toward the bag on the chair next to her. "So is it someone's birthday?"

"Oh, no. Just some things I'd made a list of, that I thought I'd pick up while I had the chance. I could probably have arranged for them to be sent somehow, but sometimes the way that you're used to ends up being quicker. These computer procedures can be so confusing—especially when they're automatic, and they think they know what you want better than you do. It seems that every time they *assume* anything, that's when it all goes wrong. I'm particularly wary of anything that calls itself 'smart.' They're always the first things I deactivate if I can. You *know* that the first thing they do will be absolutely stupid. And there's never any way to tell them to just shut up, don't assume anything, and do exactly what I tell you. Although, having said all that, I suppose we're on our way to getting something of our own like VISAR; or maybe having VISAR extended to manage things here too. It could only be an improvement on a lot of the things we've got."

Caldwell was already hearing again some of Danchekker's lamentations. Maybe it was just as well that she was back for only a few days. Otherwise this could go until the dawn of the next ice age.

"Oh dear," Mildred said, either reading something from his face or body language, or else there was some kind of telepathy at work. "I know. Christian tells me. I do tend to prattle on at times."

"Not at all. It's probably part of a feeling that comes with being back home. Although you seem to be making the best of things there. I'm told you're getting along just fine with Frenua Showm."

"Yes . . ." Mildred's manner became more serious. "In fact, it's in that connection that I was hoping to talk to you, Mr. Caldwell. Kind of in that connection, anyway. . . ."

" 'Gregg' is fine. I said you're family here."

"Oh, thank you. . . ." She seemed to hesitate. Caldwell waited. "As a matter of fact, it was the main reason I came back. Yes, I know you have some of those Thurien neurocoupler things at Goddard that can make you as-good-as be there in an instant. But everything that goes through them is handled by VISAR, you see. And even calling on the phone involves VISAR to connect it through . . . oh, I don't know, h-, M-physical, virtual . . . whichever of all those spaces it is. It *is* an alien intelligence, after all, built to serve alien purposes. How do you know where something you say might end up? And what I wanted to talk about is very confidential."

Caldwell raised his eyebrows and did his best to look appropriately solemn. It was a slow afternoon, anyway. In fact, the Thuriens had always given assurances that all communications traffic handled by VISAR enjoyed scrupulous privacy, and from his experience of them he was inclined to believe it. But he wasn't about to get into a pointless debate about it now. "I'm listening," he said, spreading his palms.

Mildred took a deep breath and frowned, as if not sure which of several threads to pursue. "I know it's only been a matter of months, but I've found out a lot about the Thuriens. It's the reason I went there, after all. . . ." She looked up. "But I don't want to go off on another tangent, telling you things you already know. You were involved with them from the beginning. Just to be sure we're talking the same language, what would be the most salient adjectives that come to mind to describe them?"

Caldwell scratched his brow and had to consider. This wasn't an approach he was used to dealing with. Mildred had her own way of cutting through the chaff when it suited her, he had to grant. "Oh, I guess . . . 'advanced'; 'benevolent'; 'nonviolent'; 'honest,'" he offered. "And, I suppose you could say, 'resolute,' when the need arises; 'rational'; 'realistic.'"

"Yes, it's the last ones that are significant. One of the things I've been learning a lot more about has been their history, all the way back since the time of the early Ganymeans. As you say, they're totally nonaggressive in their dealings with each other and with every other kind of race that they've encountered since their migration. Their very nature makes them incapable of anything else. But they've also shown on more than one occasion that when their existence or their way of life is threatened, they can be ruthlessly efficient in protecting themselves. And I use the word 'ruthless' quite deliberately."

She was no doubt referring to such episodes as the program to cleanse Earth of predators in preparation for colonization, which had been aborted and still gave the Thuriens feelings of guilt, and more recently their mind-blowing plan to seal off the Solar System. "I'm familiar with the cases in point," Caldwell said, nodding to head her off from any feeling of needing to explain.

He drummed his fingers on the desk. Mildred stared at them for a second or two, and then said, "When you put those two qualities together, I find it drives one to a rather sobering but inescapable conclusion. Earth's history of warfare and every other kind of violence is totally abhorrent to them. Yet they've seen how rapidly this aggressiveness enables us to advance what we think are our interests. They can have no doubt that with the situation that exists at the present juncture—Earth spreading across the Solar System despite all the attempts of the Jevlenese to prevent it, and now absorbing Thurien technology—a possibility exists that we might carry everything they abhor out among their own system of worlds, but equipped with a destructiveness unlike anything imaginable before." Now she had gotten Caldwell's interest. This wasn't new. He had gone over the same ground many times in his own mind and discussed it with Hunt, Danchekker, and others. It was a regular topic of debate among UNSA executives.

"Go on," he said.

She sighed. "The Thuriens might be benevolent, patient, compassionate, and all those other saintly things, but they are also political realists. They would never expose themselves to such a risk. If it ever started looking like developing into a real threat, there's no way they'd just sit there and let it happen."

Caldwell was beginning to revise his impressions of Mildred rapidly. He had been trying to get this point across to some career diplomats and so-called professionals in international affairs ever since the Pseudowar with the Jevlenese and the events that had led up to it—and that had been with the insights of people like Hunt and Danchekker, who had been involved with the Ganymeans from the beginning. Mildred had worked it out for herself in something like four months. "Do you have any idea what they'd do?" he asked. Naturally enough, that was the first hope that came to mind. But she shook her head.

"I don't know. But from the way things have happened before, once they decide a course of action is necessary, they go all-out. There wouldn't be anything half baked about it."

Again, Caldwell could only agree. He waited for some kind of conclusion to emerge, but that seemed to be it. He reminded himself again that this was something he had been living with every day. For Mildred, it was a new revelation. He sought for a way to acknowledge that the message warranted her coming twenty light-years to deliver. "This is all very interesting," he told her. "You've obviously given it a lot of thought. So I'm curious. Do you have some specific ideas as to what we should do?"

Mildred seemed mildly surprised, as if such a question shouldn't need to be asked. "Well . . ." She turned up a hand, seemingly at a loss for a moment. "I mean, a person like you talks to people in governments everywhere, don't you, and things like that? I'd sort of assumed that if they were sufficiently informed as to the Thurien nature and probable disposition in the event of developments they perceived as threatening, then . . ." she made tiny circular motions in the air, "well, then they'd be able to decide their policies or whatever else they do in an appropriately prudent manner."

Caldwell had to bite his lip to stop himself from smiling. Oh, that the world could be that simple! All it would have taken to avert the procession of disasters called history would have been for someone to tell leaders mesmerized by delusions of their own genius and conquerors drunk on power to behave themselves and think of others first before doing anything rash. "They seem to have been doing better in more recent years," was the best he could find to offer. "It's like anything that involves lots of people and big changes. It can only move at its own speed. We can only be patient and persevere. The way you walk a mile is to just keep putting one foot in front of the other. A city is bricks laid one at a time." It didn't really say a lot, but sounded as if it did. Caldwell could be good with things like that. "But the things you've pointed out are important. You're right. They have to be treated very seriously."

Mildred seemed relieved. "Can I take it, then, that you'll make sure they're conveyed to the places where it will do the most good?" she said. "I'd hate to see us get into some kind of dreadful trouble with the Thuriens, and have to think that it might have been because I'd been there and learned what I have, and then not brought it to the attention of those in a position to put it to the best use."

"You can rest assured of it," Caldwell replied solemnly.

And yet, Caldwell was unable to dismiss their conversation lightly from his mind. It had forced him to bring out into the light and examine things that he knew but had been pushing to the back. Maybe he had been allowing himself to go soft in these latter years of acclaim and seniority. Too much golf, weddings, and black-tie dinners.

He had never been convinced that all of Earth's troubles could be blamed on the Jevlenese. Too many people had seized on the revelations of Jevlenese meddling in human affairs as an excuse to absolve themselves, or their nations, or their creeds, or their ideologies from guilt and responsibility, as if they had never had a part in the crimes that cried out for atonement from every page of history; or if there could be no atonement now, at least for some lessons to be learned that the future might be saved from seeing them repeated. There had been no shortage of native talent willing to share in the work and eager for its share of the spoils. The sure way to seeing those instincts taking charge again would be for Earth to lull itself into assuming the role of innocent victim and believing there was nothing for it to learn, and hence nothing that needed changing.

Owen, before his retirement, had voiced apprehension on more than one occasion about some of the things that came to his attention in the course of his dealings with responsible people in all quarters of the globe. While the world at large gluttonized on self-congratulation and the media reveled in its orgy of alien-centered sensationalism, the familiar rumblings of old hatreds that continued to fester, undercurrents of unrest, and ambitions to domination were still very much alive in the world. The official story, of course, fueling a spirit of public optimism and buoyancy toward the future, was one of leadership reborn, burying hatchets and about to bring the Golden Age in a new light of understanding that external forces had obstructed before. But the heady tone had always struck Caldwell as somehow unreal. What kind of forces might be biding their time at the back of it all, conspicuously on their best behavior while they assessed the redrawn game board and immensely raised stakes that the chance of access to a whole new regime of alien technology represented? Already, items were appearing openly in more outspoken areas of the partisan press and global net likening Terrans to the tiny but ferocious bands that had subjugated the Americas, and claiming that Earth's "moment" was approaching and that its destiny was "out there."

The old quotation ran through his mind again, that the only thing needed for evil to triumph was that good men do nothing. Apart from table talk and agreeing with a lot of people who felt likewise, what had *he* been doing? he asked himself. The short answer was, "not a lot." Like everyone else, when he examined the facts honestly, he had looked to other things to busy himself with, all the time assuming in a vague kind of way that never quite crystallized consciously that "something" would happen.

In the past this had never been his way. He hadn't taken over Navcomms and built it into the largest and most dynamic division of the UN Space Arm by waiting for "things" to "happen." Things didn't just happen. People made them happen. A colleague had asked him once, back in the early UNSA days, if he really thought that a few dedicated people who believed in what they were doing could change the world. Caldwell had replied, "They're the only ones who ever have." Actually, it wasn't his own line; he had come across it as a quote by a woman anthropologist, or something, from way back. But it was a good one, and he didn't think she would have minded his stealing it. His former self was still around, speaking in his head now, asking him what *he* was going to *do* about it.

He was still tussling with the question at home that evening, missing half the things that Maeve was saying and bringing a new precipitation of frost on the domestic scene just when things had begun to thaw. About the only thing he'd done by the end of the evening, to make amends and assuage his conscience, was cancel his golfing fixture.

The next morning, a bottle of brandy arrived for him and a bunch of roses for Maeve, from Mildred. It reverted breakfast to its normal warm and sunny condition, and gave his confidence in human nature a boost after his negative musings. But Mildred had never belonged to that part of humanity whose nature he had ever doubted in the first place.

By the next day, after repeated metaphorical walks around the subject in his head to explore all possibilities and angles, he had satisfied himself that, quaint though it was, Mildred's simple suggestion didn't contain any hidden key that he should have recognized. Embarking on some kind of moral lecture tour through the world's corridors of power was unlikely to achieve anything of note except feed it into the gossip mill that the strain had gotten to Caldwell finally, and possibly—done with all due civility, of course, and the requisite honors for him to cosset in his doting years—cost him his job.

And even if he did get some serious and sympathetic attention here and there, the conflicts of interests were so tangled and the true motivations behind them so guarded that any initiative he might manage to spark would be diluted away by countermands and bureaucratic obstruction long before it cold grow into anything coordinated and effective on an global scale. He should know, having played a significant part in coordinating one of the biggest international ventures of modern times. But the Space Arm had come into being and been able to function as it had precisely because all the financial and political forces aligned behind it had stood to gain. They were unlikely to show the same capacity for concerted action when they saw themselves as being asked to renounce the very opportunities for expanding and diversifying and generally outperforming their rivals that had spurred them before.

Caldwell wasn't going to change human nature or the way it shaped the world; at least, not anytime soon. The only other factor in the equation was the Thurien disposition that viewed humans as violently disposed aliens—to be accommodated generously if their inclinations could be curbed and redirected; but if not . . . who knew what? On the face of it, Caldwell didn't see that he could do much to change that either. It would need something that lessened the distance between them emotionally and psychologically, so that the "alienness" was reduced; that made humans "family," the way he accepted Mildred within his Division of UNSA.

After Minerva's destruction, the Thuriens had shown their capability and potential willingness to form such close ties in the way they had taken the Lambian element of the Lunarians back and tried to integrate them into their civilization—later to become the Jevlenese. But that attempt had been marred by the intrusion of the Ents from the surreal world of computing symbology that came into being inside JEVEX. The Cerians, at their own request, had remained in their own Solar System after being transported to Earth and become the ancestral Terrans. The separation since then had produced the sense of alienism underlying the superficially cordial relations that existed now.

What was needed was some unifying event or experience that would overwhelm all other considerations, something momentous enough in the minds of Thuriens—and humans too—to weld their two races into one with a common future with the kind of affinity the Thuriens had been able to show for the Jevlenese. But what?

Then news came in from Hunt saying that Eesyan's group

of Thurien scientists thought they had cracked the time line convergence problem. If so, it meant they were on the verge of getting coherent information back from other parts of the Multiverse. Caldwell spent several hours in his office, studying the report that followed and pondering on its implications. Slowly, a vision formed in his mind of a time when the gulf that divided them now hadn't existed; a time when the divergent histories of Ganymeans, Terrans, Lunarians, Jevlenese, all came together at a world that had existed long ago.

Enough thinking, he decided then. It was time to give rein to his instincts and circumvent the system. The old Irish adage that "contrition is easier than permission" came to mind. A warm, invigorating feeling of the old Gregg Caldwell moving into action again surged through him. He reached out to his deskside console and entered the code to access Advanced Sciences Division's channel into the Thurien net. VISAR's voice spoke a few seconds later.

"Gregg Caldwell. Hello, it's been a while."

"Yeah, well, you don't have a building full of people and a family at home to run."

"Try a couple of dozen star systems."

"Okay, you've got me. But it's nice to talk again."

"Likewise. What can I do for you?"

"Can you tell me how Calazar is fixed? I need to talk with him. And I'd like it to be face-to-face through the virtual system, not just a call."

"When did you have in mind?"

"Whenever it suits him. I'm free right now."

"Just a second."

Caldwell tapped his fingers absently, imagining a computer out at the other star interrupting an alien in the middle of something right now. It still seemed uncanny. Boy, had the church of Einstein gotten that one wrong.

Then, "Calazar says 'hi and great to hear from you.' He's coupled into the system now, as it turns out. If it's business, how about making it the Government Center in Thurios?"

"Fine. Give me two minutes."

Cadwell got up and walked through to the outer office. Mitzi was away on some errand. He carried on through to the corridor and along to the room where the neurocouplers were installed.

He had thoughts on and off of putting one in his office but hadn't made his mind up yet. Gimmicks to impress visitors wasn't his style, and it would have better use out where it was, available for anyone. He lay back with the feeling it always gave him of being at the dentist's. Moments later he was standing in a brightly decorated room of marble walls, rich furnishings, floor coverings, and draperies, with a window looking out at towers and soaring arches. Calazar was sitting on a couch before a low table with several other seats positioned around it.

"Your timing was excellent. I was just catching up on some reading." The alien stood and gestured at one of the seats. "Join me, please."

No, he was supposed to stop thinking "alien," Caldwell reminded himself. That was what this whole visit was about.

CHAPTER TWENTY-FOUR

VISAR had abandoned its attempts to solve the convergence problem by generating a "quantum signature" unique to a particular universe, by means of which other universes could effectively be locked out. Although the concept was sound enough, it turned out that the amount of information needed to define a stable zone increased exponentially with the size of the zone. This meant that beyond trivial experiments that had little value other than to demonstrate the principle, the amount of calculation necessary to achieve a realistic operating volume capable of supporting anything worthwhile rose rapidly toward infinity, taxing the capacity of even something like VISAR. The Thurien mathematicians held hopes they might find some form of short-cut or algorithm that would render the problem tractable, but they were the first to admit that as of now they had no clear idea of what they were looking for, and the search for a solution, if one existed at all, could well take years.

The breakthrough came from a completely unexpected direction that didn't involve mathematicians or advanced theoreticians at all, but space propulsion engineers. Thurien spacecraft operated by an advanced form of the drive employed in the *Shapieron*, going back to the early days of Ganymean Minerva, whereby the ship was carried inside a propagating "bubble" of distorted spacetime. Whereas modern Thurien vessels drew their power from the interstellar grid beamed through h-space, the *Shapieron* used its own onboard generators. Some of Eesyan's group had been looking into the separate problem of maintaining coherence of the standing wave that defined an object projected out across the Multiverse, hence halting it. The method worked, but it was unstable. After a brief existence ranging so far from fractions of a second to a minute or so, the wave would break up—not observed directly, but inferred from observations of objects arriving from other universes that had done so in this one.

Eesyan's scientists had approached the space-drive designers to find out more about how this bubble was created, their thought being that something like it might be contrived to contain the standing wave pattern in such a way that would prevent it from dispersing. It seemed, when they looked into it, that adapting the technique to M-space should be fairly straightforward—it involved a longitudinal form of the same type of wave that the engineers had long experience of dealing with. But when preliminary experiments were run at Quelsang to investigate the creation of M-space bubbles, a completely unexpected result was observed.

An M-space bubble apparently kept time-line convergences contained, restricting them to the inside. Even when Eesyan gave approval for the machine's power to be cautiously increased to a level where convergences had occurred outside the transfer chamber before, nothing was detected. Tests showed that the effect was still there, but confined inside the bubble sitting in the center of the chamber. Outside, the chaos of events and objects with different past histories all being present at the same time and place was eliminated. Nobody was quite sure how this came about, which would no doubt provide the theoreticians with another area of contention that that might keep them occupied for years. But it wasn't the first time, either for Thuriens or for Terrrans, that a practical solution to a problem had preceded the appearance of an elegant theory explaining why it worked.

So the convergence problem was apparently solved—or at least, acceptably contained. When the bubble was combined with the transfer wave function as part of the pattern projected across the Multiverse, it turned out that it did indeed achieve the original aim of confining dispersion as well. So an object sent into another universe could now be induced to remain there.

Creating a bubble required a considerable input of energy.

Suitable sources couldn't be carried in the tiny test objects used in the Quelsang experiments, or even the probes being projected from MP2, which were still little more than compact signaling beacons. The method developed, therefore, was to stretch the bubble created at the projector to suppress time line convergence into an elongated filament that the projected wave function expanded at the far end to enclose the test object as well. The bubble thus took an extended dumbbell form of two contained zones connected by a filament that carried the energy to sustain the surface at the far end. When bubble experiments were performed on the transmitters being projected from MP2, it was found that the filament also acted as a conduit for the signal sent back, which if intercepted outside the trapped convergence zone, could be decoded coherently. The filaments were dubbed "umbilicals."

The nice thing about it all was that once the object had consolidated and stabilized, the energy previously fed through to maintain the pattern was no longer required, and the bubble could be switched off. It "really" existed there, in the other universe, and although there was no way of testing it yet, theory indicated that it should thereafter be capable of interacting independently with its surroundings and moving around in them freely.

Although an exemplary achievement, all this was still akin to firing an artillery shell blind and knowing it had landed somewhere. To say where would require knowing something about the surroundings and circumstances that it had landed in. But at least the scientists were now in a position to decode intelligibly any information that was sent back. The next step would be to project objects large enough and complex enough to send back more than just an identification code.

It was something like a reversed form of deja vu. There was the eerie feeling of having been through this before, but this time Hunt was on the other side of it.

He sat in the tower block lab, surrounded by exotically styled equipment, getting used again to the experience that he realized had become unfamiliar, of looking at a hard screen that was really there in front of him. The Thuriens hardly ever used them. What was the point in constructing hardware when the same effect could be generated more easily and with more versatility inside the viewer's head? But for these tests the Thurien scientists had wanted to be sure of capturing exactly what was seen and heard at the far end of the connection.

A half dozen or so of them sat or stood around the room, waiting and watching curiously. The Terrans were there too, with the exceptions of Danchekker, who was meeting with some Thurien philosophers to discuss his theory of consciousness, which he was still developing, and Mildred, away on one of her excursions into the city. The terminal was linked to the MP2 facility, several hundred thousand miles away, which was now fitted with its own internal bubble generator to contain convergence effects. With convergence suppressed, a small staff of researchers and technicians had been installed at MP2 to prepare the various configurations of instruments being despatched. However, the data transmissions back from the instruments were usually relayed to Thurien for monitoring and analysis.

VISAR reported, "The probe platform is stabilizing." On the screen, an image formed of stars in a black background of space. Murmurs came from around the room. Some of the occupants moved closer behind Hunt, although the screen content was being copied neurally via avco. The view slid by as instruments on the probe scanned their surroundings. Earth appeared from an upper corner, showing the Atlantic hemisphere, and moved toward the center, bringing the Moon into view as a three-quarter crescent on one side.

"Right on!" a Thurien voice approved somewhere nearby.

"It makes me feel quite homesick," Sonnebrandt said to nobody in particular.

VISAR announced, hardly necessarily, "Target location is confirmed. It's where we wanted it to be. Starfield distribution and positions of visible planets are consistent with specified time frame.

"Unbelievable!" Chien whispered.

VISAR again: "And we're picking up communications. Processing for system codes and message protocols. This may take a few seconds."

Duncan: "I'd thought we were still months away from anything like this."

Sandy: "These guys are good."

A Thurien: "You ain't seen nothing yet."

Another Thurien: "What does that mean?"

"An Earth saying that my children picked up. Like it?"

VISAR's previous efforts to construct quantum signatures had turned out to be not entirely fruitless. Although failing to achieve the original purpose, the logic of groups and sets that they were based on provided the basis for a method of "mapping" the Multiverse by space and time coordinates, and introducing a measure of "affinity" that could be derived from a virtually an unlimited number of dimensions and grew less as universes became progressively more "different." Exactly in what kind of way they were different, and how rapidly that varied, could only be determined by sending things to various places, trying to make sense of what they found there, and calibrating the results to some kind of scale. The task was probably in a similar league to that of a medieval cartographer of village streets and farms setting out to map the world, and would probably take years to develop into a working, quantitative science, if not generations. But, as with Shakespeare and the alphabet or Beethoven and the basic inversions of C major, everything had to start somewhere. Hunt was amazed that from all the unthinkable permutations and variants making up the Multiverse, they were able to come anywhere near this close at all.

For he was not looking just at the familiar Earth, twenty light-years away across space, that they had come from. It was Earth—an Earth—as it had been, if the crude scaling factors that represented the best that could be achieved so far were to be believed, a little less than six months previously. That would put it at not long before the Tramline group's departure—assuming that anything of such a nature had happened, or was even possible, on the world they were looking at. But the fact that they were picking up recognizable communications traffic meant that at least it wasn't a version of Earth that had blown itself up in one of the twentieth century's fits of paranoia or never managed to get beyond windmills and horses in the first place.

"London, Paris, Lisbon, Boston, New York, Rio de Janeiro are all where they should be and looking normal," VISAR reported. "We have indications of lunar bases. Lots of comsats in the synchronous belt." He shouldn't be so amazed, really, Hunt reflected. They had set the parameters that they thought determined the affinity to be pretty close. But even so, it was amazing.

"I think you might be about to go on stage, Vic," Duncan called across.

"Okay, we're into a comnet trunk beam," VISAR told them. "This is looking good. Library structure and directory listings look familiar. UNSA is there . . . Advanced Sciences at Goddard, yes . . . Dr. Victor Hunt, Deputy Director, Physics. You didn't get hit by a truck. Temporal calibration is not bad: We're within five days. Do we go with it?"

There was no reason to doubt it, but etiquette required Eesyan to confirm. "Carry on." He was patched in from somewhere in Thurios.

"Call is connecting. . . ."

Hunt felt a curious mixture of feelings: excitement; still more than a little incredulity; a delicious sense of impending mischief that the Thuriens didn't quite seem to understand but went along with; the tension that came with a glimmer of fear that it might still all mess up now. "Think I'll get an encore?" he asked Duncan, who was now a couple of feet away.

And then the view on the screen changed to show . . . none other than Duncan Watt! The Duncan next to Hunt froze, unable to do more than stare. Hunt waited for a reaction. "Yes, Vic?" A bit anticlimactic, Hunt had to admit. Then the face on the screen knotted in puzzlement. "There's a Thurien behind you. What's going on?"

"Wait till you see who's next to me." Hunt motioned for the nearer Duncan to move into the viewing angle. And Duncan ruined Hunt's act. He had read the transcript of Hunt's original encounter with his own alter ego enough times to know it by heart. Hunt had been saving the line for his other self in this universe—assuming they found him. But Duncan stole it!

"I suppose this must come as a bit of a shock."

Alter-Duncan stared back blankly. He didn't seem able to find any words. Nobody had really expected that he would. "It would take a lot of explaining," Hunt said. "But to give you a hint, think of the work that the Thuriens are doing right now, if my guess is right, to unravel what went on when Broghuilio and his bunch got catapulted across the Multiverse. Let's just say for now that we here are a little way ahead of you. Getting the drift?" The image, still glassy-eyed, managed to return a stupefied nod. "Good. In a nutshell, we've projected a relay into orbit there that's hooked into the comnet and is converting to Multiverse language. A data package should have transferred itself with this call that goes into it all. But while we're through, I was hoping to talk to me; that is 'your' me. Is he around? . . . Duncan, come on, snap out of it. You have to be prepared for some weird stuff if you're going to mess around with this kind of thing. Believe me, it gets worse. Pay particular attention to the part that talks about convergences. Is Vic around there anywhere?"

Duncan found his voice finally, "He's over in ALS . . . with Chris Danchekker."

"Put me through, then, would you? There's a good chap. Sorry it couldn't have been longer. Just saying hi as a courtesy, really."

"Yes. Of course. . . . Er . . . I'll put you through."

"See you around," the calling-end Duncan said automatically, then thought about it. "Well, probably not, actually."

In setting up a file giving the background information, they had prepared themselves better than seemed to have been the case with the group the original Hunt had represented. But then again, that group looked as it had still been working on the stability issue and so perhaps they hadn't been worried about the finer points just yet.

Sandy Holmes took the call in Danchekker's lab over in Alien Life Sciences. She stared uncertainly out from the screen for a second or two, jerked her head around to look back over her shoulder, then at the screen again. "What is this?" she muttered half to herself. "A recording? Is it some kind of joke? Hey, guys, who is this?"

"No, not a recording or a joke. it's me, Vic," Hunt said. "I'm looking for Vic."

He could read Sandy's mind: *The image is interacting. He's real.* She wrestled with the conundrum, gave up, and turned her head again. "Chris, Vic. . . . Come and look at this." The Sandy watching from a few feet behind Duncan just smiled. She didn't try to muscle in by repeating Duncan's routine of a minute earlier. There would be plenty more times. Two more faces appeared on the screen: Hunt, matter-of-fact; Danchekker looking irritable, as if he had been interrupted in the middle of something. "It's not a recording," Sandy informed them. "It interacts."

"Yes, it does. Try me," Hunt offered.

Danchekker blinked rapidly several times through his spectacles, then turned to the Hunt who was with him, "What kind of stunt is this, Vic? If it has a point, I'm afraid it eludes me. We really do have a lot to get through."

The other Hunt shook his head helplessly. "No, honestly, Chris, I don't know any more than you do. It's got nothing to . . ." He looked back from the screen as an answer suggested itself. "It has to be a VISAR creation. VISAR, are you in on this? What's the idea?"

"I am, but only as the phone operator. It isn't a creation," VISAR's voice replied on the circuit. In an aside voice that was clearly for local ears only, it inquired, "Do you want me to tell him?"

"Sure," Hunt said.

"It's you. Or another one of you, that is. We're plugged into your comnet from orbit from Thurien. Another Thurien, that is."

Hunt could almost hear the thoughts racing through his other self's head. "A Multiverse version?" the image said finally. "MV cross-communication? Does that mean you've cracked it?"

Cheers and applause came from all around. VISAR showed a copy of the panned view it was sending through of the room full of Thuriens and Terrans.

"Extraordinary!" Danchekker pronounced weakly.

The subsequent exchange followed roughly the lines it had with Duncan, but going into a little more detail.

The package of technical data was just a gift thrown in as a goodwill gesture. The people in the universe sending it could derive no benefit, since they of course possessed the information already. The real purpose of this series of tests, which would visit other versions of both Earth and Thurien, and of which this was just a beginning, would be for VISAR to extract as much reference information as it could collect describing the universe that the probe had arrived in—physical characteristics; geography; history; political and social organization; technology; arts; customs; anything that could be accessed in the time available. By correlating the results of many such searches with the settings programmed in at the projector, it was hoped to build up an enormous database that would enable the "affinity" parameter to be interpreted in more everyday-meaningful terms. The phone chat really wasn't necessary. In fact, most of the planned tests omitted it. It could only get repetitive, and the novelty would doubtless wear off very quickly. But in the meantime, the impulse to try a few just to see the results had been irresistible. It also explained, perhaps, why the original alter-ego of Hunt had been so agreeably chatty.

Hunt refrained from saying anything about investment tips for Jerry Santello. It looked as if his other self was going to have more than enough to think about. And besides, he wasn't really that sure himself what the Formaflex business was all about.

Now that it was possible to identify where and when a projected probe had arrived at, this series of tests also enabled another prediction of Multiverse theory to be verified. An intriguing thought that had occurred to everybody involved was that sending probes ahead in time to closely related universes sounded like the next best thing to being able to read the future. The energy balance equations, however, said it wasn't quite so simple. The resolution of uncertainty that events unfolding in the forward direction of time represented took form in the second law of thermodynamics, expressed as increasing entropy. Multiverse physics related entropy and energy in such a way that projecting into another universe required more and more energy as the time of the target reality came closer to "now" at the sending end, becoming infinite when the time difference became zero. In other words, an energy barrier seemed to exist that precluded peeking into the future. Whether that too might be broken one day, no one was prepared to say or even guess. The tests at MP2 confirmed, however, that the restriction was very real for the time being.

True, the transmissions from probes projected back in time were traveling across the Multiverse and into their future. But the MV equations talked about the projection energy of the defining wave function, not the subsequent flow of signal energy and information. In their case this had been supplied from the sending end.

CHAPTER TWENTY-FIVE

If Porthik Eesyan had been of an inclination to place bets, he would just have lost out spectacularly. Betting on outcomes of events was not a habit among Thuriens, and they had nothing comparable to organized gambling on sports; but it was catching on as part of the general Terran influence. Although he had wished his scientists well, his personal belief had been that it was too early yet to expect coherent communications with another part of the Multiverse. They had barely finished the tests after installing the bubble generator at MP2, and that was little more than the original lab prototype, patched and modified as experience was gained and then hastily rushed out as soon as the first consistent results were confirmed. But the instrumentation people, inspired by the glimpses they had caught of probes actually arriving from other realities, had already been pressing ahead with designs of sensor packages and communications relays of their own. When the bubble turned out to be the answer to convergence, there had been no restraining them. It wasn't like the old days of orderly, planned and controlled progress at all. Eesyan put it down to another example of Terran influence making itself felt—this time inside his own department!

Terrans!

Like most Thuriens, he still hadn't arrived at a final analysis concerning this race of emotional, opinionated, aggressive and squabblesome, pink-to-black dwarves. The aspect of them that troubled Frenua Showm was their violence—appalling enough, to be sure; and how it could be elevated to being admired as a virtue, with honors bestowed for proficiency in commanding it and whole industries devoted to optimizing its results, was a question that was surely the proper province only of psychiatrists. But Showm was a sociologist of exo-cultures and a political historian, and factors like that were central to her work. That side of Terran nature rarely affected Eesyan directly. The side of them that was more apparent from the standpoint of scientific advisor and research director, especially with regard to the conduct of this joint project he was now committed to, was their impulsiveness.

The traditional Thurien ways might seem slow and cautious by comparison, but they were solid and reliable. In the Great Age of expansion, when Minerva had been left to the Lunarians, who subsequently destroyed it, earlier generations of Thuriens had built the cores of the huge cities, created the foundations of the network that grew into VISAR, and engineered an energy conversion and distribution system that connected far-flung star systems. All of these creations did what they were designed to do, and they didn't fail. No Thurien engineer could have conceived how things could be otherwise. Would a chef be acceptable who only poisoned the odd guest or two occasionally? Eesyan had heard stories from Earth of equipment being installed with known flaws, vehicles going out of control, structures falling down—usually through overzealous pursuit of their upside-down value system that rewarded ownership of wealth more than the creation of it—but what went on there was their business.

When it started impacting programs that he was responsible for, however, it was another matter. To have come from the first successful experiments at Quelsang to launching a functioning communications probe from MP2 in six months was, to Eesyan's mind, unpardonably reckless. The greatest factor contributing to the success had been pure luck, and looking back, it had been thanks to nothing more that no irremediable consequence of convergence had been experienced at Quelsang before they realized what was happening—such as being stuck with a duplicate of somebody marooned from another universe. And even then, he had been so touched himself by the rush of enthusiasm that he had let himself be persuaded to order just that the power be reduced, when the correct thing would have been to shut everything down until they had some idea of what they were doing. He attributed it to the Terrans. They could exhibit failings and live with consequences that would condemn a Thurien to a lifetime of dejection and remorse. Most Thuriens deplored it, although some saw it as a strength that it would serve them to have more of themselves at times—for instance, over the ongoing hangups about some of the actions of their distant ancestors. Eesyan had no firm opinion either way. What he did know just at this point, however, was that he wasn't sure how to deal with it.

He was on his way to see Calazar, at Calazar's request, and was fairly certain it was in connection with Showm. He had followed Hunt's dialogue with the probe while in a g-line conveying him through Thurios to the Government Center. That the meeting with Calazar was to be face-to-face rather than conducted virtually meant it was more than just casual or routine business. More than likely, Eesyan suspected, it had something to do with the semiannual convening of the Grand Assembly, a formal affair involving delegates not only from the Provinces of Thurien but the various dependency worlds and major off-planet habitat groupings as well, due to commence in two days time. Having known Calazar for as long as he had, Eesyan had been forming the impression for some time that Calazar had been saving something important that he intended to announce at the occasion.

Eesyan's guess was that it had to do with the proposal Showm had put to Calazar a while ago now, and brought up again at intervals since, to send a series of sophisticated reconnaissance probes back to Minerva as it existed before the Lunarian schism that led to the final, fatal war. She wanted to find out if the usual depiction of the Lunarians as a cooperative and progressive race up until that time was accurate, or just a popular myth. Supposedly, it would answer the question of whether Terran paranoia and violence were inherent parts of their nature or aberrations caused by their experiences, and therefore, conceivably, redressable. If the latter, then the Thurien policy, she argued, should be one of total commitment to compassion and working positively toward establishing Earth as a member of the galactic community, with no room for talk of shutting them off from it. "Total" commitment meant dismantling the containment option. The first time he heard this, Eesyan had been astonished. Frenua had always been one of the staunchest hard-liners.

The stream of Thurien figures that Eesyan was flowing with entered a labyrinth of ports, tunnels, and multifarious interconnecting spaces extending in all directions in the lower levels of the Center. Local gravity at any place came with the architecture, and individuals detached and merged and sped away above, below, and all around. Terrans were invariably lost in seconds. Eesyan diverted toward a shaft leading up into the main body of the building.

He was against the idea. For one thing, Frenua and the advocates she had rallied were underestimating the technical problems wildly—although this might be a difficult point to convince them of in view of the successes that had recently been achieved. Sending simple instrument packages obviously wouldn't tell them the kinds of things that Showm wanted to know. It would require accessing libraries and archives in the way VISAR had just demonstrated, and that in turn presupposed connecting into the communications system. But achieving that with a closely related version of Earth that was only six months old—and Eesyan was surprised that even that had worked—was a very different matter from doing something comparable with a Minerva of fifty thousand years ago. At least the style of technology, codes, access procedures and a whole host of other factors relating to Earth were familiar, even if some of the details differed—and resolving even those had been far from a trivial matter, even for VISAR. What they would be up against in the case of Minerva, they had absolutely no idea. Nothing about the Lunarian practices or conventions at that time was known. Thuriens were reluctant to use the word "impossible"—they had managed quite a few things in the end, in their own plodding way, that left Terrans speechless—but in this instance, Eesyan thought it came close.

But more than that, this was still basic research science into a whole new realm of physics. The focus for now should be on that. Treating it as a tool to acquire historical background information for formulating a political policy would be altogether premature in the present circumstances—and open to a lot of questioning on principle at the best of times. Even if Showm's sudden change of heart should be proved to be solidly based, and the early Lunarians were ascertained to have been peaceable, it didn't follow that the humans existing today were necessarily redeemable. Eesyan didn't think Calazar would be right to abolish the insurance that the containment option provided, and he wouldn't want to play a part in inducing him to do so. Some thought that the question as to how much was inherent in human nature has already been answered by the record of the Jevlenese—but their situation was complicated by the invasion of the Ents, and so in Eesyan's estimation it didn't count one way or the other.

And finally, as was the habit most Thuriens learned from an early age, he had tried to examine his own motives without prejudice. A large part of his attitude, he had to concede, sprang from the desire to keep Thurien science pure, the way he had been trained to, which meant exercising control. He didn't want to let it become a part of the carnival of sensationalism and celebrity that he had seen passed off as science on Earth. There were exceptions, to be sure—Hunt and his group were a notable example; were it not so, they wouldn't be here—but the extent that Eesyan had seen, both in current practice and the historical record, of evidence being blatantly manipulated to support preconceptions, or argument from theory determining what was permissible as fact, appalled him. How scientists could rationalize the defense of ideas that were demonstrably wrong in pursuit of personal gain and undue credit was beyond him. To Thuriens, science brought its own reward by adding to the understanding of reality. Publicity, fame, and accolades could only make a scientific theory popular. They couldn't make it true.

The shaft deposited him in an atrium area built around a tree growing up from the levels below, with crystal-walled galleries and corridors leading away to various halls and administrative offices. Calazar had arranged for them to meet in the chambers of the staff preparing for the Assembly, where he would be today, checking on the arrangements. An aide greeted Eesyan in the ante-room, exchanged pleasantries, and offered him refreshments, which was the customary courtesy. Eesyan declined, and the aide conducted him through to a small meeting room at the rear. As Eesyan had anticipated, Frenua Showm was there too.

"Porthik!" Calazar extended both hands—his usual ebullient self; even more so. Eesyan was at once on guard. "I trust the day finds you well."

"As much so as I find in the day. And yourself, Bryom?"

"Never better." Calazar paused while Eesyan bowed toward Showm.

"Too rare a pleasure."

"A shared one, I assure you."

"We saw the news from Quelsang," Calazar said. "Congratulations indeed, Porthik! A splendid success. And entertaining! If only more of science could be that way. Do you think we could arrange for me to talk to a different version of myself in another universe too . . . in some future test like that?"

"Well . . . I don't see why not."

"I'd just like to see the look on his face. Vic was obviously enjoying himself. Yet I'm told that you didn't think it would work. Is that right?"

This wasn't going the way Eesyan had expected. The atmosphere was too convivial, too light—not right for the heavy clash of opinions that he had been bracing for. But Calazar's question gave him as good an opening for the kind of line he had prepared, he supposed. "The truth is, we were extremely lucky," he replied. "Far luckier than we had any right to hope for. The convergence suppressor at MP2 is the experimental prototype, barely tested. It shouldn't have been rushed out there in such haste, and a staff installed. We're violating all the principles. I accept that it's my responsibility, and I have no excuse to offer. Managing a mixed Thurien-Terran team seems to bring complications that I don't pretend to understand yet."

"Grave words," Calazar commented. Eesyan had the feeling that it hadn't come as a great surprise.

"It's a serious business. I can only state the situation as I see it."

"What would you recommend?"

"A thorough reappraisal of the physics, commencing with a recapitulation of the low-power phase at Quelsang. A moratorium on all further experiments at MP2 until we have consolidated our thoughts and plans. Replacement of the suppressor by a properly engineered and tested device when results from Quelsang permit." Eesyan drew a breath. What was to have been his whole argument had compressed itself into a few words. Might as well see it through, he decided. "It's more than a recommendation, Calazar. If I am to retain the capacity of director of this project, I must insist. Otherwise, I would have no choice but to step down from taking further responsibility."

Calazar and Showm glanced at each other. Well, that had put things clearly enough, they seemed to say. Eesyan waited for the querying and cajoling to begin. "It does seem that we got a bit carried away, doesn't it?" Calazar replied. "I mean everybody—myself included. I think you're right. Absolutely right. The house needs to be put in order from the ground up. We must never stray from our standards of excellence and professionalism."

"Don't take it as a personal lapse, Porthik," Showm said. "I've heard from the other scientists that It's been affecting all of them. A firm lead is exactly what they want."

Showm wasn't coming across as somebody in the process of consigning a pet project to oblivion. Her manner was detached and casual, as if it had never been more than a passing curiosity. Eesyan was off balance. He sensed that something more was afoot. "It goes without saying, of course, that this will put all thought of sending reconnaissance probes to Minerva on indefinite hold," he pointed out, more to test their reaction than to tell them anything they wouldn't already know.

"Which should please you," Showm said. "You were never keen on it anyway."

Eesyan looked perplexedly from her to Calazar. Calazar waved a hand dismissively. "Ah. . . . And what could it have achieved, really? You told us yourself how improbable it would be for us to learn anything meaningful about Minerva that way. Creeping about, spying and eavesdropping from the sky. . . . Didn't we have enough of that with the Jevlenese? And then what, even if we did? Suppose we should find answers to our questions there—Minerva before its downfall, hopeful and unsuspecting, yet with the whole ghastly story of war, destruction, catastrophe, and the aftermath all lying ahead of it. What do we do after we've collected, sorted, categorized, and catalogued our data in tidy charts and reference bases? Just pull out the probes and leave them to it like laboratory animals that have served their purpose—billions of unborn to the story of anguish, pain, torment, and slaughter that will unfold . . . for millennium after murderous millennium?"

Calazar looked expectantly toward the door. It opened to admit a house platter, which glided in to deliver a serving of *ule* with a selection of confectionaries. Timed exactly to allow him time to absorb the message, Eesyan noted.

"I didn't mention this at the time, because I wanted to reflect and be sure," Calazar said, rising to set out the dishes from the tray, as befitted the host. "Some time ago, I had a visit from Gregg Caldwell."

Now it was all taking another unexpected turn. "Vic Hunt's superior," Eesyan said, more to give himself a moment to adjust again.

"Yes. The man who was one of the driving forces that turned Terrans' energies away from violence and destructiveness, and instead hurled them out across the Solar System; who directed the investigations that led to their rediscovery of their past and the rescue of the *Shapieron*, and kept his head after they eventually made contact with ourselves, when many others on both sides were yielding to fears and suspicions that would have led us to a very different situation today." Showm flinched slightly, but Eesyan didn't think Calazar had intended it personally. Calazar handed Eesyan a goblet mixed in the way he knew from experience was to Eesyan's taste. "The *kessaya* are very good." He gestured toward the tray.

"Maybe in a moment. . . . Thank you."

Calazar went on, "A person not only of rare vision, but also with the even rarer gift of being able to turn visions into reality. Who dares to dream, and can make dreams come true. Well, Caldwell came to me with a dream. . . . Are you sure you won't try the *kessaya*?"

Eesyan had a fleeting urge to throw them at him. He shook his head.

"Terrans like him epitomize all that's positive about their race: the dynamism; the restless energy; the refusal to give in even when the cause is hopeless, and yet win. Look at what can happen in just a few decades when they turn their aggressiveness upon constructive ends."

Such thoughts weren't exactly new to Eesyan. He had discussed them on many occasions, with Showm among others. "Truly extraordinary," he agreed. They had come across nothing else like it in all the worlds they had reached.

"And we Ganymeans embody another set of qualities that are every bit as laudable," Calazar said. "You put them succinctly yourself just a few minutes ago: caution and thoroughness; commitment to excellence in all things; dignifying of the moral over the material. We've seen what each of these combinations has achieved on its own. But can you imagine, Porthik, what they might be capable of *together*?"

Eesyan looked at Showm, who was watching him intently. She seemed to be brimming with things to say of her own, but just at this instant not wanting to interrupt Calazar's stride. Eesyan wondered if he was missing a point somewhere. "Yes, I hear what you're saying," he said, turning back to Calazar. "But isn't that what we have? The Jevlenese menace has been uncovered and neutralized. Earth is showing signs that it might have mended its ways finally. They seem to be absorbing our science and adapting to our technology. . . ."

Calazar waved a hand and shook his head rapidly. "That isn't what I meant. What we have is Earth with all its scars and bruises and blemishes, and us on the other side of a divide that began opening tens of thousand of years ago, struggling to get to know each other again like adult siblings that were separated in childhood. I'm talking about the potential that existed with the human race as it existed *then*, before they were forced back to animal survivalism, and then had their recovery sabotaged; when no gulf existed. Where might Thuriens and a race like that be today, do you think? Still striving to trace the origins of the codes that direct life, to discover what agency devised them and for what purpose? Or would we long ago have become fully alive and conscious beings, knowing ourselves and our role in the multiplicity of realities that we are even now just beginning to glimpse?"

Eesyan had a sudden, jolting premonition of where this might be going. He licked his lips and glanced at Showm again. She nodded as if reading his thoughts. "And it was the lead we got from Terrans that put us on the right track, even now," she reminded him.

Calazar became expansive. "I'm not talking about sending probes and prying eyes, and sitting back here like gawkers at some awful Terran movie, passively watching the Lunarians marching toward their fate. I'm talking about *going there*, to the time before the war ever happened, and *doing something* to change it!"

Eesyan reached for one of the *kessaya* and unwrapped it shakily. Just for the moment, his mental faculties seemed to have seized up.

"Think of it, Porthik!" Showm urged. "The full, true potential of humans and Thuriens in combination, that should have been realized—just as the potential for Minerva should have been realized. A whole new reality that was meant to exist. It still can. We can create it!"

For a brief moment the sweet, smooth taste of the candy distracted Eesyan from the turmoil of his thoughts. Minutes ago, Calazar and Showm had agreed that the current program had gone beyond the bounds set by prudence and needed tighter control. Yet what they were proposing instead exceeded it in boldness and audacity on a scale that took his breath away. Objections poured into his mind reflexively.

They wouldn't be "creating" anything; the physics of quantum reality said that everything that could possibly exist did exist.... But no. He checked himself. That was according to the old way of assuming things, arrived at from a literal interpretation of the mathematical formalism. Danchekker had produced some good reasons for supposing that the intervention of consciousness was able to change that, making some futures by no means automatic. Rebellious Terran thinking again. It had started a furious debate among the Thurien philosophers. Perhaps it was possible to bring about whole new futures through an effort of volition, that otherwise wouldn't have existed. At their present stage of knowledge, there were no grounds to exclude it.

"It's . . . it's . . ." Eesyan gestured weakly and looked from one to another. "Do you realize the immensity of what you're saying? . . . We've just agreed that even the present project is in drastic need of complete overhaul. What we're talking about here is on a totally different scale of—"

"We've agreed that we need to stop what we're doing and get back to a program of sound, professionally managed research and solid engineering," Calazar cut in. "Perfect. That means we can begin from the basics, observing all the right principles."

Eesyan extended his hands pleadingly. "It's not just a question of technicalities. You're talking about sending *people* . . . Thuriens, Terrans, both; I don't know . . . not just robots. The whole underlying philosophy changes. They'd need autonomy to be able to adapt to whatever local conditions they encounter—to provide for their own safety, or even survival. So they'd have to go in some kind of ship. But they wouldn't even be able to move around. Ships draw on the h-grid for power. There was no h-grid at Minerva fifty thousand years ago."

Showm seemed to have been expecting it. "You're forgetting one ship that doesn't need the h-grid," she said. Eesyan looked at her blankly, his mind in too much of a whirl to make the connection. "The *Shapieron*. Right now, at Jevlen. An old Ganymean starship with independent onboard drives, everything self-contained."

"But even if we did what you say . . . the totality of the Multiverse is so vast. They would be so few. Could it make any difference that matters?"

"What are you saying, Eesyan?" Showm chided. "That sounds like some kind of petty profit-and-loss accounting that you would expect from Earth. Do you not feed a hungry child because you cannot feed all of them? Do you let a sick person die because there are other sick people in the world that you can't help? Our very concept of civilization lies the principle of caring, compassion, and love being extended outward from the primitive family to embrace a progressively wider community: town and village, then nation, planet, until today we feel kinship across many worlds. Isn't this the next step that whatever power brought all this into being is calling us to? Imagine, a community of universes that were isolated, just as the stars were once isolated. Where it will lead, or what will one day come out of it, nobody can say. We will be true pioneers and discoverers again. That is why we have no choice."

Objections started welling up inside Eesyan again, but then he met Frenua's eyes. They were bright, inspired, shining with a light that he hadn't seen anywhere for a long time. He could sense the same intensity of feeling radiating from Calazar. Something inside Eesyan the scientist was responding to it. And as it grew and swelled deep down inside his being, the negative fixations that had gripped him seemed to shrink to dimensions fitting to the business of a jobbing-shop clerk.

Visions were stirring in his own mind now, of the Ganymeans long ago who had cast out from the havens of their warm, familiar-sun systems into the daunting voids between, who had dared to dream of constructions the size of moons and taming the power of exploding stars. Were the unknowns and the challenges that they had faced any less than of the prospect that was beckoning now? Could the things they stood to gain and to learn have been any greater?

"*Yes!*" he heard himself whisper. It was involuntary—not he speaking, but the spirit that was motivating him inside; yet even as he the word, he knew that it was right. Calazar turned away, fidgeting with his hands, seemingly having difficulty keeping his feelings under control. Showm was on her feet, looking as if she were fighting back an impulse to throw her arms around Eesyan and hug him. "Yes!" Eesyan said again, louder this time. "We will do it! Our race has lived in security and complacency for long enough. It is time for us to rekindle the flame and know again the adventure of true discovery. You are right, Frenua. Minerva will live again, and become what it should have been—maybe even in a new reality that we will create! This was surely meant to be."

PART TWO

Mission to Minerva

CHAPTER TWENTY-SIX

"**K**les! Look! Bears!" Laisha shouted excitedly above the noise of the engine and the rotors. They were riding with the supply flight that went up to Ezangen two or three times a month. Klesimur turned his attention away from the mountains ahead above the pilot's shoulder, crowning the skyline like white fangs, and looked below where she was pointing. Disturbed by the sound and seemingly being pursued by the spinwing's shadow, two adult bears were herding four cubs away from the river bank and up a slope showing streaks of snow toward the cover of some rocks and fallen trees, probably where their lair was.

"Brown tundras," Kles confirmed. "You'll see plenty more when we get to the camp. Don't try getting too near them, even if they do look cute. They can be nasty. But they stay away from people in groups. So no straying off on your own up there." He looked up at her. At twelve, only two years younger than himself, she still had many of what seemed the ways of a child. But her family had moved to the town when she was at an early age, and she still spent most of her time there. And she learned fast. Her face was bright and eager, a little pink in the cabin's heat with her heavy hooded jacket, happy at the thought of being away and free for a couple of weeks. Kles grinned reassuringly. "But we'll take good care of you. Haven't I always?"

The crackle of a radio coming to life came from somewhere forward, followed by, "Ezangen camp calling. You reading, Jud?"

231

The pilot acknowledged. "Hi, Urg. This is Jud."

"How's it going up there? We may have some weather coming in."

"We're just approaching the bottom end of the lake now. Should be, aw . . . another ten, fifteen minutes."

"That should get you here ahead of it just fine. Kids okay?"

"Sure. I'll let 'em tell ya." Jud turned and passed back a hand mike on a stretch cord. "Hey, Kles, wanna say hi to your uncle?"

"Thanks. . . . Hello? Uncle Urgran?"

"Right here, buddy. It's been a while. Everyone's looking forward to seeing you back around the camp again. We've got some interesting new things to show you."

"Giants' things?" As was true of many young people, Kles had always had a particular fascination for the lost race that had lived on Minerva long ago. There was a scientific name for them that meant "long-headed sapient bipedal vertebrates," but for most people they were simply the "Giants."

"You bet. More bones—three complete skeletons, at least. Parts of some buildings."

"Fantastic!"

"And pieces of machines . . . but all pretty flaky and corroded. We're not sure what most of them are."

"Maybe Laisha will know. She's the one who wants to be an engineer, like her dad. Can she say hi too?"

"Sure."

Kles held the mike toward her and nodded. Laisha took it. "Mr. Fyme?"

"Well, that's nice, but it's generally Urg to everyone around here. So you're going to be our guest for a couple of weeks, eh? Know much about archeology?"

"Not a lot, to be honest. As Kles just said, I'm more into science and technical stuff. But it sounds really interesting, and I can't wait to get there. Thanks so much for inviting me!"

"Well, I'm warning you, two weeks of the air up here and food the way the Iskois cook it, and you might not wanna go back. But one thing at a time, huh?"

"One of the people my dad works with showed me a piece of Giants' supermass once," Laisha said. "It was only the size of a fingernail, but you couldn't lift it. That was really weird."

"I've seen some of that too in my time," Urgran answered. "Well, we'll see you soon."

"Okay. 'Bye."

Kles passed the mike and its cord back to Jud. "You never told be about that supermass before," he said to Laisha.

"Yes, well, er . . . it wasn't really me," she confessed, coloring. "But I heard my dad talk about it."

Kles shook his head. "Don't ever say anything to Uncle Urgran that isn't absolutely straight," he said. "He's got this way of sounding easygoing and all that, but underneath he's real sharp. He'll catch you out. And once he does, he'll never quite rate you the same again."

"I'll remember," Laisha promised.

The archeologists' camp was set up near a settlement of a local tribe called the Iskois, who built their houses over excavated pits from cemented rocks and bricks of frozen soil. They did domestic chores for the scientists in return for tools, clothing, and supplies from the equatorial-zone cities, and made good housekeepers. That evening, after a supper of venison stew and a savory mash called *lanakil*, made from some kind of tuber and herbs, Urgran took Kles and Laisha across from the cabin that served as the general mess area, where they had eaten, to the lab shack, which also housed the generator. The night was cold and clear, with the hills and scattered clumps of scrub trees looking white and ghostly in the light of a thin crescent of moon. Earth was just rising, low in the sky to one side of it.

"The place we're digging at the moment is about six miles north," he told them as he opened the outer door of the threshold, turned on the lights, and ushered them through. "Seems to have been some kind of heavy construction, maybe part of a spacecraft base. Laisha should be interested. We'll go up and have a look at it tomorrow. For now, I thought we'd show her some of the bones. I know you've seen this before, Kles." Laisha had seen all the usual things about Giants in books and mythical adventure movies, of course, and a few skeletons in museums, but it wasn't a subject she had ever gone into in much detail.

To Kles this was incomprehensible. He devoured every piece of new information on them to be published. His room at home was a miniature museum of Giants models and trophies, with most of one wall taken up by a map showing a reconstruction of Minerva in the vanished Age of the Giants. He and some of his like-minded friends had visited the excavated ruins of some of their cities, and gazed in awe at the massive foundations and bases of structures that experts said had towered above the landscape, sometimes for thousands of feet. They had built spacecraft powered by principles that Lunarian scientists, racing to develop the means for staging a mass migration to Earth before Minerva became uninhabitable, had still not uncovered. A legend read by some into the fragments of Giants' writings that had been recovered and interpreted told that they were not extinct as skeptics maintained, but had migrated from Minerva themselves to a new home at a distant star. The reason why was not clear. Some thought the climate might be cyclic, bringing about conditions before that had been similar to those threatening the Lunarian civilization today. According to the legend, the star was one located twenty light-years from the Solar System, that had come to be called the Giants' Star. It was not visible from the latitude of Ezangen, but Kles had stood gazing up at it for what must have added up to hours over the years, hoping that the legend was true and trying to picture the kind of world the Giants would be living in now.

The room held two large work tables with sinks, laboratory glassware, a couple of microscopes, and other scientific apparatus, with walls of closets, tool racks, and shelves of bottles and jars. Kles recognized specimens of Giant skeletons both on the work tops and in several containers of preservative to one side. Although there wasn't an example of one complete and assembled, a large wall chart showed the overall plan. The adults had stood eight to nine feet tall. Urgran moved over to it, at the same time picking up a plastic cast of an elongated skull.

"You have to have seen this before," he said, addressing Laisha. "No one could be around Kles more than five minutes without hearing about it. See, they didn't have receded chins and flat faces the way we do. They were kinda more horselike, with this down-pointing snout that gets wider at the top to give you a broad spacing for the eyes—which are more forward-looking than a horse's. Then on the back, instead of a round braincase like ours, you've got this protruding shape that counterbalances the weight. . . . And the shoulders, completely different with these overlapping bone plates—almost like some kinda armor. Not just some spindly collar bone that wild kids like Kles are always breaking." Urgran gestured toward the far wall. "We've got some parts over there."

Laisha stepped forward to peer more closely at the center section of the figure shown on the chart. "It is true they had six . . . you know, arms, legs, whatever?"

"Hey, she's not so slow, Kles! Right . . . see there." Urgran pointed to two sets of bone structures set on either side of the thick hoop of bone braced by a forward-pointing strut, girding the bottom of the rib cage—the Giants didn't have a splayed pelvic dish in the way of humans; they were thought to have carried the internal abdominal organs more by suspension than by support from below. "Vestigial limb structures. You're right. Although these guys walked on two legs and used two arms the same as we do, the family of life that they're part of has a different body pattern based on three pairs. Original native Minervan life."

"The way you can still see in the fish," Kles put in, although Laisha was aware of it. The original Minervan land dwellers had been hexadic too, but predators were unknown among them, and they had been replaced by the the current types, which had appeared suddenly in the period immediately following the disappearance of the Giants. Nothing that anticipated the new population with its quadrupedal architecture existed in Minerva's earlier fossil record, and there was little doubt that it was descended from ancestors imported by the Giants. Most scientists believed Earth to have been their place of origin, although this had never been proved. Flyby probes had confirmed that it was teeming with life, but the first landers were still en route and not due to arrive for several months. But if it was true, it would add a whole new significance to the planned migration. For the imported population had included the ancestors of humans too. It meant that the Lunarians would be going home.

They were still talking about the plans for tomorrow, when they heard the outer door open and close. Moments later, April, the Iskois woman who took charge of domestic matters around the camp, knocked and entered to let them know that bunk spaces for the two arrivals were prepared. She nodded at Kles and smiled. "Welcome back. I suppose there will be mischief. And this is your friend?"

Kles introduced Laisha. "Anything you need or want done, Opril is the person," he said. "She knows everything there is to know here. And how are Barkan and Quar, Opril? . . . Her sons," he explained to Laisha.

"Away hunting with their father and others from the village. They should be back late tomorrow. Then there will be full bellies and dancing for days."

"Good timing. Jud brought a couple of cases of good hooch," Urgran said.

"We'll show you how to handle a *rangat* before you go back," Kles told Laisha. "It's great fun, especially over the rapids."

"Watch those three. They'll have you drowned first, more likely," Opril said.

"Well . . ." Laisha stifled a yawn. "Oh, excuse me. . . . So long as it isn't tonight." In his enthusiasm, Kles hadn't realized how tired she was looking.

"Come on. I'll show you where you'll be staying," Opril said. "I've put your things there already."

Urgran eyed Kles inquiringly. "I'm heading back to the parlor for a mug of something hot before I turn in. Want to join me?"

"Sure." Being treated like one of the men felt good. Urgran turned out the lights to leave just the generator drumming in the darkness at the rear, and they went back out into the cold. At the entrance to the mess cabin, Opril said goodnight and continued on with Laisha in the direction of the sleeping hut—part dugout, Iskois style. Kles and Urgar went into the cabin. The air was close and warm inside, with the stove throwing out heat. Jud was at the table, a glass in his hand, looking mellow and contented. A bottle stood amid the litter of used dishes. Another man was sprawled in an easy chair near the stove, large in girth, with red curly hair and several days of stubble, clad in a thick sweater, fur pants, and heavy boots. Kles hadn't met him before. Urgran introduced him as Rez and said he was a mining surveyor and geologist. Urgran checked a pot that was standing on the stove, added water from a jug by the sink, and put the pot back. Then he took another glass from the shelf above, rinsed it, and poured himself a shot from the bottle. "Gotta do something while the hot stuff's heating," he explained to Kles. "Care to try a nip?"

"Well . . . okay, I guess."

"Attaboy. There's still some things the Iskois can't get right." He passed over a glass with a shorter measure. Kles sipped it, coughed and choked, and hoped the tears in his eyes didn't show.

"Went down the wrong way," he said.

"Yeah, right." This was Uncle Urgran, Kles reminded himself. Who did he think he was kidding?

The TV up on its corner shelf was on, but with the sound turned down. It was showing the Cerian president, Marlot Harzin, looking serious and talking against the backdrop of a picture of Minerva. The caption at the bottom read, DIVISION THREATENS CONCERTED SPACE EFFORT. "What's this, something new?" Urgral gestured with his glass.

"It's a repeat of what he said this afternoon," Jud told him.

"What'd he say this afternoon? I've been up at the hole all day."

"They just can't seem to get their act together with the Lambians. They're serious, Urg. Harzin says we're going to have to be better prepared—as a precaution. Perasmon is saying our ways won't work, and going half and half is just going to take everyone down. It's their survival as well as ours."

Urgran downed half his measure and shook his head. "So his answer is to start diverting part of what they've got? Now we have to do likewise? Doesn't that strike you as just a little bit crazy? Or is it me? Every functioning brain and pair of hands on the planet should be working to get us off of here. But when you've got leaders starting to talk crazy. . . . I never heard the like of that. What do you do if they're not making sense? Aren't they supposed to have it all figured out for the rest of us?"

"I don't know, Urg. I just fly the spinner. Maybe when things get this serious, having that kind of responsibility drives you to it."

"Perasmon can't be serious," Rez declared. "Not at a time like this. It has to be a bluff. Not the kind that I'd say was very smart. Even being able to conceive something like that should be enough to disqualify him from office. Maybe it's because nobody's quite sure yet what the right way is to deal with our kind of system. But it can't be for real."

Urgran scowled and leaned across the table to top up his glass.

Kles stayed out of it, occupying himself by ladling out another bowl of the stew, which was still hot. He raised his eyebrows inquiringly toward his uncle and indicated the pot. Urgran shook his head. "Not for me. . . . Thanks."

Kles didn't follow the politics that the adult world seemed to spend half its time talking about these days. Giants and buried cities, life in the fringe regions, and finding out about animals was more interesting. He didn't understand why they couldn't all get along the way the archeologists and geologists got along with the Iskois.

Minerva had two major populated land areas, called Cerios and Lambia, each straddling the equatorial belt between oceans that became ice-locked in the north and south alternately with the winters. It hadn't always been that way. Long ago, when the ice caps had been much smaller, the oceans had connected all around the planet. The civilization of the Giants had extended into regions that were now covered by permanent ice sheets, which was why so little of it had been found. There were probably the remains of whole cities and who knew what else still waiting to be discovered. The mix of gases in the atmosphere, along with a thin crust that permitted a high flow of heat from the interior, had kept Minerva significantly warmer than it would otherwise have been at its distance from the Sun, for as long as reliable records of the past could be reconstructed. But in recent centuries that had been changing. Towns that had once flourished lay abandoned to the snow, and former farmlands turned into frozen deserts as year by year the advancing ice sheets pushed the populations centers relentlessly back to the equatorial belt.

Earlier peoples, aware of the trend and under no illusions as to the fate that it portended, had resigned themselves to accepting that, like all things and every individual, their world would eventually come to an end and nothing they could do was going to change it. Amassing vast fortunes or striving to gain fame and prestige for themselves in the future was all pretty pointless, since there wasn't going to be one. They applied themselves instead to the arts of civil and harmonious living, the enjoyment of culture, catering to the needs of the young, the sick, the elderly, and the unfortunate, generally pooling what they had to make the experience of life as comfortable as possible for all while the time lasted. Some said that it should never have changed, that people had never been better than in those days. Trying to fend off the natural end to the spell that had been allotted to a world was like propping up a wilting flower that had lived out its days, and in the end just as futile. Didn't the skies show that new flowers were forever budding? The Lunarian word for universe meant "never-ending garden."

Then learning and experiment led to the emergence of science, engineering, new technologies, and the harnessing of revolutionary forms of energy. Machines opened up regions of vast untapped resources beneath the ice, and when the dream of artificial flight became a reality, followed rapidly by the development of regular air travel, the notion took root, inspired by the legend of the Giants, of moving the Lunarian civilization to Earth, closer to the Sun. This became the racial quest.

Most of the various tribes, clans, nations and so forth that made up the population were ruled by some form of the hereditary monarch or popular chieftain that Lunarians had traditionally turned to for ordering their affairs. As the goal of survival by migration became the common enterprise, the pattern of previous history led them to merge and combine their efforts until, apart from a few fringe communities, the map had consolidated into the two major groupings of Cerios and Lambia.

Kles and Laisha were Cerians. Why such things should matter much was a mystery as far as he was concerned, but as the pace of life quickened with the coming of the new technologies, and change seemed to become the rule for everything, Cerios had replaced its royal house with a president heading a congress of representatives that the people appointed. Some kind of theory that most Cerians apparently supported said that this would lead to a decentralized system of research and production in which many different groups competing with each other would produce better results faster. The Lambians, on the other hand, believed this could only result in chaos, duplication, and ruinous waste, and the old, proven methods of central direction and coordination were the only way of achieving any coherent program; in any case, this wasn't a time to be tearing down what had been shown to work and replacing it by something unknown that might not. So Lambia still had a king, with the people being represented by a limited parliament.

The two powers had coexisted in this way since Kles's father's time with neither demonstrating anything that was obviously superior. The advocates on both sides emphasized their own successes and the other's failures, while the critics of both said that ability and knowledge were what counted, not theories on how they should be motivated—as if the present circumstances required any additional motivation, anyway.

The more ominous development that Urg, Jud, and Rez were talking about was fairly recent. Taking the traditional Lunarian view that resources belonged to all, the Lambian king, Perasmon, had accused the Cerians of squandering a future that belonged to the Lambians as much as to themselves. If the Cerians were not going to safeguard it responsibly, Perasmon said, then the Lambians had the right to take charge of it themselves, forcibly if necessary. He was setting aside a sector of Lambian industry to develop appropriate equipment for a contingency force to be armed and trained accordingly. Now it sounded as if President Harzin was saying that Cerios had no choice but to follow suit.

Kles was still too numbed by the implications to even want to think about it. Kings, presidents, all other the kinds of leaders who had headed communities . . . were there to serve people, to organize ways to help them live better. It was why people had always listened to them and trusted them. But this talk now was about designing and making things to kill people. Not just hunting weapons, or the kind that sheriffs and town marshals and sometimes companies of volunteers needed for stopping criminals or dealing with the bandit gangs that appeared in outlying areas from time to time, but for threatening ordinary people who hadn't done anything.

Long ago, there had been barbaric tribes and even upstart nations that tried to live by violence and preying upon their neighbors. But they had never lasted long among a vaster majority once the majority was driven to take action, and civilized ways had spread to become universal to the point where most Lunarians were probably incapable of conceiving anything else. To hear a king talking now about organizing to violently attack another nation was like the thought of being ruled by bandits. Perasmon said he had no choice. Kles didn't know what choices kings did or didn't have, but it seemed unbelievable that the whole adult world with all its complexities and resourcefulness couldn't come up with some other way of resolving the problem. He had seen the corpses of animals felled by bullets and spears, and once, when he was younger, the charred remains of two occupants of a car that had gone off a cliff. His mind conjured up a picture of something like that happening to Laisha—not from an accident or one of the misfortunes that life brought sometimes, but inflicted deliberately by someone, with a device that others had designed and made for the purpose. The thought was so horrifying that Kles felt unable to finish his stew.

But it was only for a moment. The stew was Opril's best. He pushed the morbid images from his mind and buttered a hunk of crusty bread to mop the dish.

"How is it?" his uncle asked.

"Mmm. . . . Good."

"You've gone very quiet. It's not like you."

"Just hungry, I guess. It's been a long day."

Urgran looked at him. "Don't take too much notice of all the talk, Kles. They're just posturing. It can't get that bad. Everyone knows that."

"Urg's right. Perasmon can't be serious," Rez said again.

CHAPTER TWENTY-SEVEN

The Multiporter project was taking on characteristically Thurien dimensions. The original Quelsang transfer chamber, built to handle no more than tiny specks of matter to prove the principle, had been scaled up to the version contained in MP2, which could accommodate devices like communications relays and instrument probes. MP2 was now superseded in turn by MP3, otherwise known as the "Gate."

It took the form of a volume of space defined by an array of sixteen projection generators hanging at controlled positions a few hundred miles from MP2, which was where the control center for MP3 was located. They were called "bells," although each was more the shape of a tapered cylinder flaring at the wider end into a truncated hollow cone—a shape vaguely suggesting a common pattern of desk-lamp shade. In both diameter and length, however, the bells measured almost a thousand feet. The power to drive them came via the Thurien h-space grid. They were positioned and oriented in a spherical configuration that focused their outputs onto a central "transfer zone" a little over a half mile in diameter. This configuration was the "Gate" from which objects projected out across the Multiverse were launched. The Gate transfer zone was large enough to accommodate the *Shapieron*.

Experiments had not reached the stage of sending the *Shapieron* anywhere yet. The ship had been moved from Jevlen, however, and was currently being refitted at a construction and overhaul facility elsewhere in the Gistar system. At the same time, it was being equipped with its own M-space bubble generator, which later tests performed at MP2 had shown would be necessary for transferring objects significantly larger than simple instrument platforms and communications relays.

With such a smaller device, the elongated dumbbell bubble that suppressed convergence effects at the sending end, at the same time preventing dispersion while the projected object was stabilizing at the remote end, was created using energy supplied by the projector. However, this method would not be adequate for producing a remote-end lobe large enough to contain something the size of the *Shapieron*. The connecting "umbilical" filament couldn't be made to carry the load. Therefore, an additional source would be necessary at the remote end, and the obvious way to get it there seemed to be to build it into the transferred object itself.

The test "raft" centered in the Gate was a dummy structure half the size of the *Shapieron*, containing an instrument and sensor platform, and a duplicate installation of the *Shapieron's* intended on-board M-wave gear. It also carried a selection of plant and animal specimens for ascertaining the effects on biological processes. Hunt sat in the MP3 Control Center at MP2, taking in the situation from screens commanding the floor, plus VISAR-supplied avco visuals. He was here physically once more. There was no nonexistent observation room, complete with virtual bar, this time.

Almost a year had passed since the group's first arrival at Thurien. However, with acceptance of the new mission that Calazar had called for in his dramatic presentation to the Thurien Grand Assembly, the workload had not only intensified but widened, as everything that had been pieced together concerning Lunarian Minerva suddenly became relevant. On top, there had been Eesyan's insistence on reverifying the engineering from the ground up. Without Thurien methods and the computational resources of VISAR to back them up things, things would never have gotten even close to progressing this far.

All the same, most of the group had managed to fit in at least one trip back to Earth during this time. Sandy and Duncan had broadened the interpretation of their role of assisting Danchekker and Hunt to involving themselves with the Thuriens in analyzing as much as was known of Minervan history in the period leading up to its destruction, but at the same time managed to fit in a couple of weeks skiing in the Andes as well. Danchekker had spent most of the interim at Thurien immersed in his biological and philosophical pursuits, returning once or twice in response to summonses from Ms. Mulling involving official duties that he was unable to evade. Sonnebrandt was currently back there, having been called home on some family affair, and when he would be returning was as uncertain. Mildred had completed her researches and returned to Earth to work on her book, while Chien had not been back at all, but stayed on to follow the progress of construction at the MP3 Gate. She was the only other Terran present with Hunt at MP3 to observe the test.

In fact, Hunt's work had taken him back to Earth the most, involving long sessions with Caldwell to redefine Tramline's part in the new overall strategy. Caldwell was patched into the proceedings too, coming through from Earth in an avco window. Hunt was pretty sure that more had gone on behind the scenes to all this that involved Caldwell somehow. Caldwell was showing more interest in the day-to-day details than was usual for his kind of management style. Hunt had picked up rumors among the Thuriens that the vision with which Calazar had dazzled the Assembly owed much to Caldwell in its earliest stages of conception. But when Hunt tried to raise the subject out of curiosity, Caldwell had been evasive. Hunt knew from long experience that when Caldwell decided he didn't want to talk about an issue, that was the end of the matter.

Since Minerva at the time the mission was aimed at had been inhabited by human Lunarians, it had been agreed humans should be included in the team to be sent on it. Anyone suggesting otherwise would have had a tough time dealing with Hunt and the others who had been there from the beginning, in any case. Caldwell had made it clear that no one among them needed to feel any commitment to the new mission, but the thought of not going hadn't entered any of their heads. As was to be expected, when the news went around back on Earth, various other interests had made their presence felt, wanting to get in on the act and send people too. But they would have been negative assets, resented as an intrusion into the team. Caldwell was alive to the mood, and since disruptions at this point would have compromised the effectiveness of his people who were on the spot, he took it as part of his business to mount defenses on the home front. Hunt could only conclude that in this Caldwell was fully successful, since none of the wrangling and background politics had percolated through to Thurien.

The object of the present experiment was to send the test raft to a marked alternate reality of the Multiverse, and then bring it back—a pretty important prerequisite to have mastered if they were going to be sending Thuriens and Terrans. It was still not possible to "map" the Multiverse in terms of the attributes pertaining to a particular reality, for example, "A universe where Genghis Khan wasn't recalled after defeating the Prussian defenders of Europe, overran the West, and the dominant civilization that arose to colonize the world was Asiatic." No ready way had been found to connect "change," as perceived subjectively in the countless directions making up the Multiverse, with anything that could be measured as physics; indeed, whether such a connection existed at all was by no means certain. VISAR had been trying to refine the concept of "affinity," which yielded rough measure of how far a different reality was from the familiar one, but it could be notoriously unspecific when it came to indicating *how* they were different. A universe where Earth had no Moon, one in which Mars still possessed oceans, and another where Jupiter was missing two of its principal satellites all registered comparable affinity indexes. Why this should be, nobody even had a theory. At this stage it was impossible to say if sense would ever be made of it.

The affinity index was useful nevertheless in that it provided a crude way of marking off the swathe of Multiverse in which realities possessing a certain family resemblance—the Minerva of fifty thousand years previously, for example—were likely to lie. The approach was a bit like highlighting a newspaper ad with a tar brush, but in a situation where it reduced possible solutions numbered at "almost-infinity" by an amount "almost-infinity-minus something," the result was a problem that VISAR could generally find manageable. In short, while it wasn't possible to hit a specific target by its characteristics, they could usually lob a shell onto more or less the right continent.

Given some indication by the data fed back of where and

when they were within those limits, the technique then was to try and hop the device closer by sending it a series of corrections. The corrections didn't always have the expected effect, but correlating the directives sent with the result returned was producing the fragments that it was hoped would one day connect together into a map. But nobody yet knew what the scale was, and to make matters worse the scale seemed to vary in every one of innumerable directions. VISAR said it was nice to have something challenging to do.

The voice of the Thurien supervisor directing the operation came over the local circuit. "Beacon lock-on is holding steady. Bell distributor drawing h-input and charging. Drone wave function registering on all matrixes. Pilot beam synched." An exchange of numbers and status checks with VISAR followed. It meant that the raft out in the Gate was ready to go, and the array of projectors positioned in space around it was almost up to power. The "beacon" was for VISAR to home the raft on—a probe that had been sent through about thirty minutes previously to a fairly "nearby" location in the Multiverse that could be identified with some confidence. A fix from the returned astronomical observations and intercepted Thurien communications signals put it about a half million miles from an unremarkable planet of one of Gistar's neighboring systems, and several months in the past.

"Well, with luck we'll soon know if you were right," Hunt said to Chien. The test involved an aspect of the return-wave that she and some of the Thuriens had been investigating. An object was brought back by reversing the projection process—effectively creating a progression of wave representations in the return direction. It had been demonstrated successfully with a series of small objects sent via the old MP2 chamber. The raft would be the first attempt with a larger body, using the Gate.

"Being sure about the part that gets us home again is something that interests me greatly," she replied dryly.

"Vic, by the way," Caldwell said from his window in Hunt's head. "Owen stopped by to visit today. Asked me to say hi. He was hoping to be in on this too, but he couldn't stay." The test had been postponed a couple of hours due to some last-minute changes out at the Gate.

"That's too bad," Hunt said. "How's he liking retirement?"

"Doing okay. Catching up on his reading and traveling, he says, and still thinking about writing that book about his UNSA days. But I think he misses the firm. Did I ever tell you I thought about retiring too around a year or two ago?"

Hunt's eyebrows arched in surprise. "No, you never did. Seriously?"

"Sure. It was touch and go. Maeve talked me out of it in the end. I think she was terrified of the thought of having me under her feet all day, every day. I'm glad she did. I think I was going through a—"

VISAR cut in "Excuse me, but Bytor is asking to have a word with Gregg." Bytor was one of Thurien engineers assisting near the supervisor's panel.

"Back in a second, Vic."

"Sure."

Caldwell vanished. Hunt returned his attention to the screens. The views from the raft's imagers showed the sixteen projector bells as disks of blue-violet light spaced around in all directions against the background of stars, with MP2 showing as a bright light on one view and the distant globe of Thurien beyond. The Thuriens around the Control Center sat intent at their tasks. By now, nobody expected any real surprises. Hunt reflected on how quickly even something like this, which a year ago would have been viewed as outlandish, could come to be accepted as routine. The countdown was approaching zero.

"Sequencing out. . . . Transferring."

And the gate was empty. That was it. There were no spectacular effects. One moment the raft had been there, centered at the focus of the array pattern, and then it was gone—across several light-years of space and several months back in time, if all was according to plan.

"Looks like another good one," Chien said, her eyes busy taking in displays and numbers.

"And we're sitting here getting ho-hum about it. Do you realize how staggering this all is, really?" Hunt shook his head.

VISAR confirmed that the data link to the raft was functioning. The readings coming back showed that it had found the beacon. Moments later, a visual channel opened up, showing an altered view of stars and space, this time without any bells, no MP2, and a planet that wasn't Thurien, farther away and smaller.

"There it is." Chien indicated with a nod. The beacon was coming into view in another shot, riding at a distance that VISAR reported as being eleven miles.

"We're probably causing some excitement there already," Hunt said. There could be no hiding something the size of the raft from the Thurien monitoring system of whatever universe they had connected with—not that there was any particular reason to want to hide it. In fact, quite the contrary.

Caldwell popped back into his visual field. "It's looking good. The raft got there," he said.

Hunt nodded. "Seems like it, Gregg."

"Access established. We're presenting our calling card," VISAR informed the company. It meant that via the raft's communications relay, it was in contact with its counterpart—the VISAR that existed in the target universe. In fact, this was one of the more valuable parts of the exercise. Instead of having to decode its way into an unfamiliar system, this way it was able to transfer enormous volumes of information describing the reality the raft was in. After a series of repeat performances with probes, they were no longer initiating person-to-person contacts. The routine had gotten old, and the individuals on the receiving end were usually too dumbfounded to supply much in the way of anything useful enough to be worth the time.

"Wow!" VISAR didn't often insert exclamations. "You're lucky you weren't with this outfit. They didn't power down at Quelsang and move the action out to MP2. There was a major accident—sounds like a matter clash. It took out half the Institute. The group was wiped out except for Danchekker and Mildred, who weren't there. I've given them our records, but I don't know if it will do any good. Their whole project is shut down. It's causing a major political scandal all over Thurien and back at Earth."

"Jeez!" Caldwell murmured. Hunt could only whistle silently, too taken aback to form any words.

"Eesyan permitted it?" Chien said, sounding surprised and a little disbelieving.

"It seems their Eesyan resigned from the program early on," VISAR replied. "There were disagreements. . . . Pressures from Earth that he wouldn't go along with."

"Don't tell me, I can guess," Caldwell said. "My other self there is about to be fired, right?"

"You're not there," VISAR answered. "You took an early retirement over a year ago."

The supervisor announced, "Wave pattern is stable. Switching over to local control now."

"Link deactivated to standby. Bubble manifold dissolving," another voice reported.

This was the crucial part of the experiment. The transfer of power through from the Gate had been cut. The bubble of local M-space and its extension forming the umbilical to the raft's locally generated bubble was no longer being sustained. The raft was now a self-contained entity, free to move around in the foreign universe, all communications severed. It simulated the situation that would exist with the *Shapieron* when it was sent back to Minerva. The blank screens and inactive readouts confirmed that all information flow back from the raft had ceased. The homing beacon that had been sent ahead, on the other hand, was still connected to the projector at MP2 via its own umbilical and sending back a view of the raft, captured telescopically from about fifty miles away.

The beacon would play a crucial role in bringing the raft back. Multiverse navigation was still far too much of an inexact business for VISAR to be sure of finding the same place again by aiming blind. "Place" meant not only a given point in space at a some moment in time, but also a particular variant among countless shades of "likeness," and tests had shown that repeating what appeared to be the same parameters was no guarantee of returning to the same one; in fact, it had never yet succeeded in doing so once. But having an active beacon already there gave VISAR something to "home" on—hence, its name. The schedule called for a five-minute pause before they attempted reestablishing contact. Around the room, Thuriens were leaning back into more relaxed positions, stretching, and turning to talk to others.

"Oh, and I meant to tell you," Caldwell said. "We've had Lieutenant Polk bugging us here again."

"From the feds? You're kidding."

"He found out you were back just recently. Now I'm in trouble. Seems I should have notified them. Talk to them or do something, will you, Vic? Get him off my back."

"Okay. But I'll need to figure out what angle to take on it," Hunt promised.

Formaflex had recently gone public after a trial of marketing a method of duplicating objects using Thurien scanning and nano-assembler technology. They claimed that they were limiting the process to areas that couldn't be tackled profitably by conventional methods, but the manufacturing sector saw it as the thin end of a wedge and were panicking. The rise of Formaflex's stock price had set records, which of course was what the original tip had been about. Hunt didn't think he would have passed anything comparable on in like manner himself, even without the trouble he had experienced. He could only conclude that there was at least one version of himself loose in the Multiverse somewhere that had even less of a head for the world of finance than he did.

"You know it will spread," Chien commented. It was a topic she returned to regularly. "Earth is going to have to adapt to Thurien values eventually. The money system is designed to tally the checks and balances of a zero-sum economy. Every credit in one book has to be balanced by a debit somewhere else. But once Thurien technology is introduced, the exchange of material goods that the system assumes ceases to be the dominant factor. Their wealth lies in their knowledge, which is subject to a different arithmetic. Sharing what you have doesn't lose you anything. The more that's given, the richer everyone gets. The sum is an exponential growth."

"I don't think Wall Street is quite ready for that yet, Chien," Hunt said.

"It's going to have to learn. The genie is coming out of the bottle."

"I think Maeve already understands it," Caldwell told them.

Hunt realized that consternation was breaking out among the Thuriens. "Vic!" Chien exclaimed at the same time. He followed her gaze back to the screen showing the transmission coming back from the beacon. The most extraordinary thing was happening. Where there had been simply the image of the raft floating in space against the background of stars, now there were two rafts. Even as he watched, one of them vanished, then reappeared moments later in a different position. Then there were three rafts; then nothing at all.

As the chaotic pattern continued, voices among the Thuriens called for the test to be aborted. But Chien cut in on avco, addressing the Controller. "It started as soon as the connection was broken. Try restoring it."

Several seconds went by while he wrestled with the decision. Then, "We'll try it. Power the bubble back up." The Gate bubble was restored and projected using the homing information provided by the beacon. After a couple of corrections, the screens feeding from the raft came to life again. At the same time the view of the raft being sent by the beacon stabilized. Five minutes elapsed, ten. . . . No further sign of the problem appeared.

"We will continue as scheduled," the Controller announced. The last part was to bring the raft back again. It went without a hitch. The bells were brought up to full power, VISAR initiated the reversed phase sequence, and seconds later the raft reappeared in the Gate, looking as if it had never left. The views from it showed the universe as seen from MP3 again. In the cages, the animals were scampering about, feeding, scratching, or just sitting lost on their own brooding, all as if nothing had happened.

Clearly, what had been observed was some kind of timeline convergence effect. Hitherto, convergence had been a phenomenon occurring in the vicinity of multiporting projectors, such as the Quelsang prototype and the scaled-up chamber at MP2. But there was no projector on the raft. It carried only instrumentation and communications gear, and the test model of the onboard bubble generator intended for the *Shapieron*. Lots of probes fitted for instrumentation and communications tasks had been sent over many months without anything like this happening before. So the effect had to be caused by the onboard bubble generator. But it had only happened when the umbilical connecting back to the Gate-end bubble was severed. This suggested that it was a consequence of something that was inhibited while the bubble existed in its double-ended dumbbell form.

Further experiments were performed using observer probes fitted with MV-wave analyzers to monitor events around the raft from close quarters. It was found that the core region of the Gate bubble, inside which the projector-end convergence zone was trapped, also extended as a thin filament inside the umbilical to the far end. Here, it formed a convergence lobe inside the remote-end bubble too, but as long as the two bubbles were connected, a "tension" between them kept it down to a small core region—so much so that its existence hadn't even been suspected before.

However, when the Gate-end was deactivated, the onboard power source at the raft end expanded the remote bubble and its core convergence zone to produce bizarre observable effects. The solution was to deactivate the remote bubble as soon as the projected standing wave had stabilized and was unable to disperse. While the precise physics was still to be worked out, repeated tests showed the method to be reliable. An interesting point to note in the course of all this was that they had believed the convergence problem to be solved, gone ahead accordingly to the next step of sending instrumented probes equipped for communication back, and then discovered that convergence was a more subtle business than they had thought. This perhaps explained the episode of the similarly conceived device from another reality that had precipitated the virtual craziness a while back, which had puzzled Hunt.

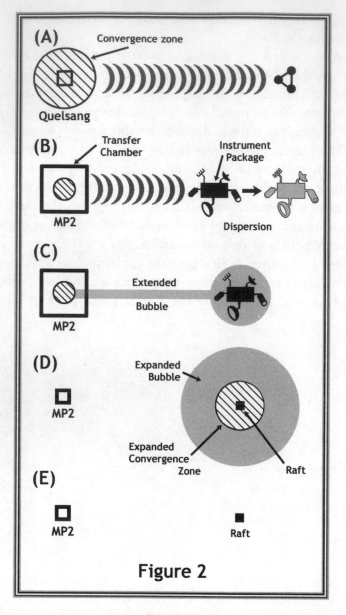

Figure 2.

(A) Quelsang prototype. See p. 132.
(B) MP2 bubble contains convergence, but dispersion of test object not eliminated. See p. 208.
(C) Extended bubble prevents dispersion. See p. 209.
(D) Detached bubble. Onboard power drives expansion of bubble and remote-end convergence zone. See p. 250.
(E) Collapsing of remote bubble after stabilization eliminates convergence. See p. 252.

CHAPTER TWENTY-EIGHT

Hunt would never have believed he'd see the day when humans showed sentimentality over a computer. After further successful tests involving the raft, the next major step was to scale things up to operational dimensions by repeating the experiment with the *Shapieron* itself—the size of the Gate configuration had been decided with this as the eventual aim. The *Shapieron* was the only ship of its kind in existence, and if anything went wrong, it would be irreplaceable. But everything leading up to this crucial test had gone well enough to satisfy even Eesyan, and eventually the time came when the moment of decision had to be faced.

The first trial of dematerializing the entire ship would be just that—involving the vessel only, with no Ganymean or human presence aboard. Such a precaution was the routine approach, but in this instance there was an unusual complication. An integral part of the *Shapieron* was its distributed control and computing entity, ZORAC—in some ways a diminutive precursor of VISAR—which had been doing invaluable work plugged into the planetary net while the *Shapieron* was based on Jevlen. In fact, VISAR's informal, whimsical style of interacting had been modeled to a large degree on the interface designs of the old starship systems, which had been popular among the crews. ZORAC had been the first alien intelligence that Hunt, Danchekker, and the other Terrans present at the time had actually talked to when the *Shapieron* first appeared at Ganymede after its strange exile. To them, and others who had gotten to know ZORAC in the subsequent period of Ganymean-Terran dealings out at Jupiter, or later during the *Shapieron*'s six-month stay on Earth, it had a distinct personality that warranted classing it as a sentient being in its own right, in every sense of the word. And this was even more true of Garuth and his Ganymean crew, for whom ZORAC had been not only a totally dependable manager of the ship and everything in it upon which their lives had depended for twenty years, but also a companion, advisor, and mentor in a way that made it as much a fellow member of the mission as any Ganymean. In short, by universal accord, it would be a shame to lose the ship, but if that was what it came to they could live with it; but they weren't prepared to jeopardize ZORAC.

ZORAC itself was unperturbed about the prospect, having concluded from the record of experiments up to that point that the probability of anything going seriously amiss was not something to be wearing out any circuits over. The electronic and optronic devices that had been transferred through M-space and recovered had continued functioning normally, and likewise the animals. It was just another case of soggy biological carbon-based minds getting emotional again, and so best left to them to come up with something that would make them happier. What the biological minds came up with was that as an insurance, before the trial was conducted a full backup of ZORAC would be stored by VISAR. At least, this information would enable ZORAC to be recreated in some other form later if worse came to worst—exactly what such a form might be was something they agreed to worry about when and if it should become necessary.

In the event, the worries turned out to have been misplaced. The first trial in which the *Shapieron* was dematerialized from the Gate was a very cautious affair that involved merely shifting it a few hundred miles to a beacon positioned not far away in the Gistar system of a reality that was very "close." ZORAC almost caused coronaries by faking a system crash for several seconds before announcing that it was fine and the experience had actually been less unsettling than a regular transfer through h-space. As confidence grew, the scope of the tests was gradually increased until pitching a beacon out across the Multiverse (exactly "where" to was still not something that could be predetermined with any exactness), sending the *Shapieron* to home on it, and then bringing the *Shapieron* back had been demonstrated as a task that could be repeated at will. And that brought them finally to the second hurdle that there was no way around: the first trial involving living people.

It was their project, the Thuriens pointed out; the privilege of sending the first being should be theirs. The Terrans reminded them that it was they who had been contacted by the relay bringing the message that had put them all on the right track, so they should have the first shot. Nobody was quite certain of the logic by which this conclusion followed, but it was the best argument that anyone on the Terran team could come up with, so they all pretended not to be aware of the non sequitur. Wrangling continued until the matter got back to Caldwell, whose reply was simply, "Why not send one of each?" Why not? Like so many obvious things, it was obvious once somebody had said it.

Then, of course, the question became, Who, from each? Since Hunt was officially the leader of the Terran group, there was no question in his mind that it meant him—there was an old principle about officers not expecting the men to do anything they weren't prepared to do themselves, and in any case it suited his temperament. Duncan Watt disputed this on the grounds that Hunt's experience made him less expendable, which Hunt read as a cheap ploy by Duncan to get himself some glory. The Thuriens were at a bit of a loss to follow these intricacies, since the concept of personal glory meant little to them anyway. Danchekker contacted Caldwell privately to confide the view Duncan was right in maintaining that Vic shouldn't be put at risk, small though the risk might be, and suggested it might be appropriate for Caldwell to pull rank and take the decision out of Hunt's hands. Caldwell, however, knew that seeing the leader overruled wouldn't be good for the group and elected not to interfere, leaving it to Hunt to assert his position by pulling rank instead—as Caldwell knew he would. That much having been settled, the Thuriens took a dissent-free view that if the Terrans were putting forward the head of their group, the Thuriens would do likewise. So Hunt and Eesyan, it turned out to be.

✳   ✳   ✳

They had to travel out to MP2 for the test, and wear space suits. The original transfer chamber at Quelsang wasn't big enough to take a single human, let alone an eight-foot Thurien as well. The reason MP2 had been built remotely in space and projected its test objects into distant regions was to avoid the hazards associated with things rematerializing inside solid matter. The same considerations applied when it came to projecting people—if anything, more so. Hence the suits.

They stood gripping a handrail on a raised grating in the metal-walled chamber. A clutter of monitoring heads and instrument mountings filled the space around them, packed between the apertures of the projector barrels angling in from all directions. In several places, eyes looked in on them through observation ports. Below the grating was the five-foot diameter sphere containing the convergence suppressor. No doubt the strange things that happened with time would become a subject for further research one day, but for present purposes they would remain confined in there. As a test object, Hunt and Eesyan were well below the size where carrying a local bubble generator became necessary.

Although Hunt had maintained a light-hearted attitude all the way through to now, this all had a sinister and oppressive feeling. He felt like the victim in some macabre, over-elaborate execution ritual. His usual inclination toward banter had deserted him. The suit readings were all good, projector systems counting down; there was nothing much to be said. Although Caldwell was patched in from Earth again, he was being reticent this time. It was as if he could read Hunt's mood. Typical Gregg, Hunt thought to himself.

"Everything okay?" the Thurien supervising scientist's voice inquired inside Hunt's helmet.

"All okay."

"As ready as we'll be," Eesyan said.

The black mouths of the projectors flickered yellow for an instant, then stabilized to a uniform, depthless indigo. "Sequencing out. . . . Transferring."

And Hunt was floating in space. This was not some virtual illusion manufactured by VISAR, that he was experiencing in a neural coupler somewhere. He was really out here—several thousand miles from MP2, if all had gone as scheduled. It seemed to have—Hunt could see one of the beacons at a distance he judged to be a mile or less away. With live beings involved in the test, Eesyan had stipulated sending a backup beacon ahead in addition to the regular homing beacon. As Hunt gyrated slowly, Eesyan came into view, sliding by with the starfield. His long Ganymean face was turning this way and that inside the headpiece of the Thurien space suit as he took in the surroundings. Hunt could feel his gloominess of only a few moments ago giving way to a strangely exhilarating sense of awe.

He had to remind himself of what had just happened. Every one of the particles that composed his body had been converted to a component of a wave pattern projected and stabilized a short way across the Multiverse. There, drawing on energy beamed through by the projectors, the wave components had condensed into the nodes that define material particles, reconstituting the configuration that equated to Victor Hunt.

This *was* him now, a structure frozen out of vibrating local energy condensations, just as the one back at MP2 had been. A containment bubble sustained through the M-space umbilical from the projectors was keeping the pattern together while it found a local energy balance and stabilized.

"How are we reading?" the supervisor's voice checked.

"Everything appears to be admirable," Eesyan replied.

"Vic?"

"Oh . . . fine. Just fine."

"It's looking good from here. Are we clear to go to the next phase?" There would have been nothing to be gained by not completing the process once they had gotten this far. Eesyan looked across. Hunt gave a double thumbs-up with his gauntlets and nodded.

"Proceed," Eesyan said.

"Dissolving bubble now."

They allowed several seconds to elapse. The indicators on Hunt's sleeve panel that monitored the status of the link channel changed to null readings suddenly. "This is Eesyan, calling Control. Testing." There was no response. Hunt tried and got the same result.

"I guess we're on our own," Hunt said over the local channel.

"Sobering to contemplate, indeed."

For the MP2 that Hunt could make out as a point of light gleaming in the direction opposite to Gistar was not the MP2 they had come from. He was staring out through his helmet visor at a different universe. And he and Eesyan were now part of it. There could be another Hunt inside this MP2 there, right now; and if not, there would almost certainly be one somewhere on the Thurien behind his right shoulder, looking the size of a dime. The beacon that had appeared over ten minutes ago now was probably causing consternation already. Hunt grinned to himself as he pictured the reactions if the Thurien senors had resolved in addition two space-suited figures floating miles from anywhere in space.

The sleeve panel indicators registered activity again. VISAR having remained locked on to the beacon throughout, had reformed the bubble. "Control checking. Your readings look good."

"All fine," Eesyan reported.

"Fine," Hunt echoed.

"I suppose you realize you've just made history?" Caldwell's voice came in, judging with perfection that Hunt was in a sociable mood again.

"It seems to be becoming a daily thing here these days, Gregg," Hunt told him.

"Seen enough?" the supervisor at MP2 inquired.

"One could never see enough of this," Eesyan replied.

"Well, it will have to do," the other Thurien quipped. "It's all we have scheduled, and there's this very meticulous boss I have to deal with. Sorry, people, but it's time to bring you home."

After that, there were trials that involved sending the *Shapieron* with occupants to a succession of targets progressively "farther" away in the Multiverse. There were no new surprises. At last the time came to put final touches to the planning for the mission that it had all been leading up to, which had been proceeding at its own pace in parallel with the engineering. Eesyan and Hunt had a final meeting with Calazar, Showm, and a deputation from the Assembly that was reporting on the project. There seemed no reason why everything shouldn't be ready for a departure in two weeks.

CHAPTER TWENTY-NINE

Imares Broghuilio experienced the feeling close to panic that comes with being aware of having regained consciousness, but of nothing else. He didn't know where he was, or what had preceded the present instant. He just . . . "was." Peculiar patterns of light seemed to shrink and grow and whirl in his head. It was if his mind had somehow disintegrated into a billion fragments and was now only beginning to form itself together again. He was lying on a hard, uncomfortable surface and felt stiff and cold, as if he had been there for some time. The only sounds were the muted hum of machinery and a steady whoosh of air blowing from a ventilator.

He opened his eyes. For an indeterminate time that could have been anything from a few seconds to a matter of minutes, the farrago of objects, shapes, patches of color, and centers of light that he found himself looking at refused to take on a coherence that conveyed meaning. The side of his head hurt, as if he had struck it. Then a flat, synthetic, voice from somewhere intoned, "Unstable resonance condition abating. Reintegrating to normal space after unscheduled h-transfer. Arrival coordinates unknown. Locator call not being acknowledged. No grid activity detected. Evaluating."

The words cued the pieces of visual imagery to assemble themselves together to become the interior of the bridge deck

of a Jevlenese spacecraft. A groan from nearby completed the
process of nudging Boghuilio's mental faculties back into motion.
Crisis. . . . Local JEVEX nodes down. . . . Thuriens and Terrans
have thwarted the plan. . . . Get away and regroup. . . . Emergency
transfer to Uttan.

It was coming back to him now. Five Jevlenese ships carrying
Broguilio, recently proclaimed premier of what had turned out to
be the short-lived Federation of Jevlenese Worlds, his immediate
circle of accomplices, and a hard core of followers, had taken
off from Jevlen in a bid to escape to their secret fortress-factory
planet, Uttan, where they would be able to hold out while they
reconsolidated and made new plans. But the *Shapierion*, which
by rights shouldn't have been anywhere near Jevlen, had appeared
out of nowhere, bearing down in pursuit. After the underhanded
dealings that had evidently been going on for some time between
Calazar and the Earth, the *Shapieron* could have been carrying
Terrans with Terran weaponry. The Jevlenese ships would never
outrun an old Ganymean, self-powered starship in normal space.
Broghuilio had ordered immediate h-space transfer to Uttan.

Uttan was where the real JEVEX system had been secretly
relocated. The activity supported at Jevlen, which was all the
Thuriens had known about for years, was a shell operation. But
when JEVEX attempted to project a spinning black-hole transfer
port for the five ships, some other force attempting to counter
it had intervened, causing the vortex to go unstable and creating
conditions of violently tangled and convulsing spacetime. It could
only have been VISAR, trying from light-years away to block
the transfer, but with nothing to guide it apart from inadequate
information from one of the *Shapieron*'s reconnaissance probes
dogging the Jevlenese's heels. Attempts at evasion came too late.
Impelled on an irreversible gravity gradient, the five Jevlenese
ships had plunged on, into the turmoil of scrambled Relativity.

The groan came again. Broghuilio mustered his energies, winced
as his head lifted from the deck plates, and hauled himself up
sufficiently to turn and sit with his back against the base of a
console. Wylott, the former Jevlenese Secretary of the Exterior,
since appointed Commanding General of new Federation's military
forces, was hunched over in one of the operator-station seats,
holding his face in his hands. A trickle of blood had run down
from between his fingers onto his sleeve. Broguilio brought a

hand up to feel his own face and his beard. He found nothing wet or sticky. Garwain Estordu, the scientific advisor who had been with them, was lying along an aisle between cabinets and equipment panels, still unconscious. Around them, the captain and other members of the crew who had been in the vicinity were either motionless in assorted crumpled and splayed positions, or slowly beginning to move and show signs of life. "Full evaluation not possible at this time," the computer that had spoken before reported. "Matrix and system files have been disrupted. Necessary to run deep-scan diagnostics, repair linkages, and reconstruct. Acknowledgment requested. . . . Repeat, acknowledgment requested. . . . Proceeding."

Broghuilio registered the situation dully. His eyes drifted upward to take in the main display screen overlooking the bridge deck. It was showing a view of space and stars. So at least that much was still working. . . . To one side of center was the disk of a planet. It was not Jevlen. Nor was it Uttan. It wasn't a world that Broghuilio recalled seeing before at all.

There was no doubt about it. The planet was Minerva, accompanied by its moon. The spectrum, size, and mass of the parent star, something like three hundred million miles away, were identical to that of Sol, and then a telescopic survey of the surroundings had picked out Jupiter. The star pattern was as projected from that point in space—except that it had to be corrected to allow for the passage of fifty thousand years. There was no signal of any kind to indicate any presence of the Thurien h-grid, and nothing on any of their communications, navigation, or data bands. Nor should there be. There was no Thurien presence in this part of the Galaxy. VISAR, as such, didn't yet exist. The Jevlenese ships were back at Minerva, before the time of its destruction.

Even Broghuilio was too numbed by the realization slowly seeping into his brain to show much of his customary bellicosity. "How is this possible?" he whispered to Estordu, now recovered sufficiently to sit in one of the crew stations, but still shaky.

The scientist ran his gaze over the displays for the umpteenth time as if a part of his mind still retained a hope that their message might have changed somehow. "What we entered was a total dislocation of spacetime. It has jumped us to another region of the quantum totality. I can't tell you how. Nothing in physics has ever predicted anything like it."

"So how do we get back?" Broghuilio demanded.

Estordu shook his head bleakly. "The energy concentration that it took could only be created by systems with the capacity of VISAR and JEVEX focusing through the h-grid. There is nothing like that here. We have no way of getting back." Broghuilio's face colored and began to swell. "You can shout as much as you want, Excellency, but it won't change anything," Estordu said. "What we should be thinking about are the options we have here. There is no other choice."

Such talk from the normally obsequious Estordu was so out of character and unexpected that Broghuilio stopped as he was about to speak, deflated, and for a moment just stared. Maybe Estordu was still more traumatized than he showed. The Captain and other officers within hearing, and other members of Broguilio's staff who had appeared, digested the information somberly.

Wylott had a mild gash on one cheek but nothing worse apart from a bruise or two. "So we are without primary h-grid power?" he concluded. "Just the auxiliary system?"

"So it appears, General," the captain said.

"We will need to put down somewhere soon," Wylott observed.

A barb congratulating Wylott on his brilliance began forming reflexively on Broghuilio's lips, but then died. Sarcasm would get them nowhere. "Captain, convey the situation to the commanders of the other vessels," he ordered. "Have them stand by for further instructions."

"Aye, aye, Excellency."

Broghuilio paced across the floor to stand staring up at the main display, still showing the view of Minerva, while he thought. He still needed to keep a hand on one of the consoles to steady himself, he found. He wished now that he had made the effort to learn as much as was known about precataclysm Minerva when the opportunity had been there. But he had concentrated on the Earth surveillance program, managing the information reported to the Thuriens, and secretly building up the Jevlenese military capability. His face was turned toward the future, he had been fond of telling his subordinates. What was past was past and didn't concern him. The words had an ironic ring to them now.

He had talked about Earth as the new power base of the Cerians, but that was more for the propaganda value. He really didn't know that much about the Cerians, other than that they were one of the two superpowers whose eventual catastrophic war had destroyed Minerva. The Thuriens had taken the survivors of the other side, Lambia, back to their own part of the Galaxy, eventually installing them on Jevlen. That made the Jevlenese "Lambians"; it followed that the Cerians were the enemy. Broghuilio's historical analysis and any ideology stemming from it had never really gone a lot deeper than that. He looked at the moon, half lit behind Minerva's disk.

"JEVEX." The prompt was a mental reflex. There was no response. Of course, JEVEX wasn't there. He turned his head to speak over his shoulder. "Advisor Estordu. What can you tell me about the Lunarians' technical capabilities at this time? Military organization and weapons capability in particular."

"The most we have to go on is the events of the final war—which obviously hasn't happened yet. But even by that time, the phase they were at was still primitive—rudimentary nuclear and beam weapons; off-planet capability just sufficient to contest near space and establish long-range bombardment installations on their moon, and some robot surveys sent to Earth. But indication are that most of the advances necessary to produce even that occurred toward the end, as militarization on both sides accelerated."

"So they're probably still in the early stages down on Minerva," Broghuilio said, his eyes still fixed on the screen. "They aren't present on the moon to any significant degree yet."

"Possibly so, Excellency. A telescopic survey of the surface would tell us more. Also a profile of communications traffic."

Broghuilio stared up at the image for a minute or so longer. Although ostensibly Jevlen-based transports, his five ships were fitted with armaments that the Thuriens never knew about. Also, they were still holding cargos of the kinds of weapons that he had been bringing in from Uttan as part of his buildup. Between them they were carrying somewhere between two thousand and three thousand of his supporters, most of them trained and with experience of the war games staged in remote places—the exact number was uncertain, due to the haste in evacuating from Jevlen. He turned, his hands clasped behind his back. "Very well. You have all had time to consider the situation," he told his aides. "What plan do you recommend?" He looked at Estordu.

"What? I . . . That is . . ."

Broghilio's eyes shifted to Wylott. "General?"

"Well, it's hardly . . . I mean, in view of the suddenness of the changed situation."

Broghuilio took in the rest of the company. "The experts do not have a plan," he informed them. "I, however, do have a plan. We do not know at this stage how effective the Minervan space surveillance systems might be. Since they don't have any inter-planetary activity worth talking about, I would expect them to be minimal. But let us not take chances. Until we have formed a clear strategy, we would prefer our presence not to be known. Out here in space, we are vulnerable to detection. Assuming that the moon turns out to be still sparsely occupied—which I predict will be the case—we will put down there and effect a temporary camouflaged base. A small landing party will be dispatched to Earth to reconnoiter the situation and make contact with such authorities as seem advantageous to our interests. If they are in the early phases of growing hostilities, working to develop weap-onry and tactics, it isn't as if we have nothing of potential value to bargain with. I trust you take my point, Gentlemen?"

Wylott began nodding slowly. "Ye-es. Of course."

"Advisor Estordu, commence arrangements at once for a survey of their moon," Broghuilio ordered. "I want a report of any visible surface installations and communications activity."

"Yes, Excellency."

"Captain, send orders to all craft to maintain orientation with minimum radar profile toward Minerva in the meantime. General Wylott, we need an inventory of the weapons complement we are carrying, along with a personnel count and breakdown by skill rating and specialty category. Also a schedule of equipment to be readied for a surface base."

"Sir."

As the seniors relayed orders and the bridge area began bus-tling into life, Broghuilio felt himself slipping back into his familiar role. So those amateurs down on the planet thought they knew something about war preparations, eh? Maybe he could introduce a few concepts they hadn't thought of yet. And who knew? It seemed that the ambition he had nursed to become the warrior overlord of Jevlen had been frustrated. If there was no going back, then there was nothing to be done about that. But, maybe, a different world instead, perhaps? His face was to the future. What was past was past. He surveyed the scene around him with satisfaction.

"Evaluation completed," the bridge deck computer announced proudly. "We are at the system of Sol, positioned eight hundred thousand miles from the planet Minerva, time-shifted negative fifty thousand years."

"Turn that idiot thing off," Broghuilio snarled.

CHAPTER THIRTY

The Gate controller recited the by now familiar line.

"Sequencing out. . . . Transferring."

But this time it was the real thing. The huge disks of the Gate projection bells went to blue, from blue to blue-indigo, and then were gone. A different starfield surrounded the ship.

Hunt's first time aboard the *Shapieron* had been shortly after it made its appearance at Ganymede. He and Danchekker had been at an exploration base there, set up to investigate the wreck of an old Ganymean spacecraft discovered beneath the ice. A signal from a a piece of equipment reactivated by UNSA engineers had been picked up by the *Shapieron* and brought it to that location. The *Shapieron* then had been virtually a self-contained small town, crammed with Ganymeans of all ages, from those numbered among its original mission, down to the youngest of the children born in the course of its strange exile. Its interior then had shown the wear and tiredness of serving as the only abode its occupants had known for twenty years. When Hunt walked around the familiar corridors and galleries some days previously, all gleaming and new after the ship's refit, it had seemed like a deserted cathedral. Just Garuth, his senior officers, and a skeleton crew were manning the half-mile-long starship. It was being used for its ability to operate autonomously, not because of its size.

The Terran contingent comprised the original group with

the exception of Mildred, back on Earth writing her book, and Sonnebrandt, whose affairs had detained him in Europe. They followed the event from the vessel's Command Deck, which at least had almost the normal complement of crew at their stations and felt something like old times. This was Hunt's first time back aboard since the expedition to Jevlen, when they had mounted the Pseudowar. It was strange how events had led to this circle. The revelation that Broghuilio's ships had somehow been thrown back to ancient Minerva was what had inspired the whole project of Multiverse research, which now culminated in their going back to that same place and time.

Well, not quite the same. The hope of the mission was to create a new reality from which would spring an entire family of futures in the Multiverse that so far didn't exist. The new world view challenged the formerly held belief, which had been derived purely from physical considerations, that everything which could happen did happen "somewhere." The newer line that Danchekker was developing with the Thurien philosophers held that consciousness was able to alter quantum probabilities. With consciousness now intervening to initiate changes across universes, the suggestion that new realities could be created was gaining currency. It had certainly provided the main inspiration for the mission.

The hope was to bring into being a variation of the past in which Minerva was saved: a new twig amid the immensity of the Multiverse's diverging branches that would grow and bear fruit as all the histories of humans and Ganymeans that might follow. Some still insisted that this was impossible. Others argued that, on the contrary, it was the very reason for the Multiverse's existence; that surely, being able to bring about morally meaningful change was what consciousness was *for*. But two things could be said with certainty. First, nobody knew. And second, now that their vision and sense of a purpose had been inspired, the likes of Calazar, Showm, Caldwell, and just about everyone else involved in the project, were not going to wait for the philosophers to come to a consensus. In any case, philosophers of both races had done that too many times on innumerable occasions before, and then changed their minds.

The object, then, was to appear at Minerva before the calamitous war had ever happened. Yet, despite all the effort expended on discussions and planning, exactly what was supposed to happen then was far from resolved. It wasn't that the Thuriens and Terrans were unable to agree on goals or a strategy for attaining them. It was simply that surprisingly little was known about the war and its times, and even less about events over the years leading up to it.

Practically all of Minerva's libraries and records had been destroyed with the planet. Probably influenced by the guilt they still felt aeons later over their disastrous attempts to depopulate the Earth of predators, the Thuriens had adopted a policy of staying out of Lunarian affairs and developing their own part of the Galaxy centered on Gistar. Only in the war's final days, when monitors that they had left on the fringes of the Solar System registered the explosion that signaled Minerva's end, did they throw together a hasty mission to investigate—so hasty that they ignored their normal rule of not projecting gravitationally disruptive transfer ports into planetary systems. The upheaval caused by the port created for the rescue mission launched Minerva's orphaned moon on the trajectory that eventually brought it to Earth. It also impelled the largest intact piece of Minerva outward to become Pluto.

Miraculously, some Lunarians survived on pieces of what had been Minerva; but unsurprisingly, there had been very few. They were recovered from niches they had found in proto-Pluto and other fragments; as bands scattered across the lunar surface—itself a devastated waste from the conflict; and from assorted craft and orbiting stations left adrift amid all the wreckage. Preserving political texts and historical records had not been high among the priorities the survivors had been concerned with at the time. It was only much later that accounts were obtained from the Lambians brought back to Thurien, who would later give rise to the Jevlenese. Those accounts had been almost entirely verbal and reproduced from memory. The people they came from were disproportionately from such groups as soldiers, space crew, mining and construction workers, farmers, hunters, villagers, and other from areas remote from the war zones, rather than urban dwellers, scholars, or professionals likely to have studied such matters.

The tactic adopted for the Minerva mission, therefore, was the straightforward one of aiming somewhere "downstream"—i.e., a time following the war—as best as could be gauged, and working back "up" in a series of reconnaissance from which it was hoped to glean enough information to determine a more propitious intervention point.

VISAR had sent the beacons into the appropriate region accordingly—two beacons was now the norm, although there had been no failures. Preliminary readings indicated the time period to be about right. The astronomical fixes had located Jupiter and Saturn but not Minerva, but that didn't mean a lot, since it could have been on the far side of the Sun. There was some electronic chatter, but it couldn't be interpreted because the Lunarian communications procedures of the period were unknown. The only way to find out more would be for the *Shapieron* to go there and have a look around.

A tense but curious silence pervaded the Command Deck as all eyes took in the images from outside being presented on the screens. "The beacons are here," ZORAC reported. "We're at the right place, anyhow. The channel back to home is up and working." Images of Calazar, Caldwell, and anxious faces watching from MP2, the lab at Quelsang, and a location somewhere in the Government Center at Thurios formed a montage on the main screen.

"Well, I guess this is it," Caldwell said. "We'll talk to you again when you check in later." The M-connection from Thurien to the beacons would remain, and the beacons would still be capable of relaying via a regular communications beam. However, the *Shapieron* would be cut off from regular communications when it activated its main drive, which created an encapsulating manifold of deformed spacetime that electromagnetic signals couldn't penetrate.

"It won't be long," Hunt answered. "When we've just had a quick check around."

"Good fortune be with you all," Calazar said.

"We have no doubts about it," Eesyan replied.

"Take it easy with that thing, Junior," VISAR said—aimed at ZORAC, to amuse the bioforms.

"Junior? I was driving this ship before you were a design spec."

"Report local status," the supervisor requested.

"Wave function consolidated and stabilized," Garuth responded. "Ready to detach."

"Dissolving the bubble."

"Local bubble deactivated," ZORAC advised.

The screens showing he link from Thurien cut out. The *Shapieron* was a free body, now part of a different universe, as it had existed somewhere around fifty thousand years in the past.

"ZORAC, go to main drive," Garuth instructed. "Take us to the first reference."

This began a series of stops and checks around the Solar System to verify that the *Shapieron* was operating normally under main drive conditions, and to assess where and when they were. Minerva was not to be found. Its moon was located, already on a course that would carry it inward toward the sun, and nascent Pluto, emerging from the dispersing cloud of planetary debris. A long range view from closer in showed the recently arrived Thurien rescue ships commencing their thankless task. The *Shapieron* was able to pick up identifiable Thurien crosstalk on the regular local bands and in h-link mode. There was little talk around the *Shapieron*'s Command Deck. Garuth decided that they would not announce themselves. The rescuers out there had enough to think about without the situation being complicated further.

One more thing needed to be verified before they departed. Broghuilio and his Jevlenese were thought to have appeared at Minerva at around the time that the Lambian-Cerian rift was developing. Whether the Jevlenese had actually caused it was unknown. But even if not, the warlike disposition and ambitions of conquest that Broghilio had displayed on Minerva suggested that they would have been involved in escalating tensions to the eventual outbreak of war. Since the *Shapieron* was witnessing the termination of that war, it had obviously arrived at a point in time that lay after the arrival of the Jevlenese. Exactly how long after, nobody could say. The Thurien interrogators at the time had asked no questions about Jevlenese, for Jevlenese didn't yet exist, while the Lunarian survivors had said nothing about any mysterious aliens showing up at some point in the past. And that was hardly surprising. For if events had indeed followed the course that was surmised, it meant that one side was being aided by an alien intrusion whose existence could only have united the general Lunarian population in opposition had they known about it. Hence, Broghuilio and his cohort, and whatever Lunarian element had thrown its lot in with them, would have every reason to conceal the fact of the new allies' origins—which the fully human form of the Jevlenese would have facilitated greatly.

From the fragments of Lunarian records available at the time of the original "Charlie" investigations, it had been guessed that the Jevlenese arrived at Minerva a century or two before the war. The more recent researches that Duncan and Sandy had helped with now put it at far less. The Lambian leader at the time the war escalated to destroying the planet was a dictator called Xerasky. He had come to power upon the death of his predecessor Zargon, which few at the time doubted Xerasky had engineered. Zargon had been a former military general of the last of the Lambian kings, Freskel-Gar. Zargon was an unknown who came rapidly to the fore in initiating and commanding an advanced militarization program. He later ousted Freskel-Gar and proclaimed a dictatorship, taking charge himself. The suggestion that Zargon might have been Broghuilio was obvious, but it was still speculation. Zargon had appeared abruptly somewhere around twenty years before Minerva's destruction.

When the Jevlenese ships exited from the turmoil of spacetime that had tunneled them from another universe, they had been followed by the probe whose last transmitted image of Minerva had gotten back before the tunnel closed. Hunt, Danchekker, Garuth, and others aboard the *Shapieron* now had been present when that image came in. The probe was from the *Shapieron*, which had been pursuing the Jevlenese. Fifty thousand years later, orbiting on the edge of the Solar System and carrying still functional h-band equipment, it would relay the first signals that opened up contact between modern Earth and Thurien. If it had arrived at Minerva twenty years previously with the Jevlenese, that probe should be out there somewhere now. This was the one final thing to check.

ZORAC used the ship's communications gear to scan a circle around the ecliptic, sending out the appropriate call codes. And sure enough the probe returned an acknowledgment and fix from a position not too far from Minerva—it would have fifty thousand years to find its way out to the edge of the Solar System. It meant that, yes, Broghuilio and the Jevlenese had arrived. But they were already a part of Minerva's past. The *Shapieron* needed to move farther upstream against the flow of events.

"That's all we need to know," Eesyan told Garuth. "There's no more for us to do here."

Garuth brought the *Shapieron* back to the vicinity of the primary beacon. A call via the beacon when the ship had powered down from main drive reestablished contact with Thurien.

"Lock on to ship's compensator confirmed," the supervisor's voice advised. "Suppressor compensation positive. Stabilizing the bubble. . . . You're set to come home."

"You guys don't seem very talkative," Caldwell commented, back on the circuit. Silence hung heavily for a second or two.

"I guess there's not really a lot you can say, Gregg," Hunt answered finally.

CHAPTER THIRTY-ONE

The voice of Top Sergeant Nooth yelling at the newest squad of recruits, accompanied by the rhythmic thud of boots crashing in unison, came from outside the barrack hut window.

"*Hup*-two-three-four. *Hup*-two-three-four. What's the matter, Frenitzow? Frightened of pulling a muscle? Worry about it when you've got some. Pick those feet up. *Hup*-two-three-four . . ." The sounds faded in the direction of the parade square, giving way to the intermittent *rat-tat-tat* of small arms from the firing range.

Lieutenant Klesimur Bosoros stretched back on his bunk and set aside the magazine with the article on biological writings of the Giants that he had been reading. At least, he was still known as Kles. That much of his life hadn't changed. Just about everything else had, in ways that he would never have thought possible. He didn't get much time to think about his former interests these days, although when he was alone on night sentry duties he would still pick out the Giants' Star and remember his boyhood dreams. The situation between Lambia and Cerios had deteriorated to the point where actual conflict had broken out between them under different pretexts on a number of occasions. Only a matter of years ago, such things had been all but unthinkable. Now, so the sociologists said, they were recognized as an inevitable consequence of societies becoming more complex and developing ideas they were not prepared to compromise. So the world was busily learning and improving its new arts to defend them.

Kles's unit had been fortunate enough not to be involved in any of the fighting so far, and some of the barrack-room psychologists and political experts assured them all confidently that they wouldn't be, because the fit of insanity would soon be over. The Cerian president, Harzin, had issued an appeal to the Lambians, calling for Minerva to come to its senses before it was too late. The whole issue of which kind of system would most quickly produce the technologies needed to migrate to Earth—Lambian centralization and command, or Cerian multiplicity of choice and competition—which had triggered the original dispute, was itself the single biggest factor holding back all of them. After years of the two powers vying to outdo each other, the single most significant conclusion, if either of them would only care to admit it, was that it didn't seem to make much difference. Both sides were developing and deploying similar weapons, both were mounting comparable efforts to extend into near space and establish a foothold on the Moon, and now academics on both sides were talking about the efficacy of attacking civilian populations as a means of exerting political pressure and blackmail. The barrack experts could be right, Kles conceded. But he wouldn't be placing any bets. There had been this kind of thing from politicians before, and every time it had broken down into another squabble.

"Hey, Kles." Corporal Loyb turned his head from the group sitting around the table by the stove halfway along the room. He was shuffling a card deck. "The game's just starting. You want in?"

"What's the matter? You're asking for trouble. Didn't I clean you out enough the last time?" Kles threw back.

"Hey, man, that's what it's about. I want it back."

"Dream on."

"Full moon leads, quarter a bid," Oberen said, rubbing his hands. "I feel lucky."

"So did Loyb." Quose sniggered.

"Good for the house?" Loyb asked, looking back at the others. They assented with nods. "You'd better get over here if you're playing," he called to Kles as he showed off a few flourishes prior to dealing.

Kles swung his legs down from the bunk, picked up his magazine again, and stretched his arms back. "I'll pass. I think I'll take a walk, get some air."

"But hey, that's my money you're walking out with there, man."

Kles patted him on the shoulder as he passed on his way toward the door. "Wrong, Loyb. It's mine."

The sky outside was cool and cloudy. Wind from the north carried the feel of rain. Kles turned the collar of his fatigue jacket up around his neck and his ears and thrust his hands in the slit pockets while he walked along the path between I and J huts, and then across a corner of the parade square to Admin. The desk sergeant in the Day Room was Yosk, who was okay. Kles motioned pointedly with his eyes in the direction of the door to the Signals Office at the rear. Yosk turned his head the other way, and Kles moved on through. Lance Corporal Aab was on watch duty, as Kles had known he would be.

"What's new? Are we at war yet?" Kles inquired.

"If words were bullets, it would be a slaughter. Lots of talking."

"The usual, eh?"

"Suits me. They're easier to duck."

Kles nodded at the console by Aab's desk. "Anything for me today?"

"Yeah, there was something. . . ." Aab tapped at keys, consulted a screen, and glanced toward the doorway. "University net mail. Looks like it's from your uncle."

"Run me a copy."

Aab shot a nervous look at the door again. "You'll get me a week on scrub detail. How long is this gonna go on?"

"It's okay. Yosk is straight. You still want to borrow that forty for your date tomorrow? How else am I supposed to read it?"

Aab nodded and moved back, while Kles leaned across and entered the decoding key, followed by a string that would delete the original. Aab touched a button, and the printer came to life with a whine and a judder that told of a long life of battering and heavy-handed use. Two sheets of copy chugged their way out into the tray. Kles picked them up, glanced at the top one, folded them, and tucked them into an inside pocket. "You're okay too, Aab. Here, why don't I take care of it now?" He dug in a back pocket for some notes, separated a twenty and two tens, and passed them across. "Here, have fun. Don't do anything I wouldn't do."

"That gives me a pretty free hand," Aab said after a moment's reflection.

It was a letter from Laisha. She was in Lambia as a technical translator with a delegation sent by the Cerian government in an attempt to convince the Lambians of President Harzin's claim that in technological capability the two sides were as close as made no difference. But conducting private communications between a military base and somebody involved in sensitive issues in what was effectively enemy territory would have been foolhardy at best and a guarantee of no end of trouble if discovered. So they had worked out a way whereby Laisha sent her letters to an electronics consultant she used, who ran a department at the same university that Kles's uncle Urgran worked with. The consultant routed them to Urgran, who forwarded them wrapped up as university traffic.

Kles left the building and went next door to the canteen, where he filled a mug from the urn at one end of the serving counter and then found himself a secluded spot in a corner. It was a quiet time of day, apart from the clatter of cooks in the kitchen getting ready for the evening rush. Kles took the letter from his jacket, propped open the magazine that he had brought with him in front of him on the table, and unfolded the pages inside it. It read:

> Dearest Kles,
>
> Sorry—I know it's been a few days. We've been so unbelievably busy here. And, I confess, I did take some time out to go with a party of us to see something of the city. Escorted everywhere by official Lambian guides, of course. And the sights were no doubt carefully selected. There was the big monument to King Perasmon and his lineage along by the river, a washing machine factory to show how efficiently a planning agency handles things, and lots of children doing gymnastics and some heavy cultural things in the evenings—but I do like their roast eth! And they have a kind of brandy afterwards that's warm and hits your throat, that reminds me of that stuff your uncle Urgran and the others used to drink up at Ezangen. I thought it was ghastly when I tried it, but I've quite taken to the Lambian stuff. In fact I got a bit

tipsy. Does it mean I'm an adult now, do you think? Ezangen seems so long ago now. Those were such happy and innocent times, looking back. Or is that just how children see things?

But there's some really interesting news that I probably shouldn't be telling you but I will anyway, because you know me. We really might be making a breakthrough this time—with the technical talks, I mean. The Lambians actually seemed impressed, and just about ready to concede that this whole stupid rivalry is costing us all more than it could ever be worth. And guess what. Perasmon came here personally yesterday to hear it for himself. I even saw him for a few minutes! Kind of big and round, with a red face and little white beard. Quite cuddly. (Not really—just to make you jealous.) But I don't think he's really as bad underneath as all those things in the papers say. Like a lot of things, maybe it just takes someone to make the first move. And that could be what we've done. Isn't that an exciting thought! Then there was a rumor going around this morning that President Harzin might be invited from Cerios to meet with Perasmon formally. Wouldn't it be fantastic if they managed to straighten everything out, and all these horrible things that have been going on could be forgotten? Well, they wouldn't be forgotten by those poor families and friends who have lost people already, of course. But if something were learned for the future and not forgotten again, then perhaps knowing that it was not entirely for nothing might be of some consolation to them.

I'm so glad you haven't been dragged into any of it. The only thing that could spoil it all, from what I hear, is Prince Freskel-Gar, who has been jealous for his stepfather's throne for years. He sounds nasty. I don't like him. It was his faction who made such a big thing of this centralization-command dogma and set Persamon on the road to a militarized confrontation in the first place. But here I go getting serious and political again, and I know you can only stand so much.

How is life at the base? It sounds as if you're making an interesting variety of friends, even if they could be in a *nicer line of business. Congratulations on the promotion—although, to be honest, I still picture you more easily in furs and snow boots, laughing with Barkan and Quar, falling out of a rangat, or stealing cookies from Opril's kitchen than wearing a uniform, shouting at recruits, or carrying a gun.*

When are you due for some leave back at home again? Say hello for me to your mother and father, and your brother when you do. Oh, and that Giant electrical gadget that your friend in Solnek sent did arrive just before I left to come here. Tell him thanks so much. It's in remarkably good condition. I didn't get a chance to look at it very closely, but will get around to it when we're back. It looks interesting.

And so, that's it for now, Kles. I'm rushing this off during a break and will have to go soon. Be careful. I do so much hope that these omens come true, and that everything will change for the better before you do end up in real danger.

All my love as always (but you already knew that),

Forever,

Laisha

Kles drained the last of the contents of his mug, returned the letter to his pocket, and sat thinking for a few minutes about the things he had read. Then he got up, dropped the mug on the tray provided for used dishes, and walked to the door. Outside, he stopped to take in the scene of squads doubling this way and that on the parade square, mechanics working on an engine inside the open doors of the truck depot, a sergeant counting boxes stacked in front of the quartermaster store. Cerian kids being trained to mindlessly kill and maim Lambian kids they had never met, and who had done them no harm. How had it all happened? The more he tried to read the histories and the political diatribes, the more he was able to follow the inescapable logic of the details, but lost sight of any underlying sense. How wonderful it would be if what Laisha was a part of turned out to be the beginnings of the whole idiocy unraveling and Minerva getting back onto the path that it should never have strayed from. But no. . . . The thought was too momentous to get emotional about by hoping for too much if she were wrong.

And besides, he had less than half an hour to get his kit ready for supervisor shift at the main gate. He pulled his collar up around his chin and set off briskly back toward his hut.

CHAPTER THIRTY-TWO

General Gudaf Irastes, second-in-command of the Prince's Own Regiment of the Lambian Royal Guard, didn't know who the foreigners were, where they had come from, or how they had made contact with the prince. They wore strange, outlandish garb that suggested some kind of air crew tunic, and their speech, though seemingly derived from Lambian, was barely recognizable. But Irastes took a simple, pragmatic view of life. When it was deemed his business to know more, he would know. In the meantime, he just followed orders. And his orders were to go with the leader of the deputation that had made the contact, who was called Wylott, back to a base they had established somewhere, and escort their chief back to meet with Freskel-Gar at Dorjon, his stronghold in Lambia.

Irastes had with him a detachment of two officers and eight troopers. Wylott and four of the deputation that had appeared with him would accompany them, while the other four remained at Dorjon with the samples of weapons that they had brought. It was understood that they were being kept as as hostages to ensure good behavior, although nobody had been so indelicate as to say so. Irastes was intrigued by what seemed to be communications accessories that the foreigners wore on their wrists and belts, and also their sidearms. They appeared to be of extremely advanced types, completely unfamiliar. He hoped this wasn't representative of Cerian work that had been going on, and which he had never heard of. If it were, the implications were alarming. Small wonder that Freskel-Gar had been very interested in the weapons. Irastes wondered if he was working some kind of deal with a renegade Cerian group who had access to developments that had been kept a secret.

Following directions from the foreigners, a Lambian personnel flyer carried the mixed group over the hills to the south of Dorjon and then across the plateau region to the wilderness of scarps and folds forming the eastern base of the Coastal Range. Irastes couldn't imagine where the foreigners could have come from in this direction. Presumably, they had traveled to Dorjon in a vehicle of their own that was also being held there somewhere with the hostages; but it wasn't his place to ask.

An incoming call sounded from the copilot's panel, speaking in the foreigners' peculiar tongue. Irastes was able to make out what sounded like " . . . identify . . ." but the rest was lost. The copilot looked around for direction. Wylott nodded to him, accepted a microphone, and went into a brief dialogue." Evidently the foreigners had been monitoring Lambian transmission frequencies. The aide of Wylott's who had been helping with the navigating tapped the pilots shoulder and made hand motions to indicate a large shoulder of rock buttress ahead, projecting from the side of a steep ridge. "There. . . . Around, yes? Then down. You see where."

A tight turn around the shoulder brought them over a canyon that opened out below suddenly. Lying in it was an aircraft unlike anything Irastes had seen before—as seemed to be the case with just about everything else connected with these foreigners. It was dull gray in color, and curvy and bulbous, flaring at the tail into two stub wings that seemed impossibly small for its bulk, each tipped by a vertical stabilizer extending above and below. Irastes put it at about the size of a military staff carrier or a small commercial airliner. There were figures outside, watching as the Lambian flyer descended. The craft had insignia on its wings and sides, Irastes saw as they approached for touchdown. But they were not Cerian.

The flyer landed; a crewman opened the door and extended the steps. Wylott stepped out with two of the foreigners, indicating for Irastes and his party to follow, while the rest from the flyer closed up behind. The foreigners outside were armed but carrying their weapons slung. They turned to move with the arrivals back toward their waiting craft. Evidently, the journey was not over yet. Irastes halted. "How long is it likely to be before we get back here?" he asked Wylott.

"*Iz wazza gi fadid zo say?*"

Irastes motioned toward the aircraft. "How long?" He pushed his sleeve up to show his watch and pointed. Then waved a circle in the air and pointed at the ground. "Back here?"

"Oh . . ." Wylott held up a hand showing four fingers, then extended his thumb as well. "Hours." Irastes detailed one of his officers and two men to remain behind and guard the flyer they had arrived in. He nodded to Wylott, and they proceeded up the extended ramp of the foreigners' craft.

Its inside was even stranger. The structure and fittings seemed more in accord with the interior of a luxury yacht than anything economized by necessity in the manner of every flying machine Irastes had ever seen. And there were none of the panels, equipment racks, banks of cabling, and all the other paraphernalia of typical military interiors that he would have expected. Instead, there were screens flanked by arrays of what looked like luminous crystals, and areas of wall and ceiling that seemed to glow internally, illuminating the cabin. The seats seemed to mold themselves to any posture that was desired. He was still marveling at it all, when he realized the ramp had retracted beneath doors that closed from somewhere, and in moments they were moving. From the views on the screens, they were going straight up, but uncannily there was no feeling inside the cabin of lying back—or even of accelerating, though the rate at which the ground image was shrinking told that the rate was fearsome. The outline of Lambia was already visible in patches between clouds; then ocean, fringed by a brilliant line that had to mark the edge of the ice sheet. The horizon became distinctly curved. Above, the sky was darkening, showing stars. And still they were going up. Only then did the realization hit Irastes fully: This was more than just an aircraft; it was a space ship!

Broghuilio stood on the bridge of the Jevlenese flagship. Screens showed the drab surroundings of gullies, ridges, patches of ice and dusty rock making up the area of Minerva's moon where the ships had put down. Although it seemed unlikely that the Lunarians would have established any regular surveillance of the far side yet, the ships were lying in hollows selected to be in shadow for much of the time. Surface tractors with g-shovels had scattered lunar debris over and around them to obscure their outlines.

Things were moving well, and surprisingly rapidly. A reconnaissance party sent to Minerva with General Wylott aboard one of the ship's daughter craft had established the period as being the early years of strain between the Lambians Cerians, before the onset of major hostilities between them. Given the peculiar circularity of the situation as it related to Jevelenese origins, which Estordu and the scientists prattled about incessantly, it had seemed logical to approach the Lambians. Wylott had made contact accordingly with a member of the ruling faction called Freskel-Gar, who was at once enticed by the samples of weaponry that Wylott had taken with him for precisely that purpose. The plan had been simply to establish some sort of rapport with the Lambian leadership and then play things from there. However, Wylott reported that Freskel-Gar was opposed to the official Lambian policy of seeking an understanding with Cerios, and represented a dissident movement who wanted to take a harder line. Wylott attributed Freskel-Gar's readiness to divulge all this to the lure of the Jevlenese weaponry, which suggested that he perhaps harbored ambitions that went beyond merely registering dissent. This could suit Broghuilio even better, and he had requested arrangements to be made for him to meet this Freskel-Gar himself without further delay. Wylott communicated back that he would be returning with one of Freskel-Gar's military commanders to bring Broghuilio there. Even better. An honor escort. It wouldn't have done to have been told to come and knock on the door, like a beggar at a kitchen.

"Orbiter reports contact," an operator called from one of the consoles. "Lander locked onto homing beam, delta v-h two-seven-fifty and five-five thousand."

The bridge Duty Officer turned from inspecting system monitors. "They're on their way down. Landing in about four minutes."

"Put General Wylott on the screen," Broghuilio instructed. The pinkish, somewhat puffy countenance with its slicked-back silver hair appeared a few seconds later. "A commendable performance,"

Broghuilio acknowledged—which was about the closest he came to lavishing outright praise.

"Your Excellency is too gracious."

"What is the arrangement?"

"Major Krebe and a detachment have remained at Dorjon. We will proceed to a rendezvous point on the surface, where a Lambian craft is waiting to take us back. The scout has been concealed at Dorjon. Freskel-Gar awaits at your pleasure."

Broghuilio nodded. "Satisfactory."

Wylott indicated the direction over his shoulder and behind him with his eyes, and lowered his voice. "Shall I present Freskel Gar's General Irastes now?"

Broghuilio took in the figure slumped in a seat in the background, still evidently in some kind of mild shock. His mouth puckered in mild amusement behind his beard. "How well do things work with the language?" he asked.

"Difficult. The similarities are . . . distant," Wylott admitted.

He would cut a more impressive figure if Irastes were to meet him as part of his first experience of entering the command bridge of a converted Jevlenese interstellar transport, Broghilio decided. Maximizing effect was half the art of command and leadership. "I will receive him here," Broghuilio replied.

The lander appeared overhead minutes later, completed a slow descent, and docked in its mating bay of the transport. Shortly afterward, General Irastes and his staff and escorts were conducted through, gaping from side to side in total stupefaction. Broghuilio waited imperiously at the head of the grouped bridge officers, his arms folded. They would depart without delay, as soon as the visitors had absorbed enough to produce the required mood of receptiveness. There was no need to tell them that without h-grid power the ships' systems were running on reserves to maintain life support for the occupants, the main armaments were useless, and the secondaries only good for as long as reserve power lasted. When that ran out the ships would be little more than piles of scrap metal on the lunar surface. Minerva possessed no industries that were capable of refueling them.

Prince Freskel-Gar Engred stared again at the object lying on the table in his private chambers of the fortress at Dorjon, alongside the weapons that his experts had still been examining and questioning the foreigners about when General Irastes and his party returned. Irastes had brought it back as a token of the importance he attached to the events that had burst upon them that day. It was a rock from the far side of the Moon. Irastes had been there since the last time they spoke. The prince was still struggling to take in the things he had just been hearing.

Aliens that were human? . . . Somehow speaking a mutilated smattering of Lambian. . . . Some kind of time warp from the future; but a different future. How could you have a different future when you didn't have a future yet? All of that was beyond Freskel-Gar. What was clear to him, however, was that they possessed weapons of immense potency; and even if the stocks should be limited, or if Lambia was unable to supply the materials to operate and maintain the weapons, the knowledge that these aliens possessed could be of immeasurable worth.

Freskel-Gar's deputy, Count Rorvax, who had been making some progress with following the aliens' speech translated the words of the their leader, a stormy, black-bearded man called Broghuilio. "You . . . I think he means on this world . . . *don't know* . . . War. *Organizing for war.* . . . *Plans and designs, yes, and a few* . . . puppy snaps? *Skirmishes. But what of* . . . I don't quite get that . . . *the minds of the people? What of* . . . the same word. I think it means *shaping the country, state,* I guess . . . *into a,* not sure . . . *can wage war? We can* . . . *make you into a* . . . *war leader* . . . *who will unite and* . . . something like *carry* . . . *all of Lambia.* . . . This bit's awkward. He's talking about a *force Cerios won't be able to resist.* . . . *Lambia and Cerios will be/become one, with one king* . . ." Broghuilio gestured pointedly at Freskel-Gar, "*and* . . . something grand-sounding, to do with destiny."

The prince gazed again at the piece of dull, crumbly rock. Irastes had said their ships up there were the size of ocean liners. And they were willing to bargain. For reasons that Broghuilio seemed disinclined to elaborate, they were not able to get back to wherever they had come from. There were over two thousand of them up on the lunar surface in need of sanctuary and sustenance, in return for which they could no doubt render valuable services. Freskel-Gar's eyes gleamed at the pictures that Broghuilio's words had painted in his mind. He felt he had the basis of what could be a very profitable deal here. For a long time now, he had been working toward the day when he would unseat Perasmon. His followers were ready; the equipment was in place. But he had never felt sufficiently sure of having the margin that would ensure them the edge. This could be it.

The other factor had been to await the right opportunity. And that could just have been answered, too. Rorvax had brought the news that President Harzin of Cerios was coming to Lambia to meet with King Perasmon, following the negotiations that had been going on for some time between their technical advisers. It could only mean that a truce between the two powers was in the offing, after which Perasmon would be a hero, and Freskel-Gar's chance of power and fame would be gone permanently. If he was going to make his move, it seemed it would have to be very soon, or never.

CHAPTER THIRTY-THREE

"*Attack! Attack! Battle stations!*" The passages and decks of the Lambian corvette *Intrepid*, patrolling in northern waters, erupted in a frenzy of bodies tumbling out from doorways, pulling on pieces of kit as they scrambled to clamber through hatches and up ladders. Petty Officer Jissek came out of the wheelhouse onto the starboard bridge as the crew of Number Four gun were frantically finding their positions, just in time to see the black shape diving out of the night to the east. The torpedo struck amidships thirteen seconds later.

The concussion pitched him over the rail, into the signal bay above the foredeck main gun. He lay crumpled, semiconscious, pain shooting through seemingly every joint in his body. The sounds of shouting and screams penetrated through the ringing in his ears. He hauled himself up dazedly, using the mast stanchion by the flag locker. The deck beneath him was already tilting alarmingly. As he looked up, the center of the vessel lit up in a sheet of orange, silhouetting debris and bodies thrown into the air. Figures staggered out onto the bridge above him, and promptly disintegrated along with the door and companion way behind them as the aircraft made a second pass, firing rockets and cannon.

The sea was choppy under a squally wind, its gray just a little darker than the sky. Jissek could feel the cold creeping into his bones through his wet, oil-sodden clothes and the rubberized canvas floor of the raft. They couldn't last long in this, he knew, barely fifty miles from the ice shelf. But it would have been unbecoming to say so.

There were just two of them now. Two of them alive, anyway. The sonar operator who had lost a leg had died maybe an hour before, but he was still lying with his head on Ensign Thorke's lap. Kept as a shred of extra cover from the wind? Or was it that they simply hadn't had the energy to lift the body overboard? Perhaps they just didn't see any point in it. The cold made thinking difficult and sporadic, an effort of will in itself.

Thorke was hurt, too, having taken something in his back—a bullet, or piece of shrapnel or flying debris. His breathing was heavy, and he coughed intermittently, which brought trickles of blood to his mouth. Just nineteen, his first operational trip. But he hadn't complained. Jissek felt little more than a boy himself. Inwardly, he was bracing himself to the thought of having to face the rest of whatever was ahead alone. He looked at the boy's face. It was paler, developing a greenish tint. Thorke licked his lips dryly. Automatically, Jissek started weighing the risk of wasting their limited provisions. Then, catching himself and repulsed by his own meanness, he unscrewed the cap of the water flask and offered it across. Thorke took a sip, nodded gratefully, and passed it back. Jissek screwed the cap on without taking any himself and returned the flask to the survival box.

He had seen other rafts being inflated and figures hauling themselves or others into them in the light of the flames from the sinking corvette. But if they were still anywhere, they had drifted out of sight before daylight came. The only reminder from one cheerless horizon to the other that the *Intrepid* had ever existed was a corpse floating grotesquely about forty feet away, which had stayed with them doggedly along with some pieces of floating wreckage. It seemed strange. If the other rafts had drifted out of sight, why hadn't this local patch of flotsam dispersed too? Currents did funny things, he supposed. A shape that he had noticed earlier on the skyline seemed nearer and looked like ice. Did it mean they were being carried northward?

He thought about Ilia, fussing with her plants and painting the walls in the flat they had finally scraped together enough for, and Lochey just toddling the last time Jissek had been home on leave and seen him; about his parents, pottering in their garden and always worrying about him. If the end was going to be long and drawn out, he hoped they'd never know. Hunger was knotting his stomach. Time to measure themselves a breakfast, maybe. Or would it be more practical and sensible to wait until . . . He was doing it again.

"Sir . . . ?" Thorke's voice came as little more than a dry croak but sounded suddenly urgent. Jissek looked up. Thorke was staring at something high up and behind him. Jissek turned himself stiffly to look over his shoulder.

How it could have come up on them without making a sound, he didn't know. It looked like a huge metal egg, the size of a truck, hanging in the air about a hundred feet away. "What is it, sir?"

Jissek shook his head. "I'm not sure." He had never seen anything like it.

"Is it theirs?" the ensign asked fearfully.

"I can't tell."

After apparently inspecting them, the object moved closer. Jissek felt his own mouth go dry. It came to just feet away, looming over them, and then descended to immerse its lower part in the water so that the vertical part of its surface was alongside the raft. A panel that had been invisible opened to reveal a chamber with an inner door, beyond which was a larger, orange-lit space showing glimpses of fittings and equipment panels. "Can you hear me?" a voice called from within.

Jissek nodded numbly. "Yes. . . . Who are you?"

"That would be too much to go into right now. Besides, you don't look as if you've exactly got all day to sit there listening. This is about as close as I can get. Can you make it across? There's plenty of room for three."

"No," Jissek replied. The compulsion to correct was reflexive. "Just two."

They were progressing back in time, toward the war's beginnings.

The *Shapieron*'s doctor pronounced that the uninjured sailor from the raft had slept, eaten well, and was strong enough for visitors. His companion was still unconscious after surgery, with chances of recovery that were not good. The situation did not call for the pestering of a crowd of interrogators. Frenua Showm, who was technically in charge of the political mission, decided that she and Hunt would talk to him. His name was Jissek, the medics had established, and he appeared to be a Lambian.

ZORAC had increased its proficiency as a translator rapidly with the contacts made in the course of these reconnaissance visits. Approaches had been restricted to isolated individuals, which did have the risk that the individual approached might have little of value to tell them. Hunt had suggested keeping things simple and saving time by putting a probe down in the middle of a university campus with a concentration of people who would be able to answer anything, and wrapping the whole thing up in one operation. Danchekker, however, felt that in all the hysteria and excitement that a stunt like that was likely to cause they would probably end up being too deluged with questions and demands for explanations themselves to have much chance of asking any, and the present policy had prevailed.

Showm was silent as Hunt walked with her along the corridor of pale yellow walls and glowing luminescence panels to the clinic and medical bay. Her decision to handle this herself was more than just to complement his scientific perspective and show a Thurien presence, Hunt knew. For her this had become a deep personal matter, involving aspects of her nature that she desperately needed to understand better and to master to progress toward in the inner development that Thuriens regarded as the fulfillment of existence. Hunt had seen her shaken reaction when one of the *Shapieron*'s probes sent back views of the aftermath of a Lambian air strike on an industrial suburb of a city, and watched her face as an intercepted news broadcast showed young orphaned children, some blinded, others missing limbs, telling their stories. For her, the possibility of creating even a sliver of reality in which such things could be avoided was becoming an object of almost religious fervor.

An orderly admitted them to the room. Jissek was sitting in an easy chair by a small table in the outer room of the suite, wrapped in a robe, with baggy hospital pants and fluffy house socks. ZORAC had mentioned ahead that he had expressed a reluctance to receive visitors in bed. He stared at Hunt in surprise. Hunt was the first human Jissek had seen since coming aboard. He had watched over his companion through the probe's trip back to the *Shapieron*, and lost consciousness as soon as the Ganymean medics took charge.

Showm began. ZORAC's translation came from a grille above the table. "The doctor tells us it would be comfortable for you to talk now." Jissek's eyes strayed back to Hunt. "My name is Frenua Showm. We are here just for a short time, from a world that is far away. This is Dr. Hunt, a scientist. We would like to ask you some questions."

"Is there news of Ensign Thorke? The one who was with me. I was told he was being operated on."

"It does not look good, I'm afraid," Showm told him. Typically Thurien, Hunt thought. Incapable of bending anything, even a little. Jissek nodded. He seemed to have been ready for it. Hunt sat down in the other chair at the table. Showm took the couch by one wall.

"You are the Giants, who inhabited Minerva long ago?" Jissek said. "The stories we've heard are true? You went to another star?"

"That is correct."

Jissek looked at Hunt in puzzlement again. "So . . . are you a Lunarian?"

Hunt clasped his hands together on the table, looking affable. "This could get complicated. We've probably all got lots of questions to ask. But you owe us . . ." He paused while ZORAC queried Jissek for a translation of the phrase. "So why don't you answer ours first?"

Jissek nodded. "I'll try."

Hunt looked toward Showm. She consulted some papers she was carrying and verified Jissek's name, that he was from Lambia, a naval officer, and other details that the doctor had already established. It was just to get a dialogue moving. Showm came to the subject of the war. "How long has it been going on now?" Jissek seemed unsure how to answer.

"Was there a formal declaration at some point?" Hunt asked. "A day when Lambia or Cerios announced that a state of war existed with the other?"

Jissek shook his head, as if such an idea were new to him. "It just . . . grew, year by year."

"How did it begin?"

"There was always a problem with the Cerians, for as long

as I remember. They were driven by private greed and corruption, even at a time when the survival of all of us depended on working together as one race. We wanted to move everybody to Earth. . . ."

"Yes, we know about that," Showm said. The Cerians they had talked to put a different interpretation on it, of course.

Jissek went on, "Our king had tried to reason with them, to make them see that what they were doing would destroy the chances for everybody. But they said they would make us do things their way, and they began manufacturing weapons. Lambia had to do the same, to defend itself. The Cerians sent planes over our country to spy on us. One of their spy ships came into our coastal waters. When Lambian naval craft went out to turn it back, it fired on them, and it was sunk in the engagement that followed. That happened before my time in the Navy. But it was probably when the actual fighting began."

"You're talking about the Cerian frigate *Champion*," Showm said, glancing at her notes.

Jissek's eyebrows went up in surprise. "Yes."

The Cerian version was that the *Champion* had been attacked in international waters.

"And that was how long ago?"

"Two to three years. . . . Something like that."

"Does the name Xerasky mean anything?" Showm asked. Xerasky had been the Lambian dictator at the time of the final war.

"No."

So Xerasky hadn't succeeded Zargon yet.

Showm went on, "You mentioned your king. Do you still have a king in Lambia now?"

"Yes."

"King Perasmon?"

Jissek looked surprised again but this time shook his head. "No. He was killed. Freskel-Gar is king now."

Showm glanced at Hunt pointedly. This was interesting. Freskel-Gar had been the last of the kings before Lambia became a dictatorship under Zargon. "How about the name Zargon?" Hunt inquired.

Jissek nodded. "Oh yes. He's one of the king's generals. Very powerful. He commands the advanced weapons program. Highly secret. Cerian Intelligence has been trying to penetrate it—and with some success, due to Lambian traitors and double agents."

"What kind of weapons are we talking about?" Hunt asked curiously. When no immediate response was forthcoming, he prompted, "Nuclear fission, fusion? Particle and radiation beam? Advanced nucleonic?"

"I . . . don't know anything about such matters."

Hunt let it go at that. "How about this General Zargon? Can you describe him?"

"Yes, everybody has seen him in the news and on TV. Not all that tall but very broad." Jissek brought his hands up to indicate his chest and shoulders. "Darkish skin, like a heavy tan, and a black beard—short beard, trimmed and neat. Big chin, pugnacious teeth." Hunt leaned back in his chair and gave a satisfied nod. It sounded like Imares Broghuilio all right. He would have staked an arm on it.

"Tell us about Zargon's background," Showm said. "His career, his record. Which part of Lambia is he from?"

"Not a lot is known about that," Jissek replied. "He seemed to come out of nowhere, very suddenly."

"When would this have been?"

"Again, around three years ago. It was before the *Champion* incident, but not very long before it. . . . Six months, maybe." Jissek hesitated, then added, "If you want my opinion, I think Zargon might not be from Lambia at all. I think he could be a Cerian."

That came as a surprise. "Why would you think that?" Hunt asked.

"He appeared on Freskel-Gar's staff with a group of followers who were very secretive. I don't know even today how many of them there were. But they brought new weapons technologies with them, and set up a program that involved all kinds of advanced scientific knowledge." Jissek made a gesture that asked what else could be made of it. "You see my point? It sounds as if it could have been Cerian armaments specialists from some other part of Minerva, who defected en masse. Just my theory."

"If they were Cerians, why would Cerios need to mount an espionage operation to find out what they were doing?" Hunt asked, smiling faintly.

Jissek had to think about it for a moment. "Maybe they were trying to get it back—if Zargon brought the whole program with him. It would explain all the secrecy, anyway." Hunt nodded that the answer was good enough.

Showm came back in. "Getting back to King Perasmon, you said he was killed. When was this?"

"Three years ago."

"Around the same time, then?"

"I suppose so."

"Had General Zargon actually appeared on Freskel-Gar's staff by this time? Was he around when it happened?"

"I'm . . . not sure."

"So how did it happen?"

"There was a time when many people thought the problems between us and the Cerians could be solved. I'm not sure of the details. . . . Something about the differences between us not being so important after all. I don't think anyone wanted the war. In those days such things were difficult to imagine—the kind of thing you saw in horror movies. So there were hopes everywhere that it could be avoided. The Cerian president—his name was Harzin—came to Melthis to meet the king personally . . ." Melthis was the Lambian capital city.

"Perasmon?"

"Yes. And they made a big speech together saying they had come to an understanding, and from then on all of Minerva would work together. They would keep their system and we could stay with ours. It seemed like a nightmare that had ended." Jissek paused, poured a glass of water from a jug on the table, and took a sip.

"And?" Showm said.

"Afterward they were supposed to fly from Melthis to Cerios for Perasmon to visit there. But their plane was shot down."

Showm had to cover her eyes for a moment, even though she had been hearing a lot of this kind of thing by now. "Who did this?" she asked.

"Cerians. A rogue unit within their military establishment. You see, it was this obsession of theirs with self-seeking and private interests again—instead of thinking of common goals. The state of armed tension gave them a lot of power. They weren't prepared to give it up."

"And after that?" Hunt queried, although it wasn't difficult to guess.

"Oh, there could be no more compromising after that. Freskel-Gar became king. He turned out to be the strong leader that we needed, who wasn't deceived the way Perasmon had been. The Cerians had been arming all along. It was probably Zargon who saved us. Without the defenses he's built up over the last three years, it's practically certain that Lambia would have been invaded by now."

The pieces fitted. Broghuilio and his Jevlenese had arrived when Cerios and Lambia were on the verge of settling differences that had been building up over many years, but which as yet had resulted in no more than skirmishes. But the two leaders who had brought about the reconciliation were assassinated before it had taken any effect. The Cerians had a different version that put the blame on a Lambian plot engineered by Freskel-Gar. The timing invited the suspicion that Broghuilio might have been involved too, but that couldn't be concluded for sure. Whatever the true explanation, Freskel-Gar, the hardliner waiting in the wings, had seized his opportunity, and with Broghuilio either already on the scene or appearing soon afterward, the road toward intransigence, escalation, and eventual all-out war was set. At some point that still lay in the future, Freskel-Gar would reap as he had sown, when Broghuilio-Zargon judged the time right to get rid of him.

This information at last provided a clear pointer to where in time the mission should be aimed. Around three years previously, Minerva had been ready to take a completely different course. The markers to look for were that Freskel-Gar was still a prince in Lambia, and Perasmon and Harzin were still alive. But it also needed to be before the Jevlenese arrived, to enable Harzin and Perasmon to make suitable preparations for dealing with them. But precisely when the Jevlenese had arrived was not known, and further questioning was unlikely to establish it, since the installation of Broghuilio and his entourage had been carried out in secrecy. The secrecy surrounding their presence and origins also meant that simply failing to find any sign of their ships couldn't be taken as indicative of anything—there was no sign of them now, but the Jevlenese were surely here.

The final marker to look for would be the absence of a response from the *Shapieron*'s daughter probe that had followed the Jevlenese ships through the spacetime tunnel. ZORAC had signaled it on every reconnaissance visit and found it functioning, and it was there now, functioning normally, on this visit. When they reached a point upstream in time where no response could be evoked, it would mean that the probe wasn't there yet, and so the Jevlenese couldn't have arrived yet either.

Chien thought that the optimum psychological moment for the *Shapieron* to make its arrival would be as close as possible to the joint announcement of the new understanding by Perasmon and Harzin from the Lambian capital, Melthis, when the whole of Minerva would be optimistic and hopeful. Showm agreed, and the proposal was drawn up for Calazar to approve formally.

There was still the other side of the bargain to be fulfilled. After some clothes had been found for him from the Terran stores, Jissek was taken to the *Shapieron*'s Command Deck to meet the other members of the mission. There, as he had promised, Hunt explained as fully as was pertinent the strange story of where the ship was from and why it had come back to Minerva. After the events since his rescue, however, it seemed that Jissek was capable of believing just about anything, and he accepted the account phlegmatically, though not pretending to comprehend all of it. The ship's doctor then called to break the news that Jissek's companion, Thorke, had died as feared.

Frenua Showm looked at the young officer with obvious concern and compassion. "Before very much longer, your world will end horribly and violently. We know that. It cannot be changed. But for you, it doesn't have to be that way. You can come back with us, to a world of peace and wonders that you are unable to imagine, with the rest of a life to look forward to, and a future."

Jissek stared back at a screen where one of the views of Thurien that they had shown him was still displaying. Smiling distantly in a resigned way, he told about his wife, their new son, and the parents who worried about him. "If such things are to pass, they will need me there all the more," he replied. "I thank you, but that is where I must be."

Hunt and Showm went with him in the transit tube to the stern docking bay where the probe was waiting. It would take him to a cove along the coast, near to a Lambian naval base. Jissek waved a farewell from inside as the doors closed. A minute later, they watched on a docking bay monitor as the probe exited from the ship and shrank away into the starfield. Frenua Showm's face was making strange twitching movements. It was the first time, Hunt realized, that he had seen a Ganymean cry.

CHAPTER THIRTY-FOUR

Laisha felt upbeat and lighthearted, with hopes for the future that she hadn't known for years. It was as if a growing burden inside that she had ceased being aware of was suddenly lifted. And on top of that, there was the sense of gratification and accomplishment that came with the thought that she had played a part, even if a minor one, in bringing it about.

President Harzin had been in Melthis for two days. The interim bulletins released to the world's news services were encouraging, and it had just been announced that they would be making a joint statement to the peoples of both Cerios and Lambia at noon that day, before Harzin's scheduled departure. The gossip around the offices in the Agracon, the complex of government buildings in the center of Melthis being used by the delegation Laisha was attached to, was that it would be the accord that all had been awaiting. It had also been noted that King Perasmon's calendar showed no fixtures for the few days immediately ahead, which perhaps indicated a surprise program to be unveiled at the same time. Laisha sat at her desk in the translators' room, tidying up her notes and records. There was little work going on that morning. She conjured up pictures in her mind of Minervans working together, and the fleet of ships taking shape that would one day carry them to Earth.

Uthelia stuck her head in through the doorway from the press office. "Hey, Laisha Engs. You've got a phone call."

"Me? Who from?"

"Well, I don't know. You'd better come and find out. Try to make it quick, though. We need all the lines we can get this morning."

Laisha got up and went through to the clutter of paper-strewn desks and beeping phones where the Cerian journalists and reporters worked. The Lambians had supplied lines to their offices back home. Uthelia gestured toward a handset off its cradle on a table stacked with files in a corner. Laisha picked it up. "Yes? This is Laisha Engs speaking."

"Hey, how proper and formal! Very professional. I'm impressed."

"What? . . . Kles, is that you?"

"Ha-ha! Surprised? Happy Birthday."

"But it's not my birthday."

"So? Birthdays are supposed to have surprises. Where's the surprise in being told Happy Birthday when it is your birthday and you're expecting it?"

"Oh, Kles, you're so daft. So where *are* you?"

"Still on base. We've got a class going on here, to do with communications and codes and stuff. It made me think of Wus Wosi, that guy I knew at college. You remember him?"

"The ball player?"

"That's him. Well, I remembered he's working with the NEBA news bureau in Osserbruk now. I figured they must have some way of talking to you guys over there in Lambia, so I called him on a special cleared channel that we have here. And guess what. Here I am!"

Laisha shook her head despairingly but smiled. "You're crazy. But it's great to hear you voice. Especially today, after all the work we've been putting in. It tops off the good news."

"Let's hope it is good news, anyway. But I have to make it short."

"I know. Me, too. But I'm glad you thought of me."

"I do all the time. You know that."

"And me."

"Well, take care with that Lambian brandy. I have to go. Maybe we'll see you back soon."

"I hope so. Goodbye, Kles."

"And . . . well, you know. There's guys around."

"I know. Me, too."

Laisha replaced the phone and turned to go back. Uthelia was watching her. Her face had a pinched look, as if she were mildly resentful. Perhaps she just begrudged anyone's using the office's time. Whatever, it was her problem, Laisha decided as she walked back through to the translators' room.

Now back in his flagship aground on the lunar far side, Imares Broghuilio paced restlessly across the floor of the bridge deck. Estordu and a group of aides were standing behind a signals operator's console, watching a picture being picked up on one of the Lambian news channels. It showed King Perasmon and President Harzin addressing a crowd from the center of a group of figures out on a balcony at the front of the Agracon. Another screen showed Freskel-Gar, his adjutant, and Broghuilio's general Wylott at the fortress-palace of Dorjon, twenty miles from Melthis. Freskel-Gar was conferring with two officers updating him on the state of the preparations.

Everything seemed to be going smoothly. Freskel-Gar had been dissatisfied with Perasmon's rule and laying plans for a coup to seize power himself for some time. However, an opportunity had just presented itself to get rid of Perasmon and take over as the legal successor, which happened to coincide with Broghuilio's arrival. At the same time, it promised to bring about just the kind of irreconcilable split between Lambia and Cerios that Freskel-Gar needed. Perhaps feeling that he needed to impress Broghuilio and gain his confidence if he was going to be given Jevlenese weaponry, Freskel-Gar had been surprisingly generous in sharing details of the situation and his plans.

From his own intelligence sources, Freskel-Gar had divined that following their address to the people, Perasmon would be returning with Harzin, the Cerian president, to make a symbolic reciprocal visit to his guest's home country. In a hastily devised operation designated Hat Rack, a missile would be launched from a flight of three Lambian interceptors flying at high altitude when Harzin's presidential plane was over the far side of the ocean. Waiting until it was closer to Cerios would make a cover story implicating a rogue faction of Cerians more credible. Planting an on-board bomb would not have looked good on a Cerian plane that had taken off from Lambia, inviting accusations of failed security if nothing else.

Although Freskel-Gar would succeed automatically when news came of Perasmon's demise, there was always the chance of some kind of opposition emerging and impeding a rapid establishing of control. in some form. He was mobilizing his forces accordingly as a precaution. The units assigned to securing key points and installations were ready to move; Freskel-Gar's own picked troops were heavily represented in the roster of duties around the Agracon; and prominent legal and political figures ready to endorse the legitimacy of the succession were standing by. If necessary, the moves to secure his position and place the right people in office would be carried out under the justification of emergency provisos following the assassinations.

Wylott and his advance contingent of Jevlenese had been installed at Dorjon, but they would not be taking an active role in the events planned for that day. The Jevlenese would be integrated into the national scene gradually and invisibly, avoiding the risk of a public reaction that could unite Minerva in opposition. Wylott's part would be to prepare the way for bringing the rest of the Jevlenese down from the Moon. That night, while Minerva was still in confusion, the five ships secreted on Farside would slip in to deliver their occupants to a transit site being prepared in a remote part of Lambia. The ships would be stripped of as much as would be useful, and then sunk in the ocean. It was regrettable, but once their power was exhausted they would become more of a liability than anything, while having to account for them in the event that their existence was discovered would create impossible difficulties.

"Excellent," Freskel-Gar said. While he dismissed the two officers, Wylott came back to look out from the screen. Broghuilio looked back at him inquiringly. "Reception parties to meet the ships tonight are being organized," Wylott informed him. "Temporary accommodation is being made ready, along with supplies of clothing and provisions."

"Good." Broghuilio nodded.

Freskel-Gar joined Wylott. "Will we need to do something about recovering scuttling crews after the ships are sunk?" he asked.

"That won't be necessary," Broghuilio replied. The ships would simply be sent down into one of the deep trenches on automatic control, and opened to the ocean.

A muted roar from the crowd sounded at the screen Estordu and the others were watching. Broghilio told the operator to turn up the volume. The two leaders had declared a truce between them as had been widely anticipated. Then, while the noise was still abating, they went on to announce Harzin's invitation to Perasmon to visit Cerios, and their imminent journey together—precisely as Freskel-Gar had predicted. Broghuilio had already marked Freskel-Gar as shrewd, calculating, able to wait until his time was right, but at the same time possessing the nerve to move swiftly and surely when he saw his opportunity. An invaluable resource to have around for securing their position in the period immediately ahead, Broghuilio had decided. And in the longer term, dangerous.

At that moment the bridge-deck computer interrupted with an announcement. "Attention. We have an anomalous surveillance alert."

"Report to Station 5." A crew officer brought screens and indicators to life.

Broghuilio moved across, frowning. "What kind of alert? What's happening?"

The officer studied the displays. "Something strange, Excellency. Intermediate C-band has picked up an unidentified object. It seems to have just suddenly . . . appeared, about a million miles out."

"Object? What kind of object?"

The officer took in more data. "It's not one object. It's two. There's another one a few hundred miles away from it."

Freskel-Gar was watching the activity from the screen connected to Dorjon. "What's happening up there?" he demanded.

"We're not sure," Broghuilio told him.

They were still debating the anomaly, when the computer came again: "A larger disturbance is building up, registering seventeen-six in beta octave."

The officer reported, "About a thousand miles from the away from the first. This one is much larger. It's transmitting some kind of signal in h-mode."

For several seconds, Broghuilio just stared. It didn't make any sense. "That's impossible," he declared.

Nothing had existed in the age of Lunarian Minerva that could produce h-radiation.

"Homing beacon is locked on and checking positive. Backup beacon is functioning. You're set to go. Good luck, *Shapieron*. Sequencing out . . . Transferring."

They were back at Minerva, now six months before the sinking of the Cerian frigate *Champion*. The silence dragged while ZORAC scanned for the probe that had always been the indicator that the Jevlenese had arrived. Every previous reconnaissance had found it not far away from Minerva—which was to be expected if it had only recently arrived. But it used Ganymean h-space signaling, so there would be no noticeable turnaround delay in any case.

"Negative," ZORAC announced. Startled looks, some disbelieving, flashed around the *Shapieron*'s Command Deck. Was this really it, finally?

"Repeat the scan and confirm, ZORAC," Garuth instructed.

A sort delay, then, "No response registering. There's no sign of it."

No probe; no Jevlenese. The mission had arrived.

Hunt ran his eye over the faces. They were tense. This was not another reconnaissance. It was the real thing, what the whole mission had been leading up to. Eesyan was looking at him questioningly. Showm was watching. Danchekker looked on impassively from one side. Hunt returned a faint nod.

"We go with it," Eesyan said to the team waiting at the other end of the link back to Thurien. Calazar and Caldwell were connected in again. It had become a sort of custom. On this occasion they just sent silent salutations.

"Wave function consolidated and stabilized," Garuth confirmed. "Ready to detach."

"Dissolving the Gate bubble."

"Local bubble deactivated." The *Shapieron* was on its own, a free creature in its natural element once again.

The next thing was to establish the exact date. They knew by now when the Harzin-Perasmon assassination had taken place, and could tune into Lunarian broadcasts. As had previously been decided, VISAR had aimed for as close to that date as its coarse scaling would allow. They expected having to make a few fine corrections to edge closer—ideally to within a couple of days of the incident, which would have Minerva in a hopeful mood, while at the same time allow the mission some margin to make contact and communicate its message to the right people. Hunt moved to where Chien was standing, behind one of the Ganymean crew operators, watching him sift through the Lunarian communications spectrum. A reference to Harzin indicated him to be still alive. Things were looking promising.

"So, are we merely following a path between our reality and this one that was always here?" Danchekker's voice asked from behind Hunt. It was a mild gibe at naturalist materialism. "No, I refuse to believe it. Frenua was right. We are creating a new reality. Whole worlds will come into being from this, Vic." Danchekker had been entertaining some radical departures from his customary habits of thought since getting involved with the Thurien philosophers. Four years ago, Hunt wouldn't have believed it. Once one of the most ardent and inflexible defenders of the theory of mind as simply an emergent property of matter, his latest assertion was that mind is no more an accidental product of nervous systems than the plays of Shakespeare were an accidental product of marks on paper.

"You'll be taking up politics next, Professor," Chien said impishly. "Enrolling in the diplomatic corps."

Danchekker rubbed his nose with the crook of a finger. "I'm inclined to suspect that we may have done that already. What else would you call this escapade?"

The Ganymean operator gave an over-the-shoulder glance that said, *How about this?* Hunt leaned forward to see. The screen showed a crowd in what appeared to be some kind of city square, cheering a group of figures up on a balcony. Moments later, a switch to close-up showed the two in the center to be Harzin and Perasmon. The operator gestured to the bar across the bottom of the screen in a way that said there was no need to comment.

Hunt read the details. "Oh God!"

Eesyan came over. "What?"

"VISAR was right on. We're *too* close, Porthik." Hunt pointed. "It's today!"

CHAPTER THIRTY-FIVE

Broghuilio stared incredulously at the image framed in the long-range surveillance shot. There could be no mistaking the form with its sleek curving lines, flaring at the stern into four swept tail surfaces. The last time he had seen the *Shapieron*, it was closing in on his ships fleeing from Jevlen. If it hadn't been for those Ganymeans from the past and their accursed starship, the whole conspiracy of circumstances that had resulted in him and his Jevlenese being flung into this predicament would never have happened. A vein began throbbing in his neck. He could feel the self-control and sense of staying on top of events despite all that had taken place starting to slip.

"How did *that* get here?" he whispered, turning his face belligerently to Estordu.

The scientist made a helpless gesture. "I can only conjecture that it came through the tunnel with us."

"I thought your experts assured us there was no trace of anything else. They said it was just us."

"I . . . must take it that they were mistaken."

"Experts!" Broghuilio spat that word and turned away malevolently, his hands clasped behind his back.

"What's happening?" Freskel-Gar demanded from the other screen, having overheard.

"Copy the image through to Dorjon," Broghuilio told the operator.

Freskel-Gar's head turned as he took in the presentation from a different direction. "What is that vessel there? Are you telling me now that your ships were not alone?"

"It's too much to go into now," Broghuilio said. "There seems to be a complication that I was not prepared for. It may call for some quick action."

Freskel-Gar studied him penetratingly from his screen for several seconds, then nodded tightly. "Right now, you obviously know more of the facts than I do. Tell me what you want done." A fast thinker and a realist, at least, Broghuilio granted inwardly.

Broghuilio paced across the bridge, stopping to stare unseeingly at the unmanned flight engineers' stations of his grounded craft while he thought furiously. Then he turned, regarded Estordu and the others for a moment, and wheeled finally to face Freskel-Gar again.

"Another race inhabited Minerva long ago—a race of different beings."

"The ones we call the Giants?"

Broghuilio nodded. "That ship is one of theirs. My ships here are fitted with armaments that they are not aware of, so the advantage is with us."

"They know you are here, then?" Freskel-Gar said.

"Not necessarily."

"Are you saying they didn't follow you? Why else would they be here?"

"It's a complicated matter to go into now. They could be simply searching for our whereabouts. I expect them to try and make contact with you somehow. If we can entice them down to Minerva to negotiate, we will have the potential of surprise on our side. How are communications routed from your satellite ground stations?"

"Via the national telecom net."

"And messages intended for the ruling authority would find their way . . . where?"

"To the communications room at the Agracon in Melthis. It has direct links to the Military Command Headquarters also."

"It may be necessary to move parts of the plan forward," Broghuilio said. "We need to be in control there. Can your people take over inside the Agracon, now? It's especially important to secure the communications."

Freskel-Gar nodded. "I've got my men in most of the key places already. The important guard details are all ours. They are at mobilization alert."

"Order it at once. How long would it take you to get there from Dorjon to take charge?"

"My staff flyer is manned and standing by. Ten minutes at most."

Broghuilio nodded. "Go there. General Wylott can complete our arrangements at Dorjon." He thought for a moment longer, then added, "And get Hat Rack airborne, in case that needs to be brought forward too."

Freskel-Gar seemed to check through the items in his mind. "Very well," he said, and turned to begin reeling off a list of instructions to his adjutant. Broghuilio turned back to Estordu, who was consulting various data displays.

"What are those other two object that appeared first? The smaller ones. Have you established that?"

"Unfortunately not, Excellency."

"They aren't probes from the *Shapieron* again, like that one you said was right behind us?"

"No, they are something else. They appear to be of unfamiliar design and purpose."

Broghuilio scowled. The probe had provided the eyes and intelligence for the *Shapieron* when it was pursuing them. "I don't like it." He called to the ship's captain, who had been obtaining confirmatory readings from one of the other ships. "Bring your secondary laser batteries to firing readiness and keep them trained on those things. Also, have all ships brought up to flight standby." The captain passed on the orders.

"Can I ask our plan, Excellency?" Estordu inquired.

"We have no indication that they are aware of our presence down here. And there is no reason to alert them to it," Broghuilio answered. "We wait."

"It's too close." Eesyan shook his head. "We need to be a few more days further back."

"Call Thurien via the beacon for a correction," Shilohin, the *Shapieron's* female scientific chief said. "Can VISAR can pitch it finely enough if we're this near?"

"It should be able to," Eesyan answered.

"ZORAC," Garuth called. "Call—"

"*No!*"

Surprised heads turned toward Frenua Showm.

"No," she said again, and looked around imploringly. "Think what you are saying." She half turned toward the screen next to which Hunt, Danchekker, and Chien were still standing. They had just caught the end of Harzin and Perasmon's address. The two leaders had announced that Perasmon would be returning with Harzin in the Cerian presidential aircraft, and they were already disappearing back inside the doors at the rear of the balcony from where they had been speaking. Some of those who had been with them were following, while another in a uniform had stepped forward and was delivering some closing words. Showm went on, "There's a world full of people down there who have just been given the first hope they've known for years. Real, warm, alive, flesh-and-blood people, like us. They have homes, children, loves, dreams. But we know, you and I know, because we've been in their future, and we've *seen* the horrors that are in store for them . . . all the way through to the militarized nightmare that their world will turn into, and its final total destruction. And you're saying that we just call Thurien and go home, and let it happen! How could we, after the things we've seen? The rotting corpses; the lame, the blind, the crippled; the burning cities. How could any of us sleep easily again?"

"We're too close. There isn't enough time—" Eesyan started to say again.

"There *is* enough time! So Perasmon and Harzin are flying today. How long does a journey halfway around Minerva take with an aircraft of their period? Four hours? Five? We know the plane won't be destroyed until it's approaching the Cerian coast. A missile from something flying at high altitude. The plane's electronics officer even caught it coming in on radar just before it hit. Never mind the spectacular landing and public theatrics that the mission strategy talks about. All we've got to do is access somebody high enough in the chain to divert the flight. The explanations can come later."

"Would we be able to convince them in time?" Duncan Watt asked dubiously. "They have no idea who we are."

"We have several hours," Showm insisted. "Put me on and let

me talk to them. A Ganymean. One of the Giants who inhabited Minerva in the distant past. Don't you think that would get their attention?"

Danchekker was shaking his head, at the same time showing his teeth, as if looking for a way to put something delicate without offending. "What you say is true, of course, Frenua. It's all most distressing. But even were we to succeed, it's still merely one infinitesimal sliver in a totality of unimaginable immensity . . ."

"It's a *world* of people. Living, thinking, feeling, *people.*"

Hunt pinched his eyebrows together with his thumb and fingers. Danchekker was right, of course. What Danchekker might also have been trying to remind Showm of but wasn't saying was that the future of this world was fixed anyway. Nothing could change it, anymore than a past that had already happened—which of course was what it was. What the mission could hope to achieve, what the physicists and philosophers were still arguing over, was whether an action initiated across the Multiverse would give rise to a new future that had not existed previously. But emotions were running high, and he wasn't about to get into it.

"Whatever we do, I suggest we get on with it," Chien said. "They could be on their way to the airport already."

Although Eesyan was technically in charge of the mission until they made contact with the Lunarians, he inclined his head to concede Showm the floor. "Garuth," she said, "Can you get us a connection? We need the Lambian government system in Melthis—whichever department is the most closely involved in Perasmon's affairs. The best place to start would probably be the Agracon."

The white phone beeped on the desk of Vazquin, the head of the translation section. That was the Agracon's internal system, not connected to the outside. Vazquin was away from his desk at the moment. Laisha turned in her chair and took it. "Cerian translators. Laisha Engs speaking."

"This is Farissio. I'm in the communications room in the main building. We need a translator here. Can you get over immediately?" Farissio was a senior negotiator with the Cerian delegation. He sounded strained.

"Well, yes, of course. What—"

"Just do it, please." Another voice in the background, clipped and harsh, said something that Laisha didn't catch. Farrissio hung up. Mystified, Laisha threw a pen and notebook into the bag that she carried for office chores. The translators' offices were located in one of the peripheral buildings at the rear of the Agracon complex, outside the secure zone that included the main building. To get to the communications room she would need to check in at the guard desk and get a Lambian escort. She made sure that she had her ID and clearance papers, and hurried for the door, followed by one or two curious looks.

Downstairs, Laisha exited through a side door that she had learned led to a short cut, and followed a narrow alleyway along the rear of the VIP transportation garage to a path leading to one of the access roads. Something about the atmosphere of the whole place had changed. Although there was no outward noise or fuss, Lambian soldiers were everywhere, moving swiftly and purposefully. Sudden misgivings seized her that something had gone terribly wrong.

Another alley brought her to a side door of the restaurant and staff cafeteria. Cutting through to the main entrance would bring her out opposite one of the guard posts into the secure zone. She had just entered the building and was following the corridor past the kitchens toward the dining areas, when Mera Dukrees, one of the delegation's technical specialists, came hurrying toward her, apparently taking the same route in the opposite direction. He looked distraught, casting anxious glances back.

"What is it?" Laisha asked.

"I'm not sure. There's some sort of takeover going on. Soldiers herding people around. They've got the whole place sealed off in there."

"How did you get out?"

"An argument broke out at the gate just as I got there. I slipped through. I think it might be a move to overthrow Perasmon." Raised voices and shouts of protest sounded inside the building from the direction of the dining areas. Dukrees gripped Laisha's arm to keep her attention. "But don't you see what it means? If that's what's happening, this is only a part of it. That plane isn't going to get there!"

Laisha shook her head and brought a hand up to her mouth. "Oh no!"

"Were there soldiers back at the offices when you left?" Dukrees asked her.

"They were around outside, but nobody had come in yet."

"There might still be a chance to get word out. Communications from inside the secure zoneare all blocked. Come on."

A short passage off the corridor where they had met led to rest rooms and some stairs. On the wall in a recess by foot of the stairs, Laisha spotted one of the white internal phones. "There's no sense in both of us getting stopped," she said. "You go ahead. I'll try from there." She pointed. Dukrees looked, nodded curtly, and hurried away. Laisha went to the phone and hammered in the number for the press office behind the translators' room. At least, in the side passage she was out of sight from along the corridor. She wasn't even sure what she planned on asking anyone to do.

Ri-ing. Ri-ing. "Oh please, please . . ."

"Cerian Press Office."

"Uthelia, is that you?"

"Yes. Who's this?"

"Laisha. Look, there isn't time to explain. That line you had to that person at NEBA in Osserbruk earlier. Is it still open?"

"It should be. Why—"

"I need you to call him again. His name is Wus Wosi."

"Really, all this is most irregular, you—"

"*Uthelia, shut up!* There isn't time for that! Just call him!"

Laisha's tone was enough. "What do you want me to say?" Uthelia asked, sounding shaken.

Voices sounded at the end of the corridor from the dining areas. "Get three men over here. Check down there. Secure all outside doors."

Laisha forced herself to speak slowly and clearly. "Listen very carefully. There is a Lieutenant Klesimur Bosoros, at a Cerian army base. Wus knows how to contact him. The president's plane is in some kind of danger—I'm not sure exactly what. Bosoros needs to get the message to Cerian High Command." A warning via the military, originating from the Agracon in Melthis, seemed more likely to get attention than an allegation by someone at the NEBA news bureau.

"Are you serious?"

"There's some kind of coup going on. They'll be over there any moment, Uthelia. Just do it."

"Wus Wosi at NEBA. Lieutenant Klesimur . . . Bosoros?"

"Right."

"*You!* Phone. No!" The Lambian trooper barked in broken Cerian, at the same time motioning menacingly with his rifle but not pointing it.

"It's okay. I speak Lambian," Laisha said as she replaced the handset.

"Who were you talking to?" an NCO demanded, appearing behind the trooper.

"It's the internal house line. I'm a translator with the Cerian delegation. I was called to the communications room, but I lost the way. I was trying to call for directions."

The Lambian NCO peered at her badge. "Your clearance?" Laisha produced the papers from her bag and waited nervously. "Come with me. I will take you to the security gate out front. You two, carry on."

"Sir."

Laisha emerged with the NCO from the passage just in time to see Mera Dukrees being led back in through the outside door at the far end of the corridor.

The figure looking out of the main screen on the *Shapieron*'s Command Deck was lean and hawk faced, with dark, mobile eyes like a bird's and a pair of tapered mustachios. He wore the uniform of a Lambian field marshall. More figures were standing in the background, some also wearing uniforms, others in civilian clothes. He seemed about as composed as anyone could be expected to be, who within the last few minutes had found themselves talking to a company that included beings from a race that had vanished long ago, speaking from a starship standing somewhere out in space. In fact, Hunt thought he seemed too composed; it was almost as if something like this happened every week.

"The king is at this moment out of the country on state business," Freskel-Gar informed them. "As First Prince of the Realm I am fully able to represent him." News reports from Minerva had confirmed that the plane carrying Perasmon and Harzin had left during the time it had taken the *Shapieron* to establish the right contact.

"You must have a means of communicating with him," Frenua Showm said.

"By our constitution, I *am* the official acting head of state in the king's absence," Freskel-Gar replied smoothly. "I welcome you on behalf of the Lambian Crown and its dominions on this truly momentous historic occasion."

"Insisting on going over his head could be offensive," Danchekker said from the side. ZORAC would edit it from the outgoing audio. "We don't know enough about their ways to be able to judge. I wouldn't advise risking it."

They knew that as Perasmon's successor, Freskel-Gar would eventually take a harder line in his dealings with Cerios. But that didn't mean he was committed to such a course today. There was nothing that specifically linked him with the assassinations. All kinds of factions and intrigues abounded on both sides on Minerva, and Freskel-Gar would succeed as king whoever had been responsible.

"The most significant factor, perhaps, is that Broghuilio and the Jevlenese have not arrived here yet," Shilohin offered. After two years of being stationed on Jevlen as planetary administrators on behalf of the Thuriens, the *Shapieron* Ganymeans had no doubt who had been the cause of the deterioration to all-out war that had followed. "It will be four years before Broghuilio overthrows this Freskel-Gar and proclaims himself dictator. A lot can happen in four years."

Monchar, Garuth's second-in-command on the ship, endorsed the point. "The assassinations would be enough on their own to send things into decline, even without Broghuilio. Especially if each side suspected the other. Preventing them from happening could be the single most important result we could achieve. Failing to do so could make everything else futile."

Showm took a long breath while she composed her words. Then she looked back up at the screen showing Freskel-Gar. "How we know the things that we know is a long and complex story that is better told at a more fitting time. The fact of our appearance should be enough to give ample weight to our words. The aircraft that has just departed from Melthis carrying your two heads of state is in imminent danger of being destroyed. I don't wish to

harp over details. There may not be time. But it is imperative
that you issue orders immediately for the flight to be rerouted
to the nearest safe landing facility until the circumstances are
investigated. Then, there are events shortly to befall your world
that will have calamitous consequences for all of Minerva if they
are not averted. After those things are dealt with, we can talk
about the uniqueness of the occasion and the development of
relationships between our races."

All eyes around the Command Deck were fixed on the main
screen. Freskel-Gar's features knotted as he took in the strange
mixed company of vanished aliens and unfamiliar humans. They
could almost read his thoughts. *Appearing from nowhere and
claiming to know our future?* And then, again, *But beings whose
civilization was advanced before we even existed, and a craft that
travels from the stars?*

"How can you know such things?" he demanded.

Showm emitted a sigh that conveyed impatience being controlled only with difficulty. "I have already said, there isn't *time*
now. All will be explained in due course. For now, just do as we
ask. Call down the flight."

Freskel-Gar stared uncertainly for a few seconds longer. Then,
seeming to make his mind up, he turned and conferred with the
others who were with him. They murmured and gesticulated among
themselves for what seemed ages. Hunt caught Danchekker's gaze
and just raised his eyebrows. Chien watched impassively. There
was nothing for any of them to say.

The deliberations on the screen ended finally, with nods and
a couple of people hurrying away. Freskel-Gar advanced the
forefront again. "Very well," he said. "Instructions are being
issued in accordance with your wishes. We are calling the
flight controllers now, and making alternative arrangements for
landing." The sighs of relief aboard the *Shapieron* were audible.
Frenua Showm had to put out a hand to steady herself. "And
now, perhaps we can give consideration to hearing the rest of
what you have to tell us in more propitious surroundings befit-
ting to the circumstances," Freskel-Gar suggested. "It shall be
our honor to receive you here, personally, as guests of Minerva.
We await your account with considerable impatience and limit-
less fascination."

✳   ✳   ✳

Silence endured for a while in the communications room at the Agracon after the screen showing the transmission relayed from tracking stations had cut out. Troops of the Prince's Own Regiment who had secured the building stood at their posts by the doors. Perasmon's staff had all been removed. Freskel-Gar's people manned the consoles and monitor panels.

"Are we done?" the communications major who had taken temporary charge checked.

"Link down. We're off the air," a technician confirmed. Freskel-Gar relaxed and looked inquiringly toward the screen showing Broghuilio and his staff on the bridge of the Jevlenese ship on lunar Farside.

"Splendid!" Broghuilio acknowledged. "An impressive performance, Your Highness. I could almost have believed it too. But I do you a disservice; it is 'Your Majesty' now. . . . Or very soon to be, anyway."

CHAPTER THIRTY-SIX

Freskel-Gar advised that the aircraft carrying the two national leaders was on its way to a safe landing ground, and he had received a message of compliments and respects from them to pass on to the *Shapieron*. They would receive a deputation from the ship jointly, possibly in Cerios, as soon as their own revised itinerary was put in order. In the meantime, a preparatory meeting at Melthis would facilitate arrangements greatly, and the landing there should proceed as he had suggested. It was neither Calazar's nor Caldwell's style to insist on being involved in every stage of every decision. The strategy for the mission had been set, and it was up to the people on the spot to determine the best way of implementing it. Frenua Showm sent a report to Control at Thurien via the primary beacon on the latest happenings, and turned her attention to preparing for the meeting with Freskel-Gar.

They made the descent in one of the *Shapieron*'s general utility shuttles—a craft larger than the reconnaissance probe that had rescued Jissek, but smaller than a surface lander, which would have been too large for the helipad area inside the Agracon complex, where the Lambians had directed them. Eesyan and Showm were the principal Thuriens, accompanied by a small staff; Hunt and Danchekker represented Earth; Monchar and two of the ship's officers went too, on behalf of Garuth. The *Shapieron* moved closer in to launch the shuttle but remained within the

Moon's cone of visual eclipse from Minerva. It seemed fitting to let the planet's governments announce the vessel's presence to the population in their own time, rather than have it revealed prematurely by an outbreak of pandemonium among the astronomical community.

Hunt was quiet as he sat in the cabin of the shuttle, watching the orb of Minerva enlarging on one screen, while the Moon, which they had passed close by, slowly shrank on another. His mind went back five years to the discovery of "Charlie"—the spacesuited corpse on the Moon that had been the first trace of the Lunarians to come to light. The subsequent investigation, orchestrated mainly by Gregg Caldwell while the rest of the UNSA chiefs were trying to draw lines between who should do what, was what had first brought Hunt and Danchekker together. One of their first major achievements had been the reconstruction of Charlie's world from information contained in documents found on his person and other evidence that had shown up later. That was when they had christened it Minerva. Hunt's group had built a six-foot-diameter model of it in his laboratory at Houston, from where the UNSA investigations had been coordinated. He remembered spending long hours gazing at that model, trying to bring to life in his mind the picture of a lost world that had existed fifty thousand years ago. He had gotten to know every island and coastal outline, the mountain ranges and the equatorial forests, the inhabited areas and major cities sandwiched between the advancing ice sheets. What he was seeing on the screen now looked entirely familiar. But this wasn't a model in a lab or a computer's reconstruction. It was real, and it was out there. They were on their way down to its surface.

The Moon, on the other hand, presented an unfamiliar countenance—one that was smoother and with less features than the pictures he had known from science books and encyclopedias since childhood. The Moon that looked down on the unfolding saga of human history, the emergence of its various races, the struggles of their earliest ancestors to survive, had carried the scars of the ferocious battle fought across its surface in the final days of the war before it was obliterated by billions of tons of debris when Minerva broke up. But those events were twenty years in the future yet. The Moon that attended Minerva was still unsullied and serene.

"A strange, circular course of events, don't you think?" Danchekker's voice said from nearby. Hunt looked away from the screens. "Long ago, Minerva's orphaned Moon traced its solitary course to Earth, bringing the ancestors of our kind. Now here we are, the descendants of fifty thousand years later, returning to where it all started. Rather in the manner of paying homage to our place of origins; a pilgrimage, as it were." Danchekker had evidently been entertaining similar thoughts of his own.

"A bit like salmon," Hunt said.

Danchekket clicked his tongue. "You really can be quite Philistine at times, you know, Vic."

Hunt grinned. "Probably a touch of New Cross coming through," he said. That was the area of south London where he had grown up. " 'Every inch a working man, an' proud of it,' my dad used to say. He didn't have a lot of time for high-falutin fancy stuff. 'The 'igher a monkey climbs, the more of an arse 'e looks to the rest of us,' was another one. He could never fathom the kinds of things I got into. Said the only thing I'd be good for was going off into other worlds. I suppose he was right enough about that." Danchekker blinked through his spectacles, not quite sure how to reply.

Monchar and the two crew officers from the *Shapieron* were silent. They alone among all those in the descent party had actually seen Minerva before. They were not Thuriens. For them it was the lost home they had departed from millions of years ago—somewhere over twenty years by their own reckoning—magically restored once again.

The shuttle broke through a high layer of cirrostratus. Below, Hunt recognized part of the southern Lambian coastline showing intermittently against the gray ocean between patches of lower cloud. "You've got company coming up," ZORAC observed, speaking from the *Shapieron* but reading the shuttle's radar via a probe positioned off to one side of the Moon. The screens showed interceptor jets rising and spreading out into an escort formation around the descending craft—whether as an honor guard or to keep a wary eye on it was impossible to say. They were swept deltas design mounting side-by-side engines in a flattened fuselage beneath twin tail fins—uncannily like some of the Terran designs of the turbulent period around the late twentieth century. As with things like sharks and dolphins, shapes that worked were probably restricted within quite narrow limits and likely to be found universally, Hunt guessed.

"You're on course and looking fine," the Lambian ground controller who was seeing them down reported. "The landing area is clear."

"We have your approach beam," the Ganymean copilot acknowledged. "It's looking like just over three minutes."

"Check."

"Does it look familiar?" Eesyan asked Monchar and the two *Shapieron* crew officers.

"No," Monchar replied, staring at the images. "Everything has changed."

The city of Melthis took shape and resolved into progressively finer detail until a cluster of buildings that the descent radar identified as the Agracon steadied in the center of the view. They opened out and grew, transformed slowly into profiles of roofs and windowed facades sliding slowly upward on the screens showing the side views as the shuttle came down between them, and then were stationary. The mild humming that was all the shuttle produced to mark its exertions, died.

"Landed. Powering down. We are on the planet Minerva," the pilot announced.

"It's been a long time," ZORAC said, presumably for the benefit of the three original Ganymeans aboard. They seemed a bit too overcome to respond.

The views from outside showed that they were in an open space surrounded by high gray buildings that looked imposing and solid, with a scattering of gray, scrubby plants sprouting in beds by the wall and along paths across patches of gray lawn. Hunt was already forming the impression that this whole world might be a composition of grays, like an old black-and-white movie. Vehicles were parked around the edges of the area: an assortment of ground cars and trucks, and some helicopter-type craft crammed to one side as if they had been moved out of the way. The cars, like the buildings, looked solid and indestructible, but utilitarian and boxy. Detroit stylists would have despaired. The predominant colors seemed to be black, a kind of khaki . . . and shades of gray.

No Lunarians had been visible when the shuttle touched down.

But after the engine cut, figures began appearing through what seemed to be the rear entrance of one of the larger buildings flanking the square and moved out toward the craft. For the most part, their garb was of the monotonous, tuniclike patterns that the *Shapieron*'s previous visits had shown to be characteristically Lunarian, along with variations of common themes that suggested uniforms. A number of topcoats and hats were in evidence. "I think it might be cold out there," Hunt said.

"Nine-point-three Celsius," ZORAC supplied.

Frenua Showm and Eesyan moved up to stand facing the inner door of the shuttle's lock, with Hunt, Danchekker, Monchar, and the two *Shapieron* officers behind them. An indicator showed the lock pressures to be balanced. The inner door opened. They moved forward. Then the outer door opened. A wave of cool, damp air met them. It carried a hint of the odor of tunnels that pervades subway stations and was slightly pungent.

In a typically Thurien touch, Eesyan and Showm did not pause at the top of the ramp, where they would have eclipsed the two smaller Terrans squeezed in the lock chamber behind them, but descended at once to where there was space for all to spread out and be presented equally. Although basic information had already been exchanged via the communications connection, it seemed that the occasion required a few formal words. Showm gave the customary Thurien head-bow of greeting, introduced herself, and proceeded to name the others with her. The link back to ZORAC, via a relay connection in the shuttle, made it available as a translator, but the distance of the *Shapieron* created a turnaround delay of three to four seconds. Interacting was not as sophisticated as the methods developed later with VISAR. The party wore headbands carrying audio and video pickups, with information from ZORAC delivered through clip-on ear pieces and wrist screens. Showm concluded, "We have come from a world known as Thurien, a planet of the star that you know as the Giants' Star."

The central figure of the group facing them wore a uniform with lots of braid and a peculiar three-cornered hat—the uniforms were noticeably more ornamented than those that would come into use later, when the war got serious. He was of stocky, rounded build, and light brown in countenance like the others, with a flattened nose and narrow eyes that lent a vaguely

Asiatic appearance. He held himself upright and replied stiffly. "Gudaf Irastes, Commanding General of the Household Forces to Crown Prince Freskel-Gar of Lambia and its dominions." Iraste hesitated, his eyes flickering uncertainly in the direction of his retinue. Then, evidently deciding his wasn't about to go through the list of all of them, "Greetings on behalf of Minerva. Freskel-Gar is waiting inside to receive you. If you will follow this way . . ."

They proceeded in through the entrance that the Lunarians had emerged from. Hunt noticed several figures in the background following them with what looked like movie or TV cameras. Inside, a short hallway brought them to an open vestibule area of marbled floor, surrounded by square columns going up to overlooking galleries. Corridors led away left, right, and ahead, between clusters of alcove spaces and doors. They went past the main staircase leading up to the galleries, and behind it passed through an archway to stairs leading down. At the bottom were sturdy double doors attended by guards. Beyond the doors, they followed a stone-floored corridor through surroundings that seemed severe compared to the halls above. The thought was just forming in Hunt's mind that this seemed an odd kind of setting in which to receive the first diplomatic delegation from an alien race of another star, when they entered a room where a number of uniformed Lambians were working at desks and consoles. It turned out to be an anteroom to a spacious, brightly lit area filled with screens and communications gear. Armed Lambian soldiers were stationed along the walls. More entered behind the party and took up stations inside the door. Prince Freskel-Gar was waiting with members of his staff at the far end. His expression was not that of a host about to welcome guests, but stony and hard.

But the sight that caused the arrivals to stop dead in disbelief, Thurien and Terran alike, was the group of figures framed in a large screen facing the floor. They were human, but not Lunarian. The leader standing at their head leered, his teeth showing white in a huge chin behind a short black beard as if he had been relishing this moment. ZORAC wasn't needed to translate his words. Hunt, Danchekker, and every Ganymean present were conversant with Jevlenese.

"Most obliging of you. My compliments go out to Calazar. I

couldn't have planned this better myself," Broghuilio said. "I'm so sorry that I could not be there to receive you personally, but it would not have been convenient. However, I'm sure we will not be deprived of that pleasure for very long. We are not far away."

He looked aside and nodded to a Jevlenese wearing what looked the uniform of a ship's captain, who signaled affirmatively to somewhere. "Fire the lasers," a voice off-screen instructed.

Wearing shorts and a house robe, Caldwell sat on the arm of one of the chairs in the summer room of his home outside the city in Maryland, watching as dutifully as any grandfather would while his ten-year-old grandson, Timmy, tongue-between-teeth, produced a commendable rendition of Mozart's Drawing Room theme on the baby grand. It was one of those balmy summer days that were made for forgetting that organizations like UNSA and places like Thurien existed. Outside, Caldwell's daughter, Sharon, was with her husband, Robin, by the pool. Maeve was in the kitchen with Elaine, the housekeeper and cook, discussing ideas for dinner—or whatever else women discussed in kitchens.

Timmy finished with a flourish and emitted the breath he had been holding in his concentration. "Bravo!" Caldwell said, patting his palms appreciatively. "New York next season? Or will we have to wait a little longer?"

"I know all the scales too. Pick one—any one you like."

"How do I do that?" Caldwell was about as musical as a tin wash tub.

"Just pick a key then."

"Umm, okay. . . . That one." Caldwell pointed at a black one.

"That's A flat. Now say major or minor."

"Oh, with me, I guess it has to be the major."

Timmy proceeded to run up the octave and back down. It sounded right, anyway.

Robin came in through the patio door. Clinking sounds from outside told of Sharon picking up dishes and glasses. "What's this? Showing off to grandpa, is he?"

"Sounds pretty good to me," Caldwell said. "I still think a crotchet's some kind of knitting."

"Are we having dinner in or going out? Have we decided yet?"

"The manager of that department is discussing it now."

Robin pulled a shirt over his shoulders and began buttoning it. "Sharon tells me you've got some kind of Open Day coming up at Goddard."

"Right."

"What's that all about?"

Caldwell raised his eyes. Even ten years previously, with secrecy and security still a hangover from the days of militarization, it would have been unthinkable. "Don't remind me. I was just enjoying my day off. It's on Tuesday. The powers that run our world have decided that since the public pays for most of what goes on at Goddard, the public has a right to see for itself. So we've got lectures, lab exhibits—you know, the usual kind of thing." A phone rang somewhere in the house.

"Sounds interesting. I might try and get along. Tuesday, you said?"

"If you don't mind hordes of tourists and kids taking over the staff dining room. It's a blessing Chris Danchekker isn't around right now."

"Gregg, it's for you." Maeve called from the next room.

"I'm incommunicado." Caldwell refused to carry a compad on his days off.

"It's Calazar. They put him through from ASD. He seems really serious."

"Oh. That's different. . . . Excuse me, Robin." Caldwell went through to take the call.

Robin turned his head to Sharon, who was just coming in carrying a tray. "Calazar? Does he mean the Thurien leader?"

"That's right."

"Everyone knows that," Timmy put in.

Robin shook his head. "My father-in-law gets calls at home from other star systems? I'm never going to get used to this."

In the next room Caldwell moved around to face the screen. "Byrom, hello. What's up?"

"I've just got word from Gate Control. They've lost contact with the beacon. Everything went dead at once."

It was certainly strange for Thurien engineering to malfunction. But did it really warrant a call like this? "So we go to the standby unit," Caldwell said.

"That's dead, too. They both went out at the same time."

The implication was at once clear. Yes, it did warrant a call like this. The only explanation for both beacons going out together was that some agency had deliberately destroyed them—they had been spaced far enough apart to avoid simultaneous stray impact hazards.

But even worse, the beacons were VISAR's locator. They provided the only way to find that particular universe again. Without them, there was no way to bring the mission home.

CHAPTER THIRTY-SEVEN

Back up in the *Shapieron*, the rest of the mission personnel had been monitoring the progress of the shuttle's landing party as relayed from their headband pickups. Not having been part of the previous Jevlen expedition, Chien was the only one among them who didn't recognize Broghuilio immediately. Duncan and Sandy were speechless. Garuth was still staring bemusedly at the view of the screen down in the Agracon showing the Jevlenese, when ZORAC interrupted. "Commander, I think we may have a serious emergency. I've just lost all contact with both the M-space beacons. Hi-mag scan shows rapidly dispersing debris at both locations."

Garuth was too nonplused by the succession of bolts out of the blue to respond immediately. Shilohin had joined him when Broghuilio started speaking from the screen inside the room beneath the Agracon.

"They were obviously destroyed," she said. "It could only be the Jevlenese."

"Is there any indication of a direction that something might have come from?" Garuth checked with ZORAC.

"Negative."

It still made no sense. How could the Jevlenese be here? The probe that followed them through the tunnel would also have to be here, but careful checking and rechecking had shown no sign

333

of it. Yet every one of the checks carried out in the reconnaissance visits further on in time had confirmed it to be out there and functioning, so how could it not be working now? Unless they had just happened to hit on a universe in which, unlike every other one that they had sampled, the probe had malfunctioned. . . . No. Garuth rejected the probability. But if the Jevlenese were here ahead of the *Shapieron* after all, why was there no sign of their five ships? Nothing was adding up. He realized with a start that Broghuilio was speaking to him.

"I assume that the proceedings in Melthis are being followed by the rest of you out there in the *Shapieron*." Garuth noted the words "out there." So the Jevlenese were somewhere that was "in." Broghuilio went on, "It probably hasn't escaped your notice that we possess considerable firepower. You may take what just happened to your scouting devices as a demonstration of its potency. It is now trained upon your ship. In case your vision is still clouded in some way, allow me to summarize the situation as it now exists. You no longer have VISAR and the Thuriens to hide behind. A most interesting change of perspective, I think you must agree."

Garuth was under no illusions as to what that meant. After the *Shapieron*'s eventual departure from Earth, Broghuilio had attempted its destruction in order to prevent a true picture of Earth from reaching the Thuriens—as opposed to the distorted one that the Jevlenese had been drawing. Only the timely establishing of direct communications between the Thuriens and Caldwell's UNSA group had prevented it. As Garuth continued to listen, still in a semi-daze, Chien's voice came through in his ear piece. The tone was subdued, indicating that ZORAC was connecting her privately.

"Garuth and Shilohin. You realize what this means. Freskel-Gar's whole performance was a ruse. Therefore everything he told us was false. No message of acknowledgment was received back from Perasmon and Harzin, for none was ever sent. There have been no orders to divert the Cerian aircraft. They're still in danger . . . if it isn't too late already."

Garuth froze and then groaned. His concern had been so much for those down on the surface who had just walked into a trap, his ship and the threat posed by the Jevlenese, to think through the further implications. It also helped to be able to think like a Terran.

"Of course!" Shilohin whispered.

"We are the only ones who can stop it," Chien said. "It will have to be through the Cerians. Obviously no one in Lambia can be trusted."

Garuth stared at the image of Broghuilio on screen, but he was not hearing the words. Chien was right. It was up to them now. His mind raced frantically. "ZORAC."

"Commander?"

"Local," indicating that what Garuth said was not to be repeated over the channel to Minerva.

"Acknowledged."

"I don't know what their plans are or if I'll be able to communicate freely. What I want you to do regardless is this. Get access to the Cerian military command system, their space operations agency, or the department of government that handles the president's affairs. Warn them there's a plot in motion to destroy the aircraft flying from Melthis with President Marzin and King Perasmon aboard. We think it will be brought down by a missile. The flight must be turned around or diverted immediately."

"I'm working on it now."

Seeing the helplessness written across Garuth's face was a gratification in itself. The *Shapieron* and its occupants were the greatest personal anathema in Broghuilio's existence. He recognized Garuth, of course, from the storm of publicity that had followed the appearance of the *Shapieron* at Ganymede and its later six-month stay on Earth, when Broghuilio had directed the Jevlenese surveillance operation reporting to Calazar. That ship had been responsible for bypassing him and the Jevlenese to open up direct contact between the Thuriens and Terrans, and the unraveling of everything Broghuilio and his predecessors had been planning for generations. It had been the instrument for perpetrating the deception that brought down JEVEX, costing Broghuilio his overlordship of Jevlen and putting an end permanently to his ambition to assert himself over Terrans and Thuriens alike. And here it was now, as defenseless as a puppy brought to heel. It had evaded his attempt to destroy it once before, making him appear a fool in the process. He had no compunction about the thought of settling that score now and finishing the job.

But as he continued looking at it, a new line of thought began to develop in his mind.

Why destroy the *Shapieron*? As he had just pointed out with great relish to Garuth, a most interesting alteration of the entire perspective had taken place. He had five ships here on Minerva's moon, all-but immobilized and barely carrying the power reserves to transport him and his followers down to Minerva, after which they would be good for nothing more than scuttling in the ocean. But here, hanging as a telescopic image on the screen right in front of him, was a fully self-contained starship, not only equipped with its own on-board power sources and designed for independent operation and endurance, but which had sustained its population of Ganymeans for something like twenty years. They didn't have to go to Minerva as refugees and beggars after all, forced to share their superiority and trade their natural advantages for a place to sleep and scraps from Freskel-Gar's kitchens. With something like the *Shapieron*, fitted with the weapons he had been about to consign to Minerva's oceans and starship power available to energize them, they would be able to dominate a planet like Minerva within a week.

The more Broghuilio dwelt on the thought, the more it intrigued him. However, like any prospective owner of real estate, he would want to inspect the property himself before deciding his offer and terms. But what kind of unknowns would he be risking, walking into a ship full of Ganymeans from the past that he had no experience of dealing with? Even if they turned out to be as fawning and indisposed toward a fight as Thuriens, he knew nothing about the AI that managed the ship and how it might react. He summoned Estordu across with a motion of his head. "In the days when that ship was built, there was no planetary executive intelligence comparable to VISAR. Is that correct?"

"That is so, Excellency. Full integration was effected later, after the move to Gistar and Thurien."

"So this ZORAC that we heard about while that ship was at Earth. What kind of system is it?"

"The earliest Ganymean starships had integrated control and system management directors that became surprisingly versatile and in fact provided some of the design philosophy later incorporated into VISAR. The *Shapieron* is probably one of the later models. ZORAC would be an intermediate development between a rudimentary autonomous intelligence and a hyper-parallel distributed architecture of full interstellar capability like VISAR or JEVEX."

"I see." Broghuilio didn't, but the words intended nothing in any literal sense. He stared at the image of the ship again. "What would be the way to go about attaining control of something like that? Does it automatically obey whoever commands the vessel? Or does is develop a more complex allegiance that builds up in some other way over time? What is its mode of operating?"

Estordu followed Broghuilio's gaze and saw which way his thinking was going. He replied, "Please understand that I have no personal experience of such systems, Excellency. But my understanding is that its primary characteristics are those of a multiply connected, self-referential learning hierarchy driving an auto-optimizing emergent associative net." He saw color rising above Broghuilio's collar and explained hastily, "That means that its behavior is shaped more by its experiences than by the initial design parameters. It would most likely have evolved a strong commitment to the present complement of officers and crew—especially so after their long, enforced period of isolation from the familiar spacetime environment."

"Hm." It obviously wasn't the answer that Broghuilio had been hoping for.

Estordu went on, "However . . ." His tone caused Broghuilio to turn his head. "The system builds itself on an underlying foundation of core directives that cannot be modified, ignored, or overridden. They define its essential design role and character. One of the most fundamental would be that other considerations are subordinated to ensuring the safety and survival of the bioforms that it has formed its principal attachment to. In the present case, such a tendency would have become extremely pronounced. Anything else it might judge to be right or wrong, or as being likely to have preferable consequences in the longer term, would be rendered immaterial. I, er . . . trust you take my point?"

A gleam of comprehension came into Broghuilio's eyes. "You mean that if it was the only way of protecting the skins of those fossil Ganymeans in there, it would follow our orders? It wouldn't refuse?"

"More than that, Excellency. It *couldn't.*"

"Hm . . . I see." And this time, Broghuilio really did. Maybe he had a solution to both of his immediate concerns.

He contemplated the image of the *Shapieron* for a while longer. Before it followed his ships through the tunnel—for that was the only way to explain how it came to be here—it had been conducting a secret deception operation at Jevlen. He didn't imagine that it would be carrying much more than the minimum number of occupants and crew for such a mission. And that suited his purpose well.

Broghuilio moved back to confront the screen connecting him to the *Shapieron*'s Command Deck.

"These are my instructions," Broghuilio said from wherever it was that the Jevlenese were concealed. "You will embark yourself and all occupants of your vessel in auxiliary craft and remove yourselves. I want the ship left available for boarding, with a clear zone around it of fifty miles. Immediately."

Garuth stared at him incredulously.

"We can't," Shilohin whispered beside him. "Look what just happened to the beacons." And the Jevlenese hadn't hesitated before, when they attempted to destroy the *Shapieron* after its departure from Earth.

"You're insane," Garuth replied. If they wanted the ship, it seemed that the crew would be safer inside it. "Do you think we're going to—"

"You seem to forget that you are not in any position to bargain," Broghuilio cut in. His image shrank to a half screen, the other half showing as a reminder Eesyan, Frenua Showm, Hunt, Danchekker, Monchar, and Garuth's two other officers now being covered by Lambian soldiers with leveled weapons, with Freskel-Gar looking on. "This is no idle threat. Would His Highness confirm?"

"On your order," Freskel-Gar said from the screen.

"Perhaps we'll begin with just one," Broghuilio said.

Garuth found that his mouth had gone dry. His instinctive urge was to call on ZORAC for advice, but he fought it down. This was the commander's decision to make. Staying where he was would mean sacrificing his subordinates and friends for certain—and he could end up losing the ship even then. Complying would possibly be to invite his own demise, in which case what would happen to those down on the surface was unclear. With the latter alternative, nothing was certain. Shilohin seemed to read the further implications too and held back from making things any tougher.

"We must have time," Garuth said.

"I have no time to waste playing games." Broghuilio waved a hand in the direction of the prisoners, indicating the more junior of Garuth's two crew officers. "Have that one step forward."

It was the most agonized and humiliating decision Garuth had ever taken. "Very well," he agreed. "It will be as you say."

The message still showing on Frenda Vesni's desk display in the headquarters of the Cerian Department of Internal Security had come in from an office of the National Aerospace Directorate that operated the satellite tracking stations. The NAD divisional chief who passed it on had appended: *I don't know what to make of it. Your call.*

The door from the adjoining room opened abruptly and Negrikof came out. "*What is this?* Calls from talking starships? . . . Doesn't someone think we have better things to do? There are some really sick people out there, I'm tellin' ya."

Vesni hesitated, biting her lip. "You don't think we should alert the President's Office . . . as a precaution?"

"What? And look like the biggest idiots in the Department? It's some student hacker or somebody, who's gotten into their system."

"But isn't that what we're here for? To convey information?"

"Yes. And also to *evaluate* information. I've been around since longer than yesterday. Any nursery-school kid could get through NAD security. I'm going to see Grat along the hall. I'll be back in a couple of minutes."

"What do you want me to do with this?"

"Oh . . . tell Dira to file it in case someone needs the details some day. You never know, they might get smart enough to track it down." Negrikof continued muttering as he crossed the office. "As if we didn't have enough to do with Perasmon deciding he's coming here all of a sudden. . . . Talking starships." He left, closing the door noisily.

Vesni looked at the message for a few seconds longer. She still thought it was a sloppy way to be going about things. But . . . the boss had spoken. Reluctantly, she tapped in an addendum and flagged the item for Dira's attention. In her estimation, Negrikof wouldn't have been risking much if it did turn out to be a hoax. She already thought he was one of the biggest idiots in the Department anyway.

The officer commanding at the base watched from behind his desk as Kles was ushered into his office. "Lieutenant Bosoros, Sir," the unit commander announced, and remained standing inside while the orderly sergeant closed the door. The OC studied the note again and had the lieutenant repeat the story.

"And you got this information from where?" he said dubiously. "Somebody you know at NEBA? A journalist?"

"It was just passed on by him, Sir," Kles replied. "The information originated from somebody who is in Lambia, with the technical delegation at the Agracon in Melthis."

"Might I ask who this person is, Lieutenant?"

"Er . . . my fiancée, sir. . . . I think. . . . I hope."

"Oh, I see. She's there in what capacity?"

"A technical translator with the delegation, sir."

"Her name?"

"Engs, sir. Laisha Engs."

"Hm." The OC made a note and stared some more at the sheet of paper. "You're telling me that this was communicated from inside the Lambian Agracon, to you in a military base here in Cerios?"

Kles bit his lip and drew a breath. There was no way around this. "Yes, sir."

"You're aware of the gravity of such an admission, I take it?"

"Yes, sir."

"This delegation is under whose direction? Which department do they report back to? Do you know?"

"I think it's NSRO, sir."

The OC thought for a few seconds longer, then snorted and reached for his phone. "If this turns out to be in error, Lieutenant, you're in deep trouble with a lot of explaining to do. . . . Yes, get me General Oodan's office at Division immediately, on the secure line. There's something extremely urgent that I think they need to check with the Scientific Research Office. Extremely urgent." He replaced the handset, sat back, and looked at Kles. "If it's genuine, I won't ask how it was done."

"Sir," Kles acknowledged.

CHAPTER THIRTY-EIGHT

They had been moved from the place where they were taken first to meet Freskel-Gar, which had seemed like some kind of war room or communications center, to plainer surroundings of painted walls, padded plastic seating, and office-style metal furniture. The seats were ill-suited to Eesyan and Showm, who alternated between perching on the edges uncomfortably and standing. Two armed guards were posted inside the door, with more outside. There seemed little question that they had walked in on the middle of something much bigger than just a ruse prepared for their benefit. Freskel-Gar had seemed in a hurry to dismiss them after Broghuilio had his chance to gloat, which showed an odd lack of curiosity toward a ship carrying live aliens, arriving from the future. The proceedings throughout had been interrupted by ceaseless calls and messengers coming and going. It was as if they were being put off while matters even more pressing were dealt with. To Hunt, it felt as if they had arrived in the middle of a revolution.

Danchekker, who was sitting in a swivel chair next to Hunt, turned his head a fraction. "I rather fear that if—"

"No talk!" one of the guards barked from the door. Danchekker lapsed back into silence. They had picked up enough Jevlenese during their stay there to know that it had a distant resemblance to Lambian, and were able to recognize a few words. The Lambians had relieved the captives of their headbands, ear pieces, and wrist screens, depriving them of communication with the *Shapieron* and of ZORAC as a translator. It also meant that conversation with the Ganymeans who were with them was no longer possible.

Danchekker's disposition was to remonstrate and make a fuss when there was a chance it could have some affect on things, but when that ceased to be the case he would lapse into a resigned silence to await what couldn't be altered. Hunt was the opposite—more like Caldwell. Sitting, doing nothing, and waiting simply wasn't in his nature. Whatever the odds might be against its making a scrap of difference, his compulsion was to *do* something.

The most immediate concern was the plane with Harzin and Perasmon aboard, at that moment on its way to Cerios. If Freskel-Gar's whole line had been phony, it was a safe bet that his assurance of the flight's having been diverted was a deception too. In fact, as Hunt thought about it, and taking into account his admittedly scrappy knowledge of the events that were due to unfold in the years ahead, it seemed pretty clear now who had been behind the downing of the flight. His feeling of having come in halfway through a revolution wasn't so farfetched at all. It was right on!

The irony of the situation was that it had been the assassination of the two leaders that had put Freskel-Gar in his position as successor to Perasmon, which a strong Lambian element had been opposed to. The hard line that Freskel-Gar had taken, encouraged by the general and close advisor Zargon—clearly Broghuilio as had been suspected—had led to the irreparable animosity that had set Cerios and Lambia on their course for war. Yet from the things learned in the *Shapieron*'s reconnaissance visits, it needn't have happened, even at this late stage. *The Cerians knew.* Their military had gotten wind of the plot and sent a warning to the security people, but somebody there sat on it. The affair caused a scandal, heads rolled, and jobs were lost, but that all came too late to change the course of events.

Garuth and the others up on the ship might have figured it out as well, of course, but Hunt had no way of knowing that, or what they might have been able to do about it if they had. So that left Hunt and the rest of them here, down on the surface. But what could they do, locked up under armed guard and without communications?

The only possibility he could think of was to find some way of rocking Freskel-Gar's confidence before his position became unassailable, which might cause him to have second thoughts. Hunt did a mental tally of the resources at their disposal that might be brought to bear. They didn't amount to much. They had arrived in a starship that was far beyond present Minervan technology, but so had Broghuilio and his Jevlenese—in fact, five starships, no less. True, the *Shapieron* was capable of independent operation whereas the Jevlenese ships depended on facilities that didn't exist yet in this universe, but the point probably wouldn't impress itself upon Freskel-Gar in the space of the next few hours, which was what mattered. They were in the company of aliens of a kind that had vanished from Minerva in the distant past, and while that would be a source of boundless interest to scientists, academics, archeologists, and the like, it was unlikely to overwhelm somebody of Freskel-Gar's practical disposition. The kind of aliens more likely to capture his attention would be ones who talked of war and brought weapons, and he already had those in the form of Broghuilio and the Jevlenese.

The only thing left, then, was to resort to bluff. They knew, and Freskel-Gar would have no way of explaining how they knew, that the Cerian presidential plane was about to be shot down by a missile that it seemed pretty likely was Freskel-Gar's doing. If strangers appearing from another world knew about it, wouldn't it seem probable that many other interests on Minerva that could prove problematical were likely to find out too? Freskel-Gar came across as a sharp calculator. Maybe he could be induced to reconsider letting the assassination go ahead if it seemed more likely to lead to consequences that would undermine his situation rather than solidify it. At least it was a tangible aim. Whatever happened after that could follow as it came.

That much having presented itself, and not a lot else, Hunt indicated by gestures to the guards that he wanted to talk. One of them motioned him across. Hunt got up and approached, accompanied by curious looks from the others. The guard indicated for him to stop a good eight feet away. "There, you [something-something]."

"Talk Lambia prince." Hunt indicated the door. "Freskel-Gar."

The guard shook his head. "No talk. Highness [unintelligible] other man." Trying to bridge between old Lambian and later

Jevlenese was tedious. Having ZORAC around made a big difference. The thought suddenly gave Hunt an idea of how he might
be able to use this to get access to ZORAC. He mustered what
he could recall of the smattering of Cerian he had picked up in
their reconnaissance interviews and strung a few words together
in an improvised sentence. The guard shook his head again.

"Cerian, no understand."

Hunt gestured again and made his voice urgent, mixing Lambian and Cerian words as if he didn't know the difference.
"Must . . . important . . . Freskel-Gar . . . danger." The other guard
muttered something and tapped on the door. It was opened from
the other side, and he left.

"Stay," the first guard commanded. Hunt complied, feeling a
bit like a dog being trained. He hadn't exactly been planning on
going anywhere.

After a wait the door opened again, and the second guard
reappeared. "Come talk [something] prince [something] quick."

The guard brought Hunt back to the communications center
where they had been before. Things were still hectic. Freskel-Gar
was talking to some officers and consulting a battery of screens
displaying terrain and city maps. One showed the *Shapieron*
hanging in space. Whether it was coming from a Minervan
astronomical observatory or surveillance gear deployed by the
Jevlenese somewhere, there was no way of telling. To his alarm,
Hunt saw that one of the full-size surface landers was pulling
away from it, having evidently just detached. The only reason to
be using it would be to carry everyone who had been on board.
But before Hunt could think any more about what it might mean,
Freskel-Gar turned.

"Well?"

"Hunt," Hunt said, pointing to himself.

"What do you want?"

Feeling mildly foolish, Hunt smiled ingratiatingly and went into
his act of mixing up the languages again. Freskel-Gar frowned as
he tried to follow. "Apologies," Hunt said. "Know Cerian more.
Easier with starship translator computer." It was one way of getting access to ZORAC, anyway. Quite ingenious, even if he did
think so himself.

"Not necessary," Feskel-Gar said. "We can get you a Cerian
translator."

※   ※   ※

Laisha sat with Farrissio and the other Cerians who had been inside the Agracon's secure zone. They were in a dingy room that looked like some kind of store, somewhere on the level where the communications room was situated, below the main building. She was still bewildered and had no idea what was happening. The crash from the euphoria she had been feeling less than an hour previously had been so total and sudden that she still wasn't capable of thinking clearly. This *couldn't* be happening, not after Harzin and Perasmon's speech, the reconciliation between their two countries, and everything it implied. She had tried to tell herself several times that at was all a bad dream and force herself to wake up. But there wasn't any waking up. It *was* happening.

After she saw Mera Dukrees being led back inside after trying to get back to the delegation's offices before they were occupied, the Lambian NCO took her to the guard post outside the restaurant building and waited with her until an escort appeared to conduct her to the communications room, where she had been heading in response to Farrisio's summons. But she never got as far as the communications room. She and her escort were stopped along the way by a Lambian officer with some soldiers and diverted to another room, where Farrisio and the others with him were by then being held. Farrisio hadn't realized the situation at the time he called her over, and had attributed it to a misunderstanding when he found himself suddenly being hustled out of the communications room. Prince Freskel-Gar had appeared with an entourage as the Cerians were being brought to their present location. The only thing Laisha could conclude was that he opposed Perasmon's position and was making a bid to take control of Lambia himself. She didn't know if Uthelia had managed to get the warning off to Kles's friend at NEBA, or even if she had attempted to, because Dukrees never arrived at the press office. So now all she could do was sit and stare at the stacks of boxes and the bare walls, ducting, and pipes, nursing a remnant of hope that she might still wake up.

The sound came of the door being unlocked. Everyone looked up. A Lambian woman in some kind of uniform stepped in, leaving a guard framed in the doorway behind. "There is a translator here?" the woman said, addressing the room in general. The Cerians exchanged uncertain looks among themselves. Some came to rest on Laisha. She tried to speak up, found that her voice caught in her throat, and had to swallow to clear it.

"I am a translator."

"You are wanted. Come this way."

Accompanied by the guard, they followed corridors full of hurrying figures to a set of double doors with guards posted on either side, and then through to an anteroom where uniformed clerks were working at desks and consoles. The woman signed for Laisha to wait there with the guard and went forward to say something to an officer stationed in front of the inner door. He nodded and disappeared inside, giving a momentary glimpse of a bright area filled with screens and communications equipment. Laisha gulped as she recognized the sharp-faced, mustachioed figure of the Lambian crown prince, wearing the uniform of an army field marshall, at the center of a gaggle of officers and aides. They waited while figures entered and left. Couriers arrived at intervals through the outer door to deliver messages to the clerks.

Eventually, the officer who had gone inside reappeared with another, wearing a Lambian colonel's uniform. Another man was with them, of unusual appearance. His clothes were unlike any that Laisha had seen before, and he stood tall and long-limbed, with uncommonly fair skin, more pink than brown, and hair that was light too, and bent into waves. His eyes were also lighter than any she had seen, and were, quick, missing nothing. They lingered for an instant on the guard and the woman who had brought Laisha from the room the Cerians were being detained in, came back to Laisha, and seemed to read the situation immediately. He caught her gaze and grinned. Laisha didn't know how to respond and glanced away, keeping a straight face.

"The Cerian translator," the woman in uniform said.

"We need help with this stranger." The colonel turned his head toward the light-skinned man, inviting him to speak.

The fast clipper from Thurien docked inside a bay in the central part of MP2. Calazar and a group of scientists from the Quelsang Multiporter were met by the Assistant Controller for the MP3 Gate and an assistant. The party hurried through to the facility's control center. Virtual travel was conventionally regarded as suitable for conducting routine business or for relaxation and pleasure, unless no alternative was possible. On this occasion, it would hardly have been considered appropriate.

"What's the news?" Calazar asked when they arrived at the glass-walled gallery looking out across space toward the distant array of projector bells and associated constructions. Caldwell was already connected through from Earth, superposed visually in an avco window.

The Controller looked grave. "Nothing, I'm afraid. There's not a trace. It's completely dead."

Calazar had pretty much known. If anything had changed, he would have heard. He gestured imploringly. "Is there nothing that can be done? It's not possible for VISAR to conduct some kind of search?"

"There's nothing to search *for*. If the beacons are dead, they are invisible in M-space. So is the *Shapieron*. The only way to find the universe it's in would be by sending an instrument probe to try and match the environment and look for it. The number of times you'd have to do that to have any chance of success appreciably greater than zero makes it simply not practicable."

"But there's a huge number of universes out there that will have versions of the same thing going on, right?" Caldwell said. "Doesn't that even up the odds a bit?"

"Marginally," the Controller agreed. "But you're still up against the sparse distribution statistics that we encountered earlier." He rubbed his brow for a moment between his two thumbs. "Also, even if we were extraordinarily lucky and did hit on a universe with the *Shapieron* there, we'd have no way of knowing that it was 'our' *Shapieron*, if you know what I mean. In fact, the overwhelming likelihood would be that it wasn't. With an operating beacon, its umbilical connects uniquely back to our universe here. There might have been countless versions of it, but that made it 'our' beacon, in the same universe as 'our' *Shapieron*. Now that no longer applies."

"As long as they got back, I'm not sure they'd be too particular," Caldwell answered.

The girl had the typically short and round build of a Lunarian, with what would have passed for Mediterranean skin on Earth. Her hair was straight and black, with almond eyes that looked Oriental and made her quite pretty. She was dressed in a plain beige trouser tunic with a high neck, a brown sleeveless over-vest, and carrying some kind of bag. The woman with her had said "the Cerian translator." The girl hadn't been brought through into the communications room, where the *Shapieron* was still showing on one of the large screens. An armed guard was standing a few paces back. Hunt guessed that the word was meant literally, and the girl was from the Cerian technical delegation known to have been in Melthis as a prelude to Harzin's visit. That made it somewhat difficult for him to be too explicit in revealing what he knew about the assassination plot. Bluntly stating the facts through somebody from the other side would place her at an unknown risk, which would be unconscionable. Hunt couldn't even be sure that the Lambian officer who had brought him out to the ante-room was in on it. Banking that the woman and the officer were not linguists, Hunt switched to more coherent Cerian than he had shown previously, when he was trying to gain access to ZORAC.

"Officer represents prince? *Are you a Cerian prisoner?*"

The girl looked startled for a moment but composed herself, catching on quickly and translating the first question only. She relayed back the colonel's answer, "You may talk to him. Freskel-Gar is very busy at present." Then added, "*Yes, with the Cerian technical group.*"

"Tell him the visitors know things. Very important Freskel-Gar be aware. *Plane is in danger.*"

"The colonel asks, what things? *Who are you? How do you know?*"

"We know the action, event planned today that involves missile. We know who is responsible. If we know, others will know. Lambia will stand . . . guilty, to be blamed. *Very complicated. Don't endanger yourself.*" The officer's expression conveyed that it didn't mean much to him. Hunt persisted, "Freskel-Gar should know that ships of other visitors have limited power. Cannot be refilled. Soon useless. Bad bargain. The large ship is good . . . for a long time. Without limit. *The Giants have returned.*"

The girl's eyes widened. "The colonel says yes, he will pass that back. Is that all? *From the stars?*"

"Freskel-Gar must stand by Perasmon. War will be . . . ruin, end . . . of Minerva. *We know your future. Bad. Trying to change it.* Please stress urgency."

The officer listened, nodded, and went back through the inside door.

"How can you know the future?" the translator asked.

"No talking now," the woman escorting her snapped.

"Putting you through to General Oodan now."

"Oodan."

"Hovin Lilesser of NSRO for you, General."

"Hello? Lilesser here." Lilesser was the person Oodan had tasked to try and locate the member of the National Science Research Office's delegation in Melthis who was allegedly responsible for originating the warning.

"Yes. Oodan speaking."

"This is uncanny. We've been trying to contact the delegation in Melthis for almost an hour. Communications seem to be out. The Lambians say there's a computer down or something. But how did you know?"

"What do you make of it?" Oodan asked.

"I'm not really sure. It's very unusual. They should have backup for this kind of thing."

"There could be something strange going on, then?"

"Well, I don't know. That's not really for me to say. Why? Is something else happening?"

"I'm not sure. . . . Leave it with me. Thank you. You've helped as much as you can."

"Any time."

Oodan replaced the phone and stared at it for almost a minute. A remarkable coincidence, he decided. Coincidences always made him suspicious. The Internal Security people needed to be in on this. They were the ones who dealt directly with the President's Office. He picked up the phone again.

"General?"

"Who do we know at DIS? I need to talk to somebody there right away. Find out who handles the President's personal security, or someone to talk to whoever does. This can't wait."

"At once, General."

CHAPTER THIRTY-NINE

Prince Freskel-Gar watched the screen showing the Giants' ship while he listened to the colonel's summary of the message from the human accompanying them who had called himself Hunt. With all that was going on that day, he hadn't had time yet to discover what the story was behind this awesome-looking vessel whose appearance had troubled even Broghuilio. It was coasting in space, maintaining a position that kept the Moon interposed between it and Minerva. The view was being captured by one of the Broghuilio's ships on the Farside surface. It was being relayed too, from the Agracon, to Wylott and his advance group of Jevlenese at Dorjon. The Jevlenese were also human, but they seemed different from the two who had landed with the Giants. It sounded as if this was going to be a complicated story.

The last-minute decision to bring forward the takeover at the Agracon had been pulled off surprisingly smoothly, with the world outside still unaware that it had happened. It was important that news of Perasmon's end be known first, before Freskel-Gar began moving overtly to consolidate his position. As expected, there had been a barrage of calls and messages querying the apparent hitches with communications, and some visitors had been inconvenienced, but by and large the cover stories had stood. Later, an explanation could be concocted attributing the early moves in the Agracon to security precautions taken in response

351

to an intelligence alert that had been recognized only later as pertaining to the assassination. To minimize the time for which the action at the Agracon would need to be concealed, Hat Rack had also been brought forward and would now be executed over mid-ocean. That part of the operation was being directed by Freskel-Gar's deputy, Count Rorvax, from Dorjon. For obvious reasons the details had been made available only to an absolute minimum who had a need to know.

All in all, Broghilio's show of nerve had paid off. His improvised amendment to the plan to accommodate the sudden change in the situation appeared to be working. This surely wasn't a time for Freskel-Gar to be losing his nerve and over-reacting. So the big news from Hunt, the colonel was telling him, was that the Giants knew about "an action" and "who was responsible." All very vague, with nothing specific stated explicitly. Freskel-Gar didn't see how they could know—even the colonel who was delivering the message didn't know what it was in reference to. Most likely, Freskel-Gar, thought, with their advanced surveillance resources the aliens had detected the Hat Rack flight climbing and moving on an interception course, made a lucky guess, and the rest was pure bluff. So Broghuilio was intending to scrap his ships because Minerva didn't have the resources to refuel and maintain them. Well, wouldn't that apply equally well to the ship that the Giants had arrived in too? Hunt said no, but that was no doubt just another part of the bluff. And if their ship was so superior, why were the Giants evacuating it right now, as he watched? They didn't seem to have much ability to resist whatever Broghuilio was threatening. No, just at the moment Freskel-Gar saw no reason to reverse his decision.

Broghuilio appeared on the channel being maintained to Farside and announced that he intended taking command of the Giants' starship. "I will inform you when I have completed my assessment," he said. And with that, the link cut out.

The essence of gaining the controlling hand in this kind of situation lay in assertiveness. Freskel-Gar had acquiesced when Broghuilio tested his mettle by presuming to give orders. The thing now was to keep to the precedent. To have consulted first about taking over the *Shapieron* would have been tantamount to seeking approval, conceding Freskel-Gar the territory. Keeping the channel open would have been fitting for a subordinate reporting progress.

Broghuilio would decide his course of action independently, in his own time as it suited him, and then announce it.

"Auxiliary compensators stabilized. . . . Thrust vector balanced," the computer advised. "All ships ready to lift off."

The captain scanned the bridge-deck readouts. "Proceed."

Broghuilio stood watching, arms folded, as the side-view displays showed the other four craft shedding their coatings of rubble and dust as they rose from the lunar surface. Although the altering surface perspective showed his flagship to be climbing too, with inbuilt Thurien-type g-localizers there was no sensation of movement. The five ships formed into a V with the flagship at the head and turned onto a course directly outward from Luna, in the direction of the *Shapieron*. If he transferred his followers and installed the armaments now, the complications of having to land his ships on Minerva and then dispose of them there could perhaps be avoided. Why should they live like thieves in hiding among hostelries provided by Freskel-Gar, when they could base themselves in a functioning starship?

He had more running in his favor than just the weaponry, the ship, and knowledge of how to use them, Broghulio had decided. There was also the psychological factor. The Lambians and the Cerians walked around in uniforms, held exercises, and drew plans on maps, but they were still playing at being soldiers. He had the records of two thousand years of Earth's history to go on. Having been entrusted with its surveillance by the Thuriens had definite advantages.

So they were playing that kind of game, were they? Freskel-Gar was conscious of his staff officers around him, outwardly impassive but waiting to see his reaction. He reassessed his situation rapidly. The destruction of whatever the objects had been that Broguilio ordered taken out had demonstrated the potency of his weapons. But before the Giants' craft arrived, Broghuilio had been willing to join Lambia as an equal partner. Now, all of a sudden, he was foregoing all else to get his hands on the Giants' ship. So maybe there was some substance after all to Hunt's claim that it had things going for it that Broghuilio's ships didn't. Freskel-Gar was feeling less sure about the formidable ally that he had thought he could count on. He needed to improve his own bargaining position drastically.

"The Jevlenese general Wylott is asking what's happening," an aide reported, gesturing toward one of the consoles a short distance away. The transmission from the ships on Farside would have been lost at Dorjon also.

"Tell him we're looking into it," Freskel-Gar replied.

Broghuilio was not in control of the Giants' ship yet. Maybe there was a way of leveling the situation. Hadn't Hunt said something about the translating device being the starship's computer? It would presumably have a picture of the situation out there on the other side of the Moon that it might be disposed to share. If nothing else, that would show Freskel-Gar's staff that they didn't need to await Broghuilio's pleasure to be informed as to what was going on.

Freskel-Gar indicated the screen that had been displaying the starship. "Do we still have the connection via that shuttle they landed in that's standing out back?"

The colonel checked with the engineering chief. "It's still there. There's just nothing coming over it."

"Can we activate it somehow?"

The engineering chief moved behind the chairs of the operators manning a section of equipment. "It seemed to be voice driven." He raised his tone and addressed a grille. "Hello? . . . Testing? . . . This is Melthis calling the ship." There was no response.

"Try Cerian," someone suggested. "The aliens spoke some Cerian." It did no good.

"How about these?" Another engineer produced the collection of headbands, ear pieces, and wrist sets that had been taken from the captives. Nothing worked.

"There's probably some kind of activation code word," the engineering chief said.

Freskel-Gar frowned in annoyance. "Is that human who wanted to talk to it still out there?" he asked. "The one called Hunt."

"Yes, Your Highness."

"Bring him back in."

The colonel went out to the ante-room and came back with Hunt. Using signs and words, the engineering chief explained the problem. Hunt turned to the grille that was connected to the channel being relayed through the shuttle.

"ZORAC?"

"Yes, Vic?" a voice replied.

✳   ✳   ✳

ZORAC integrated the data from its external sensors to compose a representation of the five Jevlenese vessels closing in around the *Shapieron* to command it from all sides. As instructed by Garuth before he and the others evacuated the ship, ZORAC had opened the main docking bay doors. As it watched, processing and evaluating the incoming data, three things happened simultaneously.

A communications processor forwarded a message received via the probe positioned to provide a signal path around the Moon. It was an acknowledgment from the Lambian embassy in Osserbruk, the Cerian capital. This was ZORAC's latest try at getting through to the Cerian President's Office, after its attempt via the National Aerospace Directorate hadn't worked.

Vic Hunt reappeared, after a long delay, on the channel to the shuttle that had landed in Melthis.

And the Jevlenese leader, Broghuilio, initiated contact over the link that Garuth had told ZORAC to keep open to the Jevlenese flagship. "I am calling the *Shapieron*."

"*Shapieron*. I hear you," ZORAC replied.

"Am I talking to the ship's controlling AI?"

"You are."

"We are about to come aboard, as was previously advised."

"I understand."

"Confirm that the vessel had been evacuated of all occupants."

"Confirmed." They were now in the surface lander that had withdrawn far outside the screen of Jevlenese ships. Garuth had yielded to the threat of violence against those down on the surface. ZORAC concluded that bioforms had their built-in operating directives too.

Broghuilio appeared less sure of the fact, however. ZORAC read the expression, pattern of muscles tensions, and intonations of voice that it had learned to associate with human uncertainty and apprehension. "I just wish to remind you of the fate of the Thurien devices that appeared here immediately before the *Shapieron*," Broghuilio said. "The weapons responsible are trained on your ship, and also on the lander that is standing off outside the limit. We expect to be received aboard the *Shapieron* without interference or any clever surprises. I hope the implications are clear. Do I make myself understood?"

"Perfectly."

ZORAC had no surprises waiting. Even if it had conceived any, with the Ganymeans and their human friends in jeopardy it would have been unable to act on it.

Frenda Vesni sat listening to Negrikof bellowing in the next room. She had just put a call through from a secretary at the Lambian embassy in Osserbruk, saying that a message purporting to be from an alien spacecraft in the vicinity of Minerva had warned that President Harzin's plane was going to be shot down. Ironically, the Lambian had ended up being routed through to the same desk as the alert from NAD earlier.

"Look, what is this? Doesn't anyone have any sense of discrimination left anymore? . . . No, I don't take it seriously. . . . Because we've had it going on all day. There's some hackers loose who are having what they think is fun, and that people like you and me have got nothing better to do. . . . No, because if I did that every time . . ."

Another indicator flashed on Vesni's desk. The head and shoulders appeared of a man in Army uniform. "This is Frenda Vesni."

"Is that Intel Dir? I was told I need to speak with Zumo Negrikof. It's very urgent."

"He's on a call to the Lambian embassy right at this minute. I'm his second. Can I help you?"

"I'm not sure it can wait. I really need to talk to someone in the President's Office, but I was told we have to go through you. Can you interrupt him, please?"

"What's it about?

"I'm with Chief of Staff Headquarters. We've received a warning through one of our locations that has contacts in Lambia that the plane that's on its way here with the President and the Lambian King aboard is in imminent danger. The President's Office has direct contact with the plane and also with ground control. They need to know."

Vesni turned her head for a moment. Negrikof was still yelling. If this had come through on its own, she would have let Negrikof deal with it. But there had been *three* warnings now. And this one wasn't claiming to be a talking starship. Her terms of office authorized her to act on her own initiative if her chief were unavailable and it was a matter of national security or an emergency. Well, this certainly qualified. She thought about the probable reaction from Negrikof if it turned out to be a hoax or a misunderstanding of something. Then she weighed that against the consequences if the warning was genuine. She took a deep breath. There were times in life when you just had to hope you were right.

"Taking all the details would just lose more time," she said. "I'll connect you through to the President's Office directly."

In the Lambian communications room, the views being sent back by ZORAC of the five Jevlenese ships positioned around the *Shapieron* were distributed across several screens. A daughter craft of some kind was detaching from one of them. It was obvious to Hunt now. The Jevlenese had to have been on the Moon somewhere. His spirits sagged as he watched. Even at this early stage, the alliance between Broghuilio and Freskel-Gar had proved itself durable enough and flexible enough to seize a new opportunity when it presented itself, virtually without even faltering in their stride. Now they had a functioning starship as well as Jevlenese weaponry. So much for the mission and its hope of averting a planetary war. About the only consolation Hunt could see was that at least this way, the advantage would be so devastatingly to one side that it might be over sooner, without spreading to dimensions that would engulf the whole of Minerva. So the mission might have created a new reality after all that was at least an improvement, if not the ideal they had hoped for. And that was something, for with the beacons gone and the *Shapieron* now taken over by Broghuilio, it was beginning to look very much as if they might be stuck in it.

He stared at the images of the Jevlenese craft seen from the *Shapieron*, hanging seemingly motionless in the void against the background of stars. Different stars—not a pattern that would have been visible from the Solar System of the time that he belonged to in a different universe. How many ships and constructions against a backdrop of space had he seen since that first trip from Earth to take part in the investigation after the discovery of "Charlie" on the Moon?

The last time had been when he went out physically to MP2 with Chien to observe the first tests involving on-board bubble generation out at the Gate. The blunt, boxy shapes of the Jevlenese vessels reminded him of the raft that it had been installed on. They'd thought they had the convergence problem solved, only to have it reappear once more when the local bubble at the raft was detached. That had been their second encounter with convergence-induced craziness—involving not virtual objects that time, but real ones. The versions of the raft multiplying and vanishing before their eyes had been solid, material bodies. The bubble had to be deactivated after stabilization to suppress the effect.

Convergence suppression. The words repeated themselves in Hunt's mind. Something insistent was trying to make itself heard from his unconscious. Something significant.

Convergence suppression. . . . The bubble generator that the *Shapieron* was fitted with had to be deactivated for the same reason, when the umbilical was broken to allow the ship to operate autonomously. Otherwise the resulting imbalance would expand the local bubble along with its core convergence zone. Out to what kind of radius? Hunt didn't know. But the raft's on-board power source had produced one extending far enough to materialize multiple versions of it. And dematerialize them. . . .

The bubble generator aboard the *Shapieron* was driven by a starship's power.

Like something materializing from another realm, an impossible thought took shape in Hunt's mind. He *had* to find a way of getting through to ZORAC!

Hunt turned to the Lambian who seemed to have been assigned as his handler. "I have known Broghuilio before," Hunt said, speaking better Lambian than he had effected before. "Not to be trusted. You make a mistake."

"You talk when we tell you," the Lambian said.

Hunt nodded at the console still showing Wylott protesting about being abandoned. Presumably he was at some other location. "Look. They don't even trust each other."

"Quiet!"

In the room that Hunt had been brought from, the rest of the party from the *Shapieron* sat resignedly under the watchful eyes of the guards standing inside the door. In the nearest alternative to action that offered itself, Danchekker wiped imaginary smears from his spectacles for the umpteenth time. He had tried to initiate some kind of communication with the guards but decided they were robots. An interesting conundrum, he reflected. Minerva had no military history worth talking about, and yet the mind-set was the same as he had encountered everywhere on Earth, and when he was on Jevlen. Did the military do it to people, or were certain kinds of people drawn to the military? He observed that he was making an unwarranted assumption of a dichotomy—that the two answers were mutually exclusive. ZORAC would have pulled him up on it.

He realized that he was playing mind games with himself to evade facing the feeling of isolation that was trying to steal up from some lower recess of consciousness and seize him with something akin to panic. They were marooned on an alien planet in a remote era of a past that wasn't even of their own universe, with apparently no way of getting back. Now even the link back to the *Shapieron* was gone. He had no idea what Hunt was trying to achieve, since they hadn't been permitted to talk. There was little Danchekker could see that he could achieve. It had all the marks of an act of desperation about it—Hunt's way of avoiding a confrontation with the same issue in his own mind. What the Ganymeans were thinking was lost to Danchekker behind their inscrutable expressions. He removed his spectacles and took his handkerchief from his pocket to wipe them.

In addition to having similar apprehensions, Showm and Eesyan were dealing with undergoing actual coercion and experiencing the threat of force for the first time. While they were aware of Earth's ways and its history, it was awareness in an intellectual sense, recorded second-hand; knowledge about, but not knowledge of. To be compelled to submit to the will of another by the threat of physical attack was unknown to anyone raised in the Thurien culture, and virtually unthinkable. The part that nothing had prepared them for was the deeply disturbing feeling of helplessness, humiliation, and shame. Showm tried to picture the effects of a race's entire history being rooted in such ways to the degree where many of them—maybe the majority, even—were incapable of conceiving how a society could exist otherwise. What crippling of the emotions and the mind did it produce? What shackling and distorting of all that was creative? What needless terrors and obstacles to be overcome? With just this small taste, the true meaning of the mission and the significance of what it might have accomplished took on a whole new dimension. She moved from one undersize, uncomfortable human seat to another to relieve her cramped limbs, and tried not to think about it.

Probably the least affected by the predicament that they all found themselves in were Monchar and the two crew officers from the *Shapieron*. The thought of being marooned in the wrong universe carried no great impact with them, for they had been marooned in a different manifold of space and time for most of the past twenty-four years anyway. Their home, as it had been, was gone. Despite finding descendants of their kind, the times of Earth and Thurien that they had returned to were very different from everything they had known. Wrong universe or not, in many ways this one was more familiar. They were the only ones who had known Minerva before.

But with all their different psychologies, experiences, and strategies for evasion, there was one question that all of them had been asking ever since they walked into the communications room and found Broghuilio staring out at them from the screen: why had there been no response from the probe that should have told them the Jevlenese were here?

CHAPTER FORTY

The Jevlenese lighter nosed its way into the *Shapieron's* cavernous main docking bay amid service gantries and access ramps, located the marker flashing over the assigned berthing doors, and attached. The bay could be closed and filled with air for extended loading and unloading or maintenance work on the ship's daughter vessels, but it was not necessary on this occasion.

Broghuilio led his party through the lock cautiously. The huge, deserted vessel seemed somehow sinister in its emptiness and quietness, as if beckoning them on into a trap. They found themselves in a large open area with conveyors and freight-moving machinery, and wide corridors leading away in the direction of the interior of the ship. Broghuilio stopped and looked around. The construction was of the solid, heavy engineering of a bygone era, not like the light and colorful Thurien designs that he was used to. He felt more as if he were in the lower levels of an old, abandoned city than the inside of a spacecraft. As a warship, fitted with the weapons from his own craft, it would be invincible.

Even with the emptiness, there was an uncanny feeling of being watched. Maybe it was the emptiness that produced the feeling. He looked warily from side to side. "Where is the controlling system?" he called out. "Can you hear me?"

"I hear you," a disembodied voice answered, echoing in the

vaults and chambers. It sounded as if it were coming from a tomb. Beside Broghuilio, Estordu shivered nervously.

"We will require guidance in making our inspection," Broghuilio said.

"To where do you wish to be conducted?"

Broghuilio tried to muster more effort to sounding like someone in charge. "Let's start with the Command Deck. We will view the plans and layout charts of the vessel there."

"Follow the blue lamps to your right. They will lead you to a transit access point. A capsule will be waiting."

"Follow me," Broghuilio said to his party. Best to fit into the role right from the beginning.

In the *Shapieron*'s surface lander standing fifty miles off, Garuth watched the progress of the Jevlenese despondently over the link that ZORAC was maintaining. Shilohin, the rest of his crew, and the three Terrans who had remained up on the ship looked on silently. They knew his anguish and sympathized, but there was nothing they could say that would alleviate it. They had all known him long enough not to hold any blame. The calculation he had been forced to make was brutal, and every one of them would have reached the same answer. But to be driven from his own ship, and now have to sit out here like some exile in banishment, watching Broghuilio strut around assessing his property. Garuth still couldn't bring himself to look any of his crew in the face. He didn't think he would ever feel like a starship commander again.

Shilohin had approached. She spoke from nearby behind him. "Don't torment yourself, Garuth. You chose as you had to. We are not Terrans. We have no experience of dealing with threats of violence against others, or of gauging the seriousness of such intents. All of us are alive and unharmed. That is your first responsibility. You could not have risked the threat of Broghuilio's weaponry. What did you have to bargain against it?"

Garuth sighed heavily. "The worst is this feeling of . . . of utter helplessness. It doesn't sit well with a commander. You say we are alive and unharmed. That is true. But for how long? What incentive does Broghuilio have to complicate his situation by keeping us around once he has control of the ship?"

"Perhaps a very strong one," Shilohin said. "Alive, we are hostages.

It's the only way Broghuilio can keep command of ZORAC. You see my point?"

Shilohin did have a point. And being honest with himself, Garuth admitted inwardly that he had allowed himself to get too focused on what he saw as his ignominy to have thought of it. "Yes. And it's a valid one," he replied. "But not much of an existence to look forward to."

"But it's an existence. And it gives us the one thing we desperately needed after walking in unprepared to such a shock as we did. It gives us time."

A communications supervisor brought a message to one of the aides, who conveyed it to Freskel-Gar. "Count Rorvax is calling from Dorjon. Maximum priority." Freskel-Gar strode over to the screen indicated, where his deputy was waiting, looking worried. The implication was that there was a problem to do with Hat Rack.

"What is it?" Freskel-Gar asked.

"It's been turned around. The flight. Cerian ground control has rerouted it and ordered it down to a low level. They're not divulging its destination. Cerian interceptors are already airborne and heading for the area. Obviously they know."

The news came like an unexpected punch in the face. It couldn't be. . . . Not when everything had been going like a smoothly running machine. It was one of those rare moments in Freskel-Gar's life that his thinking processes seized up, if only for an instant. The mystery human, Hunt, was looking at him across the floor from where he was still standing with the colonel. From that distance, he seemed to know; as he'd said he did. Who else knew?

This was desperate. It called for fast thinking. "We need to be the first to go public," Freskel-Gar said. "Make it sound like a Cerian hijack. Kidnaping Perasmon. . . ."

Rorvax shook his head. "Perasmon is already on the air, saying the Cerians have nothing to do with it. He's calling for Lambian military units to remain loyal." Even as Rorvax was speaking, stirs began breaking out around the room, with officers signaling for Freskel-Gar's aides to get his attention.

"We have to abort Hat Rack," Rorvax urged. "The world is watching that flight now. The Cerians are publicizing that they have received a threat alert and have diverted it. Nobody could imagine that Cerios was responsible if it's downed now."

Freskel-Gar stared hard at the screen, his mind fighting against the capitulation that acceptance would signify. But there was no way around it. He nodded heavily. Rorvax turned away to issue instructions.

One of his staff approached. "Your Highness. Forgive the directness, but it is imperative that you see this. The king and President Harzin are speaking to both nations. They say a plot has been discovered."

Freskel-Gar moved across and listened numbly. Reports began coming in elsewhere of movement orders being given at the regular army's central barracks in Melthis; a call to the commander at Dorjon to lay down arms and open the gate; signs of hesitation, suddenly, among some of Freskel-Gar's own units. Never had he known such a well-conceived and executed plan to unravel before his eyes in so few minutes.

He looked again at Hunt, still watching him. The strange light-colored eyes seemed to be laughing, mocking. Fighting down the uncharacteristic spasm of anger that he felt flaring up inside suddenly, Freskel-Gar clamped his jaw tight and moved over to him. "So, you knew. And what else do you and these Giants from the past know?" he demanded.

"Midnight to Hat Rack Leader. Acknowledge."

"Hat Rack Leader. I hear you."

"Abort and return to base. Repeat, abort and return to base. Do you read?"

"Understood. Confirm, returning to base. . . . Hat Rack Leader to Flight. Form on me and turn at one-eighty. The show's canceled. We're going home."

A frequency-monitoring processor interrupted to inform ZORAC of an incoming signal and request for response. ZORAC activated the message analyzer subsystem and requested it to report. The transmission was from the probe last seen entering the region of spacetime convulsions on the heels of Broghuilio's fleeing ships, fifty thousand years into the future of a different reality. The probe's self-repair diagnostics had completed a lengthy reintegration of the onboard software after a major system disruption, and was standing by for further instructions.

✳   ✳   ✳

" . . . And what else do you and these Giants from the past know?" Flurries of activity were breaking out around the room, with Lambians at different stations calling to Freskel-Gar's staff and vying for attention. Hunt was unable to make out exactly what was going on, but from Freskel-Gar's shaken manner and expression it was evidently serious. Wylott seemed to be suspecting Broghuilio's motives. Somebody on the screen that Freskel-Gar had just been speaking at had mentioned the words "Hat Rack," but to Hunt they didn't convey anything. He knew only that he had to get his thought through to ZORAC somehow. But even if he talked to ZORAC, he would never be able to get the message across with Freskel-Gar's people all around him. . . . But maybe the others would! Hunt played the only card he had.

"Can't trust Broghuilio," he replied to Freskel-Gar. "The Giants from the starship. What is happening?"

"You saw. They are removed from the ship."

"Out in space. Defenseless targets."

"They have not been harmed."

"I wish to see myself."

"You see there, on the screen."

"I see just a surface lander. I wish to talk to the Giants' captain."

"How?"

"The computer will connect us."

"The computer controls the starship. I won't let you talk to it."

"I just want to talk to the captain. To know they are safe."

"Broghuilio assures us they are safe."

"Pah! Broghuilio's own general doesn't trust him. If the Giants are safe, I will bargain. You will learn what else we know besides Hat Rack, what else can happen. Otherwise, I have nothing to tell you."

Freskel-Gar didn't look happy about it, but Hunt's mention of Hat Rack seemed to make an impression. He nodded curtly. "A brief word only. Then we talk."

Hunt was led over to the panel where he had addressed ZORAC before. Freskel-Gar and aides stood behind and around him. "ZORAC?"

"Yes, Vic?"

"Is Garuth out there in that lander?"

"Yes."

"With the remainder of the crew and the three Terrans?"

"Yes."

"You have a link to them from the *Shapieron*?"

"Stop." One of Freskel-Gar's officers interrupted, raising a hand. "What is this *Shapieron*?"

"The name of the ship," Hunt told him. Freskel-Gar nodded for him to continue. "Can you connect me?"

"No problem."

"Audio only," the officer who seemed suspicious of everything instructed. A few moments passed.

"Vic?"

"Vic speaking. Is that you, Garuth, in the surface lander?"

"Yes. I—"

"I must be quick. Being monitored by people *converged* around me. Checking on your safety. We see ships *converging* around. I feel an *expanding bubble* of anxiety that I am unable to *suppress*. Please confirm."

There was a pause. Hunt could almost sense Garuth's bewilderment at the strange choice of words. Freskel-Gar shuffled impatiently. "We are unharmed so far," Garuth answered finally. "I understand your concern, and am grateful." Another pause. "I *do* understand."

"Enough," the officer pronounced. Hunt was moved away, back across the floor. Somebody across the room relayed a message that Hat Rack had been aborted. Suddenly, an instinct told Hunt what it referred to. His hopes took an upturn. Now, all he had to do was play for time.

CHAPTER FORTY-ONE

Garuth's mind raced frantically through what Hunt had been trying to say. *Converge, expand bubble, suppress. . . .* Obviously it was referring to the *Shapieron*'s M-wave gear. But how did that apply to their present situation?

He looked back at the image of the *Shapieron*, surrounded by Broghuilio's five craft.

The others around him were picking up on it too. Moments before Hunt called, they had been stunned by an announcement from ZORAC that the probe thought to be absent had suddenly commenced transmitting. It had been out there all along! The passage through the spacetime storm had caused havoc with its on-board system programming. Possessing only lightweight processing capacity compared to something like ZORAC or the kinds of system carried in the Jevlenese ships, it had taken until now to repair the damage.

"He was trying to tell us something," Duncan said. "Vic's word games again."

Garuth looked back at the *Shapieron*, standing there empty apart from the Jevlenese, with nothing else in the vicinity.

"He talked about expansion," Chien said. "When a detached onboard generator is powered up, it creates a vastly expanded bubble."

"And its convergence core zone," Shilohin mused. "That must be what he meant."

"The raft!" Chien exclaimed suddenly. "The Thuriens' first experiments with the onboard bubble generator. Before we realized that the bubble has to be collapsed after stabilization. The *Shapieron* can do the same thing."

Shilohin saw at once what Chien meant. "Garuth, can I handle this? Vic sounded pressed down there."

"Go ahead."

"ZORAC," Shilohin called.

"Ma'am?"

"Reference the early Thurien experiments on convergence containment and wave stabilization. Specifically, the rafts built to test onboard bubble creation. When the local bubble is not balanced via an umbilical connection to the Gate projectors, an expanded convergence zone results. Are we in agreement so far?"

"I'm with you."

"With the *Shapieron*'s onboard generator driven at maximum, what kind of size would the bubble extend to?"

"I don't have access to VISAR's data right now. Impossible to say."

"Hundreds of feet? Thousands? A few miles, maybe?"

"Possibly. . . . I think I see your reasoning."

"Not mine. Vic Hunt's."

"That figures."

Shilohin hesitated. Glancing at Garuth but still addressing ZORAC, she said, "Synchronization of the collapse would have to be external. It couldn't be coordinated within the convergence zone."

"I could create a direct switch from the lander into the control circuit to collapse the bubble," ZORAC replied. "But the ship's functional integrity might be compromised. It would require authorization by the Commander."

It took Garuth a few seconds to follow what they were talking about. But if they didn't try, Minerva would be at Broghuilo's mercy. The mission would have failed. If they tried and succeeded, and as a result the *Shapieron* became no longer functional, they would be unable to get home. But it was already looking very much as if they weren't going to be able to get home anyway. The alternative they stood to face was becoming part of a world dominated by Broghuilio. Garuth met Shilohin's eyes. Once again, he had to make an agonizing decision, but with no real choice.

"I authorize it," he confirmed.

"Reconfiguring generator net for maximum power," ZORAC responded. "Commencing bubble inflation now."

Broghuilio stood with his entourage on the Command Deck of the *Shapieron* and surveyed his new domain. In terms of style and engineering it was admittedly primitive in some ways, with its reliance on voice and screens—not even avco to afford permanent visual and audio sensory integration, let alone the full-neural capability of something like VISAR or JEVEX. But in a different way it had its own kind of splendor. Without direct neural interaction, and featuring less automatic system integration than Thurien designs, the older architecture used greater numbers of screens and operators, making the vista more grand and imposing. The supervisory dais with its positions for commander, deputy, and engineering chief looked out at the main displays over the bays of operator stations and instrument panels in the grand manner of thrones. Very fitting. It would suit Broghuilio well. In his mind's eye he could already picture the extension that would be added for the targeting and fire-control sections when the armaments from his own ships were installed. The whole vessel had obviously been refitted recently throughout, and he had established from its controlling AI that the power generation and drive systems were fully refurbished and charged. He would be unchallengeable effectively indefinitely in this. Even in its former condition, the ship had been good for over twenty years—and at the end of that, still up to attempting a voyage from Sol to Gistar. Yes, Broghuilio decided, this would suit him very well indeed.

"You see," he said, turning to Estordu and the others. "We have been here for a time measured only in days, and we are established. Our situation has already improved dramatically from the poor relations that the Lambian prince would have us be. As a revolutionary, he is an amateur. Did not I, the true revolutionary, promise you that one day we would settle the reckoning for that insult? It seems the day may come sooner than I anticipated."

"His Excellency spoke truly," one of the party said.

"Luring the *Shapieron* here to be dealt with away from the Thuriens was an act of brilliance!" another effused. "The mark of a true genius."

Even Broghuilio blinked at that one. It hadn't quite been that way. But it was fine by him, if that was what they wanted to believe.

The captain of Broghuilio's flagship, who had also come aboard for the tour, looked up from speaking via compad with his second-in-command. "We are still receiving requests from General Wylott and from the Lambians to reconnect, Excellency," he advised.

"We will talk to Minerva when we have completed our inspection," Broghuilio replied. Nobody was going to be telling *him* what to do very soon now, and for a long time to come. They might as well get used to it.

"The *Shapieron* would give us a fast and regular connection to Earth," Estordu remarked. "A warmer climate; richer and more diverse habitats. Suitable for the exclusive refuge of a ruling elite, perhaps? Surroundings conducive to an appropriate lifestyle. A small population of serving classes . . ."

Broghuilio looked at him in surprise. Even the scientist was thinking positively for once. "A proposition with merit," he pronounced. "We will give it full consideration in due course."

Broghuilio strode forward to stand in the aisle of primary control stations immediately below the supervisory dais. "ZORAC." He was getting to know the system better by now.

"Acknowledging."

Broghuilio hadn't quite summoned up the nerve to direct it to address him as Excellency yet. The loss of face if it were to find some grounds for refusing in front of his followers would be intolerable. He would tackle the matter when he was more sure of himself.

"Are the plans and blueprints of the ship available as I requested?"

"They can be viewed in the holo-display tanks of the Navigation section, forward to your right and up the blue steps."

Broghuilio moved along the aisle and stopped to survey his realm from this new perspective. "You know, ZORAC, you have no choice but to learn to get along. You have to cooperate while we hold your previous associates. And I have to preserve them as long as I need your cooperation. We both have the basis for a deal."

"I understand."

And, of course, there was always the possibility that in time it might come to evolve new loyalties. Broghuilio turned and climbed the steps up to the dais itself. From this elevation, the panorama looked even more spectacular. He imagined it all lit and alive, the stations manned, the panels and screens active. And *his* to command.

"Bring up the main displays," he ordered. "I want outside views all around the ship."

One by one the large screens facing the dais came to life to show the five Jevlenese vessels against a slowly moving carpet of stars. The brilliant cloud-streaked disk of Minerva stood in the background on one, and a part of the Moon off on an edge in another. A holo image below and in front of the dais showed a three-dimensional representation of the *Shapieron* with the screens indicated around it in their correct orientations and directions.

In the center behind Broghuilio, the commander's chair and console faced out over it all. Broghuilio turned and regarded it. He straightened his shoulders, puffed up his chest, and approached his future seat slowly, almost with reverence. This was a solemn and symbolic moment. His followers watched silently from below.

And then Broghuilio stopped abruptly.

Another Broghuilio had appeared out of nowhere, already sitting in the Commander's chair. The expression of rapture that had been on his face lasted for an instant, then switched to one as bewildered as that on the face of the Broghuilio who was standing stupefied, gaping at him. The Broghuilio sitting recovered first. "*Who the hell are you?*" he demanded.

"I could ask you the same thing," Broghuilio standing shot back. The questions were reflex. It was obvious to both who the other was. What was far from obvious was a sensible question to try and make sense of it.

"What are you doing dressed like that, in my ship?"

"*Your* ship? What do you mean? This is—" Broghuilio standing faltered as Broghilio sitting vanished in front of his eyes.

"*Who the hell are you?*"

He turned dazedly. Another Broghuilio was halfway up the steps to the dais. At the same time, consternation was breaking out among the rest of the group below as two Estordu's recoiled from each other as if they had like charges, while the flagship captain disappeared from one place to reappear in another. The whole area below the dais dissolved into a mélange of figures popping in and out of existence randomly. On one of the screens, the image of a Jevlenese ship disappeared, leaving just an empty starfield.

And suddenly Broghuilio was back on the bridge in his flagship, looking at screens showing surroundings of the terrain on Luna. General Wylott was there somehow. In the background, Estordu was jabbering something unintelligible. Another Broghuilio came onto the bridge, stopped dead, and gaped.

"What's happening?" Broghuilio from the *Shapieron* demanded. "How did we get here? And who the hell are you?"

"I could ask you the same question."

"What happened to the Ganymean ship?"

The other Broghuilio shook his head, obviously not comprehending. "What Ganymean ship?"

Fifty miles from the *Shapieron*, Garuth stood with the others in the surface lander, watching incredulously as the pattern of craft clustered in space fluctuated crazily. The five Jevlenese ships performed a dance of vanishing and reappearing, jumping from one spot to another. At one instant there would be six or seven, an instant later, just two or three. In a zone extending for an uncertain distance, the time lines from scores or more of realities in which they had happened to take up different positions were converging and becoming entangled. At the center, the *Shapieron* itself seemed to shift back and forth spasmodically. The channel from the lander's local control system was connected through to a simple circuit breaker that would deactivate the bubble that defined the expanded convergence zone. All Garuth needed was one specific combination. Below his chest in front of him, his hands opened and closed as he flexed his fingers unconsciously in anticipation.

The number of Jevlenese ships shrank to three, two . . . he tensed . . . then, suddenly, six. If none of the time lines impinging on the *Shapieron* included a Jevlenese ship, it followed that the *Shapieron* couldn't contain anyone who had been brought to it by one, and therefore it would have to be empty.

Then, just for a moment, the *Shapieron* stood on its own in space. Every one of the five Jevlenese craft and their various alternative versions were momentarily in some different reality.

"NOW!" Garuth called. An icon on a display changed to confirm the transmission. Would the signal get there fast enough?

On the screen, the image of the *Shapieron* steadied itself. Nothing else changed.

Everyone waited breathlessly. Nothing. Not a sign of any Jevlenese ship.

"I think you've done it, Garuth," Shilohin whispered.

"Magnificent," Chien complimented.

In the background, Duncan and Sandy quietly clasped hands and smiled at each other reassuringly.

Garuth swallowed disbelievingly. The picture replayed itself in his mind of the strutting oaf parading himself inside his ship. The memory came back of the humiliation he had been forced to accept. And a slow smile of satisfaction formed on his face. He felt like a starship commander again.

The lander closed with its regular port in the *Shapieron's* main docking bay. Garuth had waited a further fifteen minutes before returning. A systematic search of the ship confirmed that no trace of Broghuilio and the Jevlenese was to be found.

It was necessary to search the ship physically because another result that had been feared was also confirmed. During the wait, nothing further had been heard from ZORAC, and no response could be evoked from it either from the lander or upon entering the *Shapieron*. In the same way as had happened with the system in the probe, the riot of desynchronization had scrambled ZORAC's internal processes to the point where it ceased functioning coherently. But the network that formed ZORAC was far more complex than the probe's equipment, and the energy concentration at the core of the disruption induced by starship power was more intense than anything the probe had come through. After analyzing the logs and records, Shilohin's scientists announced that not enough was left running for the damage to be repaired. ZORAC was irrecoverable.

That was why ZORAC had requested authorization by the Commander before proceeding.

ZORAC had known.

Rodgar Jassilane, the *Shapieron's* engineering chief, restored the channel to the shuttle down in Melthis. The interface that ZORAC had created into the Agracon system was working. Garuth got ready to deliver the news as best he could without ZORAC available to translate. He asked Jassilane to prepare a replay of the event sequence as captured from the lander.

A Lambian was calling something about an armored column on the move toward the Agracon. Somewhere else, an infantry regiment had declared for the king. In the middle of it all, Hunt and the officer watching him stood to one side, seemingly forgotten. The atmosphere in the communications room was tense. Nothing more had been heard from the Jevlenese. But from the bits that Hunt could pick up, Freskel-Gar was having other problems. The regular forces and the nation appeared to be rallying to Perasmon. Although Freskel-Gar was visibly under strain, whether he would try to brazen it out using the prisoners as bargaining chips, or concede now and make things easier was unclear. It could go either way.

And then a voice that Hunt recognized as deep, Ganymean guttural articulating a mixture of Jevlenese and broken Lambian came through above the hubbub from the console where he had talked briefly with Garuth. "No. Not Prince or Lambian. Victor Hunt, talk with." ZORAC was evidently unavailable. Freskel-Gar moved across, followed by his aides. The voice came again from behind the group of figures. "Victor Hunt, only. Talk with Earth human. Was there before." Freskel-Gar looked back and nodded to the officer to bring Hunt over. As the company parted to let Hunt in, Hunt saw that a screen was connected into the circuit this time, showing Garuth. Freskel-Gar stopped him with a gesture as he was about to move through.

"What did that Giant mean, 'Earth human'?" he muttered. "How can you be from Earth?"

"More to this than you could dream," Hunt replied. "Best for you to end now. Believe." It was pure bravado. Hunt had run out of everything else. Freskel-Gar interrogated him silently with a long, penetrating look, and then motioned for him to continue.

"Garuth," Hunt said, facing the screen.

"Vic. We win, as you guess. Watch how. You see now." Garuth's features were replaced by a view of the *Shapieron* riding in space, surrounded by Broghuilio's five craft. Garuth's comments continued as a voiceover. "See from lander, where we are. ZORAC expands bubble." The scene became chaotic as ships began vanishing, multiplying, shifting from place to place. Freskel-Gar took a pace forward to stand beside Hunt, peering in bemusement.

"I don't understand. What's happening?" he demanded. Even though it had been he who put the idea to Garuth, Hunt was too astounded himself at seeing it actually happening to be capable of saying anything.

Then the *Shapieron* was on its own; a voice shouted something in Ganymean; and nothing further changed . . . except that after a few seconds it became evident that the image had stopped juddering and was stable again. "Back in ship now," Garuth's voice informed. "Broghuilio, Jevlenese, all gone. For good. But Perasmon plane . . ." Garuth made hand motions in the air as he sought for words.

Freskel-Gar was looking pale and tight-faced. He seemed to have gotten the message. "Translator computer is down," Hunt told him. "Bring back other Giant here. Easier talk, yes?" Too numbed to argue, Freskel-Gar just nodded to the officer, who hurried away. Hunt made the best of his opportunity to pile things on.

"It's over, Highness. You saw. Five ships, many years ahead of all that Minerva has. But all gone." He snapped a finger and thumb in the air. "Like so. Was nothing. You can't win against Giants. Wylott knows. Perasmon lives. Harzin lives. So now you have all Minerva to fight, too. Not possible. Smart thing is end now. Best answer. I tried to tell before. Now obvious."

Frenua Showm was brought in. By means of signs and bits of Jevlenese, Hunt conveyed the situation. Showm gasped at the news, took a few seconds to absorb it and adjust, and then, radiating exhilaration, turned to Garuth on the screen. From bits of the exchange between the two Ganymeans, Hunt followed Garuth saying that ZORAC had been trying . . . something to do with the Cerians . . . but Garuth didn't know because ZORAC was . . . it sounded like "finished." Hunt broke in to tell Showm that the flight had been diverted and two leaders were fine. The remark about ZORAC was alarming, but he had no time to dwell on it. Showm passed the news to Garuth, and it was his turn to be incredulous. Some indecipherable Ganymean exclamations and expressions followed, and the two aliens began emitting snorting noises accompanied by peculiar shaking movements. Only Hunt out of all those in the room had seen a Ganymean laugh before. But there could be no mistaking it.

Neither Freskel-Gar nor any of his staff were making any attempt to interrupt now. The realization of the inevitable seemed to permeate the room, as voices died and one by one the figures all around ceased tasks they now realized were futile.

The final report came from a station on the far side of the central map table. Infantry and armor were taking up positions around the Agracon and had sealed off all access. The commander of the Prince's Own defending units inside was requesting orders. A column was also heading toward Dorjon. Total silence fell. All eyes were fixed on Freskel-Gar. He looked from Hunt, to Showm, to Garuth watching from the screen, and over the expressionless faces surrounding him. As Hunt had said, it was over.

"Tell him to stand down," Freskel-Gar said.

Outside in the anteroom, where she had been told to remain in case she was needed again, Laisha was still recovering from the shock. A few minutes before, the colonel who had taken the light-skinned man inside had hurried back out, disappeared, and then come back through with somebody he had evidently been sent to fetch. Or would some "being" have been more correct? Laisha's mind was still in a turmoil. Obviously something extraordinary was going on. Her biggest regret was that Kles couldn't have been here to see it too. The being that had accompanied the colonel back, followed by two armed Lambian guards, was darker in hue than any Minervan, with an elongated head, dressed in a yellow tunic with strange fastenings and accessories, and standing over seven feet tall. But there shouldn't have been one any closer than millions of years in the past, or light-years away—if they still existed at all. Laisha had seen a real, live, Giant!

CHAPTER FORTY-TWO

Kles was working through the week's requisition lists but his mind was not really on the job, when the phone rang on Corporal Loyb's desk. The rest of the unit were drawing kit for a forced route march. Typically, Loyb had gotten himself excepted for office duty.

"Yes, sure, I'll tell him." Loyb replaced the phone and looked up. "Lieutenant Boros to report to the OC's office," he said. "At once."

"Oh ... sure. I'm on my way." What had he started now? Kles nodded, stood up, buttoned his jacket, and pulled on his hat as he turned toward the door.

"Looks like they've got it in for you today," Loyb called after him.

Kles tried rehearsing explanations in his head as he headed toward the Admin block. He hadn't realized it was a security violation. . . . No, that wouldn't wash. If he didn't know that, he qualified for being busted back to private. They'd done it to test the security measures, but he hadn't had a chance to report it. . . . So why hadn't he reported it when he delivered the message from Wus Wosi at NEBA? He didn't have an answer. He'd just have to resign himself to taking whatever came of it, he told himself.

The orderly sergeant rose, beckoned, and opened the OC's door as soon as Kles entered. Kles went on through. The unit commander was already there. It looked serious. Kles removed his hat and saluted. "Lieutenant Boros reporting as ordered, Sir."

"At ease, Lieutenant," the OC said.

Surprised, Kles relaxed. Then he saw that the OC's expression was not critical; in fact, it seemed more a mixture of curiosity and disbelief. He shifted his eyes to find the unit commander staring at him wonderingly.

"Well," the OC said.

Kles waited. Then, "Sir . . . ?"

"You don't know?"

"Know what, sir?"

"Haven't you heard the radio anytime in the last hour?"

"No, sir. I've been on duty in the stores."

"Oh, I see. The President's plane was diverted. There was a Lambian plot to overthrow King Perasmon, but it has been stopped. My first assessment would be that a course that would almost certainly have led to full-scale war has been averted."

"I . . . didn't know," was all Kles could think of to say.

The OC regarded him expectantly for a few seconds. "You might be wondering how that could be known so soon, and how we can say already that your warning was genuine," he said. Kles was too confused just at that instant to have said with certainty what day it was. "The confirmation came via an agency of an astonishing nature that has only just revealed itself—as far as I can make of it at the moment, anyway. I'm still not sure I believe it myself. But we have someone here who can apparently explain it better." The OC nodded to somebody on the desk display facing him, said, "He's here now," and pivoted the unit around for Kles to see the screen. It showed an office or some kind of working environment, with figures in the background. A couple of them were wearing what appeared to be Lambian uniforms. Kles looked back at the OC questioningly. And then a somebody moved into the viewing angle, leaned forward to adjust a control, and then her face broke out in a smile of delight as she recognized him. It was Laisha.

"Kles! I don't know where to begin. You know you saved the president and King Perasmon, don't you? It was part of something bigger that involved a revolution here. But there's even a lot more to it than that. I don't understand most of it myself yet. But I've got a couple of people here who were very concerned about it all, and you've saved some kind of complicated plan that they've been involved in too. They want to say thanks to you personally. Will you talk to them?"

"Well ... sure ..." Kles's mind was turning too many somersaults to take it all in. Laisha was biting her lip, as if to stop something exciting from bursting out.

"Here they are. There might be a problem with language because their computer that normally translates has got problems, but I'll do my best. Er, get ready. This might be a bit of a surprise. ..." Laisha looked away. "This is Kles."

Kles's jaw dropped, and his eyes bulged as the two Giants moved into view on the screen. . . .

The room could have been intended for meetings or informal conferences. It had a couple of massively solid tables surrounded by upright chairs, along with an assortment of couches and more commodious seating around the sides. Two large bay windows with heavy, braided drapes looked out over what appeared to be the front area of the building. The walls were decorated in somber, subdued patterns giving way at intervals to alcoves containing vases and ornaments, and pictures of important-looking Minervans. A bit old and staid by contemporary Terran standards, Hunt supposed, and the carpet had seen better days; but it was a big improvement on the place they had been held in previously, down in the basement.

Following Freskel-Gar's surrender, forces loyal to Perasmon had taken over the Agracon and removed the prince and his would-be revolutionaries to oblivion or whatever retribution would be decided. Wylott and a handful of Jevlenese who, for whatever reason, had been left behind at another location outside the city were also being rounded up. Thankfully, none of that was Hunt's concern. He had been joined here not only by his own companions but also by the Cerian girl that he had met briefly, along with the remainder of the Cerian delegation that she belonged to, who had been similarly detained. Apparently, there were more Cerians in another building somewhere.

The Lambians had provided food and drink and were trying to make everyone comfortable. An officer that Hunt took to be on the commanding staff of the force now in control had explained that they were awaiting the return of the two national leaders, who wanted to meet them all personally. Meanwhile, three Lambians had been left sitting near the door, by a table where an urn containing a hot beverage of some kind had been placed. They were there to take care of anything more that might be wanted, not as guards. The room's strange mix of occupants gathered that they were definitely to consider themselves no longer captives, but guests.

Most amazing of all to the Minervans, of course, was the presence of the Giants. Although the full story would have to be recounted for Perasmon and Harzin, the Lambians who had been coming and going to check for anything that might be required or on other pretexts were unable to contain their curiosity. In return for the snippets they managed to pick up, they provided as much news from outside as was available at the present time.

Nobody knew if any message from ZORAC had played a part in causing the Cerians to divert the flight. One of the Cerian delegates, however, had recognized the danger as soon as Freskel-Gar's soldiers began taking over inside the Agracon, but he had been apprehended before he could get a warning out. However, another person whom he had told *had* managed to send a message to her soldier boyfriend—of all people—and checking with the Cerians had confirmed that their Presidential Office had indeed acted in response to information received via the Cerian military. She was none other than the translator that Hunt had met downstairs. Her name was Laisha. She and her boyfriend, as far as anyone could tell, had done as much to bring about the day's outcome as anyone.

Frenua Showm seemed the most moved by Laisha's story. Laisha had responded that there was something the Giants could do if they really felt they were in her debt. If the Lambians could get a connection to the boyfriend in Cerios who had alerted the Cerian authorities, would they let her introduce them to him? Hunt hadn't been able to piece together through all the clumsy language and improvised translation exactly why it was so important, but in characteristic Thurien fashion, Showm and Eesyan had gone away with Laisha and a couple of Lambians to see what could be done.

The *Shapieron* was moving closer in to Minerva, and the latest over the link to the shuttle, still standing outside the back of the building, was that a party headed by Shilohin was on its way down in the lander, flying under manual control. For Hunt, the news about ZORAC was like losing a personal friend. The few computer specialists who had come with the mission said they would try, but the chances of restoring it appeared next-to nonexistent. Even something like VISAR would have had little to work on with code that had been essentially randomized. It seemed that something of the same nature had incapacitated the missing probe, which had been out there all the time, engaged in some lengthy self-repair operation that its simpler structure and less severe condition had at least made possible.

Apart from those considerations, the main concern was the prospect of having to remain here. If they had indeed created a new reality, the irony now was that they seemed destined to live as a part of it. The knowledge hung heavily in the background of Hunt's mind like the funereal Lambian window drapes but he didn't feel up to dealing with it yet. It wasn't as if he were pressed for time, he told himself wryly.

With most of the more immediate questions at least partly answered, the company had broken up into talking in low voices with its own kind—Cerian and Cerian; Ganymean and Ganymean; Thurien and Thurien. Maybe it was because struggling to understand and make oneself understood was fatiguing. In Hunt's case, it meant he was limited to Danchekker, who just at that moment was polishing his spectacles. It was usually a prelude to speaking when he had been reflecting on something.

"It occurs to me, Vic, what an extraordinary book cousin Mildred would have been able to produce if she had returned for the mission. It would have had much more going for it than all those statistics and sociological observations, I would have thought. . . . But then again, she wouldn't have had access to her market for it, I suppose. Unfortunate in many ways. You know, I would never have believed I'd ever hear myself saying this on the day you talked me into this antic, but I rather think I'm going to miss her."

"What do you mean, I talked you into? Wild horses wouldn't have held you back. And as I recall, Gregg Caldwell had more than a little to do with it as well."

"Yes, Gregg. And there's another one." Danchekker sighed and placed his spectacles back on his nose. "A lot to get used to. I think, given the alternative, I would willingly accept Ms. Mulling as part of the package if it meant returning. Is it really so beyond the bounds of possibility?"

"With no beacon for VISAR to home on, there's no way to locate us. Think of a needle in Jupiter made of hay."

"Um." Danchekker lapsed into a resigned silence. Hunt hoped Danchekker wasn't about to go off into a protracted nostalgia trip. He was still far from being up to confronting the implications fully in his own mind yet. After a minute or so, Danchekker said, "It's an intriguing thought. Right now, as we sit here, there is a Thurien out there at a Gistar, twenty light-years away, with Ganymeans on it descended from the ones who migrated from here long ago. Also, we have the *Shapieron* in orbit above us here. Back in our own universe, it was the *Shapieron* that enabled us to establish contact between Earth and Thurien. So why shouldn't it perform the same function here? You see my point. With contact to the Thurien that exists in this universe, we might be able to furnish them with enough information to create the means necessary to get us out of this situation and back where we belong."

Hunt looked at him sharply. It *was* a intriguing thought. Hunt had been too preoccupied with Freskel-Gar to give any thought to longer-term issues. But then, as he followed it through, he realized that there was a flaw. "But we're fifty thousand years in the past," he pointed out. "I'm not sure that the necessary know-how existed on Thurien then. In fact, I think they were still going through their period of stagnation. We could always try, of course, but I'm not sure there would even be anyone listening there."

"Um."

But Danchekker had a point nevertheless. If the means existed to make contact with Thurien, it meant that the potential was there for a joint Ganymean-human culture to come about as soon as the circumstances were propitious, without suffering the setback of Minerva's destruction and all the consequences it would engender. So, after everything, the mission was back on track, for precisely that result had been its whole purpose. The only problem was that as far as Hunt could see, it wasn't likely to happen while he was still around to see it.

A Lambian came in and informed them haltingly that the lander from the *Shapieron* was down in an open area not far away, and the Giants who had come with it would be arriving shortly. As the Lambian was about to leave, Eesyan and Showm were ushered back into the room, accompanied by Laisha. Eesyan nodded to Hunt in a way that conveyed it had been a worthwhile gesture, and then went with Showm to join Monchar and the two *Shapieron* officers. Laisha came over to Hunt and Danchekker, chuckling in the way of one who had just pulled off an enormous practical joke. "Wonderful!" she told them. "Kles was just too . . . how would you say?"

"Amazed?" Hunt offered the Jevlenese word.

"More than amazed. Was like his face is going to fall off. Wish you had been there. You see, all his life he has had . . . Interest? Fascination?"

"Okay."

"For the Giants of old. Then, to see them real. . . . It was like in his dream. You understand?"

"I think so. " Ganymeans had been causing more than their fair share of astonishment all-round in the space of the last few years, Hunt thought. One of the other Cerians said something that Hunt didn't catch. Laisha turned away and began talking with them.

Hunt got up from the chair, yawned, stretched his arms, and moved over to one of the windows. Below was a paved court bounded by a wall of narrow stone columns like an enormous balustrade, through which two gates guarded by sentries gave access to a larger outer area. A railed fence on the far side ran in sections between square pillars surmounted by statues. Beyond was a wide street lined with stubby gray trees and buildings of massively square line and proportion, echoing the style of the furniture in the room. A twin-rotored helicopter type of machine was moving slowly above the rooftops. Everything seemed solid and gray. The type of city, Hunt thought, that a designer of early twentieth century battleships might have conceived. He wondered how typical this might be of what was looking like becoming the future home that he was going to have to get used to.

Just about everything else that his former life had been built around and toward which it had seemed to be heading was suddenly irrelevant. That was the fact, he told himself. Get used to it. At least he didn't have relatives who were all that close, or dependents to burden his conscience.

What alternatives were likely to present themselves in place of all those things now? Obviously they could look forward to

a permanent special status here, with a reasonable expectation
of enjoying just about anything that it was within the power of
Minerva's rulers to grant. Hunt could certainly think of worse
ways to start a relationship with a new world. "Never say, it can't
be done because," was another thing his dad used to tell him.
"Always say, it could be done if..."

With the Cerian-Lambian rivalry seemingly defused, the
Shapieron here as a scouting ship, and a little Ganymean know-
how thrown in, the program to move Minerva's population to
Earth should move ahead rapidly. Helping to develop the physics
needed for the requisite technologies would make an ideal role for
Hunt—that alone could keep him usefully occupied for the rest of
a lifetime. Seeing Earth as it had been would be a fascination in
itself. Pioneered by a race that was already spacegoing, it would
avoid the perils of being buried in people before they developed
the means of expanding outward, giving it the kind of head-start
that had benefitted Thurien. Definitely not all bad, he decided.
Which was just as well, considering.

A movement nearby caused him to turn his head. Danchekker
had collected a cup of the Lambian brew and come over. Hunt
eyed it undecidedly. "What's it like?" He had been too strung-out
by the effort of trying to keep up with events to have an appetite
for anything himself yet.

"Quite agreeable, I have to say. Reminiscent of strong, sticky tea
with honey. Also, an undertaste of what I recall vaguely as being
not dissimilar to Irish whiskey, which should be to your liking."
Danchekker took another sip and joined Hunt in his contemplation of the world. "All very solid and imposing," he commented.
"Immutability in stone."

"It reminds me of some of those old black-and-white newsreel
clips of winters in Russia," Hunt said. The difference was that
Melthis wasn't far from Minerva's equator.

"Little concept, it would appear, of throwing up trashy piles
of work pens purely for the purpose of maximizing short-term
rentals. It seems somewhat odd. One would have thought that
with migration to Earth being the race's single-minded objective,
expressions of permanence would be low among their traits. An
unconscious collective desire for security and a long-term future
manifesting itself, do you think?"

"Could be. At least, all that's more likely to happen now."

Hunt had the feeling that Danchekker was perhaps unconsciously expressing similar assurances himself. Hunt went on, "And you and I and the Ganymeans are hardly going to be short of work to do in the middle of it all. Just imagine, Chris, the whole Earth as it was. All those early animal forms that you've speculated about and tried to reconstruct for years, walking around, alive and breathing."

Danchekker's expression lightened a fraction as he continued staring out through the widow. It seemed that aspect hadn't occurred to him. Several seconds went by before he answered. "A fascinating thought. Fascinating indeed. . . . It would certainly help with some of the notions of evolution that I've been reconsidering. The same genetic programs expressing different adaptations to varying environmental cues. The Thuriens have a completely different picture from our traditional view. Changes occur suddenly, all at once, in the form of repopulation by new forms and body plans following catastrophic mass-extinctions." Danchekker was about to go on, but Hunt drew his attention to a bus with a small escort of cars front and rear that had entered from the street and was crossing the outer space toward the stone fence.

"It looks as if Shilohin and the party from the lander might have arrived," Hunt said.

"I do believe you're right."

They realized that Laisha had come back over and was looking at Hunt. He raised his eyebrows inquiringly.

She spoke in an amalgam of pidgin Jevlenese-Lambian. "Can speak more? Sorry."

"It's okay."

"Cerians cannot believe ship is from future. Too many . . . what makes no sense with itself?"

"Contradiction?"

"Yes. We have more questions."

Hunt sighed. There was going to be a lot of this ahead, he could see, and without ZORAC it wasn't going to get any better. He might as well start getting used to it now. Just then, a uniformed Lambian hurried in and muttered something to the three sitting by the door. One of them called something to Laisha. She went over and talked with them for a minute or two with much head shaking and gestures, and occasional glances back toward Hunt and Danchekker. They waited. Then Laisha called them over. Hunt shrugged at Danchekker, and they joined her.

"From . . ." She waved a hand. "What is place where I was? First see you."

"Communications room."

"Okay. Is connection there to . . ." Laisha made an expansive gesture in the air. "Communications for all Minerva. Phones. Computers. You know?"

"Okay."

"Message comes in. Nobody knows where from. They think maybe is for Giants."

"A message has been received by the planetary net," Danchekker interpreted, trying to follow along with Hunt.

"What does it say?" Hunt asked.

"Not sure. Nobody understands. But is from person you know? Someone who says is VISAR."

CHAPTER FORTY-THREE

By this time, Harzin and Perasmon had landed, boarded a waiting helicopter, and were due back in Melthis shortly to receive the visitors from the *Shapieron*. So Hunt and his companions had to wait before learning what had happened. But at least they enjoyed the benefit of having VISAR available online as a translator at their meeting with the two leaders.

Many forms of physical system are analogous in that they involve quantities playing similar roles, related by the same kinds of mathematical equations. Electrical voltage, current, and resistance, for example, correspond to the pressure, flow, and friction in hydraulics. Inductance and capacitance find their counterparts in mechanical inertia and elasticity. The Thurien scientists were beginning to piece together a theoretical construct that enabled many peculiarities of Multiverse to be viewed in terms recognizable in more familiar physics. The analogies were not exact, of course, but they could often serve as an aid to clearer understanding. One area that was proving fruitful in this respect was electrodynamics. In fact, the bizarre zones of time line convergence were found to influence each other remotely across MV space in a manner evocative of the way electrical charges do across ordinary space. The "umbilical" conduit connecting the Gate projectors to the bubble zone of an on-board generator could be thought of as carrying a current between them.

When a magnetic field collapses rapidly, it induces an electromotive force, or voltage, in the circuit carrying the current responsible for the field. The induced voltage acts in such a direction as to try to keep the current flowing. The system exhibits "electrical inertia." An apparently similar situation held when Garuth collapsed the expanded convergence zone built up around the *Shapieron*. A huge "voltage" was created, which in seeking an outlet found a path to a complementary "pole" in the form of the MV charge concentration at the Thurien Gate, which was operating following a directive from Calazar to launch search probes, forlorn though the scientists said the hopes of success would be.

In effect, a connecting path was created between the Gate and the *Shapieron*—somewhat like the filament of ionized particles that an electric field creates between a thundercloud and the ground, opening the path which a lighting flash will follow. The result was that the wave defining the probe that VISAR was in the process of launching, instead of going where it was meant to, followed the trail back. The probe's instruments quickly established the presence of the *Shapieron* and went into beacon mode to mark the location. VISAR was unable to raise ZORAC, however, and so resorted to establishing contact via the Minervan planetary net in the way that by now was routine.

So, they would be going home after all. But there was more. Mainly because of Eesyan's misgivings when the first full Gate test involving the *Shapieron* was due, VISAR had stored a backup copy of ZORAC—just in case. Now that contact to VISAR had been reestablished, restoration of ZORAC became first priority.

The part of the team who were down in Melthis were taken to the Agracon's communications room to follow the event via the link to the *Shapieron*. Reloading and linking took awhile because VISAR was restricted to operating via the beacon connection. It could have been carried out more quickly back at Thurien, but Garuth wanted to bring his ship back under the control of the entity he had known for years, and nobody was going to spoil it.

"Integration complete and checking indicators good," VISAR pronounced. "It's all yours." Everyone on the Command Deck looked toward Garuth.

He took a moment to prepare. "ZORAC."

"Commander?"

A wave of relief and elation surged around the company watching from the surface. Some Lambians and Cerians were present also. "Just checking on current status and the schedule for today," Garuth said. "What do you have?"

"Eesyan has approved the last series of raft tests to assess collapse of the local bubble after stabilization. All results affirmative. No anomalies detected. We're cleared for full-scale tests on the *Shapieron*. On Eesyan's insistence, VISAR has stored a backup of yours truly." Smiles went back and forth among those watching both in the ship and down on the surface. ZORAC was exhibiting the computer equivalent of amnesia, reporting what had been the situation months before. It hadn't realized yet that it *was* the backup.

"Would you care to analyze the surroundings of the ship, evaluate, and report?" Garuth invited.

A short silence ensued. Nobody expected that it would take a system of ZORAC's logical capability very long to arrive at the correct conclusion.

"I gather that I have some catching up to do," ZORAC responded finally. "And am hugely indebted to Eesyan, to put it mildly. Okay, you've got it. No more wisecracks about the pedantry of biominds." An outbreak of applause greeted the statement.

"Welcome back," Garuth said.

It was agreed that the *Shapieron* would remain at Minerva for a further week for the story to be explained in full. With the perspective that the mission was able to bring of the future that continued rivalry and escalating hostility would lead to, few doubted that Cerios and Lambia would quickly overcome the differences that had begun to emerge between them and devote themselves to the common goal that represented the only progressive future for all of them.

It was going to be a busy week. Besides providing the entire story of Earth, Thurien, and everything that had happened from the departure of the Giants from Minerva, to the decision to mount the *Shapieron* mission from Thurien, it would be necessary to advance their understanding of physics—the Minervans still hadn't been able to make any sense of quantum phenomena. On top of that there was insatiable curiosity among Minerva's public and news media to be addressed. Adopting a policy of starting the way they meant to carry on, the leaders of the two powers decided against any blackout of the aliens' presence. It would have been short-lived in any case. Even in its parking orbit a hundred miles above the surface, the *Shapieron* extended over half the diameter of the full moon and passed overhead several times a day as a brilliant pencil of light or a silhouette, depending on the position of the Sun.

But for now, all that the members of the mission really wanted to do was get away for a while, rest, and come to terms, each in their own way and in their own mind, with the feeling of sudden reprieve from the exile that they had inwardly been preparing themselves for. After staying for a dinner in Melthis that evening that Harzin and Perasmon insisted on, which could hardly be refused, the Ganymeans and the Terrans down on the surface boarded their craft to return to the *Shapieron*. Of course, the Minervans were all eager for a chance to visit the starship too. But not now. None of them pressed the point. That could come later, in the days they had ahead. They all understood.

It had been a long day at UNSA's Goddard Center too. Caldwell had tried to maintain an air of sanguinity commensurate with the spirit of the occasion as he smiled and nodded his way through rooms where staff dutifully explained their work to gum-chewing tourists in baseball hats and beach shorts, and past school groups depositing sticky fingerprints around the exhibit hall in the lobby and in the computer graphics room. He'd survived worse, he supposed.

One of the most popular items was the Thurien neurocouplers in the bay along the corridor from his office. All day long there had been a line of people waiting for their turn to walk among the towering cityscapes of Thurien, gaze in awe at real dinosaurs and jungles on another world, or be whisked through a virtual tour of the Galaxy, courtesy of VISAR. Within half an hour of opening, Caldwell had been approached by interests wanting to get in on the ground floor of a Terran commercial end of the operation. He wouldn't talk to them. That was what UNSA had a Public Relations department for.

"This is Mr. Caldwell, Director of the Advanced Sciences Division," Amelia, who had been doing a gallant job as tour guide, said to the couple in the matching shirts. Things were quieting down at last. They were among the last to be leaving. "ASD handles most of our dealings with the Thuriens."

"Do you think it's safe, allowing these aliens to come straight into people's heads here like this?" the woman accosted. "They could be setting us up for an invasion. After all, look what happened to the Jevlenese."

"We do keep a close watch on the situation at all times," Caldwell assured her.

"Psycho-socio sympathetic resonances," the man said. "Tuned to the cortical subliminal modes." He looked at Caldwell expectantly. Mercifully, Caldwell's phone beeped.

"Excuse me," he muttered.

It was Mitzi. "Gregg, I've got Calazar on the line."

"I'll be right there." Caldwell did his best to look apologetic. "Sorry, but I'm being called." He turned his head as he hurried away, still holding the phone in his hand. "I'm sure Amelia will be happy to answer your question."

He walked through the door of the outer office bearing its sign, NO ADMITTANCE, and closed it behind him. "What's up?" Mitzi gestured to a screen showing Calazar at the far end of the Thurien link. Caldwell pivoted it to face him fully. "Hi, Byrom." Caldwell was up to date on the news, of course.

"Gregg. How was your social day?"

"Almost over. I noticed that none of the administrators who dreamed it up were here to help deal with it. Anyway, what's new?"

"The mission people are back at the *Shapieron*—mainly to rest and recompose themselves, I suspect."

"I can imagine. I think I would be too."

"Since it's going to be another week at least before we bring them back, I thought it might be appropriate for you and I to join them." That was the Thurien way of talking. Calazar meant virtually, via neurocouplers. "Symbolically showing that we've been with them, as it were. And what better way could there be of celebrating VISAR's reconnection?"

"Sounds like a good idea. When did you have in mind?"

"Now, if you can manage it. Is there a coupler available there? You said earlier people were lining up to try them."

"Things are quieter now. Just a second. I'll check." Caldwell looked over at Mitzi. "Can you raise Amelia and find out what the coupler situation is out there? Calazar wants me to take a trip to visit Vic and the guys."

"Sure will."

"Some of the scientists from Quelsang will be joining us too," Calazar said. "There's one last aspect of this whole business that they're getting excited about. They want to tell the others about it, especially Eesyan and Vic."

"Oh? And what's that?" Caldwell asked.

"I'm not sure I fully understand it myself. But it's to do with this business about the *Shapieron*'s bubble implosion creating some kind of low-resistance path back to here."

Caldwell followed that much. "Uh-huh."

"All the activity that's been going on would involve many other universes apart from ours, all doing much the same thing. Well, the theory is that the entire local region of the Multiverse that was affected—centered on Minerva, fifty thousand years ago—somehow created a similar kind of pathway to the disturbance that projected those five Jevlenese ships back. So . . ." Calazar paused as Caldwell began nodding rapidly, already seeing what he was getting at.

"I know what you're going to say. That's a question I've been asking for a long time. The coincidence was too much to buy. This answers it."

"That why they ended up where they did. Anyway, it's another whole area of theory that we're about to get into, I'm told."

Cadwell realized the Mitzi was waving. "Just a second, Bryom. . . ." He raised an eyebrow.

"Amelia says, no problem. It's clear out there."

"The couplers are free," Caldwell told Calazar. "I'll see you . . . wherever. Where are we going?"

"I thought we'd go there, to the ship," Calazar said. The *Shapieron* had been fitted with Thurien neurocouplers for its stay on Jevlen.

"Sounds good. I'll see you fifty thousand years ago in a couple of minutes."

Caldwell cleared down and went back into the corridor. The building was quiet and felt back to normal. He saw Amelia coming the other way. "That couple aren't still waiting somewhere to ambush me, are they?" he said.

"You're safe. They left."

"And the coupler room is free?"

"Yes. . . . Oh, there's just one guy left in one of the cubicles but I don't think he'll be a problem."

"Great job. You've earned a day off."

"I'll hold you to that."

Caldwell went on through to the coupler area, let himself in to one of the vacant cubicles, and settled himself down in the recliner. The sensation came of his mind opening up into a void that told him he was connecting to VISAR. "So how was your day here at UNSA?" he subvocalized.

"Oh, pretty lightweight but varied," VISAR replied. "I trust my service was at its customary level of excellence?"

"I haven't heard any complaints. So, you know the deal with Calazar?"

"Yes. You're all meeting at Minerva, aboard the *Shapieron*."

"Let's go."

Hunt relaxed back in one of the *Shapieron*'s neurocouplers. Although he was aboard the ship physically, he needed to be coupled neurally to interact with the others from Thurien and Earth. The impression of being together would be an illusion shared by all of them.

"VISAR, you have absolutely no idea how great it is to be doing this again," he said. "We thought we were isolated here for the rest of the duration." It was intoxicating.

"It was most fortunate," VISAR confessed. "I had run out of viable options. You know that."

"But you tried all the same."

"That was Calazar. In a situation like that, I just follow orders."

"I think I'm beginning to understand why Thurien loves him. So he's coming here too? And Gregg?"

"They thought it was the least they could do."

"Where are we meeting?"

"Garuth thought, the officers' mid-decks lounge."

A good choice, Hunt thought. Relaxed, informal, but dignified and comfortable. "Is anyone there yet?" he inquired.

"You're the first."

And Hunt was standing in the officers' lounge amid outsize Ganymean seating of black upholstery arranged in booths and around low alcove tables. The newly paneled walls showed dynamic murals, and there was a virtual buffet set out on the counter running along one side.

"You have a call," VISAR said. "Someone from Goddard connected neurally, asking if you're available."

Goddard! The word sounded beautiful. Hunt had thought he would never see it again. Only now was it coming home to him fully that the nightmare was over. Everything was fine. He was back in his familiar world again. In his rising euphoria he didn't care who it was or bother to ask. No doubt somebody from the firm wanting to check on him. "Sure," he said. "Bring him through." A moment later, a figure in a blue suit, wearing a white shirt and tie, popped into existence in a human-scale chair in front of him. For a moment he just sat staring around, looking bewildered. Hunt couldn't place him. He was heavy set, smooth-shaven and fleshy, with hair combed back from a round, moonish brow.

"Good evening," Hunt said. "Er, do I know you?"

"I'm looking for a Dr. Victor Hunt."

"This is he, at your service. And you are Mr. . . . ?"

"Lieutenant Polk, FBI, Investigations Branch, Fraud and Finance Division." Polk reached automatically inside his jacket for his badge. VISAR had no way of knowing what he intended, and improvised a card with a smiley face. Polk stared at it with the expression of one who had just opened his safe deposit box to find a rubber duck. But academy training prevailed, and he recovered himself quickly. "Could I ask you some questions concerning your relationship with a company called Formaflex of Austin, Texas, Dr. Hunt?"

Hunt blinked. This wasn't real. "You've come a long way," he remarked, more for something to say. "You do know where this is, I take it?"

"Not really. The computer or whatever it is just told me you'd said you were available."

This was going to be even trickier than Hunt had thought. He frowned, searching for the best way to handle it. "Can I offer you a drink?"

"Not on duty, thanks."

"Oh. Of course. VISAR, straight Irish for me, please." A full glass materialized in Hunt's outstretched hand, as if caught from nowhere. Polk's eyes widened. A moment later Calazar appeared, followed by Garuth and Shilohin.

"It's a bit complicated," Hunt tried to explain. Caldwell materialized in another chair.

"Vic," Calazar greeted. "We've come to pay our respects. The least we could do in the circumstances." Frenua Showm and Eesyan were suddenly standing by the buffet counter. Polk stared from one to another of the aliens, then back at Hunt, his resolve breaking down finally in a helpless appeal for reason and sanity.

"You might as well stay now, Lieutenant," Hunt told him cheerfully. "They're all part of the story. Make yourself comfortable. Are you sure you won't have that drink? It's completely non-impairing, I promise. This will probably take a while."

EPILOGUE

In a large boulevard bookstore facing out over a bank of the Danube in Vienna, Mildred sat at a table piled with copies of *The Thurien Soul*, as well as a selection of her earlier works. It was doing respectably well, and the line of readers and buyers waiting for autographs hadn't abated all morning. Her current project was to organize into book form a collection of her thoughts on the philosophy and physics that she had found herself drawn into in the course of researching it. The tentative title she had in mind was, *Learning to Live With the Multiverse*. Collecting her thoughts together on anything was always a daunting business.

"If you'd written it two thousand years ago, it would have done a better job than the Bible," the woman in the red dress who has just had her copy inscribed to "Inga" was saying. "It spells out exactly everything that's wrong with this materialistic, legalistic system of ours."

"It does make us look a bit like children showing off their toys to each other, doesn't it?" Mildred agreed.

"And it proves it isn't inevitable, the way all our experts used to say. Just imagine, honorable individuals working for knowledge and wealth to be used to create a better life for everyone. The part on Frenua Showm's feelings about war was wonderful. All the things I've wanted to say for years. I couldn't stop thinking about it for days. Thank you so much."

"On the contrary, thank you for stopping by." Mildred smiled.

After almost a whole morning, she was content to let others do the talking. Actually, she had persevered at the discipline she'd set herself while on Thurien, and it must have shown because several of her friends had commented on it. She was beginning to think that maybe her previous tendency to chatter had been a defense against self-images of inadequacies that she need never have felt. After all, when a biologist and a physicist both tell you that you've caused them to rethink some fundamentals in their own fields, it could only be good for one's confidence. But it wouldn't do to let herself go too far the other way and be carried away by overly grand notions of self-importance, she reminded herself. Such as when she had made a trip all the way back from Thurien to see Caldwell, because she thought she had something to say that he needed to hear. The very idea! But the *Ishtar* was back at Earth again now, and Mildred was looking forward to hearing more about the later activities that had been going on at Thurien, which Christian had touched on tantalizingly in his calls and messages. The story wasn't public knowledge yet.

There was a mild stir near the door over something, but the next person in line blocked Mildred's view. He was a young man with lively dark eyes, hair tied at the back, and a short, pointy Vandyke beard. "Fantastic stuff!" he said.

"Thank you."

"Do you really think the Thuriens are right about all of us being extensions of some greater consciousness in a bigger realm? It seems so . . . I mean, why don't we know anything about it?"

"Should I make this 'to' anyone?"

"Oh, yes. To Ulrich, if you would."

"What made it clearer to me was one time when I was having dinner at a house on Thurien, and watching the serving robot," Mildred said as she wrote. "Although it acts autonomously within its own limited range of local awareness, it's connected to their whole network that exists across star systemss: VISAR. But it doesn't know anything about VISAR, or the higher concepts that VISAR deals in. Does that help?"

"Hm, maybe. I'll have to think about it. . . . And could you make this one to Anna, and say Happy Birthday?"

"Your ladyfriend?"

"My sister."

As Mildred complied, she only half noticed another copy, opened at the title page, being slid across the table in front of her. Then she registered that the hand holding it was huge, dark purple-blue in color, and had two thumbs. She looked up disbelievingly, then dropped the pen and was on her feet.

"*Frenua!*"

"I decided it was time I came to see this world of yours for myself."

They embraced warmly, if incongruously—diminutive Mildred and Showm's seven-foot frame. "But . . . why didn't you tell me?"

"Terrans are supposed to like surprises. The *Ishtar* was due back. So . . . And anyway, I wanted to see the book. We arrived yesterday."

"We . . . ?" Then Mildred saw Christian and Vic Hunt, standing and grinning a few paces back. "Oh my . . ."

The line of people looked on, waiting patiently and good-naturedly, all happy that they were getting to see a little extra for their money. A customer who had stopped to watch came across and tested Showm's arm and a shoulder approvingly. "Say, you know, that's pretty . . . Oh, my God! You're real! I thought it was a publicity stunt for the book."

Danchekker moved closer and treated his cousin to a rare hug. "Good heavens!" Mildred gasped.

"I'm here for the week," he informed her. "You can thank the accumulation of your relentless and merciless admonishments over the years. I come in contrition to bring atonement to Emma and Martha, and yes, even to see Uncle Stefan and his firm. . . . But later. Let us not hold up the good work here."

"We've got another story for you, Mildred," Hunt said. "Whatever you were thinking of working on next, forget it. I guarantee this one will trump anything."

Two days later, after leaving Danchekker to a well-earned vacation and to attend to his family matters, Hunt boarded an Air Europe suborbital bound for Washington National direct. There were matters he could have attended to at some of the European offices of UNSA, but they could wait until another day. Reporting back to Caldwell was first thing on his list.

The blue above the plane darkened, and the horizon of Earth below took on curvature as the skyliner climbed toward the top of its trajectory. It reminded Hunt of the westbound flight he'd made five years previously with a colleague from the British company he had worked for then, going out to assist UNSA with its investigation of Charlie. He would have found it hard to believe then that a hypersonic suborbital skyliner would ever seem quaint and antiquated.

Charlie—who had lain entombed there on the lunar surface, slowly turning into a natural mummy for fifty thousand years, since the time when Luna orbited a different world. Yet only a matter of weeks before, Hunt had walked on that very world. In all probability Charlie had been alive and walking around there too somewhere, at that very time. The outlandish thought struck Hunt suddenly that there was no reason why Charlie couldn't have been Kles.

What the future relationship should be between Minerva and the Thurien-Terran culture from the future who had so drastically altered its situation had been a major issue to emerge during the remainder of the *Shapieron*'s stay. Some were for maintaining contact, arguing that the young culture would do better if launched onto its new course of history with the benefit of all the knowledge and resources available. Others were less sure, and felt that it perhaps needed a period of independence and isolation to absorb what it had learned and to discover its new identity for itself. Harzin had subscribed to the former view, Perasmon, the latter. Some Minervans had joked that they had the beginnings of a another war here already.

Another issue had been whether Minerva should attempt to contact the Thuriens who already existed twenty light-years away at Gistar in their own universe. Once again, there were mixed opinions about that. The Thuriens accepted it all as simply illustrating the fact they had long resigned themselves to, that two humans in a room equated to inability to agree about anything.

In the end, it had been decided to leave the beacon probes live but inactive for a period of quarantine. Barring some kind of emergency, neither side would initiate any contact for one year, which would give them all time to reflect and debate. At the end of that time, they would confer again.

Hunt looked out at the sprinkling of stars that were beginning to appear overhead. Not anywhere out there, because in the universe they were all part of the Minerva that had disappeared long ago, but somewhere across the greater vastness of the Multiverse that was still so veiled in mystery, there existed a realm where whatever future was destined to emerge from the changes that he and the others had wrought had already unfolded and was reality. And somehow in the turmoil of it all, the original question of whether humanity's ills were due to something innate or the product of circumstances had been forgotten. It really didn't matter. He didn't pretend to know the answer. But as Frenua Showm had persuaded them, they'd had no choice but to try.

Hunt had faced one more small perplexity when the *Shapieron* was finally brought back to Thurien. After the Jevlenese destroyed the locator beacons, Eesyan had pointed out that even if a probe projected from Thurien should, against all probability, find them, there could be no guaranteeing that it would be a probe from "their" Thurien. Countless other versions of the reality they had come from would be trying the same thing, and a probe that happened to hit on the universe they were in could have come from any.

But Hunt had allowed for such an eventuality during the earlier tests and set up means by which he could tell. Before departing, he had loaded into his compad a randomized mathematical function that could be compared against a master that he had left lodged in VISAR. If the two matched, it would mean that they had returned to the identical reality that they had departed from. If not, even though the difference might be trivial, they would have come back somewhere else.

For days after returning, he had agonized inwardly over the check and its implications. In all that time, though he had searched and watched for any inconsistency, he had found none. By every measure and criterion he could devise, he was home. Finally, he had confided his dilemma to Danchekker. Danchekker had opined that if one couldn't tell a difference, there was no difference. Hunt told VISAR to delete the function unread. Chris was right. It didn't matter. Some things were best left alone.

A few rows ahead in the cabin, people were leaning toward the windows and pointing. Hunt sat forward to peer out and up. A pearl of light was crossing the sky against the starry background. "I think it's the Thurien starship," he heard someone say.

He wondered if they would one day meet the culture that existed somewhere, developed from the humans and the Thuriens who had met long ago. What kind of world would they have created by now, that might make even VISAR and Thurien seem quaint and antiquated in comparison? After the things he had seen in just five short years, Hunt had a feeling that life still held much in store yet that would be new and exciting.

As the edge of Earth's dark side crept slowly into view ahead, the *Ishtar* moved away and diminished, finally disappearing below the horizon.

THE GIANTS CHRONOLOGY

Compiled by Dr. Attila Torkos
Szeged, Hungary
20.09.2001

Send comments to: torky@freemail.hu

Appr. 4.6 billion years ago

Birth of the Solar System. At its birth the Solar System consists of nine planets which are the following in order of growing distance from the Sun: Mercury, Venus, Earth, Mars, Minerva, Jupiter, Saturn, Uranus, Neptune.

25 million years ago

The evolution of a species, the Giants, results in the emergence of intelligence on Minerva. Rise of the civilization of the Giants. Later the CO_2 content of Minerva's air begins to rise thanks to plate tectonics. The Giants set out to normalize the situation. In order to achieve this the crew of the starship *Shapieron* performs experiments on the star Iscaris. The experiments go wrong, Iscaris goes nova, and the fleeing Giants suffer a relativistic time shift on board the malfunctioning *Shapieron* which throws them 25 million years into the future. Learning about the failure at Iscaris, the Minervan Giants import animals (proto-humans among them) and plants from Earth to Minerva and successfully isolate their gene which is responsible for their CO_2 tolerance. They plan to insert this gene into their own genome, but finally give up the plan, fearing its consequences. As they find no other solution to the CO_2 problem, the Giants move to planet Thurien orbiting Giants' Star. During the evacuation one of their starships crashes on Ganymede. Terran life conquers Minerva, reaching a new ecologic equilibrium. The Thurien giants observe the changes on Minerva via relays left on the planet.

Appr. 4 million years ago
Rise of Australopithecines on Earth.

Appr. 2.5 million years ago
Homo habilis evolves on Earth.

Appr. 2 million years ago
Homo ergaster appears on Earth.

Appr. 1.6 million years ago
Appearance of *Homo erectus* on Earth.

Appr. 150,000 years ago
Homo neanderthalensis evolves on Earth.

Date unknown
The evolution of hominids with altered gene set leads to *Homo sapiens* on Minerva.

Date unknown
Along with the rise of human civilization an ice age begins on Minerva threatening to destroy civilization. Mankind starts to develop space travel to flee the planet.

Appr. 50,200 years ago [Note: later reduced to 50,020. See p. 274]
Imares Broghuilio and his generals appear from the future with five starships. They land on Minerva unnoticed and soon

unite the peoples of the continent Lambia in a military regime. Lambians start to arm against the other continent, Cerios, with the aim that only Lambians should escape the ice age. The states of Cerios are forced to arm themselves.

50,000 years ago

The race for space leads to total nuclear warfare between Cerios and Lambia at the dawn of space travel. The war involves the surface of Minerva's moon, too, where Cerians built a base. The nuclear catastrophe shatters Minerva to pieces: a major fragment becomes the planet Pluto, the rest scatter to form the Asteroid Belt. Upon their request, Thuriens observing the war transport the moon's Cerian survivors to Earth and leave them to their fate. Lambian survivors are settled on planet Jevlen in Thurien's neighborhood and are slowly integrated into Thurien society. The moon, freed of Minerva's gravitic grip, is later arrested by Earth's gravity well and Minerva's onetime moon becomes Earth's Moon. The Moon arriving to Earth orbit causes upheavals and floods on Earth, almost wiping out the Cerian survivors, throwing them back into barbarism. In a race to stay alive they soon wipe out the Neanderthals who until now ruled the Earth. *Homo sapiens* spreads on Earth and starts his second ascension toward civilization.

Date unknown

On Jevlen the Thuriens set up JEVEX, a supercomputer modelled after their VISAR. Later, Jevlenese secretly transport JEVEX to planet Uttan and set out to extend it so that it should reach and eventually top VISAR's performance. Unbeknownst to the designers, a universe later named Entoverse evolves in the growing JEVEX. Its intelligent inhabitants, the Ents, sometimes manage to transfer to the world outside JEVEX by invading Jevlenese minds. Such obsessed Jevlenese (the so-called ayatollahs) sometimes create religious-mystic cults around themselves. The existence of Entoverse remains unknown.

Date unknown

Upon their request, Jevlenese are trusted by the Thuriens to conduct the observation of Earth. Driven by vengeance, Jevlenese leaders spread religions and superstitious beliefs on Earth via agents in order to hinder the development of civilization.

1831

A newly obsessed ayatollah, Sykha founds the Spiral of Awakening cult.

Nineteenth century

Seeing that Earth's civilization grows in spite of their meddling, Jevlenese help develop certain areas of science to provoke arming and global, self-destroying wars on Earth.

1914

Beginning of World War I on Earth.

1939

Beginning of World War II which, according to Jevlenese plans, should lead to nuclear disaster. Earth, however, avoids nuclear warfare.

After 1945

Thanks to the Jevlenese agents, Earth begins a nuclear arms race after World War II, which threatens the existence of its civilization for a few decades. In the meantime, unbeknownst to the Thuriens, Jevlenese leaders also start to arm.

1979

Birth of Joseph B. Shannon.

1992

Birth of Victor Hunt.

1999

Birth of Lyn Garland. Birth of Duncan Watt.

2002

Birth of Hans Baumer.

2015

As cold war slowly dissolves on Earth in spite of Jevlenese machinations, Jevlenese agents help demilitarize Earth. In the meantime, Jevlen keeps on arming itself in secret. The ultimate goal of the Jevlenese leaders is the isolation of Thurien, destruction of Earth, and rule over the Galaxy. Jevlenese keep on reporting to Thurien about a militarized Earth on the brink of World War III.

2027

Mankind begins to conquer space again, and finds the traces of *Homo sapiens'* earlier presence on the Moon.

2028

Exploring the mystery of the people named the Lunarians, mankind realizes the onetime existence of Minerva. Expedition Jupiter 4 discovers the Giants' starship on Ganymede. They name the race the Ganymeans.

2029

Based on Ganymean and Lunar findings, humanity reconstructs the story of the Lunarians and the Ganymeans, discovers that the Moon was once Minerva's moon, and finally realizes that Earthmen are the descendants of the Lunarians originating on Minerva.

2030

The time-shifted crew of the *Shapieron* contacts the Earth people. Using references found on the Moon, the *Shapieron* departs to find Giants' Star, supposed destination of the Ganymean exodus. Earthmen realize that their intelligence is a byproduct of the unsuccessful experiments of the Giants. Jevlenese observers fail to report the appearance of the *Shapieron* to Thurien. Earth broadcasts a radio message to Giants' Star, from which Thuriens learn about the *Shapieron*.

2031

Unbeknownst to Jevlen, the Thuriens contact Earth. After realizing that Earth is peaceful, together they drive the Jevlenese leadership into a corner. JEVEX is switched off. Imares Broghuilio and his generals escape from Jevlen, and accidentally fall 50,200 years into the past. Jevlen, liberated from its vengeful leaders, sets out on a peaceful course. At the same time, chaos devours its JEVEX-dependent society in the absence of JEVEX. Thanks to JEVEX's being turned off, life dramatically worsens in the Entoverse, and many Ents try to escape their universe. The sudden appearance of several new ayatollahs and their cults make chaos worse on Jevlen. One ayatollah, Eubeleus, travels to Uttan and tries to switch JEVEX on so that Ents can invade Jevlenese minds in great numbers. Earthmen and the Giants realize the existence of the Entoverse, and prevent the Ent invasion. JEVEX is isolated on Uttan to preserve the Entoverse.